Elizabeth Jeffrey was born in Wivenhoe, a small water-front town near Colchester, and has lived there all her life. She began writing short stories over thirty years ago, in between bringing up her three children and caring for an elderly parent. More than 100 of her stories went on to be published or broadcast; in 1976 she won a national short story competition and her success led her onto write full-length novels for both adults and children.

Also by Elizabeth Jeffrey:

Fields of Bright Clover
Mollie on the Shore
The Weaver's Daughter
Cast a Long Shadow
Ginny Appleyard
The Buttercup Fields
Far Above the Rubies
Hannah Fox
Dowlands' Mill

Elizabeth JEFFREY

To Be a Fine Lady

piatkus

PIATKUS

First published in Great Britain in 2000 by Judy Piatkus Publishers Ltd
This paperback edition published in 2012 by Piatkus

A CIP catalogue record for this book
is available from the British Library.

ISBN 978-0-7499-5809-1

Printed and bound by Clays Ltd, St Ives plc

Papers used by Piatkus are from well-managed forests
and other responsible sources.

MIX
Paper from
responsible sources
FSC® C104740

Piatkus
An imprint of
Little, Brown Book Group
100 Victoria Embankment
London EC4Y 0DY

An Hachette UK Company
www.hachette.co.uk

www.piatkus.co.uk

To my family in Richmond
Chris, Julie and their children
Katie, James and Daniel
with my love

Chapter One

In spite of the warm September sunshine outside it was cool in the stone-flagged dairy. Even so, Joanna wiped her arm across her brow as she kept the handle of the butter churn turning, for it was hot, tedious work. From time to time she stopped and took out the bung to peer inside, as much to give herself a rest as to see how the butter was coming.

'Here, let me do it, Jo.' Suddenly, she found herself elbowed out of the way by a young man in a tattered shirt and trousers, spattered with yellow swarf thrown up from the grindstone where he worked. He began to turn the handle vigorously.

She shook his arm. 'Not too fast, Tom. If it's over-churned it'll spoil and I'll get another beating from t'Mester,' she said anxiously.

He slowed down and looked at her. 'Saul Bradshaw's a cruel pig, treating you the way he does. And his sons, too. They're no better. They ought to be ashamed, and you no more than a bit of a lass.' The handle began to turn faster again as his temper rose and once again she laid a restraining hand on his arm.

'It's all right, Tom, really it is. Martha looks out for me.' She grinned at him. 'At least she sees to it I get enough to eat. Not like you, any road, half starved all the time.' She went over and fetched him a dipper of milk from a basin on the shelf.

'Thanks, Jo.' He drank it down gratefully and went back to his churning.

The door opened, letting in a shaft of sunlight, and they

1

both turned, starting guiltily. But it was only Martha, Saul's wife, a small, wiry woman whose tiny frame belied her strength. In her early fifties, her face was wizened, furrowed with deep lines; wisps of thin grey hair escaped from under her cap. She was carrying a large basket with a cloth spread over its base.

'Is t'butter done, lass?' she asked briskly as she came in. 'Aye, I can hear it is. Stop that, Tom lad, or it'll be spoiled.' She looked him up and down. 'No work today, lad?'

'It's Monday, Missus. Mester never works on Mondays. I'm supposed to clear up the hull and put fresh water ready for the trow, but I can do that later when there's nobody about.'

'You mean when my man has done for the day,' Martha said with a grim smile. 'That'll not be till the light's gone. He'd work all night if he could see to do it. Sundays, too, if it weren't the Lord's Day. And he'd have his sons doing t'same if they weren't working their own stones now. Not that he ever spends owt,' she added with more than a trace of bitterness. She smiled at Tom. 'You're a good lad to come and gie t'lass a hand. I hope she's gi'en you a sup o' milk for your pains.'

He grinned back at her. 'Aye, Mrs Bradshaw. She has.'

'Good.' She looked round the neat dairy and nodded. 'Well, I can finish up in here now,' she said to Joanna. 'While you go and fetch me some blackberries from the wood.'

Joanna looked doubtful. 'T'Mester said I'd to dig up the rest of the tatties this afternoon.'

'Caleb can do that. He's a lazy lout.' She held out the basket. 'Never you mind digging tatties, you do as I say and go and pick blackberries for me. It'll be cool in t'wood, and Tom can help you if he's nowt better to do.' She winked at them. 'I want plenty, mind, so I shan't expect you back for a while. Blackberries make lovely jelly but it teks a lot of fruit for a gill of juice. Go on now, lass, be gone in case Saul decides to come back early.'

'Thanks, Martha.' Joanna flung her arms round Martha's neck. 'You're good to me.'

'Go on, away with you,' Martha shooed them out of the door, but she was pleased. Nobody else showed her any affection.

2

She stood at the door of the dairy, shading her eyes, watching them take the path along by the narrow but fast-flowing River Porter towards the wood.

They were a strange pair. Tom, a tall, gangling youth of some sixteen or seventeen years – nobody was exactly sure how old he was – with a shock of black hair that made his pale face look even paler under its grime, and Joanna, small and slight with tangled fair curls and a peaches and cream complexion that no amount of weathering could spoil. Martha's gaze softened as she watched her tripping along beside the boy and she realised with something of a shock that it was over fifteen years now since that bitterly cold March morning when she'd found her. It had been on a morning when frost had turned everything into a white fairyland and traced such thick icy patterns on the windows that she'd somehow known something magical was about to happen as she'd wrapped herself up in a blanket and gone out to milk the cows. And she'd been right, because there in the cowshed she had seen, by the light of the lantern, this tiny bundle lying in the feeding trough among the hay. Not crying, not sleeping, just lying there, looking, its blue eyes wide and trusting. Just like the Baby Jesus, the thought had come unbidden to her mind. Only the Baby Jesus hadn't been wrapped in a blue velvet cloak like this baby.

And this baby wasn't a boy, it was a girl, the daughter she had always longed for after bearing two strapping boys, Jacob, who by that time was nineteen, already married and a father himself, and Caleb, who was five years younger.

Saul had been furious when she carried the child into the house. He had warned her to get rid of it, he was having no squalling brat in his house, taking up time she should be spending on other things. When she refused he'd even tried to wrest it from her and throw it in the river; worse, he'd threatened to feed it to the pigs.

Martha smiled grimly to herself at the memory of that day. It was not often that she stood up to her husband, the consequences were too painful. But in this she had refused to give in. The child had been put there, she'd argued, just as the Holy Child had been laid in a manger. Therefore it was their Christian duty to care for it. It was a Sign. Thinking about it

3

afterwards she was convinced that it was only this comparison that had swayed him. He was not a particularly religious man but he was afraid of the wrath of God. He didn't consider his life was blessed with good fortune as it was, but a Sign was a Sign and he was not prepared to risk God's anger descending on him further. Grudgingly, he'd agreed it could remain, as long as she kept it out of his way.

Martha was not concerned with his motives, she simply thanked the Good Lord that the child hadn't been left in the dairy.

Tom and Joanna reached Hangingwater Lane, the road that crossed the stone bridge over the river and led down into the town. It was little more than a wide tree-lined track at this point, but further along it widened and joined other roads leading down into the busy town of Sheffield. They crossed over and plunged into the cool green wood, avoiding by common consent the cart track used by the strange-looking charcoal burner who lived in the wood with his daughter, keeping instead to the small path beside the rushing, tumbling river. Here the blackberries hung shiny and succulent. Tom cut a stick with which to hold down the high brambles where the biggest berries hung and it wasn't long before the basket was full and their arms stained with a mixture of blackberry juice and blood from the bramble thorns. Satisfied with their efforts they hid the basket under the bushes and went and sat by the river to eat the packet of bread and cheese that Martha had concealed under the cloth that lined it.

They munched slowly, savouring every mouthful. When every last crumb had gone they ate their fill of blackberries, then scrambled down the bank and washed their faces and hands in the cold, clear, swiftly running water of the river.

'That was a feast fit for a king,' Tom declared, lying back contentedly and squinting up through the trees at the sky.

Joanna stayed crouched by the water's edge, letting the cool water trickle through her fingers.

'This could be the exact spot where they found my mother,' she mused. She turned her head to look at Tom. 'I told you, didn't I, Tom? She was found drowned in this river, caught up in the roots of a tree by her long fair hair.'

4

'Yes, Jo, you've told me,' he said quietly, sitting up. 'Many times,' he added under his breath.

'Look, there are gnarled roots reaching right down into the water over there on the other side.' She pointed across the river, then turned back to him. 'I reckon this was the very spot, don't you, Tom?'

He nodded. 'Could be.' He sighed. 'You're lucky, Jo. At least you know who your mother was. All I know about my mother is that she died when I was born. In the workhouse. That's a terrible place, Jo.' He shuddered. 'I was glad when Zack Wenlock took me on as his apprentice.'

She went and sat beside him. 'But he's horrible to you, Tom. How can you say that?' she said, frowning.

He shuddered again. 'You don't know what it was like in that workhouse. Anything's better than that,' he said vehemently. He stared into the water for several minutes, then shrugged. 'I don't blame Zack for the way he treats me. He didn't want me in the first place. But the workhouse people said he'd got to take a boy in, so he chose me. I suppose I looked as if I might die so he thought he wouldn't have to keep me for too long.' He chuckled. 'But I didn't die, did I? I've been with him for nearly eight years now. Only another four and I'll be out of my time and I can leave him and go down into the town and earn my own living.' He turned his head to smile at her, a smile that lit up his pale face and gave a hint of the handsome man he could become. 'And when I've made my way in the world I shall come back and take you away from all this, Jo. We'll be married and live in a fine house. What do you think of that?'

She threw her head back and gave a peal of laughter. 'Oh, Tom, I'm not going to marry a *grinder*.'

He flushed with annoyance. 'I'm not a grinder, I'm a penknife maker. At least, I will be when I'm out of my time. Any road, you'd be better off with me than living with Saul Bradshaw and his sons,' he said huffily. 'They treat you worse than a servant. You get all the rough work to do. You're nothing but a slave in that house. And it'll never be any different.'

'Yes, it will, because I'll not stay there for ever,' Joanna said firmly. 'When I find my mother's family they'll take me

5

away to live with them. They're very well-to-do, you know,' she said in a prim voice.

'Aye, so you've said.' Unimpressed, Tom picked a blade of grass and began to chew it. 'Although you're only saying that because you were wrapped in a blue velvet cloak when Martha found you. That doesn't mean owt. It certainly doesn't mean your family's well-to-do.'

'Yes, it does,' Joanna said crossly. 'It's a very good quality cloak, Martha says. She's folded it up and put it away carefully till I'm grown up.' She leaned towards him. 'And it's not only the material that's quality. It's got a silver clasp. Well, half of it's not there but the bit that's left is silver. *Real* silver. Martha hid it away so t'mester shouldn't see it and want to sell it, but she showed it me once.' She leaned back to see what impression her words had made on him.

To her disappointment Tom's expression didn't change. He continued to chew glumly on the blade of grass. 'If you come from such a well-to-do family why doesn't Saul Bradshaw treat you better?' he said at last. 'Why didn't he try and find out where your mother came from?'

'I dunno,' she said impatiently. 'Well, perhaps he did. Perhaps my mother came from a long way off. I don't know, do I?' Her expression went dreamy. 'But Martha said she was a very pretty girl. They found her in the river a few days after they'd found me but nobody knew where she'd come from. Martha says I look a bit like her.' She turned to him. 'Anyway, one day I shall find out for myself. I shall make enquiries.' She'd heard Martha use those words but she wasn't entirely sure what they meant, except that it was something to do with finding her family. She sighed. 'I expect I really belong in one of those big houses up Endcliffe way.'

Tom got to his feet. 'Well, at the moment you belong at Bradshaw's Farm and if you don't get back there soon you'll feel the weight of Saul Bradshaw's strap across your back,' he said cruelly. He had loved Joanna for as long as he could remember and it was his ambition to marry and cherish her. To hear her talk of her wealthy family made him feel jealous and inadequate and to lash out with his tongue was the only way he could give vent to his feelings.

She turned to him, aware that he was in some way upset.

6

'Don't worry, Tom,' she said kindly. 'When I get back to my rightful family I shan't forget you. I'll never forget you, Tom.' She laid her hand on his arm. 'You're my friend and you shall come and work in the stables at my house. You'll be my favourite groom.'

He shook her hand off. 'I don't know anything about horses,' he muttered, refusing to be patronised.

'Well, I'm sure I'll be able to find something for you to do.' She looked up into his face. 'I mean it, Tom. I shan't forget you. I promise.'

Suddenly, they heard the muffled sound of horse's hoofs coming along the cart track on the other side of the bramble hedge.

'It's the old charcoal burner and his daughter!' Tom whispered. 'Nobody else comes along here. Let's watch, but keep quiet so they don't see us and give us the evil eye.'

They peered through the thicket of bushes just as the cart, carrying poles from trees that had been coppiced further down the valley, came into view. It was pulled by a tired old nag and walking beside it were two people, the charcoal burner, a tall figure in a smoke-blackened coat that reached below his knees and an old stove-pipe hat, and his daughter, almost as tall as her father, wearing a tattered dress that had once been yellow and a shawl that showed shadowy remnants of a paisley pattern. On her head was a black straw hat with limp-looking greyish flowers round the brim. Both were black from the charcoal and smoke, and neither looked to left nor right as they walked. But it was the man that held a fearful fascination for the couple watching. Because almost the whole of one side of his face was missing, leaving nothing but a long, purple, puckered scar from where his eye had been to the corner of his mouth. To add to his bizarre appearance, he wore a black patch over the missing eye. It was said he had stopped a musket ball whilst fighting with Wellington at the Battle of Waterloo, but nobody knew whether or not this was true because he was not a man to question. He went quietly about his business of collecting the wood from the coppiced trees, bringing it back to his hut in the woods to burn, then delivering the charcoal to the industrial furnaces in the town. It was common knowledge that charcoal fires made the best steel and

Jack Ingram, even if he did only have one eye and only half a jaw, made the best charcoal.

Rumour had it that his daughter Liddy was a witch and with her strange dark eyes and wild, unkempt appearance most folk believed this. Indeed, Joanna and Tom had sometimes seen her at a distance in the woods gathering herbs and berries for the potions she brewed on the fire outside the hut where she lived with her father. Which was another very good reason for leaving the strange pair alone.

When the little cavalcade had gone past the two watching solemnly touched their noses and then spat on the ground because they'd seen a witch. Then they retrieved the basket of blackberries and hurried back to the farm.

Tom left Joanna to take the blackberries in to Martha while he carried on past the farmhouse and crossed the river by the rather rickety footbridge that connected the farm to the two low stone buildings opposite. In these buildings were housed ten small grinding workshops, or 'hulls' as they were known. Here Saul Bradshaw and his two sons Jacob and Caleb, Tom's master Zack Wenlock and six other grinders worked in filthy, cramped conditions, grinding table knives, razors, or pocket knives, each according to his trade. The buildings were known as 'Bradshaw's Wheel', taking their name from the ancestor of Saul's who had originally owned the property and the wheel that powered the grindstones.

But Saul's grandfather had been a gambler and he had gambled and lost Bradshaw's Wheel at the card tables, leaving his family with nothing but the rather unproductive farm. Since that time Bradshaw's Wheel had passed through several hands and was now owned by local industrialist Abraham Silkin, who lived in a big house on the hill overlooking the valley. The men working the grindstones, including Saul himself, although self-employed up to a point, paid rent to Abraham Silkin and were ultimately reliant on him for their livelihood.

This was a source of great bitterness to Saul and his dearest wish was to buy back the property that had once belonged to his family. It was a wish unlikely to be fulfilled, even though he worked hard and spent little, because most of the money he earned from grinding went towards propping up the failing farm. The land was poor, it cropped badly and was not even good grazing. And Abraham Silkin stubbornly refused to sell him the field further up the hill where the land was less water-logged and the grazing better.

Tom fetched a bucket of water and stood it beside his master's grindstone ready to tip into the trow the next day when Zack came back to work. He knew it was important not to leave water in the trough – or 'trow' – when the grindstone wasn't running because the part of the stone left hanging in the water would soak up the moisture and the whole thing become unbalanced, with the risk of bursting when it revolved up to speed.

Saul Bradshaw's hull was at the far end of the building. He was there now, crouched over his stone, putting the edge on table knives. As he worked he was sprayed with the water put in the trow to cool the revolving stone. Yellow swarf it was called because it became thick and yellow with sandstone dust and grit from the stone. He was the only grinder working that day; everybody else took Monday off, 'Grinder's Monday' they called it.

He paused in his work when he heard Tom.

'Is it tha, Caleb?' he called, peering into the gloom.

'Nay, it's me, Mester. Tom Cartwright.'

'Hast tha seen Caleb?'

'No. I've not.'

'Lazy young bugger. I sent him down into t'town hours ago. He should have been back by now. I shall be waiting on t'knives he's gone to fetch when I've finished these.' He threw down one knife and picked up another. 'Time's money and wasted time's wasted money,' he muttered as he resumed work.

Tom finished what he had come to do and made his way home to the row of grinders' cottages some half a mile down Hangingwater Lane, where Zack Wenlock and his wife gave him grudging board. On his way he met Caleb Bradshaw, who had just left his brother Jacob's cottage, which was next door to Zack's.

'Your dad's yelling for you,' Tom warned as he drew level with Caleb.

Caleb snorted. 'Me dad's allus yelling. And he can yell a bit longer. I'll not be at his beck and call all t'time. He seems to forget I've me own hull and me own living to make now. I'll not have him ordering me about like he did once-over.'

'He said he sent you down into the town hours ago,' Tom reminded him. He didn't much care for Caleb, not least because of the way he treated Joanna.

'He never sent me anywhere,' Caleb said with another snort. 'I was going down t'town and he asked me if I'd fetch his order. Well, I've fetched it.' He hitched up the bag on his shoulder. 'But he'll have to wait while I'm ready to tek it to him. I've been to beer shop with me brother, if he wants to know.' He continued on his way a trifle unsteadily, pausing only to shout over his shoulder. 'An' now I'm going home for a bit o' bread and cheese.'

Tom stopped for a word with Jacob's children, playing in the dirt, then went on into the cottage where he'd lived for the past eight years. Zack was sitting in his wooden armchair by the empty grate, snoring, and his wife sat opposite, knitting. She didn't look up when Tom entered; he hadn't expected her to. Ever since the day Zack took him in she had tried to pretend he wasn't there, apart from mealtimes, when she watched every meagre mouthful he took and complained to Zack that 't'work'us brat' was eating them out of house and home. But Tom accepted her attitude stoically. Living with Zack Wenlock was better than living in the workhouse and he was learning a trade. Once he was out of his time he would be off, into the town, to set up for himself. Until then he made sure that Mrs Zack's coal bucket was never empty and that he didn't offend her with his presence any more than was strictly necessary. That he was usually hungry and often cold he accepted as a fact of life. He went up to his attic under the eaves and flung himself down on his straw mattress where he could dream undisturbed of the day he would rescue Joanna and take her for his wife.

Chapter Two

Leaving Tom, Joanna took the basket of blackberries into the farmhouse and helped Martha to pick over the fruit before it was set in a pan over the fire to boil. Then she went and put the basket away in the cupboard under the stairs. When she came back into the kitchen Caleb was there, helping himself to a hunk of bread and a slab of cheese.

'I'd be glad if you'd go and dig the rest of the tatties up on t'field, Caleb,' his mother was saying, reaching for the bread before he mutilated it further. 'Your dad wants that field cleared before nightfall and Joanna's been giving me a hand so she's not had time to do it.'

'Well, she's time now, hasn't she?' He jabbed his knife in Joanna's direction. 'She's standing there doing nowt. Me, I've just walked back from town wi' a heavy pack, I'm not going out into no field digging tatties.' He crammed more bread into his mouth. 'Any road, it's her job, me dad told her to do it, so she can get on wi' it.'

'There's only the top corner left to do. It'd not tek you long, Caleb,' Martha said encouragingly.

He speared a lump of cheese and looked up. 'Then it'll not tek her long, neither, will it?' he said as he shoved it into his mouth.

'Oh, Caleb. It's hard work for a young lass. You'd get it done in half the time,' Martha pleaded.

'It's no use you going on at me, Ma.' He leaned back in his chair and belched loudly. 'I'm not doing it and that's flat. And if she doesn't shape herself and get up there and get on wi' it I shall tell me dad and he'll tek his strap to her. Then she'll move. By 'eck she will.'

11

A flash of fear crossed Joanna's face. 'I'd better go and do it, Martha,' she said quickly. She sidled past Caleb on her way to the door but even so he managed to catch her arm with one hand and flick it with the finger and thumb of the other. Over the years he had practised this and other tricks down to a fine and painful art. She wrenched free and hurried outside where she pulled on a pair of old boots before dragging the big old barrow up to the top of the field. Martha was right, there was only the top corner to do, Joanna had done the rest over the past weeks, often with Tom's help, but even after the hot, dry weather it was hard work, the fork was heavy to lift when it was full of claggy soil and picking up the potatoes was back-breaking work.

She pushed the fork into the ground and jumped on it to make it go deeper. It wouldn't always be like this, she told herself as she forced the handle down as far as she could and then stood on it to lift the soil. She shook the fork as best she could and then began to gather the potatoes as they turned up. One day she would find – or be found by – her rightful family. She put the potatoes into the bucket and emptied it into the barrow and then began the whole process again. Over the years she had found that thinking about her lost family, daydreaming about them, who they were, where they lived, helped even the worst tasks to become bearable. She was certain she came from wealthy stock, the velvet cloak she had been wrapped in when Martha found her left no doubt about that; but what possible disaster could have caused the daughter of some great house to run away and leave her newborn child in a cowshed on the edge of Whitely Woods and then take her own life? She must have been desperate to have done such a thing. Even in her worst moments of despair Joanna had never for a moment considered taking such a step. She smiled a little to herself as she pushed a strand of hair back, leaving a muddy mark down the side of her face. Oh, wouldn't her Family be overjoyed to discover that she was still alive? Her Family – she always thought about them possessively and with a capital letter. She straightened her back and rubbed it.

But who were her Family? The only large house nearby was Cliffe House, which stood near the top of the hill overlooking the farm. Abraham Silkin lived there with his godson and she often saw the old man walking in the fields when she was going about her work. Sometimes she even fancied he was watching her and the thought had crossed her mind that he might even know something about her, indeed could even be her long-lost grandfather! But in her heart she knew this was not possible, as far as anyone knew the old man had never been married, so could never have possessed a runaway daughter.

It was more likely that she belonged further away, up at Endcliffe perhaps, where there were several enormous houses. They mostly belonged to the big Sheffield industrialists, rich men who could afford an army of servants and several carriages. Once or twice she and Tom had crept up and looked at these houses, speculating over which one might be her rightful home, but they had never plucked up the courage to go and ask if anyone might be missing from the family. But one day she was determined that she would do just that. When she was older. Perhaps she might even go into service in one of those houses and then reveal that she was really the long-lost grandchild. What a surprise *that* would give them! They would be so overjoyed at finding her that they would dress her in beautiful clothes and let her ride in the carriage. A beautiful blue dress, all shiny satin and lace ...

Suddenly, a blow on the back of her head pitched her into the dirt.

'Get on wi' it. I don't feed and house tha to spend tha time daydreaming. Look, tha's missed half a dozen over there.' It was Saul. She hadn't heard him come up the field. She scrabbled up the last of the potatoes and tipped them into the barrow.

He watched, then nodded. 'Tha can tek the barra back to t'yard now.'

She tried to push it. It wouldn't move. 'I can't budge it, Saul,' she cried. 'It's too heavy.'

'Bah, tha's nowt but a mealy-mouthed little pipsqueak.' He gave the barrow a shove to help it on its way and strode off, leaving her to haul it as best she might the rest of the way. Back in the yard she put the potatoes in the barn with the rest and then kicked off the boots. There were broken blisters on her heels under the dirt and the tops of the boots

13

had rubbed her legs raw. She went inside.

'Ee, look at you. Come near t'fire, lass, and let me bathe them feet.' Martha bustled about fetching a bowl and cloth. She smiled as she saw Joanna's look of alarm. 'There's nowt to fret over, we'll not be caught. Saul's gone down to t'beer house for once.'

Joanna put her feet gratefully into the warm, soothing water and Martha rubbed them gently. 'Lady's feet,' she mused. 'Not feet for them great boots. No wonder your feet's blistered,' she said absentmindedly. She looked up at Joanna. 'Saul thinks Caleb's up to summat. That's why he's followed him tonight. But the lad's nearly thirty. If he's got a lass somewhere I don't see Saul's any right to interfere. It's high time he was wed, any road.'

'If Caleb was wed and had a wife to keep Saul would have to pay him more for the work he does on the farm,' Joanna said sagely. 'He'd not like that. Look how he complains when he has to pay Jacob to help.'

Martha began to dry her feet gently with a cloth. 'Aye, you're right, lass, Saul 'ud not like that. He's not one to spend a ha'penny if a farthing'll do.' She frowned. 'But if that's what the lad's bent on Saul'll not be stopping him, that's for sure.'

Joanna hoped Martha was right and that Caleb would soon take himself a wife. She had never liked him, he had always been cruel and unkind to her and lately, since she had shown signs of budding womanhood he had begun looking at her and even touching her in a way she didn't like at all. She considered confiding in Martha but she suspected that Martha wouldn't be sympathetic because she cherished the vain hope that one day Caleb and Joanna would marry. So she kept her own counsel and made sure to put a wooden wedge in the latch of her bedroom door each night. Just in case.

The days shortened, and there was a nip in the air that heralded autumn. One afternoon Joanna went into the wood to gather wood for the fire and found Tom already there.

'I keep Mrs Zack supplied with firewood,' he said cheerfully. 'Not that it does me much good. She never says thank you and I never get to sit by the blaze, but at least I'm more

14

likely to get a decent helping of stew when the log pile's high.'

They walked along together, their feet rustling through the thick golden carpet of fallen leaves that covered the ground. As they went they picked up dead branches that had fallen and left them ready to be tied into bundles on their way back and carried away.

'T'Mester followed Caleb again the other night. Martha says t'Mester thinks he's "up to something",' Joanna said, dragging another branch to the heap. 'Martha says she reckons it's a woman. I hope it is. I hope he'll get wed and go right away. I *hate* him.' She flung the branch down viciously.

'What's the matter, Jo? You're limping,' Tom said, ignoring what she had been saying.

'Didn't you hear what I said, Tom? Martha thinks Caleb ...'

'Yes, I heard.' Tom's voice was matter-of-fact.

'Well?'

He looked up. 'Well, what?'

'What do you think, Tom? Do you think Caleb's after a woman?'

'Caleb's been after women ever since I've known him,' Tom said scathingly. 'And Saul knows it. No, I reckon Saul's afraid he's got himself mixed up with the Ratteners.'

'Ratteners? Who are they?'

'It's all to do wi' trade unions. The Ratteners go after folk as don't belong to a union or don't pay their union dues.' He shrugged. 'Don't fret yourself over it, Jo. Any road, you wouldn't understand.' As he spoke he was looking at her foot from all angles. Now he pointed to it. 'There's summat wrong wi' your foot, Jo. See? It's all swollen. You can hardly get your foot into your clog.'

She waved her hand impatiently. 'Oh, I got blisters when I was digging tatties a few weeks back and one of them's gone funny. It'll be all right,' she said. 'Tell me some more about this trade union business, Tom.'

'I can't. I don't know anything much about it, except my Mester pays his dues before owt else, which makes t'Missus riled.' He frowned, his attention still on her foot. 'Have you put owt on it?' he persisted.

'Martha put some salve on but it didn't do much good.' She took her foot out of her clog and stared down at it. 'It does look a bit angry, doesn't it?' She pressed it experimentally. 'I must say it hurts a lot more than it has done before.'

He sat down on a fallen log and took her foot in his hand. 'It looks real bad, Jo. It needs binding up properly.' He glanced up at her. 'Do you feel all right?'

'Of course I do.' She nodded irritably. 'Well,' she admitted. 'To tell the truth I have felt a bit odd at times today. Sort of all hot and light-headed. And I nearly fainted when I got out of bed this morning.'

'I'm not surprised. Did you tell Martha?'

'I told her it was a bit sore so she gave me some more salve. She didn't have time for owt else because it were market day. But she said I needn't go with her like I usually do if me foot was sore.' She pulled her foot away. 'It'll be all right, Tom. It's nowt.' She put her clog back on and took a few painful steps. 'Oh, Tom! Now look what you've done. You've been pulling it about and now it's all swollen up worse. Oh, what have you done to it?'

He spread his hands. 'I've not done anything, Jo. It's swelling up because it's poisoned, that's why it hurts so much. Look, there's already a red mark going up your ankle. It'll go right up your leg if something's not done soon.' He traced the line, then looked at her anxiously. 'You should have told Martha how bad it was, Jo.'

'What more could she do? She gave me the salve.' She tried to walk again but the foot was too painful. She looked up at him with frightened eyes. 'You'll have to carry me home, Tom. Oh, I don't know what t'Mester will say. He'll be that mad if I can't get his meal.'

Tom stared at the foot for several minutes. Then he said doubtfully, 'I suppose we could go and see Liddy. Folk do say she can cure things. I've known several people who've gone to her for potions.'

Joanna's eyes widened in horror. 'But she's a witch! She might want to make me eat a frog! People say—'

'Oh, Jo, I don't think she's as bad as all that.' Tom laughed nervously. 'Look, I can see smoke rising from the kiln so we can't be very far from her hut. I couldn't carry you all the way

16

home but I could probably carry you that far.'

'No. I'm not going there. I'll walk home. I can walk if I lean on you, I'm sure I can,' she said urgently. 'Martha'll put some more salve on it when she gets back. It'll be all right.'

'I'm sorry, Jo. You couldn't walk that far and I certainly couldn't carry you.'

'Then I'll crawl.' She got down on her hands and knees.

'Don't be daft, Jo. You'll never get home like that.' He pulled her up to her feet and then swung her up in his arms, staggering a little. 'Liddy's is nearer. I'll take you there. I promise I won't let her make you eat a frog, Jo.'

'But she's a witch. There's no telling what spell she might cast on us,' Joanna whimpered.

'Don't be silly, Jo.' Tom laughed nervously as he spoke.

Terrified, Joanna clung to him as he staggered along to the clearing in the wood where the charcoal burner and his daughter lived. Jack Ingram had levelled the ground so that he could build his kilns on flat land and behind them was the hut that was their dwelling place, a wooden shack with a chimney and a rickety wooden door. Over the whole clearing there hung an acrid, smoky smell that remained even when the kiln was not firing.

As they approached Joanna could see Jack Ingram at the edge of the clearing, bent over a sawing horse, sawing timber into the right lengths for building the next kiln. Liddy was carrying it away and stacking it carefully. In the foreground a carefully constructed kiln was already smouldering gently.

Joanna felt Tom stiffen as they entered the clearing. Many times the two of them had watched the old charcoal burner and his daughter at work, but always from a distance and always well hidden because it was well known that Jack Ingram's temper was uncertain and they knew that even with only one eye his aim with stones and lumps of rock was unerring. Even more, they feared Liddy's evil eye.

Then, Jack Ingram saw them.

'Aargh! Gruugh!' He shouted, his grotesque jaw making his speech incomprehensible. He waved his arms. 'Gruughoom!' He picked up a stone.

'We mean no harm, sir,' Tom shouted bravely although Joanna could feel his heart pounding through his thin jacket. 'We need help.'

'It's all right, Pa, I'll see to them.' Liddy straightened up and came over to where Tom was standing, still holding Joanna in his arms. 'Well, what is it you want?' she asked in a surprisingly educated voice.

Joanna's arms tightened round Tom's neck. She had never been this close to Liddy before and at close quarters she was even more fearsome. Her black hair hung down in rat's tails from under her battered straw hat and her teeth were rotten and broken. But it was her eyes, black and piercing in a face that was as brown as a walnut, that frightened Joanna most. They looked as if they could see right down into her soul.

'Well, what is it you want?' she repeated, her hands on her hips.

'My friend has hurt her foot,' Tom said. 'It looks bad to me.'

'Well?' Liddy gave him no help.

He licked his lips. 'I – we've heard that you—'

Liddy threw her head back and laughed derisively. 'You've heard tell I'm a witch?'

'I – yes – *no*,' he corrected himself hurriedly. 'We've heard you can cure—' Suddenly, he felt Joanna grow limp in his arms. 'Oh, Lord, she's fainted. Look,' he said, alarmed. 'Now what shall I do?'

'Oh, put her down. I'll take a look at her,' Liddy said irritably. She stared at Joanna for several minutes, then bent down and examined her foot. Then, without a word, she got up and went off into the hut. She was gone some time and when she came back she was grinding something in a wooden mortar with a wooden pestle. This she spread on the angry red swelling.

Then she went back to the hut and came back with a tin mug. By this time Joanna had come round and was clinging to Tom.

'I'm frightened,' she whispered. 'Don't let her—'

'Drink this,' Liddy ordered.

Joanna turned her head away and put her hand over her mouth.

Liddy dragged it away, saying impatiently, 'Go on. It won't poison you.' She forced it between Joanna's lips. 'Now make

18

her lie down,' she said to Tom, 'Because I'm going to need your help.'

As she spoke she dragged a tinder box and a lethal-looking knife from the folds of her skirt. When she had the tinder alight she held the knife in the flame for a few seconds, then quickly plunged it into Joanna's foot. A stream of stinking green and yellow pus gushed out.

Tom winced and turned away to look at Joanna's face as Liddy kneaded the wound to get the rest of the poison out. But whatever it was she had given the girl to drink, Joanna was lying quite still with her eyes closed and didn't even flinch.

'You've killed her!' he shouted.

'Don't be ridiculous. Of course I haven't killed her.' Liddy was busily wrapping the wound in large green leaves, which she tied with twine. 'She'll be as right as ninepence in an hour.' She finished tying the leaves then sat back on her heels. For something like ten minutes she stayed quite still, watching the girl, an expression on her face that terrified Tom in its intensity. He stood beside her, looking first at Joanna, then at Liddy, not knowing what to do, not daring to speak, still not totally convinced that Joanna wasn't dead.

Suddenly, she sat up and was violently sick on the ground.

Liddy watched dispassionately, then nodded. 'No matter. It's done its job,' she said. 'It often takes them that way.' She got to her feet and waved them away. 'Go on, be off with you now and leave us alone.'

Tom helped Joanna to her feet. She was dazed and ashen-faced. He frowned. 'Are you sure she'll be all right now?' he asked doubtfully.

'I feel terrible. She's poisoned me. I told you she'd poison me. She's a witch.' Joanna wailed and was promptly sick again.

'Oh, don't talk such rot,' Liddy said impatiently. 'Of course I haven't poisoned you. It's your imagination. How does the foot feel?'

Gingerly, Joanna put her weight on it. 'It's still sore but I must say it feels a lot better,' she said doubtfully.

'Well, leave it wrapped till after the full moon. As the moon wanes take the leaves off, a few at a time, and bury them under a sycamore tree.' She turned to go. Then turned back. 'And tell nobody what I've done,' she warned. 'Nobody! I have enough people coming to me for cures as it is.'

'We'll not tell a soul,' Joanna promised fervently.

'We should pay you. We should give you something,' Tom said urgently. Now that he could see the colour returning to Joanna's face he was anxious to be gone, but he knew he shouldn't go without paying Liddy. If a witch wasn't paid for her trouble you were in her power.

Liddy looked him up and down. 'And what have you got to give?' she asked with a sneer. 'What do you own?'

'I could make you summat,' Tom said bravely. 'I could make you a penknife.'

Liddy nodded. 'Aye. That you could. And get a beating from your Mester for your pains.' A ghost of a smile flitted across her face. 'Well, I thank you for the thought but I'll not accept. And I'll tell you this. You've nothing to fear from me. I'll do you no harm. Nor her, neither.' She gave a nod in Joanna's direction.

Then she turned and strode off into the hut.

Tom and Joanna walked home in silence, both too shaken by what had happened to talk. When she got back to the farm Joanna found a pair of Martha's old stockings and put them on so that no one would see the leaves Liddy had bound on her foot. When she took the last of them off, as the moon waned, burying them as Liddy had ordered, there was not even a scar to show where the knife had been plunged, further proof, if Joanna needed it, that Liddy Ingram was indeed a witch.

Chapter Three

Christmas came and went, hardly noticed in the Bradshaw household where one day was very like another. Joanna still dreamed of finding her family, but as time wore on the dream began to fade in the face of reality. Once, on a snowy day in early January, she ventured as far as the gate of Whitely Wood Hall and found it ajar. With a courage born of desperation she slipped inside and stood looking at the breathtaking view of the grey stone house rising above the snow-covered grounds, the huge trees in the park showing black against the pure white backdrop. Gingerly she began to walk towards the house. She had hardly taken half a dozen steps before the lodge-keeper's wife came out, irritable at being dragged from her warm kitchen, and caught her by the hair, shoving her unceremoniously back through the gates and slamming them in her face.

'I wasn't doing any harm,' Joanna shouted. 'I was only looking for my grandfather. He lives in a big house like this. He's a gentleman and when he finds out how you've treated me it'll be the worse for you.'

'A likely story,' the woman shouted back. 'I've seen your sort before. Lying, thieving vagabonds.'

'But it's true.' Joanna pressed her face to the cold metal of the gate and rattled it desperately with hands blue with cold. 'My mother's dead. I know she came from a big house like this and I'm looking for her father.'

'Well, you'll not find him here, you lying little toad. The master's got no daughter. Nor son, neither. He's a widower. And childless. Now, be off with you before I fetch the broom to your backside.' The woman picked up a stick and poked it

21

at her through the bars of the gate, pushing her away.

She told Tom about it the next day when he walked to the churchyard with her in the snow to put some greenery on her mother's grave. This was nothing more than a grass-covered mound set in unconsecrated ground in a far corner of the churchyard because the young woman buried there had taken her own life. Joanna hated to think of her poor mother lying alone in that isolated spot so she regularly put flowers there to show that she was not forgotten; primroses and wild violets in the spring, then bluebells in their season; pink and white campion and dog roses in the summer and old man's beard as autumn drew on. In winter there was always holly with its bright berries that had to be replaced often because the birds ate them.

It was holly she had brought today and as she lovingly arranged it in the cracked stone jam jar Martha had given her the berries were like drops of blood against the white snow that covered the ground.

Tom watched thoughtfully as she adjusted the prickly branches and then sat back on her heels to survey her handiwork.

'If your mother had come from round these parts, Jo, surely there would have been notices up or something,' he remarked. 'Somebody would have heard about a missing girl, wouldn't they? Especially a daughter from one of the big houses.'

She shrugged and adjusted a twig. 'Maybe. Maybe not. Most folk I know can't read, any road, so even if there had been notices they wouldn't have known what they said.'

'Even so, Jo. Think about it. A story like that would have been all round the market in town. You know news goes round there like wildfire.' He shook his head. 'No, do you know what I think?'

'Don't see how I should,' she replied tartly. She didn't want her dream spoiled.

'I reckon your mother came from further afield. Somewhere over the other side of Sheffield, perhaps. Or Rotherham. Derby, even.' That was the limit of his horizon.

Joanna's too. Her shoulders slumped. 'Then I'll never find out.'

He gave her a little shake. 'Yes you will. One day. When I'm out of me time and earning some money we'll put notices in t'papers.' He smiled at her encouragingly. 'I promise we will, Jo. Don't give up. I promise I'll help you find her.'

She didn't smile back. For how could they put notices in the newspapers when neither of them could read or write?

The conversation with Tom made her realise the futility of trying to find her mother. Yet deep down inside she was convinced that somehow, some day, she would find her family and discover the identity of the woman who had given birth to her. And it was this conviction that sustained her through the long winter days of stacking logs, cutting up mangolds for the animal feed, hoeing turnips, digging potatoes, cleaning out the pig-sty and the cattle shed, a never-ending round of back-breaking tasks that had to be done in addition to the dairy and housework.

She went out to do the morning milking one day in late March. It was her sixteenth birthday and as she laid her head against the cow's warm side and rhythmically began to squeeze out the milk she realised that it was on such a day, when every branch and twig was rimed with frost and her breath was cloudy in the freezing air, that Martha had discovered her as a tiny baby, lying in the straw, wrapped in the beautiful velvet cloak with the broken clasp. It must have been a magical moment. Like finding a little princess. She sniffed and wiped her nose with the back of her hand. For all she knew, or was ever likely to know, she *was* a princess.

She straightened up and carried the frothing bucket of milk to the dairy to cool and be dealt with later. There was nothing magical about her life now, she thought bitterly, as she shivered under one of Caleb's old donkey jackets in the icy morning air.

She took a pitcher of milk and went indoors. The porridge was on the stove and Saul was at the table.

'Took tha long enough,' he growled as she ladled out a basinful and put it in front of him.

She took no notice, but poured him a mug of tea and pushed it across the table.

Martha looked up from cutting up a loaf of bread. 'Caleb's late this morning,' she said. 'But it was late when he came home last night. Trying to burn the candle at both ends, if you ask me.'

'Nobody did ask tha, woman,' Saul said without looking up.

23

Suddenly, the door opened and Jacob burst in. 'Where is he? Where's my bloody brother?' he shouted.

'What's up wi' you, Jacob, my son? What's to do?' Martha asked, mystified.

'I'll bet it were him. I allus knew he were in wi' t'bloody Ratteners. He's teken t'bands off my grindstone so's I can't do me work. And he's teken 'em off Billy Jenkins' stone *and* Fred Rogers'. *All* on us can't do us work because o' that bastard.'

'Calm down, tha hot-headed bugger,' Saul said, his mouth full of hot porridge. 'What meks tha think it were Caleb? These Ratteners come an' go in t'middle of t'night. Tha can't tell—'

'I'll bet I bloody can.' Jacob turned as Caleb came into the kitchen, yawning and rubbing his eyes. 'It were you, weren't it, you miserable little sod!'

'What were?' Caleb slouched down at the table and reached for a mug of tea.

'Took our bands! How can us work wi' no bands on us grindstones?'

Caleb looked up and shrugged. 'I know nowt about you an' your bloody bands. All I can say is maybe if you all paid your union dues you'd get 'em back.'

Jacob banged his fist down on the table. 'How can I pay me bloody dues if me bands are gone so I can't earn t'brass? Any road I need all I can earn to keep t'kids fed. If you'd got six kids and another on t'way you wouldn't find it so rosy, brother.'

'That's your look-out. You should keep your—'

'That'll do, Caleb,' his mother cut across his words.

'—in your trousers,' he muttered into his mug.

'That'll *do*, Caleb!' Martha banged her fist on the table. She turned to her elder son. 'How much do you owe, Jacob?'

'Ten shillin'.'

Martha's jaw dropped and she sighed. She looked at Saul. 'Well, Mester, are you willing to help t'lad out?'

'Where do you think I'm goin' to find ten shillin', woman?' he muttered.

'In the box under your bed,' she replied tartly. She went into the larder and came back with a florin which she slipped

24

into Jacob's hand. 'It's not much, lad, but it'll help,' she said quietly. She turned to Caleb. 'And what about you, Caleb? Will you stand by and see your brother's family starve?'

Caleb reached in his pocket. 'Here's a shillin',' he said grudgingly.

Saul laid five shillings down on the table. 'Get it down to t'union. They'll give tha bands back if tha pays a bit off. Go on. Now!'

'What about them others?' Jacob said, looking at the money in his hand. 'What are they going to do?'

'Same as you. Find somebody who'll help them out if they can't pay,' Saul said. 'But that's their look-out.'

After Jacob had gone he rounded on Caleb. 'I've told tha before, tha'll get thysen in real trouble, my lad,' he said, jabbing his spoon to emphasise every word. 'Folks don't like Ratteners, specially when they start Rattening on their own folk. If tha's not careful tha'll find thysen waking up dead in a ditch one o' these days.'

Caleb didn't answer. He ate his porridge noisily and when Joanna went round the table to refill his bowl he didn't look at her but shoved his hand up her skirt. She pulled away quickly, flushing. She'd forgotten she must never stand too close to him.

When the two men had gone over to begin their day's work at Bradshaw's Wheel, Martha went about her work muttering, 'Ratteners, indeed. I'm sure my Caleb wouldn't get himself mixed up wi' the likes o' them. He's got too much sense. And to accuse him of tekin' his own brother's bands ... As if he would!' She noticed Joanna standing watching her and she waved her away impatiently. 'Don't just stand there gawping, lass. Go and collect the rest of the eggs and get them wiped ready for market tomorrow. And don't forget to look under the horse trough, Biddy's very fond of laying her eggs there, these days.'

Joanna took the egg basket and went out into the yard. She had never seen Martha so agitated, so determined to defend her younger son. Plainly she was as convinced of his guilt as his father and brother. Joanna sighed. She knew nothing about the Ratteners and their ways, all she knew was that it would be nice if he was caught and imprisoned, then she wouldn't have to avoid his wandering hands, and wouldn't have to secure her bedroom door against him every night. It was a pleasant thought.

She turned her attention to collecting the eggs. There were a nice lot and she would have to be up before it was light the next day in order to walk into town to the market with them. Ever since she could remember there had been the weekly trip to the market to sell the eggs and she always looked forward to it as a break from the dull drudgery of her days. Even before she could walk Martha had carried her in a nest made by tucking a corner of her shawl into the top of her skirt and as she got older many's the time she had returned home on Martha's back because her tired little legs wouldn't carry her up the steep hills. But now on the days when Martha's legs were bad she was glad for Joanna to make the journey on her own because even though the girl couldn't read or write she was quick with figures and could count and calculate as well as, if not better than, most.

Joanna went to bed early, carefully placing the wedge of wood in the door latch so there was no danger of Caleb forcing his way in. She knew he had tried the latch on more than one occasion because she had heard it click and she was terrified that one night she might forget her makeshift lock. Worse, there was no one she could turn to for help because she knew this was the one thing over which Martha would have no sympathy. Nothing would please her more than for Caleb to marry Joanna, and if he made her pregnant first, well, it was only the way of a man with a maid.

Nevertheless, safe with her wedge firmly in place, Joanna slept like a log and woke at six to prepare for her trip to market. She dressed quickly and slipped downstairs to roar up the fire so that she could make some dripping toast and a mug of tea before setting out on the long walk into town. She was holding the toasting fork to the flames and savouring the warmth when suddenly she felt two arms round her and two hands clutching her breasts.

She wriggled round to face Caleb. 'Give over,' she whispered fiercely. 'Why aren't you still asleep?'

'Sleep? Me? I've not been to bed yet. I've only just come in.' He leered at her. 'An' I can just do wi' a little nightcap before I go up.' He held her fast with one hand and began to

26

unbuckle his belt with the other, not helped by the ominous bulge in his trousers. 'You may keep me out of your bedroom, my lass, but I'm not fussy,' he said, breathing heavily as he wrestled one-handed with the stiff leather. 'What I want'll do as well here as anywhere else. God knows you've kept me waiting long enough for it. Oh, bugger it!' He let her go briefly so that he could take two hands to undo the buckle and quick as a flash she shot round the table out of his reach.

'Touch me again and I'll have your eyes out with this toasting fork,' she warned, shaking the bread off it and holding it out towards him. 'And it's been in t'fire so it's red-hot.'

'You little—' he lunged at her across the table, trying to grab the toasting fork, but she was too quick for him and she plunged it into his arm and dragged it down nearly to his wrist, leaving four deep burning scratches.

With a howl of rage he covered the arm with his other one, hugging it to himself in agony. 'You bloody little bitch. You won't get away wi' this. I'll have you. By God, I'll have you if it's the last thing I do,' he said, between gritted teeth.

She lifted her head. 'That you never will, Caleb Bradshaw. I'll see you dead first.' She threw the toasting fork down on the table, picked up her shawl and the two baskets of eggs and walked out into the cold morning to begin the long walk to market.

She'd had no breakfast, not even a drink of water, but she wasn't hungry. She was shivering, but she wasn't cold; she felt sick every time she thought of the scene that had just taken place and that she couldn't get out of her mind. It had been sheer luck that she had been holding the hot toasting fork; without that she realised she would have been powerless against him. Next time – and she was in no doubt there would be a next time – she might not be so lucky.

Oh, God, she whispered over and over again, I wish I never had to set eyes on him again. I hate him. I wish he was dead. I wish he was dead. As she walked the words became like an accompaniment to the clatter of her clogs.

She was so busy with her thoughts and the words going over and over in her mind that at first she didn't notice the strange figure marching along the road towards her. As she got closer she could see that it was a woman carrying a long staff as a walking stick, her black shawl and skirts flapping in the breeze as she strode along, her hat rammed squarely on her long, greasy hair. As she drew level with Joanna she slowed down and stared at the girl, her black eyes narrowing. She opened her mouth as if she was about to speak, then thought the better of it and without a word, nodded and walked on.

As soon as Liddy the witch had passed Joanna put down the eggs and with shaking hands touched her nose and spat on the ground. Then she picked up her baskets again and hurried on, wrestling with the uncomfortable feeling that Liddy's black, piercing eyes had been able to see right down into her soul.

The first part of the journey had been along Hangingwater Lane, little more than a cart track bordered by frost-spangled hedgerows and tall trees whose black skeletal branches met overhead for all the world like the nave of a huge cathedral, but as the track joined the proper road and the way became wider and lighter Joanna's spirits began to rise and she forgot the bad beginning to the day. The road now was sparsely scattered with houses and shops and a few people going about their daily round and the nearer she got to the town that sprawled over the valley and up the hills beyond, the thicker the scattering became until it was so tightly packed with a jumble of houses, shops, beer houses and factories that it was all too easy to become lost in the maze of narrow streets and ginnels. But Joanna had been coming to the market ever since she could remember and as long as she kept to the streets she knew she had no difficulty in finding it. Market Day was as good as a holiday to her; with any luck the eggs would be sold before midday and Martha had told her she could buy a pie from the pie-seller before making her way home.

'And a ribbon for your hair, lass, although you'll have to mek sure *he* doesn't see it,' Martha warned. It was Martha and Joanna's secret that the money from one egg in every dozen went into Martha's pocket instead of Saul's. 'After all, he doesn't collect the eggs so he can't know how well the hens lay, can he?' Martha said with a wink.

In the town the air was thick and choking with the smoke from the factory chimneys and Joanna had to protect her baskets from the people who hurried and jostled their way along the streets, so intent on getting to work on time that they often only narrowly avoided the wheels of the carts and horse buses and the hoofs of the straining horses. It was all very exciting, but a little frightening too.

She reached the market and took up her position alongside the stalls of fresh vegetables, sweet-smelling bread, cheap and gaudy trinkets, multi-coloured ribbons and buttons, and sticky sweets and toffee. There was no need for her to shout her wares, Bradshaw's brown eggs were well known in the district and she would have no trouble in getting rid of them. So she watched the jugglers and the man on stilts who towered above the crowd and she stamped her feet to keep warm and counted the money and hid it away carefully against the pickpockets who roamed the busy market as the egg baskets slowly emptied. By eleven o'clock they were all gone.

By this time she was hungry so she bought a pie from the pie-seller and ate it as she walked round, looking at the stalls. Martha had told her she could buy a ribbon and she spent a farthing on one that was bright red. Then, as it began to rain in cold, sleety needles, she turned for home.

She trudged along. It was uphill all the way back, and she was tired, cold and wet. When she heard the horse bus coming along she stopped it and climbed aboard. She was sure Martha wouldn't mind her spending a penny to shorten the journey. After all, the ribbon had only cost a farthing. She sat down with her two baskets behind two women who, from the look of their baskets, had also come from the market. The conductor was in a garrulous mood and when he clipped their tickets he spoke of an explosion in the town. Joanna pricked up her ears. Martha always liked to be told the latest gossip.

'It were at Tyzacks,' the conductor told them. 'Did you not hear about it?'

'Aye,' one of the women nodded and the cherries on her hat wobbled. 'It were all the talk in the market. I've not heard what the damage was, but it were a hefty bang, by all accounts. Did you hear, Doris?'

'I heard it were them union men,' Doris answered, pursing her lips. 'My man says t'trade unions have got a stranglehold on industry. He says if you don't belong to t'union or if you don't pay your dues you're liable to get blown up, or at t'very

29

least t'Ratteners'll sneak in and tek the bands off the grind-stones so you can't work. It's disgusting. Never ought to be allowed.' She gave a disapproving shrug.

'My man says industry needs t'union for protection,' the other one said stoutly. 'My man allus pays his dues because he says t'union kept us alive when he were out o' work all them months two year ago. We'd have starved if he hadn't been able to go on t'box, as they call it. We was paid a few shillings, reg'lar as clockwork every week, and that's what kept us going. He says his contributions go to help any of his mates who can't work. Oh, aye, my man is a great one for t'union.'

'Not when they go Rattening and blowing up other folk's work place, surely,' Doris said, shocked.

'It's only them as don't belong to t'union, or don't pay their dues as get Rattened on. T'union looks after the workers, my man says. Meks sure a man gets a proper wage and looks after him when he's sick or wi'out work. And it can't do that wi'out money, so them as don't pay deserve to be made an example of.' The cherries on her hat nodded in complete and self-satis-fied agreement.

Joanna had to get off the horse bus at this point so she didn't hear any more of the argument, but she turned it over in her mind as she walked the last two miles home. This must be what Caleb was involved with. This must be what the trouble had been about yesterday at breakfast. She frowned. All this talk of unions was more than she could understand, but she rehearsed what she had heard carefully so she could relate it to Martha when she got home. But Martha didn't want to listen. She said it was none of their business and she was sure it wasn't anything Caleb would get mixed up in spite of what his brother had said.

But Joanna wasn't convinced and she noted that Caleb still hadn't come home when she finished her chores and crawled into bed at nearly midnight. He didn't appear at breakfast either and when Martha went up to his room his bed hadn't been slept in.

'Stop worriting, woman,' Saul said when she returned to the breakfast table and waved away the bowl of porridge Joanna put in front of her. 'T'lad's over thirty. Time he was wed, but sin' he's not it's not surprising if he has a night on the tiles now and then.'

He had hardly finished speaking when there was a commotion in the yard and the door flew open.

'Bad news, Mester.' A swarf-covered grinder snatched off his cap revealing a shock of red hair. 'We found your lad on us way to work. You'd better come and see.' He jerked his head towards the yard.

Saul never took his eyes off the man's face. He scraped back his chair and followed him out into the yard, with Martha, wringing her hands in her apron just behind him. Joanna came last.

A figure completely covered with several coats was lying on an old door in the mud of the yard. Saul bent and lifted the coats, making a strange, strangled sound in the back of his throat when he saw the drenched body of his younger son.

'He were lying face down in Porter Brook when us found him,' the red-headed man said. 'We called the Constable and he tried to pump him out but it were too late, he were already cold. He must have been there best part of all night, we reckon.'

'The Constable reckoned he must have fell in when he were drunk and then couldn't get out,' a second man said.

They stood aside for Martha, who stood looking down at Caleb dry-eyed although her face was ravaged with shock and grief. 'What's that gash on his temple?' she asked, mechanically smoothing back the hair from her son's pallid face.

'Likely struck his head as he went in, Missus. Them rocks where he fell is powerful sharp,' a third man in the background said quickly.

'Aye. I guess you're right.' She gave a deep sigh and turned away. 'You'd better fetch him in so's I can lay him out proper,' she said, her voice dead.

'Hadn't you better call somebody in to do that, Missus?' the red-headed man said, shuffling his feet uncomfortably.

Martha slowly turned and looked at him. 'Why should I? He's my son. It was me that gave him birth and it'll be me that shrouds him.' She nodded towards Joanna. 'She'll help me.'

Joanna didn't answer. She was remembering her encounter with Liddy the witch, who had seen right down into her soul and had known that she wanted Caleb dead.

31

Chapter Four

Joanna did what she had to do to help Martha while Saul sat in
his chair by the fire crying like a baby, a broken man. She
fetched water and helped her cut off Caleb's sodden clothes.
Then she stood by as the older woman lovingly cleaned and
laid out the lifeless body of her son. But all the time Caleb's
eyes, dark and staring in his waxen face, seemed to be watching her, following her accusingly wherever she moved. It was
as if he had known she wanted him dead, had somehow caused
it to happen. Not until Martha gently closed his eyes for the
last time and laid pennies on his eyelids could Joanna take her
eyes off his face.

When the task was finished Martha gently covered Caleb
over with a sheet to wait for the undertaker to arrive with the
coffin.

'I'll never believe he fell in Porter Brook of his own
accord,' she said dully as they left the room. 'Drunk or sober
he'd walked that path all his life and never tripped. But who's
to say who helped him to his death? And any road, what's the
odds? He's dead and that's all there is to it. The Bible says an
eye for an eye, a tooth for a tooth, but where's the sense in
that? Teking another life won't bring back the one that's gone,
will it?'

Joanna had no answer to Martha's logic and no will to find
one, burdened as she was with her own guilt over the death of
the man she hated. 'I'll make a cup of tea,' she said.

Saul was still sitting by the dying fire crying noisily. She
riddled the ashes, then put more coal on and pumped the
bellows to hasten the blaze. When it had flared up well she

pulled the kettle forward. It was strange, she mused, that Saul, great cruel bully that he was, should be giving way to his grief in this way whilst Martha, tiny and sparrow-like, went dry-eyed and silent about taking down cups from the dresser and fetching more milk from the dairy. But she had aged twenty years in the past hours. Her face was parchment-white and ravaged as she went about her tasks like a clockwork toy only half wound, as if any moment she would slow down and come to a sagging halt. But it didn't happen and she kept doggedly on, finding her strength in everyday tasks. Joanna could only watch helplessly and listen as Martha extolled the virtues of the paragon that had been her son, virtues that Joanna had never witnessed in all her sixteen years, in a paragon she didn't recognise.

It was much later in the day before she felt she could leave Martha and Saul long enough to sneak over to Bradshaw's Wheel. She was desperate to see Tom because he was the only person she could confide in, the only one she could unburden her guilt to.

She crossed the wooden bridge over the river and climbed the steps made from old grinding wheels to the low stone building. It was getting dusk and as she peered in at the open door she could see the men working by the light of candle stubs stuck wherever there was a space. The grindstones were all running except for the two at the far end, belonging to Saul and Caleb, which stood ominous in their stillness. The other men worked without speaking, the only sounds the whirring and rasp of the grindstones, the tapping of hammers and the constant roar of water from the dam, powering the huge wheel that turned the central drive shaft which ran through all the hulls, from one end of the building to the other. There was no question of work ceasing even though there was a death in their midst.

Next to the two silent hulls Jacob worked doggedly on; he couldn't afford to lose time grieving over his dead brother when he had hungry mouths to feed. In any case, he had little to thank Caleb for, he argued, as he adjusted the leather band that connected his stone to the drive shaft. These bands were the targets of the illegal Ratteners, for without them the grindstones had no power to turn. He hadn't forgiven Caleb for removing his, because now everyone knew that he hadn't paid his dues, but he'd walked away from the drunken scuffle last night, never dreaming it would end in his brother's death.

He shifted on his horsing, as the wooden seat in front of the grindstone was called, picked up another blade and bent forward over the revolving stone. He didn't blame himself; he couldn't have saved Caleb, in fact if he'd tried he could likely have ended up in the river with him. No, the best thing was to keep his own counsel. If the Constable was satisfied – and it would only take a shilling or two to ensure Constable Barratt didn't investigate too deeply – there was an end to the matter. His conscience salved, he picked up another blade and held it to the stone.

Zack's hull was nearest the door and Tom was working at the bench beside the stone. The air was thick with dust even though the door stood open and the window had no glass in it. It was very cold. He looked up when he saw Joanna and came to the end of the bench. 'The light'll be gone in an hour so we shall have to finish,' he whispered. 'I'll see you behind the dairy.' He shook his head. 'Bad news about Caleb.'

'Aye.' She nodded soberly. 'I'm baking you a potato,' she added.

'Thanks.'

When Tom arrived behind the dairy he was blue with cold. He took the potato that Joanna had baked for him in the embers of the kitchen fire gratefully, unable to decide whether to keep it cupped in his hands to warm them, or to eat it straight away, for his belly was rumbling with hunger. He compromised by holding it close to his chest between taking tiny, tantalising bites and listening to what Joanna had to say.

'Don't be daft, Jo,' he said, when she had poured out her fears to him. 'Caleb couldn't possibly have drowned just because you'd been wishing him dead when you saw Liddy. It doesn't make sense.' He took several bites of the potato, savouring it slowly. 'You don't *really* think she could read your mind, do you?' he asked at last, his expression uncertain.

'Oh, yes. I do.' She nodded vigorously. 'I think she could see right down into my soul. I think she knew only too well I was wishing him dead.'

He held up his hand. 'All right. I believe you.' He was

34

silent for several minutes, considering. Then he said, 'But even if she could read your mind, what could she do about it? Do you think she waited and pushed him in the water for you?'

'No, of course not.' Joanna tossed her head impatiently. 'But she's a witch. She could have cast a spell that made him fall in the water when he was drunk.'

He gave a hollow laugh. 'She wouldn't have needed to cast a spell for that! It's a miracle it's never happened before, if you ask me.' He finished his potato and wiped his mouth with the back of his hand. 'No, I'm sure Liddy had nowt to do with it, Jo. Either he fell in or someone knocked him on the head and pushed him in. He'd plenty of enemies, even in the hull over there, because nobody likes a Rattener.' He jerked his head towards Bradshaw's Wheel.

After a minute he picked up her hand and shook it gently. 'You are a silly little goose, Jo. It's only because folk say Liddy's a witch that you imagined she has some kind of magic power. And even supposing she does, she still might not have chosen to use it. After all, why should she? You're nowt to her.'

'No, of course not.' She smiled crookedly at him in the gloom. 'Thanks, Tom. I feel a lot better now I've talked to you about it.'

'Good.' His mood changed and he shook the hand he was holding more roughly. 'But why didn't you tell me Caleb had been making a nuisance of himself to you, Jo?' he asked angrily.

'Well, there wasn't that much to tell. He never actually did anything,' she said with a shrug.

'It wasn't for want of trying, from the sound of it!' He clenched his fist. 'God, if I'd known I'd have—'

She laid her free hand on his arm. 'You mustn't speak ill of the dead, Tom. He's gone now. He can't try to do me any more harm.'

He put his hand over hers. 'Oh, Jo. If only I could take you away from all this. But I will. I promise. Only a few more years.'

She didn't answer. She was fond of Tom, he was a good friend, but she knew that her destiny lay in a better life than he could ever offer.

Joanna went back to the house. Saul was still sitting in his chair beside the fire. His eyes were red-ringed, but he had stopped his awful sobbing and was just sitting and staring into the fire. Martha was dishing up the stew that Joanna had prepared earlier. Joanna looked at the scene. It was just like any other evening except that tonight the silence was one of grief and sadness rather than the usual hatred and animosity.

'You must eat summat yourself, Martha,' Joanna coaxed when she saw that Martha had only served up two plates.

'I couldn't. It'd only stick in my gullet,' Martha said, shaking her head.

'Get it down tha, woman,' Saul said, his voice holding a rare edge of gentleness. 'Tha's going to need all tha strength in t'days to come.'

Joanna spooned a few carrots and potatoes and mashed them into the gravy to make a thick broth. 'There. Eat that. It'll slip down that easy you'll never notice,' she said.

'Thanks, lass.' Martha managed to swallow a few spoonfuls and then sat staring at a burn mark on the bare table top. 'Things never work out the way they're planned, do they?' she said in a weary voice, tracing the burn mark with her finger. 'I'd allus hoped to see you and Caleb wed, lass, and grand-children playing round my feet.' She sighed. 'But now he's dead and gone so it'll never come to pass, will it.'

It would never have come to pass anyway, Joanna thought as she wiped a crust of bread round her plate to sop up the last of the gravy, but there was no point in saying that now. No point in telling Martha how much she'd hated her son, a hatred that had grown more and more over the years because of his cruel and spiteful treatment.

'It would never have come to pass.' Suddenly, surprisingly, Saul echoed Joanna's thoughts. 'The lass was never for Caleb,' he added.

Martha's back straightened. 'And why not? Did you not think her good enough for our lad! Or him for her?'

He shrugged. 'I never thought about that one way or t'other. He was never for her because she's already promised, that's why.'

Joanna's jaw dropped and her eyebrows nearly reached

her hairline as she looked from Saul to Martha and back again.

'What do you mean, she's already promised? Nobody's ever spoken for her that I know of,' Martha said, puzzled.

'Well, it just shows tha don't know everything,' Saul replied, leaning back in his chair and picking his teeth.

'Who am I promised to?' Joanna was annoyed to hear her voice come out as little more than a squeak.

He turned and studied her for several minutes, then said, 'Mr Abraham Silkin. Him as lives up on t'hill and owns t'Button Factory in t'town as well as all these places on t'Porter Brook.' He jerked his head in the general direction of Cliffe House. He turned to Martha. 'He's allus known I've wanted that bottom field of his, a few sheep on there 'ud mek all the difference to this place. But he wouldn't sell, no matter how much I pressed – well, not at a price I could pay. But at back end of last year he said I could have it for what I was offering and he'd tek t'lass in lieu of the rest. The Easter after her sixteenth birthday. That's the date we agreed on. And that's this Easter, a fortnight from now, if I don't miscalculate.' He sat back with an air of contentment and continued rummaging his teeth.

Martha stared at him for several minutes while the news sank in. Then, suddenly, she threw her apron over her head and began to cry in huge, releasing sobs.

'Oh, my lad's gone and now you want to tek my lass from me an' all,' she moaned, and Joanna registered that they were the first tears she had shed since Caleb was brought home that morning.

That morning. It seemed a lifetime ago.

She got up and went to Martha, cradling her grey head close. 'It's all right. I'll not leave you, Martha,' she said, holding her against the great shuddering sobs that racked her.

'Tha'll do as I say,' Saul said roughly. 'A fortnight from now tha'll be gone from here.' He leaned forward and in an unprecedented gesture laid his hand awkwardly on Martha's arm. 'Don't fret, woman,' he said, not unkindly. 'I'll fetch a brat from t'workus to lend a hand on t'farm.'

Martha shook him off and dabbed her eyes with the corner of her apron. 'You don't understand, do you?' she said bitterly. 'And if you did you wouldn't care. It's nowt to you

37

that the lass is more to me than flesh and blood. She's the daughter I never had.' She got up and left the room.

Joanna followed her through the door. 'I'm going to bed,' she said to Saul over her shoulder. 'I'll clear up in the morning.' To Martha she said, 'Don't fret, Martha. I'll not go and leave you.'

Martha paused half-way up the stairs and turned to her. 'If he says you've to go then you've to go, lass, and nowt either of us can say will ever alter his mind.' She gave Joanna a ghost of a smile. 'At least you'll be out of this place, love. It 'ud be selfish of me to try and stop you going to live in a big house. After all, likely it's the sort of place you belong to.' She turned and continued her weary way upstairs.

Joanna went in and closed her bedroom door. She realised with relief that there was no need for the wedge, the cold figure lying in his coffin in the damp front parlour could no longer threaten to do her harm. She laid it on the window sill, it would still be useful to stop the window rattling.

She undressed down to her shift and climbed into bed where she lay shivering, her teeth chattering so hard that she bit her tongue. Yet she was not cold and she realised that it was the accumulation of all the events of the day that was making her feel so strange and ill.

Caleb was dead, but it wasn't her fault, she said to herself over and over. Tom had been quite right. Even Liddy the witch's powers couldn't stretch that far. She began to feel calmer and was almost dropping off to sleep when she recalled Saul's words at the meal table and the shivering started up again. He had said she was promised to Abraham Silkin. What did that mean? She rolled the idea round in her mind for some time before she realised that it could only mean one thing. She was to be a servant at Cliffe House.

She tested the idea thoroughly, considering all the implications, good and bad. As far as she could see there were no bad ones, except of course that she would miss Martha. And Tom. But she would be able to visit them now and again when she had time off because Cliffe House wasn't far away, only up the hill. And being a proper servant she would be paid, so she would be able to buy Martha little presents to make her life easier from time to time. She would enjoy that.

There was nothing else she would miss about Bradshaw's Farm; not the mud, not the drudgery, certainly not the cuffs and blows Saul dealt out. The more she thought about it the more the idea of going to work at Cliffe House appealed to her. Her heart missed a beat. Living in a big house would put her in a far better position to search for and discover the identity of her mother because servants gossiped between houses. That was an exciting thought and she was suddenly wide awake, exploring all the possibilities this opened up. It was a long time before she fell asleep.

Caleb was laid to rest in the churchyard on a day that held a real promise of spring. Saul and his remaining son, Jacob, Zack Wenlock and Tom carried the coffin and filled in the grave they had dug earlier to save the price of the sexton. Afterwards Joanna left the graveside and went to stand by her mother's grave, savouring the smell of fresh grass in the warm afternoon sunshine.

Tom found her there and came and put his arm round her as she stared down at the grass-covered hump that was all that marked her last resting place except for the little pot of primroses she had placed there a few days – it seemed a lifetime – ago.

She turned and looked at him eagerly. 'I might be able to find out who my mother was before very much longer,' she told him. 'Because I'll be leaving Bradshaw's Farm soon.'

A look of alarm crossed his face. 'When? Why? Where are you going?'

'Next week, I think. That's Easter, isn't it?' She drew herself up proudly. 'I'm to go to Cliffe House to work.' She smiled and laid a hand on his arm in an affectedly genteel gesture. 'But don't worry, Tom, I shall still come and see you. When I'm allowed time off.'

He laughed. 'Don't be daft. Saul Bradshaw'll never let you go.'

'Oh, yes he will. You see he's been after Abraham Silkin's bottom field you know, the one next to the tattie field – for ages, but he couldn't afford Mr Silkin's price. Well, now Mr Silkin says Saul can have the field for what he can pay as long as he can have me as well.'

Tom frowned. 'I don't much like the sound of that. What

exactly did Saul say when he told you about it?' he asked suspiciously.

Joanna screwed up her face in an effort to recall Saul's exact words. 'Well, as far as I can remember it went like this. After Caleb died Martha said she had hoped that one day Caleb and me would have been wed so she'd have had grandchildren playing round her feet. But Saul said I was never for Caleb because I was promised to Abraham Silkin. He said I was to go there the Easter after my sixteenth birthday as part of the price of his bottom field.' She pouted her lips. 'I think he should have told me about it before, don't you, Tom? After all, Easter's only next week.'

Tom looked at her sadly, shaking his head. 'You don't understand, do you, Jo?'

She frowned at him. 'Don't understand what?'

He laid his arm round his shoulders. 'If you're promised to Abraham Silkin, it means you're to wed him, Jo, not to work as a servant in his house.'

Her eyes widened and then she laughed. 'No. Don't be silly, Tom. Mr Silkin must be at least fifty.' Her laughter died, to be replaced with a look of alarm as she saw the expression on his face. '*Wed* him? Wed Abraham Silkin? Oh, Tom, you can't be serious. Surely, he wouldn't want to wed *me!* Would he?' she added in a small voice.

Chapter Five

Abraham Silkin stood in front of the full-length mirror in his dressing room and adjusted his pearl grey silk cravat, carefully replacing his gold tie stick exactly three inches from the knot. He pulled himself up to his full height and tugged at the points of his waistcoat, checked that the chain of his pocket watch was looped just so, then turned and surveyed his profile. He was quite a tall man and his figure was – as he would put it – not fat, but ample. He gave a small, self-satisfied shrug; he felt he could congratulate himself on wearing extremely well. A fine figure of a man was the phrase that sprang to mind. He turned his back for Norbert, his manservant, to help him on with his frock coat, dusting an imaginary speck of dust from the velvet collar as he buttoned it.

'Get off, man! Don't fuss!' Abraham said tetchily, waving him off.

He turned his attention back to the mirror, to his shock of white hair and side whiskers, which he stroked lovingly as he surveyed his slightly florid complexion. Nose a trifle large, perhaps, jowls a trifle heavy, but he still possessed all his front teeth and only needed spectacles for close work.

'Not bad for a man of fifty-two, eh, Norbert?' he said, lifting his chin and surveying himself from all angles.

'Very good, sir. Very good indeed,' Norbert answered with no change in his habitual blank expression.

He allowed Norbert a final fuss with the clothes-brush and went downstairs. Bradshaw was bringing the girl today. She was only sixteen so the age difference was great; she was young enough to be his daughter, nay, his granddaughter, as

Gertrude had had no hesitation in reminding him when he told her of his intention. Gertrude did not approve of this intended marriage. But he had known his sister well enough to be sure that her innate curiosity added to her animosity towards Lynwood would ensure her co-operation when the time came. And he needed her co-operation, he realised that, because the girl would come to him with only the rags on her back and no social graces whatever. But Gertrude would teach her. He knew he could leave everything safely in her hands. She was downstairs now. Waiting.

Lynwood, of course, was quite another matter.

Twenty years old, his godson had come to live with him when his father died four years before. Abraham had promised his friend Joshua at the boy's baptism that he would look after him in the event of Joshua's death and he'd been as good as his word, taking Lynwood into his own household so that his widowed mother could go and live with her sister in Bath. In fact it worked very well. Lynwood was good company at the dinner table and not averse to a hand of cards or a game of billiards to while away a dull evening. True, he wasn't particularly interested in the Button Factory in the town where most of Abraham's money was made, nor in collecting the rents from the properties on the Porter River, but he paid lip service to it all and, contrary to Gertrude's all too frequently voiced misgivings, Abraham was confident that as the years went on and his own abilities faded the boy would take responsibility and his interest would increase.

But that was all in the future. A good way into the future it was to be hoped because with a young and attractive wife in his bed who could tell? An heir of his own was not beyond the realms of possibility. Abraham allowed himself a self-satisfied smile. Although he had remained a bachelor he was not without some experience in those areas. Off and on for over twenty-five years he had visited a little widow in a lane off Fargate and they had found mutual comfort from the association, she from his provision of a neat little house and he from her buxom body. Since she had died five years ago he had not had the heart – indeed, had not felt any particular urge – to replace her. He allowed himself the ghost of a smile. No doubt a pretty young wife would soon remedy that!

42

Abraham suspected that it was fear that the marriage might produce an heir that was the cause of Lynwood's recent morose bad temper and the reason he had taken himself off to Derby for the day, knowing the lass would be arriving.

Be that as it might, Abraham's mind was made up. He wanted a wife to grace his table and to show off to his business acquaintances. He was tired of being the only single man at dinner tables and having hostesses thrust totally unsuitable women – usually their poor relations – on him as potential marriage partners. And he was lonely. Lynwood was increasingly off pursuing his own interests and he needed a companion to share the evening firelight, perhaps to talk over the day's problems or to play a gentle game of cribbage with, or simply to watch as she worked at her embroidery, or whatever it was that women occupied themselves with. The idea was appealing. And the more he thought about it the more the appeal increased. It had taken him a long time to come to this decision but now it was made there was no going back.

And the Bradshaw child was pretty, there was no doubt about that. He pulled his thoughts up sharply. Mustn't keep thinking of her as the Bradshaw child – such thoughts were not quite healthy in a man of his age. Anyway, she was no longer a child, although it was her youth that had first attracted him. That and pity when he had observed her working on the farm, tackling jobs that should rightly have been done by a man, lugging great buckets about, wielding a spade that was nearly as big as she was, plodding about in boots that were miles too big. Either that or going barefoot in all weathers. Oh, aye, he'd felt sorry for her, all right.

He'd admired her courage, too. Whatever she had to do she got on with it and never appeared to complain. Bradshaw wasn't mean with his blows towards her, neither. It was when he'd seen the man beating her out on the field that the idea had first come to him that he would like to take her away from all that and give her a better life. And the more he thought about it the more he liked the idea. He imagined her dressed in the extravagant fol-de-rols that women of his acquaintance all seemed to wear, gracing his dinner table. It had to be said that he also fancied her in his bed, he reminded himself honestly. Well, a man needed a bit of comfort. What was wrong with that? It wasn't as if he was suggesting anything immoral. He needed a wife and if the wife he had chosen was a little young, well, it wouldn't be the first time an old – he corrected himself – a middle-aged man had taken to himself a young wife.

And Lynwood would get used to the idea. He'd already made up his mind that the boy shouldn't suffer, should a son and heir make an appearance in the fullness of time, although he hadn't felt the need to tell Lynwood that yet.

He reached the foot of the stairs and crossed the black and white tiled hall to the drawing room and sat down opposite Gertrude to wait.

'It's not too late to change your mind, Abraham,' she said, with an amused grin and a rustle of purple silk as she tried to ease her stays a little. 'You're looking a trifle nervous. Got cold feet?'

'I am not nervous. My collar is a shade tight, that's all. And I have no intention of changing my mind.' He stopped fiddling with it and rested both hands on the gold top of his cane.

'Good.' She nodded, clearly beginning to enjoy the situation. 'Ah, here's Parker. Yes, Parker, show Mr Bradshaw and his ... and the young lady in.'

Parker, the butler, raised his eyebrows. 'In here, Ma'am?' Less well trained and his voice would have held a note of shock.

'Yes, Parker. In here.'

Joanna was excited. It hadn't taken her many days to become used to the idea that she was to live at Cliffe House and her one thought was that this could prove her opportunity to find out her true identity. Her mind was so full of this that she could think about little else, not even the fact that she was to become the wife of a man she had only so far seen from a distance.

Martha had helped her to bath and wash her hair the night before, pouring hot water into the tin tub in front of the fire and scrubbing her back for her until it was nearly raw and rinsing her hair in vinegar to make it shine.

'I'll not have you going up to Cliffe House not looking your

44

best, my lass,' she had said as she combed out the tangles from Joanna's curly golden hair, her voice gruff and short to hide her true feelings.

'Am I to wear the velvet cloak, Martha?' Joanna had asked.

Martha had thought for several minutes, then shook her head. 'No, lass. Best not. But I'll keep it safe for you, never fear. Any road, the dress we got for you from Mrs Wrigley's has washed and ironed up a treat. Are the shoes much too tight?'

'No, not much,' Joanna had lied.

And now she stood in the big hall at Cliffe House beside Saul, who was nervous as she had never seen him in her life before, twisting his cap round and round and shuffling from one foot to the other till she wanted to laugh at him.

Not that she had any cause to laugh at his discomfort when her own stomach was full of butterflies. It was the sight of the house that had done it. A huge stone building with an impressive portico, grand enough for the Queen to live in, she was sure. Even the hall where they stood waiting was big enough to swallow the Bradshaw's farmhouse and still leave room for the great carved staircase that wound up to the next floor.

The manservant, dressed all in black, who had opened the door to them when they arrived and had been on the point of directing them to the servants' entrance till Saul stated their business, came back from announcing them.

'This way,' he said disdainfully, looking down his nose at them. 'Follow me.'

He led the way into a large room with a huge fire burning in the grate. Joanna's first thought was that somebody must have spent an awful long time gathering all those logs from the woods.

Then she saw Abraham Silkin. He looked different, somehow bigger and more forbidding than when she had seen him walking on the hill. Older, too, she thought, trying not to stare, although it didn't really matter because he was carefully not looking at her but directing his attention towards Saul, who was fawning over him in a way quite unlike himself.

The lady sitting opposite to Abraham cleared her throat to attract Joanna's attention. She was small and plump, dressed in the most beautiful purple gown with a shawl of gossamer cashmere round her shoulders, and fairly sparkling with jewellery. Earrings, necklaces, brooches and so many rings on her fingers that Joanna wondered how she managed to lift her hand out of her lap to beckon her over.

'Ee, you look half-starved, lass,' she said with a friendly smile. 'But we'll soon put that right.' She put her head on one side and her eyes travelled from Joanna's feet up to her neck. 'And you'll pay for dressing. Your waist'll be the envy of the town.' She looked up into Joanna's clear blue eyes, sparkling with excitement and wonder. 'Are you nervous at coming here, lass?'

'Yes. A bit.' Joanna's blue eyes met Gertrude's slightly faded grey ones openly.

'No need to be, lass. Not really. But you'll find you've a lot to learn. Life at Cliffe House'll be a far cry from mucking out pig-sties and digging turnips.'

'Good. I've had more than enough of that,' Joanna said firmly, with a lift of her chin.

Gertrude chuckled. 'Oh, aye, I can see what Abe sees in you, lass. You've got plenty of guts, that's for sure.' She picked up the hem of Joanna's dress, bought after much agonising on Martha's part from the second-hand clothes shop and altered to more or less fit, and dropped it again with distaste. 'Well, the first thing we shall have to do is get you some decent clothes. I shall enjoy that.' She leaned back in her chair and folded her hands over her stomach. 'Now that man's gone you can ring for tea, Abe,' she said, looking over Joanna's shoulder.

Joanna turned. There was no sign of Saul. He hadn't even said goodbye.

She watched Abraham as he went over to the tasselled bell pull and tugged it. This man was to be her husband; this large, rather elderly man was the man she was to marry. She couldn't take it in. The whole thing was a dream. He hadn't even looked at her. Soon she would be sent packing, back to the drudgery of Bradshaw's Farm.

She decided to make the most of the situation before that happened.

Yet another servant, this time a woman wearing an apron as white as driven snow, brought in tea, staggering under a huge

46

silver tray on which were all sorts of silver things, teapots, milk jugs, sugar bowls and a big covered dish. Following her was a smaller girl with another tray on which was the most beautiful china Joanna had ever seen.

'That's right, Milton, put it down here,' Gertrude said briskly.

Joanna found the next half-hour uncomfortable. She had never drunk tea – weak, wishy-washy stuff, not the thick black brew she was used to – from such dainty, delicate cups. She was afraid the handle would come off when she lifted it and she didn't know what to do with the saucer while she drank. She was terrified it would slip off her lap. Then there was the tea plate. How could she be expected to hold a cup and saucer and a plate and take the muffin Gertrude was offering her? She put the plate on the floor while she took the muffin, then held the muffin in her mouth while she picked up the plate again. It was a most delicious muffin, she had never tasted the like before and she was hungry. It was gone in seconds.

'I think your bride has a lot to learn, Abe,' Gertrude said quietly, offering her a second and then a third.

But Joanna didn't hear. She was too busy enjoying the muffins and washing them down with great gulps of tea, forgetting all the things Martha had told her about minding her manners.

'I rather think I shall take dinner in my room tonight, if you don't mind, Abe,' Gertrude said thoughtfully, when the tea things had been cleared. 'And perhaps Joanna would like to join me?' She raised her eyebrows questioningly.

Joanna's jaw dropped. 'Me? You mean there's to be another meal tonight?'

'Not until eight-thirty,' Gertrude said with a laugh. 'No doubt you'll be hungry again by then.'

'I'm always hungry,' Joanna said gloomily. She smiled and patted her stomach. 'Except now.'

Abraham stood up. 'I think that's a very good idea, Gertrude. In any case, Lynwood will be back later and I think perhaps it will be best if he doesn't—' He gave an almost imperceptible nod in Joanna's direction.

Gertrude nodded back, understanding him perfectly. 'I agree. And of course we shall be gone in the morning.' She turned to Joanna. 'You're to stay with me, love, until the wedding. Well, it wouldn't be right for you to stay here, would it? And there's a lot to be done. You'll need a whole wardrobe, for a start. When did you think the wedding should be, Abe? July?'

He cleared his throat and looked uncomfortable, as if he might be changing his mind after all. 'I – er, yes, about then. Early July.'

'Good. That will give me plenty of time to knock the corners off the lass, so to speak.' She nodded complacently. 'Now, Joanna, ring for Milton. Yes, that's right, the bell pull is beside the fireplace. No, on second thoughts don't bother, I'll take you to your room myself.' With some difficulty, because her legs were short, Gertrude got up from her chair and took Joanna by the hand. 'This way, love.'

In a daze Joanna followed her out of the room and across the hall, up the stairs – the stair carpet so thick and deep and soft that Joanna would have liked to take her tight, uncomfortable shoes off and walk on it barefoot – along a corridor carpeted in the same luxurious way, to a large room dominated by a bed with blue silk hangings.

'This will be your room for the present. I'm afraid it's not very big. Of course, when you're wed you'll be moving to the master bedroom at the head of the stairs.' As she spoke Gertrude went over and adjusted the curtain at the foot of the bed. 'Now, if I were you, love, I'd have a little lie-down till dinner time. You must be worn out with all this excitement.' She smiled at Joanna. 'I'll call you when it's time. And you've no need to worry. There'll only be the two of us.'

When she had left Joanna sat down gingerly on the bed. It was so soft she thought she was going to sink right through it, with downy pillows and a thick blue eiderdown. Gertrude had said the room was small but it didn't look small to Joanna and there was more furniture in it than Martha had in her whole house. Smooth, dark brown furniture, chests of drawers and a big wardrobe with a mirror in which she could see herself, a forlorn little figure sitting nervously on the edge of the bed.

Gertrude had told her to lie down and rest but she didn't feel in the least tired. In any case, nobody that she knew ever rested in the middle of the day, it was unheard of. She fingered the smooth silk of the bed curtains and then got up and went over to the window, draped with more blue silk and with a blue velvet cushion on the window seat.

She sat down and looked out. The window was at the back of the house and looked out over the hill. From where she was sitting the house seemed to be perched on an almost sheer cliff-face. Far below, Bradshaw's Farm where she had spent her life up till now straggled untidily along the bank of the River Porter in the valley. It looked dirty and run down. Her mouth twisted. The field that Saul had coveted for so long and that had been part of the bargain with Abraham Silkin looked very small and insignificant from this distance.

Her gaze travelled to the other side of the narrow but swiftly flowing river. The two long, low buildings of Bradshaw's Wheel, where Tom worked out his days in gloom and squalor, looked quite picturesque from this distance, with the sun shining on the stonework and the huge water-wheel turning at the side. Even the water stored in the dam beside the wheel looked calm and peaceful with the sun glinting on it. Away to the left was the bridge that carried the road down into the town and on the other side of the road stretched Whitely Woods where she had so often gathered firewood or picked berries with Tom. If she craned her neck she could even see a wisp of smoke curling up from the charcoal burner's kiln and she recalled her terror when Tom had carried her there for Liddy the witch to cure her poisoned foot. She turned away. She didn't want to think about Liddy the witch because it reminded her of Caleb's death.

In any case it all seemed like another life.

She went back and sat on the bed, then, not quite knowing what else to do, she kicked off the uncomfortable, too small shoes and leaned back on the soft pillows. If this was all a dream, she thought with a contented sigh, she hoped she would never wake up.

Chapter Six

It was no dream, as Joanna quickly realised almost two hours later when Gertrude came along to her room and shook her gently awake.

'Come along, lass, time for your first lesson in table manners,' she said kindly. 'I've had dinner brought to my room so we shan't be disturbed.'

She waited while Joanna splashed cold water on her face and then took her back along the corridor past the head of the stairs to a room at the end.

'This is my little sitting room,' she said proudly. 'Abe let me furnish it how I liked so that I would always feel at home when I came to stay. My bedroom's through there.' She indicated a door in the corner.

Joanna looked round. The room was far from little in her eyes and seemed to be full of red plush; red plush chairs of every imaginable shape and size, two overstuffed red plush settees and long red plush curtains at the windows. Even the small tables were draped in red plush under cream lace cloths. She had never seen so much red plush; indeed she had never before seen so much furniture crammed into one room.

'Do you like it?' Gertrude said, not waiting for Joanna's reply. 'Cosy, isn't it? Of course, it goes without saying, once you're wed I'll not intrude. I'll only visit when I'm invited. After all, it wouldn't be right, would it? But my brother's been glad of my company and my advice over the years, him being a bachelor. And since my Sam died I've been pleased to come. Now, let's see—' she glanced at the small table laid for dinner beside the fire. 'You sit there, lass, and I'll sit opposite.'

Joanna sat down and stared at the array of cutlery in front of her. Gertrude went over and tugged at the bell pull then came and sat down with her.

'Now there's nothing to be alarmed about, lass. Just remember to start at the outside and work your way in. It's quite simple.' She shook out her napkin. 'Just do as I do. Ah, here's the soup. Thank you Ivy, it smells delicious.'

Joanna watched and copied Gertrude. The soup tasted as good as it smelled although it was not nearly as thick as the broth Martha made. She soon forgot to watch and copy Gertrude.

'There's no need to wolf it down like it's your last meal ever, love,' Gertrude reproved mildly. 'Take it like so ... and gently tip the bowl away from you. And try not to slurp, love, it ain't lady-like.'

Course after course followed, with Gertrude watching her every move.

'Take small amounts on your fork, love. No, try not to use it as if it was a spoon, spear it – yes, even the peas.' 'No, not that knife, love. It's a fish knife and we haven't reached the fish course yet.' 'No, dear, don't wipe your mouth with your hand, that's what you've been given a napkin for. That's right, just dab your mouth gently with it.'

By the end of the meal Gertrude felt quite exhausted, but she could see that Joanna was an apt pupil and would soon learn.

As for Joanna, she felt that her dream had turned into something of a nightmare. Martha had always taught her to mind her manners, but she was convinced she would never remember half the pernickety little things Gertrude had told her. If this was what belonging to the gentry meant she wasn't sure she wanted any part of it.

She was quite glad to be back in her own room, where a voluminous night-gown – she suspected it was one of Gertrude's – had been carefully laid out for her. As she climbed into the big soft bed her last thought before she fell asleep was 'Oh, Martha, if you could see me now!'

The next morning, breakfast was again taken in Gertrude's sitting room, where several boxes stood strapped and ready to be loaded on to the carriage for the journey to Gertrude's house. Joanna managed this without too much good-natured head-shaking from Gertrude.

'Aye, lass, just as I thought. You'll soon learn,' she said, watching Joanna's every movement.

Soon after breakfast they left Cliffe House. As the carriage bore them away Joanna took a last look up at the windows. At one of them, on the first floor, someone was standing and watching. It wasn't Abraham, it was a young man and from what Joanna could see he looked decidedly bad-tempered.

'Who was that at the window, Gertrude?' she asked as they rumbled down the drive.

'Oh, I expect it was Lynwood. You'll meet him soon enough, lazy young puppy that he is,' Gertrude said, pursing her lips. 'The trouble is, my brother spoils him. Indulges him far too much. All Lynwood thinks about is spending money and cutting a dash, instead of helping Abraham with his business interests. I told Abe he was making a mistake when he took him in, but he wouldn't listen. Said the lad was his godson and he had a moral duty to look after him. Moral duty my foot. That boy's nothing but a sponge waiting to mop up his inheritance, anyone can see that with half an eye. Anyone except Abe, that is.' She glanced at Joanna and chuckled, a rich, throaty, infectious chuckle. 'But he'll not feel quite so sure of himself now you've come on the scene to cramp his style, will he?'

Joanna couldn't share in Gertrude's humour. Life was going to be difficult enough without an enemy. And the face at the window had been far from friendly.

She had little time to dwell on the problem of Abraham's godson over the next few weeks. She was far too busy. Gertrude took her to her own dressmaker, where swatch after swatch of beautiful material was presented for approval. Names were bandied that Joanna had never heard of, grenadine, taffeta, tarlatan, barege, gingham – and in the most delicate colours and combinations of colour, plain, striped, flowered; she had never imagined so many different materials were possible. And she had only to point to something and say, 'Oh, how pretty,' for Gertrude to order a dress to be made from it.

'That's at least six!' she whispered at last, after admiring a beautiful striped taffeta in three shades of green.

Gertrude nodded. 'Yes, perhaps that's enough for now.' She raised her voice. 'That'll do, Estelle. We need to look at evening wear now.'

More swatches of material, this time shot and figured silks, velvets and moire in even more delicate patterns and colours. Joanna was so bewildered that she left it to Gertrude and the obsequious Estelle to choose for her.

Estelle turned to Gertrude, raised her eyebrows slightly and made an hour-glass gesture with her hands. 'Before we take ze measurements perhaps Mademoiselle could step to ze fitting room?' she said in her carefully accented English.

Then followed a most uncomfortable interlude as Joanna found herself pushed and pummelled into stays stiffened with whalebone that stretched from her bosom to her hips and were laced so tightly that she could scarcely breathe.

'Aye, I said she'd have a waist that was the envy of the neighbourhood,' Gertrude said with a satisfied nod. 'What does it measure, Estelle?'

'Eighteen and a half inches,' Estelle said with a beam. 'Is it comfortable, Mam'selle?'

Joanna, who had never before had her figure restricted, but didn't want to appear ignorant, nodded and murmured breathlessly, 'Yes, thank you.'

'Zen we can manage another half inch.' Estelle put her knee in Joanna's back and laced the stays even tighter.

Gertrude, seeing her turning slightly red in the face, said, 'No, I think eighteen and a half is sufficient. We can always lace them in later when they're worn in a bit. They're always tight at first.'

More measurements were taken, patterns chosen and matched with materials until Joanna felt her head was spinning. But at last, with the promise that the first dress would be delivered within three days, they left Madame Estelle's and went to the milliner's, armed with snippets of material for matching. Then it was on to the bootmaker's for shoes, evening slippers and boots.

'You must have spent an awful lot of money on me,' Joanna whispered as they returned in the carriage to Gertrude's house on the Glossop Road.

53

Gertrude patted her head. 'Abe gave me a free hand. He said you were to have whatever I thought fit.' She frowned. 'I wonder if eight pairs of gloves is enough ...'

Joanna lapsed into exhausted silence as Gertrude ticked off everything that had been ordered. She felt more tired than after a day hoeing turnips and she simply couldn't imagine ever having use for half the extravagant items Gertrude insisted no self-respecting lady could ever be without, parasols, fans, muffs, clips attached to a chain, which Gertrude called 'pages', and said were used to hold the skirt up out of the dirt when walking, smelling bottles to be hung from the waist, the list seemed endless.

She looked down at her chapped and chilblained hands, a good deal less red since Gertrude had smothered them in a delicious oil that smelt of lavender before she went to bed last night. She couldn't imagine them in the tiny lace mittens or soft kid gloves that had been ordered any more than she could imagine her feet in the dainty satin slippers or elastic-sided boots that lay in boxes on the seat opposite.

She closed her eyes, her head spinning with the excitement of the morning. There was so much to learn, so much to remember. And Gertrude had told her they were only just beginning, for once she was properly dressed the etiquette of visiting would begin. For a moment her heart sank at the thought, then she reminded herself that this was what she had been born to. This was the life she had been meant to lead, had it not been for a cruel twist of Fate. But Fate had relented, thanks to Abraham Silkin, and set her back on her rightful path, a path that could eventually lead her back to her roots. To the grandparents who didn't even know of her existence. She pulled back her shoulders and sat a little straighter in her seat. She was determined that they should have no cause to be ashamed of her.

Gertrude had forbidden Abraham to visit for a month. When the month was up she invited him and Lynwood to dinner.

'I think you'll see a difference in your little bride-to-be, Abe,' she said excitedly when he arrived. 'She's been an apt pupil and I've enjoyed taking her in hand.' She looked beyond him. 'But I'm forgetting my manners. Where's Lynwood? Has he stayed away because he couldn't bring himself to be civil? I know he don't like me, but then, I don't like him, neither, as you well know. All the same I thought it would be a civilised gesture to invite him tonight so that he could meet his new step-godmother.'

'Yes, and I appreciate it, Gertie,' Abraham made himself comfortable on the sofa opposite his sister. 'He'll be along shortly. He's been out hunting and needed more time to clean himself up. I couldn't wait for him.'

'Too anxious to see what I've made of your future wife, Abe?' she said with a sly chuckle.

He flushed. 'Not at all. Where is she, by the way?' He looked round for her.

'Patience, man. She'll be down in a minute.' Gertrude leaned forward in her chair. 'I'm glad Lynwood's not here yet, because it gives us a chance of a few words in private. Do you know what the lass told me? She told me she's not Bradshaw's child at all. She was left in their barn when she was only a few days old. And that's where Martha Bradshaw found her. Did you know that?' She leaned back in her chair to see what effect her words were having.

He lifted his eyebrows, the only sign of his surprise. 'No. I've never thought otherwise than that she was his daughter, even though he was so cruel to her.'

'Well, it's not the case. Apparently, her mother was found drowned in the river soon after the lass was left in Bradshaw's cattle shed or wherever it was they found her.'

Abraham was silent for several minutes, then he looked up, frowning. 'Do you think she's telling the truth, Gertie?'

'Oh, yes. I'd stake my life on it. That lass is as honest as the day's long. She said Bradshaw didn't want to keep her, but Martha – she set great store by Martha, that's Bradshaw's wife – somehow managed to persuade him not to do away with her. But that didn't stop him treating her worse than a dog, cruel pig that he is.' She winced. 'I've seen the scars on her back, poor lass.'

'So who was her mother, then?' Abraham asked, his mouth turning down at the corners. He hoped there weren't going to be difficulties.

'Nobody knows. Joanna reckons she was well-to-do, from

one of the big houses round about. But I've not heard of a young gentlewoman gone missing in all the years I've lived in these parts, have you? And I reckon there would have been a pretty hue and cry if there had.'

He nodded slowly as the full implications of the story began to sink in. 'Yes, you're probably right.' He looked up. 'Maybe I should see what I can find out.'

'And maybe you shouldn't, Abe,' Gertrude warned quickly. 'Maybe it's best to let sleeping dogs lie. If you ask me she's more likely to be the bastard of a servant-girl turned out after the master of the house had got her in pod.'

'Don't be coarse, Gertie.'

Gertrude shrugged. 'It goes on, as well you know. And she'd be mortal disappointed if she found out that was the case.'

He nodded. 'Yes, I daresay she would.' He took a deep breath. 'Perhaps you're right, Gertie. Best to let matters rest where they are.' He frowned again, searching his memory. 'Now you come to speak of it, Gertie, I do seem to remember some talk among the servants about a young woman being found drowned in the river in Whitely Woods. But that was years ago.'

'Well, it would be, wouldn't it?' Gertrude reminded him. 'Sixteen years, or thereabouts.'

He nodded again. 'Well, I never did.'

Gertrude held up her hand. 'Sh. Here's Lynwood.'

The young man who entered was tall and dark, with a long, fine-featured face that never seemed to lose its attractive pallor even though he led an active outdoor life. He was a handsome man, although to Gertrude's mind his looks were marred by a coldness in his pale blue eyes. A coldness that Abraham had never observed so Gertrude wondered if it was reserved for her alone.

She held out the back of her hand to him and said cheerfully, 'Good evening, Lynwood. I trust you had a good day's hunting.'

'Tolerably good, Aunt Gertie, thank you.' He kissed the hand obediently and with a flick of his coat tails sat down beside his godfather on the sofa.

Before anything else could be said the door opened and

56

Joanna entered. She was wearing a pale blue dress of figured silk lavishly trimmed with cream lace, the style accentuating her tiny waist. Her hair, which Gertrude had despaired of taming into the modern style, was a mass of golden curls, caught up at the back and cascading down to her neck. She stood for a moment in the doorway, hesitating. The two men had immediately risen to their feet and stood looking at her. But Gertrude's eyes were on her brother and the younger man.

Abraham was staring at Joanna with a look of almost paternal pleasure, clearly relieved and delighted to have lifted her out of her life of drudgery. Just as Gertrude expected. But it was Lynwood that caught most of her attention. Expressions flitted across his face with the speed of a peepshow. Sudden, surprised admiration as his eyes swept from her head to her feet, lingering briefly on the swell of her breasts, was quickly replaced by an ugly expression of such naked jealousy that Gertrude drew in a sharp, involuntary breath. But then, as if a shutter had been pulled down on his true feelings his expression changed again and he gave such a charming smile that Gertrude wondered if she could possibly have been mistaken. And if she had not been mistaken was Lynwood jealous because he feared for his inheritance? Or because he wanted the girl for himself? Only time would tell.

She pulled herself together with an effort and went over and took Joanna's hand and led her into the room. 'Here you are, Abe,' she said proudly to her brother. 'Here's your little ugly duckling. I think you'll agree she's got the makings of a beautiful swan.'

Joanna dipped a shy little curtsy. She was awed by the two men in evening dress standing in front of her, this elderly, rather distinguished-looking man and the charming young man standing smiling beside him. Then the reality of her situation hit her. This old man with white hair and whiskers, offering her his arm in to dinner, was the man she was to marry. This was the reason for the fairy-tale month she had just spent. There was no going back.

Abraham was inclining his head. 'You look very pretty, my dear,' he said gravely. In his mind's eye he could see the men of his acquaintance – he could hardly call them his friends – men who had rather pitied him in the past for his inability, as they saw it, to find a wife, and imagined how they would gape when they saw him with this ravishing creature on his arm.

Lynwood bent over her hand, encased in a dainty cream lace elbow-length mitten. 'I must congratulate you, Godfather,' he said, not taking his eyes off Joanna's face. 'You'll be the envy of Sheffield when you walk out with this lovely young lady on your arm.' He was smiling as he spoke, but the look in his eyes sent a cold shiver down Joanna's back and she knew instinctively that this young man hated her.

She drew her hand away and laid it lightly on the arm Abraham offered. She was no stranger to hatred, she had lived with it for most of her sixteen years, but now she had a protector. She smiled up at Abraham and held her head high as he led her in to dinner, leaving Lynwood to follow in second place. With Gertrude.

Chapter Seven

From her seat at the head of the table Gertrude watched her guests with interest. She was gratified by the way Joanna was behaving; the lass had been a willing and enthusiastic pupil, a joy to have had under her wing. It only needed a discreet cough when she forgot herself and used the back of her hand instead of her napkin, or tried to cram her mouth too full, or picked up the wrong fork, and she soon remembered what she had been taught and shot Gertrude a grateful glance. But most of the time her manners were impeccable, which was more than could be said of young Lynwood, and there was only the merest hint of nervousness.

She smiled to herself. Abraham was clearly delighted with his bride-to-be. He was attending to her every need and treating her as delicately as old porcelain. Gertrude had forgotten how charming he could be when he put his mind to it. And Joanna was responding with a quaint shyness that was quite touching. Contrary to her first misgivings Gertrude was beginning to think that this rather outlandish marriage might work very well, after all.

She pursed her lips. There was only one fly in the ointment that she could see. And that was Lynwood. He had spent most of the meal in morose silence and more than once she had caught him looking at Joanna with something of a sneer on his face. She was sure it was his fault that the lass spilt her wine. It was only him staring at her that had made her so nervous that her hand had shaken as she picked up her wineglass and drops of it had spilt on to the white tablecloth. That wouldn't have been so bad if she hadn't tried to mop up the spots with her napkin, because in her agitation she had then knocked over the whole glass. It had taken all Gertrude's tact to smooth over the incident and prevent Joanna from running from the table. It had been a difficult moment and all Lynwood's fault.

He was jealous, that was the top and bottom of it, he couldn't bear to think anyone else might gain favour with his godfather. Gertrude gave a disapproving sniff as she watched the young man signal for his glass to be refilled yet again. He was drinking rather too much of her best claret. Not that she ever begrudged what her guests drank – heaven forbid – but Lynwood did tend to become belligerent when in his cups and she didn't want trouble, tonight of all nights.

She was quite glad when the time came for the ladies to leave the men to their port and cigars.

'You did very well, love. I was proud of you,' Gertrude whispered to Joanna as they left the room together.

'I was very nervous,' Joanna admitted. 'And spilling my wine like that ... Oh, dear, I'm so sorry, Gertrude.'

'Never mind, lass. It's no matter. Come along now, we can relax for a little while and put our feet up while we drink a cup of coffee and wait for the men to join us.' Gertrude settled herself and tried to ease her stays. 'I think I've eaten too much. I'd forgotten how tight these new stays were.'

Joanna wriggled in her seat. 'I hate stays. I'd never worn anything like it before and I can't get used to it. They're so uncomfortable I can't even bend down and my skin is quite raw in places.'

'You'll get used to 'em, lass, and they do wonders for your figure. Especially a figure like yours. You'll be the envy of the town with that waist.' Gertrude put her finger to her lips. 'But no more of that. Here come the men. They didn't linger long over their port, did they?' She raised her voice. 'You weren't long, Abe. Wasn't the port to your liking?'

'It was very good, thank you, my dear.'

'Yes, it was excellent. I could have drunk another glass or two, if Godfather here hadn't been so anxious to join his lady-love,' Lynwood said, throwing himself down in an armchair.

'It seemed to me you'd had quite enough to drink without more port, Lynwood,' Abraham said mildly.

'I think I'm old enough to be the best judge of that,

Godfather. Remember I'm nearly twenty-one. Old enough to hold my liquor,' Lynwood replied. He turned to Joanna. 'Well, aren't you going to entertain us at the piano, Miss? That's what young ladies do after dinner, isn't it? Gives us men a chance for a quiet nap.' He gave a wide yawn.

'I'm sorry, I'm afraid I don't have any skills in that direction,' Joanna said, with a nervous glance toward Gertrude. 'Although Gertrude assures me that with tuition I could sing a little.' She couldn't help feeling a little afraid of this worldly young man.

'Oh, don't apologise. It's the best news I've heard tonight. Saints preserve us from women who think they can sing! Or play the piano. It's a relief to hear you aren't going to bore us with that. I can't abide music.'

'And I can't abide rude young men,' Gertrude snapped.

'You're drunk, Lynwood.' Abraham said, frowning at him.

'I'm not drunk. I'm perfectly sober.'

'Then your behaviour is inexcusable. Please apologise to my sister. And to Joanna.'

Lynwood gave a great sigh. 'I beg your pardon, Ma'am.' He bent his head in Gertrude's direction, then half looked at Joanna. 'And yours, Miss,' he muttered.

Furious with Lynwood but unwilling to make further fuss, Abraham turned to Joanna and smiled. 'We'll see you have singing lessons if that's what you would like, my dear. After we're ...' he hesitated. 'Later on.'

'I think I should like that very much ...' There was a long silence while Joanna debated what to call him and with difficulty resisted the temptation to say 'sir'. '... Abraham,' she said at last.

He flushed with pleasure. 'Good.'

Lynwood got up and went over to the fireplace, leaning his arm on the mantelpiece. 'Oh, Lord preserve us from squalling women,' he said under his breath.

Abraham got to his feet. 'I think it's time we left, Lynwood.'

Lynwood gaped. 'But I thought we were going to have a hand of cribbage.'

'I think not. I need you to come down to the Button Factory with me at nine tomorrow morning and you'll need a clear head for that.' He gave Gertrude a peck on the cheek. 'Thank you for a most enjoyable meal, my dear.' He pressed Joanna's hand. 'I shall come and see you tomorrow, my love.'

'I don't think Lynwood likes me much,' Joanna said after they had gone.

'Oh, you mustn't take any notice of Lynwood,' Gertrude said with a laugh. 'He's nowt more than a spoilt brat. The trouble is, he's had it all his own way for the past four years and now Abe's put his nose out of joint, deciding to tek himself a wife. He'll come round after you're wed. You'll see.'

'I do hope so,' Joanna said on a sigh, 'For Abraham's sake as well as mine.'

The date for the wedding was set for the sixteenth of July. Until then Abraham visited Joanna every day at Gertrude's house. Often he brought her a little gift, a single rose in a silver holder, a lace handkerchief, a pretty enamelled brooch in the form of a blue bird, a necklace of tiny seed pearls, a set of silver buttons. Once he brought her a book and, embarrassed, she had to admit that she had never learned to read. He was mortified at his insensitivity and immediately began to teach her, sitting with her for at least an hour every afternoon helping her to master the art.

When the lesson was over he would stay with her in Gertrude's sitting room, holding her hand and talking of what he hoped their life together would be.

'I've been a crusty old bachelor for too long, my little love. Cliffe House needs a woman's touch,' he said one day.

'I'll do my best, Abraham, but there's such a lot to learn,' she said with a sigh.

'You're doing very well, sweetheart. You've come a long way since Bradshaw brought you to me.' He looked at her with concern. 'You don't regret leaving Bradshaw, do you, Joanna?'

She threw back her head and pealed with laughter. 'Oh, Abraham, how could you even *think* that! It seems like another life.' She shuddered. 'A life I would hate to go back to, even though I loved Martha.' She was quiet for several moments. 'And Tom was a good friend to me,' she added thoughtfully.

She turned to Abraham. 'I would like to go and see Martha, Abraham. And Tom, too.'

Abraham's face darkened. 'No, my dear. I don't think that would be a good idea at all,' he said firmly.

'But they were both so kind to me for all those years. I wouldn't like them to think I had forgotten them.' It never occurred to Joanna that Abraham might be jealous of her regard for Tom.

'It's best that you should. They are no part of your life now. You've led such a terrible existence up till now that I want you to forget it.'

'Very well, Abraham,' she said reluctantly.

He put his arm round her. 'I do so want you to be happy, my little love. Are you happy?'

'Oh, yes. I'm very happy, thank you.' She leaned over and kissed him. Then she frowned. 'Although I do worry a little about Lynwood. I don't think he likes me, Abraham.'

'He's a little jealous, that's all. But he'll come round, never fear. He's a good boy at heart. When you get to know him better I'm sure you'll like him.'

'But will he ever grow to tolerate me?' she said uncertainly.

He kissed her cheek. 'Of course he will, my dear.'

Sometimes, with Gertrude as chaperone, Abraham would take Joanna in the carriage to the Botanical Gardens so that they could admire the formal flower beds and marvel at the wonderful sights in the conservatories. Gertrude didn't walk much, she preferred to sit and listen to the band in the bandstand and when Abraham and Joanna had finished their wanderings they would join her and then the three of them would have a cream tea before starting home again.

Occasionally Abraham took them both to the theatre and Joanna had to hold herself carefully in check so that she didn't exclaim in wonder at the sight of the glittering ladies in the audience and the brilliantly gaslit stage. She was so enthralled with the scene that she didn't even notice the whisperings that went on behind ornate fans and the sly glances in her direction. Everything was so new and wonderful that she felt like Cinderella waiting for the clock to strike midnight, half-expecting to find herself pitchforked back to the squalor of Bradshaw's Farm. It was only as the carriage took them home afterwards that she realised all was not as wonderful as she had thought.

'We've still got a long way to go, Abe,' Gertrude remarked, leaning back in her seat and fanning herself wearily. 'Lady Beckwith cut us dead and what she does the rest will follow. Just like a lot of sheep, they are.'

Abraham nodded. 'Aye, it'll take time. But I was never one to bother about that sort of thing as you well know, Gertie. They'll come round. You'll see.' He patted Joanna's hand. 'They'll not resist your charms for long, my love. I'll wager on that.'

Joanna said nothing. She had noticed that nobody had spoken to her during the interval and she could hardly fail to observe that in the powder room the ladies had looked right through her when Gertrude had tried to include her in the conversation. But this hadn't worried her because it gave her a chance to observe the behaviour of ladies of fashion and to realise that their manners often left a great deal to be desired.

'I wish Abraham would allow me to visit Martha, Gertrude,' Joanna said one afternoon. 'He says I should forget my old life, but it worries me because I wouldn't like Martha to think I had forgotten her.'

Gertrude thought about it for several minutes, then she nodded. 'I think you're right, lass. After all, if it hadn't been for Martha you wouldn't be here now, would you?'

'That's what I think. Do you think I might go, Gertrude?'

Gertrude pinched her lip. 'I don't see why not, lass. Especially if I come with you.'

'Oh, you couldn't possibly!' Joanna said, shocked. 'Not to Bradshaw's Farm.'

'I don't mean I'd come to the farm. I'd wait in the carriage. Then if Abe finds out I'll tell him it was my idea.' She grinned. 'You deserve a little treat after all your hard work, learning to be a lady, don't you?'

'I'm not sure it will be much of a treat, Gertrude,' Joanna said with a rueful smile.

The next afternoon they took the carriage as far as Whitely Woods and then Gertrude waited while Joanna made the rest of the journey on foot, carrying a basket filled with delicacies for Martha.

The farm was in an even worse state than when she had lived there. It was ankle-deep in filth and the whole place stank. She wished she had thought to put pattens over her boots, but it was too late now. She picked up her skirts as she reached the yard and with them bunched up round her ankles she waded through the muck to the dairy, where she could see Martha bent over the butter churn.

She seemed to have aged, but when Joanna softly called her name she looked round and her face lit up with pure delight.

'Joanna, lass! Ee, I'm that glad to see you.' Wiping her hands on her apron she came over, her sinewy arms outstretched to embrace her. Then suddenly she stopped, her arms fell to her side and she bobbed a curtsy.

'Martha!' Outraged, Joanna almost lifted her to her feet and crushed her in a great hug. 'Oh, Martha, don't you ever curtsy to me again. I may be wearing fine clothes but I'm still your Joanna inside.' Tears were running down her cheeks and they mingled with Martha's as they clung together.

They went over to the house, Martha all the time apologising for the state of the yard and how it would muddy Joanna's boots.

'He never sweeps it and I haven't the time, not wi' everything else,' she explained as she pulled her boots off and stepped into the spotlessly clean kitchen. Joanna pulled her own boots off and stood them beside Martha's, which were scuffed and down-at-heel, with a large hole in the toe.

She sat down at the table she had scrubbed so often in the past and watched while Martha pulled the kettle forward and spooned tea into the old brown teapot. It had a crack in the lid that Joanna remembered well because it had happened one night when Saul had flung it at her in a rage and it had hit the wall. The place was full of memories, few of them pleasant. Idly, she traced the burn mark on the table, made by the hot toasting fork when she'd flung it down before escaping that morning when Caleb had threatened to rape her. Caleb. She didn't want to think about Caleb. Nor his manner of dying.

'I must say the place looks more run down than ever, Martha,' she remarked as she sipped the dark, thick tea which was all she'd been used to when she lived here, but now made her stomach turn. 'I thought the field Abraham sold Saul in exchange for me was going to make his fortune.'

Martha began to laugh. She laughed till the tears rolled down her cheeks. 'Mek his fortune! Fat chance! Nowt'll grow on that land. He thought he'd keep sheep there but it's too dry and rocky for t'grass to grow to feed 'em. And he broke a plough trying to plough it. It's not a ha'porth of good, that land. But he was so eager to own it he couldn't see—' She wiped her eyes on her apron. 'Serve him right, that's what I say. And it did you a good turn, lass. It got you out of this hell-hole, didn't it!' Her expression changed as she glanced at the clock ticking on the wall. 'But you'd best not stay, lass,' she said anxiously. 'He'll be back before long and he'll not be pleased to see you here in all your finery. It'd be like rubbing salt in.'

Joanna got up immediately. She knew that if Saul saw her it would be Martha he would vent his wrath on. 'All right, I won't stay. But before I go, Martha. Tell me, how is Tom?' she asked urgently.

Martha shrugged. 'Now you've gone he thinks of nowt but finishing his time wi' Zack Wenlock and getting down into t'town to work. He thought a lot of you, Joanna, and he misses you now you're not here.'

'Yes, I know he did. He was a good friend. Tell him I asked after him, won't you.'

'Aye, I will. He'd be reet set up to see you looking so smart, lass,' Martha said with pride. 'Ee, I'm that glad you're out of this place. You're a lady now, and it's plain that's what you were born to.'

Joanna kissed her. 'But if it hadn't been for you, Martha dear, I wouldn't have lived to be anything at all, would I?' She heard a sound and looked over her shoulder. 'Is that him?'

'Yes, he's gone over to t'barn. He'll not be in for a few more minutes.'

Joanna went to the door. 'You understand I can't come often, Martha, don't you, but I'll send you what I can. And remember, I think about you a lot. I'll go now. I don't want to be the.cause of you getting a beating from Saul.'

'Wait. I think it's time you took what's rightly yours.' Martha scuttled up the narrow stairs. While she was gone Joanna quietly slipped the old and worn boots on to her feet, leaving her own for Martha.

'Here, now. Your cloak. T'one you were wrapped in when I found you.' Lovingly, Martha laid it in Joanna's arms. 'Ee, lass, that was the happiest day of my life. Barring today. Because I'm that happy to see you in your rightful station and that grateful to think you haven't forgotten old Martha. God bless you, lass.'

Joanna stared at the cloak. It was a beautiful midnight blue and in her new position she was able to appreciate the quality of the velvet. The silver clasp, the half of it that remained, was tarnished but it was intricately chased, in itself a work of art. She realised that Martha could easily have sold the cloak. Many times over the years she would have been glad of the money it would have raised. But she had kept it, hidden from Saul, who had forgotten its existence or he would have sold it himself, because it was Joanna's one link with her past. She looked up from the cloak.

'Thank you, Martha. One day I promise I shall repay you for all your love and kindness.'

A last embrace and Joanna hurried from the house, keeping Martha's old boots carefully hidden under her skirts as she walked. At least now her old friend would be dry shod, although the smart, elastic-sided boots wouldn't look smart for long in the filth of that yard. She smiled as she imagined the look on Martha's face when she found them.

Chapter Eight

On the sixteenth of July in the year 1850, in a beautiful gown of white silk and lace and with a crinoline so wide she could hardly fit into the coach, Joanna became Abraham Silkin's wife.

It was a quiet ceremony, with only a handful of people there because, apart from Gertrude and Lynwood, Abraham had no relatives and he had few friends. And Joanna had nobody at all that could be invited although Martha was there, shabby and unseen behind a pillar in a far corner of the church, shedding a tear of happiness for her beloved lass.

To Joanna's relief Lynwood behaved impeccably, kissing her hand and saying he hoped very much that she and Abraham would be happy together. He sounded as if he meant it and had even bought them a tantalus, three heavy cut-glass decanters on a silver stand, as a wedding present. The gesture obviously delighted Abraham.

After the wedding Abraham and Joanna left in a cloud of rice and good wishes for the honeymoon, to be spent in Southwold.

'You'll like it, my dear. It's a little town by the sea in Suffolk,' he said, taking her hand as the coach rumbled along to the railway station.

Joanna felt very smart and excited in her dress of cream and green striped taffeta with a neat little green jacket to match, her tiny green hat tip-tilted over one eye, and carrying a frilly parasol of the same taffeta. She had never before been in a train and she was overawed by the noise and clatter and a little frightened by the speed at which the train lurched along so she clutched her new husband's arm nervously, which pleased him a great deal and he patted her hand reassuringly and told her there was no need to worry.

But when they finally reached their destination another surprise awaited her. She was completely overwhelmed when she caught her first glimpse of the sea from the window of their hotel suite.

'Is it all water, Abraham? As far as you can see? Reaching right up to the sky?' she asked in wonder.

He came and stood beside her. 'Yes, my dear, it's all water, as far as you can see. But it doesn't reach the sky. It only appears to, as it disappears over the horizon.' Patiently, he explained this to her.

'Oh, I see. Thank you for telling me, Abraham. I'm afraid you must think me very ignorant,' she said when he had finished. 'But I'm very anxious to learn,' she added earnestly.

'And I shall be more than happy to teach you, my dear.' He smiled at her, then cleared his throat nervously. 'I've ordered dinner to be brought to our suite tonight. Then, as we're both a little tired after such an eventful day I shall leave you and retire to my dressing room for the night.'

'Very well, Abraham. As you wish.' She hoped she didn't sound too relieved.

Later, as she put on her new lawn night-gown decorated with frills and ribbons and slid into the huge bed between crisp linen sheets, she tried to analyse her feelings. She was glad Abraham had decided not to share her bed, not because she didn't love him, she did, she was sure of it, but rather because the day had been so perfect and she was afraid that perhaps she wouldn't please him as a wife should please her husband and then Abraham would be angry and everything would be spoiled. She fell asleep determined to do everything she could to make him happy.

The next day passed in a euphoric haze. She was so proud to walk beside her new husband, wearing pink sprigged muslin as the weather was so warm, with a straw hat trimmed with pink ribbons and carrying a pink silk parasol. With her hand tucked in his arm – she wasn't wearing gloves because she wanted to show off her new wedding ring, which glinted obligingly in the sun – she didn't notice the sniggering looks that came their way at the sight of an elderly man with his young bride.

But the glances were not lost on Abraham and he was determined to prove to himself that even though he was, as he put it, no longer a young man, that was no reason why he should not be able to keep his lovely young wife happy.

They ate in the dining room that night, an opulent room decorated in gilt and plush, which gave Joanna the opportunity to show off one of the evening gowns Gertrude had chosen for her, a cream shot silk with a lace bertha that exposed her shoulders. She was very anxious to do everything correctly so she watched Abraham and copied him, following his every movement. Unfortunately, she accidentally knocked her bread roll on to the floor in her nervousness and she automatically got up to retrieve it as it rolled across the floor.

'Leave it!' Abraham hissed loudly as he signalled to the waiter to bring her another.

'I'm sorry, Abraham,' she whispered, her face flaming. 'I didn't want to waste it—'

'Never mind, my dear. Simply act as if nothing happened.' Smiling, he picked up his glass and signalled her to do the same.

After that, in spite of her anxiety the meal went smoothly and she enjoyed the food, especially the fish, freshly caught that day. She had rarely eaten fish before and then never less than three days old.

Later, as they went up the stairs to their suite Abraham whispered to her, 'We shall begin our married life properly tonight, my dear. I shall come to you in half an hour when I have finished my cigar.'

'Very well, Abraham. As you wish. I shall be ready for you,' she whispered back.

She undressed and put on the frilly night-gown and sat down at the dressing table to brush her hair. Then she climbed into bed and sat bolt upright, waiting, her hands clasped round her knees. No, that wouldn't do, she thought after a minute, it didn't look right. So she lay down among the soft pillows and pulled the covers up round her. Then she wondered if she ought to blow the candle out. Yes, she decided, it would be better if he couldn't see how nervous she was. She leaned over and blew it out. Oh, dear, now it was so dark that Abraham wouldn't be able to see his way to the bed and might trip over. She sat up and began to scrabble for the matches, but before she could find them the door connecting with Abraham's dressing room opened and he came in, carrying his own candlestick.

Without looking at her he climbed into bed beside her and blew out the candle.

The next half-hour was a nightmare.

Joanna was anxious to please him and be a good wife to him, so although his whiskers were prickly and she hated the smell of stale cigar on his breath she pretended to return his kisses. But before long she discovered that she had no need to pretend. His hands moving under her night-gown were producing the most pleasurable sensations, sensations that caused her to cry out with pleasure. And when he moved on top of her and parted her legs she made no resistance but waited for what Gertrude had warned her might be a painful though not unpleasant experience.

But nothing happened. All she could feel was something warm and soft against her and after several moments Abraham rolled away.

She waited. She had seen enough of animals coupling to know that there was more to it than this, indeed her own body felt somehow cheated. She put out her hand and touched him but he had turned his back and before long she heard him gently snoring.

But Joanna didn't sleep for a long time. Was it her fault he had turned his back on her? Was he regretting their marriage already? She wished Gertrude had been a bit more specific on the subject of wifely duties. Oh, she had known more or less what to expect – she hadn't lived on a farm for sixteen years and remained ignorant of the process of procreation – and had been prepared for it. But Gertrude hadn't prepared her for what had actually happened. Or rather had not happened. And she didn't know how to deal with it. Finally, she fell asleep, telling herself that things were bound to be better next time.

But they weren't. The same thing happened the next night and again the following night. After that Abraham didn't come to her bed at all but with no explanation slept each night in his dressing room.

Joanna didn't know what to think. When Abraham had come to her bed he had begun to rouse in her new and strange feelings that were not at all unpleasant. But it clearly couldn't have been so pleasant for him or he wouldn't have preferred to sleep in his dressing room. She was afraid that it was her fault; that she had failed him in some way, but she didn't like to ask him and he never spoke about it. He simply kissed her goodnight at her bedroom door each night and every morning he asked her at breakfast if she had slept well.

During the day he behaved in the same courteous, loving way, and they took long walks along the beach listening to the waves, then sat on the promenade and watched the seagulls or walked into the little town so that he could buy her a book – he was delighted how quickly she had mastered the art of reading – or a trinket.

One day as they were walking along the beach Joanna said diffidently, 'Do I please you, Abraham? Am I what you had hoped for in a wife?' She hesitated, 'Sometimes, I wonder—' She couldn't go on, there were no words delicate enough for what she wanted to say.

But he had stopped and turned to face her. 'Joanna, my little love, never doubt that you are all I could ever hope for in a wife. And more.' Daringly, he planted a kiss on the end of her nose. 'I truly believe I am the luckiest man in the kingdom to have found you.' He tucked her hand in his arm and held it there as they walked on. 'Do you know,' he reminisced, 'I used to watch you working the field in those dreadful boots that were several sizes too big, dragging barrows, digging turnips, doing all manner of tasks that were beyond your strength and I longed to rescue you and give you a better life. I wanted to show you that there was more to life than drudgery; I wanted to buy you beautiful things. But I realised that I couldn't do any of those things unless I made you mine. Even then I hesitated, you were so young and I—' he cleared his throat. 'Well, I was so much older. But I can only say that knowing and loving you has brought me more happiness than I had ever dared to hope.'

'Thank you, Abraham.' She didn't look at him. 'You know I would do anything to please you.'

He patted her hand. 'You do please me, my dear.' He was quiet for several minutes, then said quietly, 'If there is any fault, it is in me.'

'Oh, no, Abraham,' she said quickly. 'You must never say that. There is no fault in you. You are kindness itself to me.'

'Then there is nothing more to be said, is there?' His voice was decidedly cool. He pointed with his cane, changing the subject. 'Look, over there, at that pretty pink shell.'

She bent and picked it up, her face flaming. She had made a terrible mistake, she realised that. She should never have tried to speak to him on such a delicate subject, it was a breach of good manners or etiquette or something, she wasn't sure what the correct term would be. But whatever it was she had breached it and committed a terrible social crime, although of course Abraham would be too polite to tell her so. And it was not a subject she could discuss with Gertrude.

Miserably she realised that she had failed Abraham yet again.

Joanna was very nervous about taking up her new role as mistress of Cliffe House. She knew it would not be easy moving from a life as a servant – indeed as far as Saul Bradshaw had been concerned she had been little more than a slave – to a life in command of servants of her own. Especially as for the most part the servants themselves were only too well aware of her background. And her youth.

'Don't worry, my little love,' Abraham said as she voiced her fears in the carriage that had met them at the station on their return home from Southwold. 'I treat my servants well and they value their positions too well to step out of line. And if anyone does, Norbert will report to me and it will be instant dismissal for the culprit.' He patted her hand. 'The only newcomer will be your own personal maid, my love. Gertrude will have engaged her during our absence and I trust my sister's judgement totally. There, does that make you happy, sweetheart?' he smiled at her.

She managed to smile back in spite of her uncertainty. 'You seem to have thought of everything, Abraham.'

'I've tried to,' he answered. He lapsed into silence. Oh, yes, he'd thought of everything, he thought bitterly. Except that he hadn't expected to fail in bed. The humiliation of that went deep, so deep he could hardly bring himself to think of it. He had been sure that his impotence would be cured by the excitement of bedding an innocent young virgin, but to his surprise the reverse had been the case. He had felt nothing but self-loathing and disgust as he prepared to defile this sweet child with his carnal lusts. Perversely, to the self-loathing had been added shame at being unable to fulfil his conjugal duties. Three nights he had tried, three nights had ended in total disaster. He was not prepared to put himself through such humiliation again.

Fortunately, Joanna, innocent child that she was, wouldn't fully understand what had – or more accurately had not – happened. For that he was grateful.

He roused himself from his reverie. 'Ah, here we are. And look, Norbert has the servants lined up to greet us.'

Joanna looked out. On the steps of Cliffe House they stood waiting. Eight of them now that the groom had scrambled down from his perch on the carriage and taken his place. The only two she even vaguely recognised were Norbert, who now stepped forward and opened the carriage door and Parker, the butler. Then he introduced Mrs Osborne the cook, Milton the house-maid, Ethel the scullery-cum-maid-of-all-work, and Lily: 'Your personal maid, Madam,' he murmured in her ear. 'Employed by the Master's sister. She hopes you'll find her satisfactory.'

'Thank you, Norbert. I'm sure I shall.'

'And this is Bragg, the gardener,' he resumed in his normal voice, 'And Osborne the groom you've already met.' Again his voice dropped. 'Married to Cook. They live in a flat over the stables. Alfie, their little lad, cleans the boots and does a few odd jobs about the place.'

'I see. Thank you, Norbert.' Joanna smiled and nodded acknowledgement as each one bobbed a curtsy or bowed, reserving an especially warm glance for Lily, who looked frightened out of her wits.

That bit had been surprisingly easy, she thought with satis-faction as they all stood aside for her to enter the house. No doubt this was her natural breeding coming out, inherited from

74

her dear, drowned mother. She must remember to continue to put flowers on the grave, she reminded herself briefly.

In the hall a large bowl of red roses stood on the table by the stairs and the scent filled the air. Before she could comment on this Lynwood stepped forward out of the shadows and coolly kissed her cheek.

'Welcome home, Stepgodmother.' Unsmiling, he raised one eyebrow. 'Should I call you Stepgodmother? I'm not sure what would be considered correct—' he paused. 'Under the circumstances.' There was more than a hint of hostility in his pale blue eyes.

She ignored the tone of his voice and managed to smile at him. 'I think Joanna will be perfectly acceptable, Lynwood. Don't you agree, Abraham?' she turned to her husband.

'Whatever you wish, my love.'

Lynwood looked at the two of them, smiling at each other. It was disgusting. The old boy was quite besotted. He turned to Joanna again. She was quite a looker, by Jove, with her tumbling curls and those huge blue eyes. And she couldn't be much more than sixteen. His glance swept her figure. Nice little breasts and a waist he could easily span with his two hands, he wagered. He'd like the chance to try! Wouldn't he just! Totally wasted on old Uncle Abe, of course.

He turned away. She didn't really look the money-grubbing type, although he couldn't think why else she would have married a man of Uncle Abe's age. His mouth turned down at the corners as another thought surfaced, a thought that had exercised his mind a good deal ever since his godfather announced his plans to marry. Now she was Uncle Abe's wife of course she would be the one to inherit the Silkin fortunes. And there would be plenty to inherit, too, because Uncle Abraham was not short of a copper. So where did that leave him and his rosy expectations? It didn't bear thinking about if his fortunes at cards didn't soon take a turn for the better. Without another word he flung himself upstairs to his room so that he no longer had to look at the two of them fawning over each other.

Joanna watched him go. 'Do you think I've offended Lynwood in some way, Abraham?' she asked anxiously. 'I really don't mind being called Stepgodmother if that's what he prefers.'

'Think nothing of it, my love,' Abraham said. 'Lynwood is a law unto himself and as unpredictable as the wind.' He gave a little laugh. 'I wager he's more than a little jealous, if the truth be known. But don't you worry your pretty little head over it. Give him a few days to get used to things and he'll come round. You'll see. Now, I must go to my study and see to my post and find out what's been happening in my absence. Why don't you go up to your room and rest until dinner? Get to know your new maid, Lily, wasn't that her name?' He chuckled again. 'My sister seems to have thought of everything.' He kissed her cheek. 'Run along, now. Dinner won't be till eight so you'll have plenty of time to change. It'll be quite informal because there'll only be the three of us. Oh, I was forgetting. The master bedroom is to the right at the head of the stairs.' He cleared his throat and said in a lower voice. 'My dressing room adjoins it.'

Realising she had been gently dismissed Joanna began to mount the big sweeping staircase, her hand light on the gleaming banister, her feet making no sound on the thick Turkey carpet. As she went she gazed about her. Blue flocked wallpaper covered the walls on which gilt-framed pictures hung at intervals between crystal sconces. Sunlight glinted on the sconces, making them sparkle like tiny rainbows and it was a minute before she could see where the light came from since there were no windows above ground-floor level. Then she glanced up and saw that a huge stained glass dome high above the stairwell was shedding a soft multi-coloured light over the stairs and landing.

She pushed open the door to the master bedroom. It was a large room, filled with light from the two long windows at which green silk curtains fluttered. The carpet was pale green too and with lemon yellow striped wallpaper the room had a bright, spring-like appearance that was further enhanced by the elegant walnut furniture, chests of drawers, a small writing desk, small bedside tables and an ornate armoire. A chaise-longue covered with green velvet stood at the foot of the bed and there were several chairs covered in the same material dotted about the room. More roses, this time deep yellow, stood on a table between the windows.

Joanna had never seen such a beautiful room in her whole

life. She sank down on the chaise-longue and looked around. Oh, what would Martha say if she could see her now!

There was a tap on the door and Lily slipped in. 'Can I get you owt, M'm?' she asked nervously.

Joanna unpinned her hat and threw it on the bed. Suddenly, she was overcome with tiredness from the journey and the strain of her first meeting with all the servants and she rubbed her temples to ease the headache that threatened.

Lily came over to her. 'Is summat wrong, M'm?'

Joanna looked up at her. She was probably not much more than twelve years old and she looked frightened half to death. 'No, a bit of a headache, that's all.' She smiled at the girl. 'So you're to be my maid, Lily. That's nice. Where are you from?'

Lily gave a little bob. 'Attercliffe, M'm. Windmill Street. But my gran works in t'kitchen for Mrs Theakston and she put in a word for me.'

'Mrs Theakston?' Joanna frowned. She felt she ought to know the name but she couldn't think where she'd heard it.

'Mr Silkin's sister, M'm.'

'Gertrude! Oh, yes, of course.' Joanna's face cleared and she smiled again at the thin little wraith who reminded her of herself not so many weeks ago. 'I'm sure we'll do very well together, Lily.' She yawned and rubbed her eyes. 'Oh, dear. I do feel weary. I didn't realise travelling could be so tiring.'

'Will I get you some tea, M'm?' Lily asked eagerly. 'I know where t'kitchen is. In fact, I know where everythin' is. I've put all your things away, like Mrs Theakston said I should—' her voice trailed off. 'I'm sorry, M'm, I'm being too forward.'

'That's all right, Lily. And I'd very much like some tea, if it's no—' she stopped herself. Lily was here to do her bidding, whether it was any trouble to her or not. Giving orders was something she was going to have to learn and she could tell it wasn't going to be easy after a life of doing the bidding of others.

Lily scuttled away and Joanna leaned back on the chaise-longue and put her feet up, feeling guiltily blissful.

'This really is a most beautiful room,' she said when Lily came back with a tray holding tea things and a plate of toasted

77

tea cakes. 'I'd been staying with my husband's sister before my marriage so I hadn't seen it.' It was the first time she'd said the words 'my husband' and it gave her a little thrill of excitement.

But Lily didn't notice. She prattled on, 'Oh, yes, M'm. I were here when Mrs Theakston had it all beautified. New carpet laid, an' all. She said it had to be just right for when you got back.' She grinned. 'By, she made them men work!'

'I can imagine,' Joanna said with a chuckle.

'Will I fetch you some hot water to wash, M'm, while you're having your tea?' Lily asked, hovering over her. 'Mrs Theakston said that would be what you'd be needing.'

'Yes, that would be very nice. You've no idea how dirty the trains are. Have you ever been in a train, Lily?'

'Oh, no, M'm.' Lily looked horrified. 'I'd be scared. But I've seen them. They run not far from our house. Nearly shake the pots off the shelves they do, great roaring monsters.'

Lily left her and Joanna drank two cups of tea and ate a tea cake. She glanced at her hands. They were soft and white now and only slightly grubby; in fact in what she was now beginning to think of as her 'former life' she would have considered them clean, but Gertrude had taught her to be fastidious and had impressed on her the importance of keeping herself clean and sweet-smelling and now she felt positively grimy from the journey.

She decided against eating another tea cake and instead got up and went over to the windows. They both overlooked the garden at the side of the house, a riot of colour, roses, geraniums, lilies, whole beds of pansies, antirrhinums and salvias, all laid out with geometric precision. Beautifully cut lawns stretched like velvet between the bright borders and flower beds and just below the windows on the terraces huge urns spilled over with geraniums and roses.

And she was now mistress of all this, she reminded herself yet again. Joanna Bradshaw, Saul Bradshaw's skivvy in that other life, was now Mrs Abraham Silkin and mistress of this beautiful house and grounds. So dreams did indeed come true. Only this reality was beyond a dream. Beyond what she could ever have imagined in her wildest dreams.

It was all so perfect that there had to be a snag somewhere.

As if in answer to her thought there was the sound of heavy footsteps along the corridor and Lynwood's voice calling imperiously, 'Norbert! Where are my bloody riding boots? Hasn't that lazy sod of a boot boy cleaned them yet?' There was a pause, then, 'Watch where you're going, you stupid bitch, you nearly had me over!'

The door opened and Lily came in, flustered, her face beet-root red.

'I'm sorry, M'm. I'm afraid the water got spilt a bit. I wasn't looking—'

'It's quite all right, Lily. I heard what happened,' Joanna said. She was pretty sure she knew who it was who hadn't been looking where they were going and it wasn't Lily. 'It's of no consequence. As long as there's enough left for my bath.'

'Oh, yes, M'm. And it's piping hot.'

'You didn't scald yourself?'

'Oh, no, M'm. Well, only a bit. On my hand.'

'Let me see. Oh, Lily, it's very red. Go downstairs and ask Cook or Milton to give you some salve for it. Tell them I sent you.'

After Lily had gone Joanna smiled to herself. It was the first order she had given in her new home and it had felt quite a natural thing to do. She straightened her shoulders. Now she knew without any doubt that this was the kind of life she had been born to.

Chapter Nine

Later that evening, armed with her new-found confidence, Joanna went down to dinner. With several involuntary oohs and aahs, Lily had helped her to dress in a coffee-coloured grenadine dress, the skirt cut away at the front to reveal a coffee and cream striped petticoat and with a cream fichu to match the tiny cream cap perched on her curls. Round her neck Lily had fastened the gold enamel-backed watch on its slender gold chain that Abraham had bought her as a wedding present.

'There, you look a real treat, M'm,' the little maid had said, standing back to admire as Joanna surveyed herself in the mirror. 'Fit to meet the dear Queen herself.'

Meeting the Queen might have been less of an ordeal, Joanna decided half-way through the meal because Lynwood seemed to be at his most difficult, sapping away her new-found confidence so that she was at a loss as to how to deal with him.

He had obviously had several drinks beforehand because his eyes were bright and his face a little flushed.

The trouble was, there was nothing she could actually accuse him of. It was just that every time she glanced up she found his eyes on her. Even when he was talking to Abraham his eyes hardly left her face. It was most disconcerting, especially as she found the expression in his pale blue eyes impossible to read. She couldn't make up her mind whether he was mocking or admiring her. If it were not for his previous behaviour towards her she would have sworn his look was of admiration but that was so unlikely that she knew she must be mistaken.

Abraham didn't seem to notice anything amiss. He treated

her in his usual attentive manner, apologising for talking a certain amount of what he called 'shop' with Lynwood. She noticed that Lynwood's answers to his godfather's questions about the business were brief and evasive and she suspected that he was not in the least interested in the manufacture of buttons except that they provided him with an income.

Although Abraham had ordered a simple meal there were six courses to be sat through. Sitting opposite Lynwood – Abraham had refused to allow her to take her rightful place at the foot of the table, saying it was much too far away – she tried to keep her eyes on her plate, but every now and again, almost involuntarily, she glanced up, only to find those pale blue eyes still watching and to her consternation a frisson of something she couldn't put a name to would run through her, turning her insides to jelly and bringing a pink flush to her cheeks.

She tried conversation. 'I believe you and Abraham are in the habit of enjoying a game of cribbage, after dinner,' she said, addressing him directly.

He smiled and the pale blue eyes seemed to darken fractionally. 'Occasionally,' he replied.

'Sometimes we play chess. But not often.' Abraham dabbed his whiskers with his napkin. 'Because I always beat him.' He laughed delightedly and took a sip of claret.

'Yes. You're always the winner, Godfather,' Lynwood said quietly, but he was gazing at Joanna. Still not taking his eyes off her he went on, 'I shall excuse you from games with me tonight, Godfather. I'm sure you'll prefer to play a game with your ravishing young wife.' He hesitated a fraction too long before adding, 'Do you play chess, Joanna?'

Joanna felt her face flame. 'No, I'm afraid not. But I've no wish to interfere with your usual evening entertainment, gentlemen.' She yawned delicately. 'If you'll excuse me, I'll leave you both to your port and cribbage, or whatever you decide to play.'

They both got to their feet. 'But Joanna, my love, dessert is yet to be served,' Abraham said anxiously.

'I'm sorry. I'm very tired. Please give my apologies to Cook. Goodnight Abraham.' She gave him a dutiful peck on the cheek, then turned to Lynwood. 'Goodnight, Lynwood. Enjoy your game.'

She left the room and went upstairs, her whole body sagging

with relief at having managed the meal without mishap. If this was to be a nightly ordeal how was she going to survive? Worse than that, how was she going to keep her temper?

In the dining room Abraham toyed with the stem of his glass.

'Joanna's a charming lass, don't you think, Lynwood?' he asked conversationally.

'Indeed I do, Godfather. Indeed I do.' Lynwood only called Abraham Godfather when he was trying to be distant. At other times, such as when he wanted to borrow money, he called him Uncle Abe.

'I want her to be happy here.' Abraham paused. 'I should not like to think anything – or anyone – might upset her.' He paused again. Then looked up with a ghost of a smile. 'I daresay you might think such a sweet young thing is wasted on an old man like me ... '

'Oh, no, Godfather. Not at all,' Lynwood said a shade too quickly.

'Don't take me for a fool, Lynwood. Remember I too was young and hot-blooded once.' He took a draught of wine. 'Be that as it may, Joanna is my wife and I will not tolerate her being treated with anything less than the respect due to her.' He dabbed his mouth with his napkin. 'Now, let's see, what is your allowance at present? Is it sufficient for your needs? I think perhaps another hundred a year might not come amiss. What do you say?' He smiled at Lynwood.

'Thank you, Godfather. That's most generous.' Lynwood flushed, partly with pleasure at the thought of the extra money and partly with annoyance because he knew he was being paid to leave Joanna alone. He wanted to shout that he wouldn't touch the wench with a bargepole, but it wasn't true. Already he had dreamed of getting her into his bed, of pleasuring her – and himself – in ways this old man could never imagine.

'Good.' Abraham's voice brought him back to earth with a jolt. 'And now, what shall it be, Lynwood? Cribbage? Or chess? Or what about a game of backgammon?'

Joanna began to enjoy her new life. She loved being clean and sweet-smelling, she loved the beautiful, extravagant clothes she wore even if she did find the restrictions of whalebone stays and crinolines uncomfortable and irksome, and she loved the feel of kid slippers on her feet and the smooth whiteness of her hands. Never before had her fingernails needed to be cut; ever since she could remember they had been black and broken and she gloried in their new oval shape and delicate appearance.

To Abraham's surprise and delight she slipped into the role of mistress of Cliffe House with comparative ease. She seemed to know instinctively the best way to treat the servants, and if at times Abraham felt she erred on the side of leniency he came to understand that her compassion was born of fellow-feeling.

'Don't forget I was a servant until I came here, Abraham,' she reminded him. 'I was kicked and cuffed and made to work from early morning until I was dropping with tiredness at night. That's no way to inspire respect and loyalty.'

He soon found that she was right because before long the servants began to recognise that she was treating them with respect and consideration and they stopped sniggering and whispering names behind her back and grew to love her.

Gertrude accompanied her when she made calls. The older woman treated her less like a sister-in-law than the daughter she had always wanted but been denied and this suited Joanna, who thought of Gertrude rather in the fashion of a favourite aunt. In this way the two got on very well together.

Gertrude tried to introduce her to all the right people, but this was far from easy. Time after time Joanna's calling card was returned with the message, 'Not at home'.

'They don't like me,' Joanna said sadly. 'I'm never going to be accepted in their society. And I've tried so hard—' her eyes filled with tears.

'Ee, lass, they'll come round in time. It only teks one and the rest'll follow,' Gertrude told her. But privately she was not so sure. Word had quickly got round of Joanna's squalid upbringing and it was a barrier that would be difficult, if not impossible, to overcome.

Gertrude's only success was with the Dowager Lady Kathryn George who received them one afternoon.

'By, you kept your temper like a real lady when that old bitch was rude to you,' she said as they went home in the carriage afterwards. 'Mind, Kate's rude to everyone, she's got a tongue like a razor. They don't call her Catty Kate for nowt. But I don't pay any mind to her. She's old and crabby and there's nowt much left in life for her 'cept being nasty to people. But you handled her well.'

'I knew she only wanted to find out what my manners were like,' Joanna said crossly. 'Whether I knew when to stand up and when to sit down and how to manage the tea things. I did all right, didn't I, Gertrude? I didn't let you down?' she asked anxiously.

'No, love, as I said, you handled her well.' She gave a smug nod. 'Breeding will out, you see. Even though you never knew your mother you've plainly come from good stock.' She patted Joanna's hand affectionately.

'Thank you, Gertrude,' Joanna said seriously. 'You know, it's the thought of my mother that helps me through the difficult bits. I think to myself, "What would my mama have done in this situation?" and I try to act accordingly.' She sighed. 'I wish I could discover who she was and where she came from.'

'I shouldn't worry your head too much on that score, lass,' Gertrude said. Then she added thoughtfully, 'On the other hand, it mightn't be a bad idea to let people know a bit about your history. We can say you're well-born, even if you don't know exactly who you are.' She nodded sagely. 'I'll let a hint or two drop. It might help.'

'It might help me to find out about my mother, too,' Joanna said eagerly.

'Aye, it might, at that.'

Gertrude's ploy worked. More ladies were 'at home' when she and Joanna went visiting and Joanna and Abraham even began to be invited to dinner parties. This happened more and more frequently as word got round that the charmingly pretty young lass Abe Silkin had taken for his wife had really come from a well-to-do family. Tales abounded as to how she came to be living with the Bradshaws, tales that became more and more fanciful and romantic with each telling. Joanna smiled and said nothing, listening carefully to all that was said in the hope of uncovering some long-hidden family secret that would give her some real clue about her family. But although she learned all manner of scandal and gossip – some of it hardly suitable for the smoke room, let alone the drawing room – when the ladies withdrew leaving the men to their port and cigars, she never heard the slightest hint of a beloved daughter having gone missing nearly seventeen years ago.

'I think it's time we returned all the hospitality we've been receiving, don't you, my love?' Abraham said to her one evening as they sat by the fire together waiting for Lynwood to appear so that dinner could be served. 'I've never attended so many dinner parties in all my life.' He smiled happily. 'I know it's only because everybody is keen to meet you, sweetheart. All the same, it's quite gratifying.'

He allowed himself a smug smile. He had had a few misgivings at the beginning, he was the first to admit that, especially that first afternoon, watching Joanna wolfing down toasted tea cakes, and there had been one or two hiccups since, but under Gertie's tuition she had blossomed, taking to her new life like the proverbial duck to water. Of course, it had been a quixotic idea, to take a little ragamuffin and pitchfork her into the life of a lady, but it had worked even better than he could ever have hoped and he was growing more fond of the charming little lass every day. And he was certain his affection was returned although sometimes he felt that Joanna treated him more as a beloved grandfather than husband. He sighed. That was the one blot on an otherwise perfect relationship. Even now when he thought of those first nights they had spent together the humility and embarrassment threatened to choke him. And much as he would have liked to try again the fear of a repeat performance – or rather non-performance – prevented him and he continued to sleep in his dressing room.

How Joanna felt about this part of their lives he didn't know; it was not a subject to be discussed, but judging from the conversations of his married friends most wives submitted to their husband's attentions with resignation and were glad and thankful when they found comfort elsewhere.

The only trouble was, without consummating the marriage there would be no son and heir and that was a pity. A son would have provided great comfort in his old age. Fond though he was of Lynwood, a godson was not the same as his own flesh and blood. Perhaps if he tried again things might be better ... He shuddered. No, the fear of failure was too painful.

Resolutely he turned his attention to something else which

had been exercising his mind.

'A dinner party? Here?' Joanna said, her eyes widening in alarm as he told her of his plan. It was almost Christmas and they had been married for nearly six months.

'Well, my dear, don't you think it's time we returned some of the hospitality we've enjoyed since our marriage?' He smiled at her as he spoke.

'Yes, of course, Abraham.' But—' She had managed to learn how to cope with formal dinner parties in other people's houses, but she didn't feel very confident about holding one in her own house.

His smile turned into a chuckle. 'Don't look so worried, my little love. I'm sure Gertrude will be only too happy to help you with all the arrangements.'

She licked her lips. 'When are you thinking of holding it?' she asked.

'Let's see. It had better be after Christmas now, I suppose. What about a New Year party? That would be less formal than a dinner party and we can invite everyone at once. How does that suit you, sweetheart?'

'A party. Yes, I think a party would be better, Abraham.' She gave a sigh of relief. She could cope with that, she felt sure.

'Good. I'm glad you like the idea. Get yourself a new dress made.' He leaned over and kissed her cheek.

'But I've already got—'

'Never mind. I don't care how many you've already got. Get a new one made. I want you to be the belle of the ball. Ah, here's Lynwood. Good. We can go in to dinner. You took your time, my boy.' He gave Joanna his arm, saying over his shoulder, 'We've just been planning a New Year party, Lynwood. Don't you think it's a capital idea?'

'With an orchestra? For dancing?'

'Yes! Why not! We hadn't thought of that, had we, my love?'

'Then I think it's a simply ripping idea, Uncle Abe.' Lynwood followed them through to the dining room, his eyes on Joanna's bustle, but his thoughts far away on the dance floor, with his arm round that tiny waist, pressing her ever closer to him.

His feelings towards Joanna had changed over the past six months. He was still jealous of her, in fact he hated her, because he knew Abraham had changed his will since his marriage and that meant she had usurped his position as his godfather's heir. Not that Uncle Abe had ever said as much and he had to admit there was no difference in his godfather's attitude towards himself. They still frequently enjoyed a game of cribbage or chess after dinner, when Joanna had retired for the night. His allowance too, was more than generous – and even more so since it had been increased just after the marriage.

But although he hated her, the strange thing was, since Uncle Abe had more or less paid him to keep his hands off Joanna the temptation to get her into his bed had been almost irresistible. He found himself scheming ways to get her alone, to tease her and initiate her in the ways of a young and virile man. Heavens, if he was in Uncle Abe's position there would be no question of chess or cribbage after dinner, he would have far more interesting games in mind! God, she was wasted on that old man. Even now as he walked behind Joanna to the dining room, feasting his eyes on her white shoulders, he found it necessary to slip quickly into his place so that the tablecloth covered the rather too obvious effect she had on him.

Gertrude came to stay so that she could help Joanna to plan for the party. Invitations were sent, gratifyingly most of which were accepted, menus were drawn up and a five-piece orchestra booked. So busy were they with their planning that Christmas was almost upon them before they knew it.

'I must take a Christmas basket to Martha,' Joanna said. 'I can't let Christmas pass without going to see her.'

'Oh, lass, do you think you should?'

'Yes. I'll get Cook to make up a hamper and Osborne can take me.'

'I don't know what Abe'll say.'

'He won't know if you don't tell him.'

Gertrude shook her head. 'Ee, you're a determined lass when your mind's made up.'

It was a cold, crisp morning when Joanna again made her way along the path by the River Porter, carrying a large hamper. She had left Osborne with the carriage on the bridge, declining his offer to carry it for her, saying she had carried heavier loads in her time.

Martha was in the kitchen, making brawn, and the smell of it took Joanna back to her childhood. She had always hated it.

Martha looked up at the sound of the latch. 'Joanna!' But instead of welcome there was alarm in her face. 'What's to do? What's wrong?'

'Nothing's wrong, Martha. I've brought you a hamper for Christmas.' She heaved it on to the table and went and kissed Martha. 'You didn't think I'd forget you, not at Christmas, did you?'

'Oh, love, it's good of you. But you mustn't stay.' Martha was fluttering like a bird in her agitation. She looked over her shoulder. 'He's upstairs, asleep. He was so drunk when he came in last night he's not wakened up yet. But he'll be down any minute and he mustn't find you here. Go on, now.' She looked round again. 'Well, perhaps you've just got time to help me get this hamper into the pantry where he'll not see it.'

They carried it across the room into the pantry just as Saul's step was heard on the stairs. 'Oh, God, we're too late,' Martha moaned as the door crashed open and a dishevelled Saul stood in the doorway. When he saw Joanna, dressed in a warm cloak with a fur hood, his lip curled.

'Ah, so t'little pig thought it 'ud come back to t'sty, did it?' he snarled.

'I came to see my dear friend Martha, but I'm going now,' she replied with a lift of her chin, trying to conceal her fear.

'More like you've come to show off what a fine lady you've become.' He walked over to her and ripped the cloak open. 'Oh, my, look at t'finery.' He caught hold of the gold chain round her neck on which her enamelled watch hung and gave it a tug that broke the chain and scratched her neck till it bled. Then he held it up. 'That'll fetch me a pretty penny,' he said with a grin that showed all his brown and broken teeth.

'Leave her be, Saul.' Martha caught his arm. 'She's doing no harm.'

He shrugged her off so roughly that she fell over. 'Doing no harm! She's come to gloat over me, that's what she's come for. I let her go for a field that's worth nowt. Well, now she's here she can pay for it.' He ripped the pearl brooch off her dress, tearing it and dragged her reticule off her wrist.

'Stop it, Saul! Stop it!' Martha tried to put herself between him and Joanna. 'Go on, lass. Run. For God's sake run,' she called over her shoulder. 'And if you love me, don't come back!'

Joanna needed no second bidding. She lifted her skirts and ran, clutching her cloak round her. She didn't stop until she was safely in the carriage. Then she sobbed all the way home.

It was impossible to keep the escapade from Abraham. He was justifiably furious and for the first time Joanna discovered that her husband had a temper.

'You disobeyed me, Joanna,' he said coldly, his face like thunder. 'I expressly forbade you to visit the Bradshaws because I knew this was likely to happen, but you took no notice.' He spun round. 'You could have been killed by that man. Do you realise that? He's nothing more than a monster.'

'I'm sorry, Abraham.' She hung her head. 'Truly I am. And the things he stole – my watch, my little pearl brooch, both things you bought me. I should have thought not to wear them.'

He waved his hand. 'They're of no importance. They can be replaced. It's your safety that I care about. Look at your neck. It's black and blue.' His voice dropped. 'I care about you, Joanna, my little love. I care about you very much and it appals me that you had so little regard for your own safety. If any harm had befallen you—' he got no further but gathered her into his arms and stroked her hair. 'Promise me you'll never do such a thing again.'

'I promise, Abraham,' she snuffled, her face buried in his coat.

'And I promise you that Martha shan't be forgotten. I'll see that she is sent delicacies from time to time. There, will that satisfy you?'

She looked up at him, her face tear-stained. 'Yes, thank you, Abraham.'

He bent and kissed her. 'There. Now dry your eyes, my little love, and we'll not speak of it again.'

'You're very good to me, Abraham.' Chastened, she went to her room. She realised now how foolish she had been to visit Martha, but not because of her own injuries; they were nothing to what Martha would now be suffering.

Chapter Ten

Christmas was spent quietly because of the preparations for the New Year party. Nevertheless, everywhere was decorated with greenery; great copper jugs of holly stood in the hall and dining room and branches of it, twined with ivy and mistletoe, festooned all the pictures and doorways. There was also a large Christmas tree in the corner of the drawing room, a fashion begun by Prince Albert, prettily hung with glass baubles and tiny candles and with brightly wrapped parcels at its foot.

Presents were not opened until they arrived home from church on Christmas morning. Joanna was like a child, her cheeks rosy from the frosty air and her eyes bright with excitement as she tore the wrappings from her gifts, and clapped her hands as she watched the others unwrapping theirs. In what she now thought of as her former life Christmas Day had been much like any other, but this day had been made extra special in all kinds of ways.

For one thing she had never before had money to buy presents and she had taken great delight in searching for the right things for her new family. Finally, she had decided on an intricately carved wooden cigar box for Abraham, a pale blue silk cravat for Lynwood and a silver smelling bottle for Gertrude, and she beamed with delight at their gasps of pleasure as they opened them, almost forgetting to unwrap her own gifts as she watched them.

Abraham had bought her a set of silver-backed brushes for her dressing table, inscribed with her name, and he flushed with pleasure to hear her squeal of delight and to receive the extravagant kisses she planted over his face and whiskers.

'Oh, thank you, dear, *dear* Abraham,' she cried, sitting on his lap to give him yet another kiss. 'You are so good to me.'

'There, there, my dear.' He patted her arm, clearly pleased but a little embarrassed by her effusiveness. 'I'm glad you like them. But look, you've other things to open.'

'Oh, so I have.' She slid off his lap and hurried back to the tree.

Gertrude had bought her an ivory fan trimmed with silver lace and lined with pink watered silk to match her new ball gown.

'I had it specially made when Estelle was making your new gown. I thought you'd like it,' Gertrude said smugly.

'Like it! Oh, Gertrude, I love it.' She danced round the room fanning herself and then kissed her excitedly.

'I hope I get the same treatment,' Lynwood drawled as he tossed her a small parcel containing six hem-stitched handker-chiefs with her initial in the corner.

'Of course you do, Lynwood.' She planted a kiss on his cheek, which she couldn't help noticing was smooth and sweet-smelling, whereas Abraham's was inclined to be coarse and whiskery.

'Surely, you can do better than that, Joanna, can't you?' he whispered, turning his head and kissing her full and hard on the lips.

She backed away, her cheeks suddenly flushed to a gentle rose colour. Although the kiss had been brief it had touched something inside her that had not been wakened since those first abortive attempts by her husband to make love to her and she was both surprised and a little alarmed by her feelings.

Lynwood was smiling at her, his eyes warm. She felt naked under his gaze because she was sure he was aware of the feeling he had aroused in her.

'There's more where that came from,' he said softly. 'Any time, Joanna, dear.'

Swiftly, she turned away and began to rummage under the tree among the rest of the presents, remaining there until she was certain she had her feelings under control.

The rest of the day passed pleasantly. Abraham carved the most enormous turkey Joanna had ever seen and she was so alarmed when the plum pudding was borne in covered in flames that Gertrude had to wave her new smelling bottle under her nose.

Afterwards they cracked nuts and ate sweetmeats whilst playing four-handed cribbage, which Abraham and Lynwood won easily because Gertrude had indigestion and couldn't concentrate and Joanna was only just learning how to play.

At eleven o'clock they each went to their separate rooms, three of them to sleep and the fourth to torture himself with imagining what his elderly godfather was doing with Joanna's beautiful body.

With Christmas Day over the house became busy with preparations for the New Year's Eve party. The drawing room was cleared, the carpet removed and the floor polished so that it could be used for dancing and a raised platform was built into the huge bay window for the players who were to provide the music. In the dining room the table was extended to its full length to accommodate the buffet, with all four extra leaves inserted. There were also side tables to hold the great hams, the side of beef, an even bigger turkey than the one at Christmas and an enormous turbot, because there would be no room to carve these at the main table. The breakfast room was turned into a games room for those who preferred cribbage or backgammon to dancing.

Added to the greenery that had decorated the house for Christmas there were now great bowls of flowers. Bragg, the gardener, had been carefully nurturing huge mop-headed chrysanthemums in the heated greenhouses at the side of the house so that they should come to perfection on New Year's Eve and he had brought in armfuls of them, yellow, red and bronze for the hall and dining room, pink and white for the drawing room. Milton, the house-maid, who had a soft spot for Ernie Bragg, smuggled him in in his stockinged feet so that he could see how she had arranged the splendid result of his labours in big cut-glass and china vases and huge silver bowls. As a last resort she had even filched the large brown earthenware pickle jar from the kitchen for a striking display half-way up the stairs when she ran out of more orthodox vessels.

'Aye,' he said with a satisfied nod when he saw them. 'Aye, them's awreet.'

Lily was nearly as nervous as Joanna as she helped her to dress on the night of the party. The new dress was of coral pink watered silk, with a wide, flounced skirt held out by layers of stiffened petticoats, each of the three flounces trimmed with silver lace and caught up at intervals with tiny silver roses tied with narrow coral ribbon tails. The bodice was close-fitting, silver lace over coral pink to show off Joanna's small firm breasts and tiny waist, and a swath of coral-pink tulle dotted with more tiny silver roses softened the long, off-the-shoulder neckline enhancing Joanna's long white neck and showing off the triple string of graduated pearls, Abraham's New Year present to her. In her hair, swept up at the sides with silver combs and then allowed to cascade down in a mass of curls over one shoulder, Lily had threaded more coral ribbons. A pair of silver lace elbow-length mittens and the fan Gertrude had given her completed the picture.

'Ee, M'm, you look a real treat,' Lily said admiringly, sitting back on her heels after helping Joanna on with the tiny kid slippers dyed to exactly match the colour of her dress.

Joanna surveyed herself in the full-length mirror. The calm, elegant figure that stared coolly back at her was a far cry from the shabby little creature that had come from Bradshaw's Farm eight months ago. But the self-assured look was deceptive. Inside, she was trembling and she felt sick with fright. Indeed, so bad did she feel, that she almost wished herself back in the squalor of Bradshaw's Farm.

Almost. Not quite. Anything was better than what she had endured there. With a lift of her head she took her courage in both hands and answered Abraham's knock at her door.

He smiled at her, his face filled with admiration. 'Oh, my little love, you look absolutely charming,' he said, offering her his arm. 'You'll be the belle of the ball, there's no doubt about that.'

'Thank you, Abraham, but I'm afraid I don't feel charming. I feel sick,' she replied miserably. 'I'm sure I shall do something terrible and show you up.'

'Nonsense, Joanna, I won't listen to such talk,' he said, his

93

voice sharp. He took her hand and gave it a little squeeze before placing it on his arm. 'My sister has taught you well. Your manners are impeccable and I'm proud of you. Come along, now, we'll go downstairs and wait in the hall for the guests to arrive. Gertie's already down there, ordering the servants about, bless her.'

Joanna stood by her husband's side to greet their guests, a small wraith of a girl, pale and lovely in her fairy-tale gown beside the tall, white-haired, slightly florid, coarse-featured man. The contrast was not lost on the guests, many of whom had come simply to satisfy their curiosity, partly because of the stories they had heard about this young Cinderella and partly because Abraham Silkin had never entertained on this scale before and they were keen to take advantage of his hospitality.

The guests streamed past Joanna, briefly introduced by Abraham as they greeted her. A few she recognised from the occasions they had been invited out to dinner but most she did not. If she had been less nervous she might have seen the openly speculative looks of the wives and the naked admiration in the eyes of their husbands, but she was too intent on behaving in exactly the way Gertrude had taught her to notice and it was with some surprise as the dancing was about to begin that she found that her card was full. Abraham's name was not down.

'I don't dance, my little love,' he said when she pointed this out, a tinge of regret in his voice. 'But you go and enjoy yourself. I shall enjoy watching you.'

To her surprise Joanna did enjoy herself. She had never danced before but her partners were only too pleased to initiate her into the intricacies of the Lancers, to whirl her round in polkas and schottisches, and to hold her close – sometimes a little too close – in the Viennese waltzes by Mr Strauss that were fast becoming popular all over the country.

She was indeed the belle of the ball, a fact which didn't go unnoticed by the over-dressed wives of the gentlemen who eagerly claimed their dances with the pretty hostess, wives who had only been persuaded to accept Abraham Silkin's invitation in order to discover whether the rumours were true that this lass he had rescued from a life of squalor was in fact the daughter of a high-born lady. Judging by the way she was behaving tonight, outwardly perfectly self-assured, smiling up at her partners with just the merest hint of coquettishness, the rumour could well be true, they decided privately and grudgingly and they whispered jealously to each other behind their fans, speculating as to which of the big houses in the district she could possibly belong.

Lynwood, dashing in a blue tail-coat and a fancy waistcoat, his hair carefully curled so that one lock fell carelessly across his forehead, had put his name against four dances, including the supper dance. He was an accomplished dancer and he guided her with such skill that she felt that she was dancing on air as she closed her eyes and gave herself up to the rhythm of the music. It came as quite a shock when the dance ended and the music stopped.

'You enjoyed that waltz, didn't you, Joanna?' he whispered in her ear as he escorted her back to her seat.

'I – yes, thank you, Lynwood. You dance extremely well.' She gave him what she hoped was a cool smile, then added a trifle ruefully, 'I just hope I didn't tread on your toes too much.'

'You were so light in my arms I wouldn't have noticed if you did,' he said with a smile. 'I look forward to our next dance.' He glanced at her card although he knew perfectly well what was on it. 'The supper dance, I believe.'

'Abraham might wish—' she began.

'Abraham has gone to enjoy a quiet game of cards in the morning room,' he replied. 'He asked me to make sure you were well looked after as dancing is not at all to his taste. A task I may say I am very happy to carry out.' He bowed over her hand. 'But now I have to perform a rather less delightful duty and dance with the redoubtable Aunt Gertrude.' He sighed. 'Our regard for each other – or rather our *dis*regard for each other – is mutual. *A bientôt*, Joanna, my dear.' He disappeared into the crowd as her next partner came to claim her, a rather large man with a purple cravat who sweated profusely and trod on her feet.

When the dance was over she escaped upstairs to the room set aside for the ladies to repair the ravages of the ballroom. She felt she needed to splash on the cool eau de Cologne that

Gertrude had thoughtfully ordered to be placed there for the purpose.

The door was ajar and as she reached it she heard the tinkle of laughter and a voice saying. 'Oh aye, I agree. It makes a charming enough story. But I'm not taken in by it. Daughter of a lady, indeed! Why, did you see the way she—?'

'Come now, Connie, you're only jealous because of the way George drooled over her when he was dancing with her. I saw him, he couldn't keep his eyes off her *décolletage*.'

'That's exactly what I mean, Ruby. If she'd been a real lady she'd not have encouraged him.'

'Encourage him! He may be your husband, Connie, but I know my brother well enough to know he'd not need any encouragement! He's always had an eye for the ladies, has George, and well you know it. When they went by me the poor lass was trying to fend him off! He'd have had his hand down her dress in another minute. Right out there on the dance floor, too! I thought she managed to get herself out of the situation very well. Good heavens, she'd never have been able to carry it off the way she did if she'd not had breeding.'

'Rubbish. I'll not have you say such things about George. He's not like that. *She* was the one to blame, anyone could see that with half an eye, the way she's been flaunting herself at the men all evening. She's nowt more than a money-grubber, if you ask me. Only wed that poor old man for what she could get out of him. I thought so at the time and I'm even more of that opinion after tonight.'

'Oh, I think Abe Silkin knew what he was doing, Connie. He's not daft.'

'Then more fool him. Well, I'll tell you this, Ruby Arkwright. She'll never grace my dinner table. I'm not one to be taken in by fairy-tales. In fact, I only came here tonight out of curiosity.'

'Well, at least you admit it, Connie.'

Joanna slipped into the next room as Connie, resplendent in lemon, with a rather red face and feathers in her hair, swept out of the room and down the stairs like a galleon in full sail, followed a minute or two later by Ruby, an older, less aggressive-looking woman in midnight blue.

Joanna remained where she was for several minutes, her

hands covering her face. Had that horrible woman Connie voiced what people really thought of her? Is that what was being said behind her back? That she was nothing more than a money-grubber? How could she face the crowd downstairs after that, when all she wanted to do was to crawl away and die. She sat down on the edge of the bed, twisting her fan between her hands. She remembered Connie's husband, that awful man with the wandering hands and the lecherous look in his eye. If Connie had heard the things he'd suggested to her while they were dancing, the dirty old man, she would never have said her George 'wasn't like that'. She'd had difficulty in waiting until the end of the dance before extracting herself from his hold. Perhaps that had been the wrong thing to do, perhaps she should have walked off in the middle of the dance. Gertrude hadn't taught her how to deal with a situation like that.

There was still so much to learn.

She sighed and stared down at her hands, at the wide gold band Abraham had placed there six months before and the diamond ring he had bought her on their honeymoon. She couldn't let him down, he was such a dear, kind man. And that woman was wrong. She wasn't a money-grubber, Abraham had chosen her when she had hardly known he existed. And her mother was a lady, which was more than could be said of George's wife, the gossiping old biddy. She got up from the bed and went into the next room. It was empty now, so she splashed eau de Cologne generously over her neck and wrists, squared her shoulders and went down the stairs.

Lynwood was waiting impatiently for her at the bottom.

'I was just coming to look for you, Joanna. This is our dance, I believe, and I don't want to waste a minute of it.'

'No, Lynwood, neither do I.' She gave him a dazzling smile and allowed him to lead her on to the floor. She would not let Connie whatever-her-name-was spoil her evening.

Once again she seemed to float as he twisted and twirled her in an energetic polka that seemed to get faster and faster until her head was spinning and she was glad to feel his arm round her, holding her, guiding her. She stole a glance up at him and saw that he was looking down at her with an expression in his eyes that made her draw a quick breath.

'You're so beautiful, Jo,' he breathed. 'You're enough to drive a man out of his senses.'

'You mustn't say that,' she whispered back. He was holding her very close, too close, making her feel as if her insides were melting, yet she didn't want him to loosen his hold.

'Why not? It's true,' he whispered in her ear and she could feel his breath warm on her cheek.

The dance ended with a flourish and he spun her round so fast that she fell against him, quite breathless. Gently he released her.

'May I escort you in to supper, Mrs Silkin?' he asked formally, his eyes twinkling because he was fully aware of the effect he had had on her.

'Thank you. That would be very nice,' she answered, her voice not quite steady.

'Then please to take my arm, m'lady,' he said with an exaggerated bow.

'Thank you, kind Sir,' she answered with a curtsy. Then giggling, she allowed him to escort her to the door.

Abraham was there, watching. 'I can see you're enjoying yourself, my love,' he said quietly.

'Oh, yes, thank you, Abraham.' She relinquished Lynwood's arm and took Abraham's. 'Have you come to take me in to supper?'

'I think not. It wouldn't be right for us to take supper together, my love,' he chided her gently, extricating himself from her grasp. 'We should mingle with our guests separately. Didn't Gertie tell you that? You should go in to supper with your last dancing partner. That was Lynwood, was it not? I'm sure there'll not be any shortage of gentleman eager to wait on you when you get there.' He was looking at Lynwood as he spoke those last words.

But Joanna didn't notice. She was mortified at having said the wrong thing yet again. 'Oh, I'm sorry, Abraham. I didn't realise. I thought—' her voice trailed off.

'Never mind, my love. You'll learn.' He smiled at her encouragingly. 'In time. No doubt you've had plenty of dancing partners beside Lynwood?'

'Oh, yes, Abraham, thank you. I'm having a wonderful

time.' She knew that was what he wanted to hear.

'Capital, my dear. Capital. I'm only sorry I'm not a dancing man myself.' He patted her hand and left her, ordering food to be sent through to the games room for the guests there.

Lynwood offered his arm again.

She hesitated. 'But you're family, too, Lynwood. And I thought Abraham looked a bit—' She bit her lip anxiously. 'Are you sure it's the right thing to do?' She was becoming exhausted with trying to remember the correct way to behave every minute of the evening.

'Oh, perfectly sure.' With a laugh he drew her hand through his arm.

'Well, I can certainly do with a drink, that last dance left me very thirsty,' she said, relaxing.

He looked down at her. 'It left me feeling hungry,' he said softly, squeezing her hand and leaving her in no doubt that it was not food that was on his mind.

Chapter Eleven

Contrary to Abraham's advice Lynwood settled Joanna in a corner where he could have her all to himself.

As she waited for him to bring her a drink and some food Joanna gazed round the room at the guests. They were standing in groups or sitting at the tables, all talking and laughing, quite clearly determined to get all they could out of the evening. Milton and Norbert and the extra hired helpers were nearly rushed off their feet replenishing dishes that were emptied as fast as they were filled, and Joanna made a mental note to congratulate Cook on the spread.

'Some people are very greedy, Lynwood,' she whispered, gratefully sipping the drink he had brought her. 'You would think they had never eaten a square meal in their lives before.' Having known what it was to be hungry it upset Joanna to see the way food was being carelessly heaped on to plates, spilling over on to the tablecloth and even on to the floor, where it was trodden heedlessly into the carpet.

He grinned. 'And not a few will have fat heads tomorrow, I'll wager. And I don't just mean the men!' A bout of tipsy feminine giggles from the other side of the room reinforced his statement.

'Do you think those ladies are laughing at me, Lynwood?' she asked, casting an anxious sideways glance in their direction.

'Gad, no! Why the devil should they?' He raised his eyebrows in surprise.

She hung her head. 'I overheard what some of them were saying about me earlier.'

'And what were they saying?'

She flushed. 'They said that I was flaunting myself at the men. And that I was nothing more than a money-grubber. That I had only married Abraham for his money. It isn't true, you know, Lynwood.' She looked up at him, her eyes troubled.

'Of course it isn't true, Jo. Any fool knows that,' he said a shade too heartily since those last had once been his own sentiments if he was entirely honest. He took her hand and held it, concealed by the white cloth that covered the small table where they were sitting. At that moment he was having difficulty in restraining himself from taking her in his arms and kissing away the troubled expression on her face. 'Oh, God, you're such a little innocent, Jo. You're no match for those old biddies,' he said with a sigh. Then he smiled at her. 'But don't mind them. They're only jealous of your youth and beauty. Come on now, eat up. These oyster patties are extremely good.'

He talked to her encouragingly, allaying her fears and making her laugh, leaning forward and smiling into her eyes in a way that made her heart skip a beat. She sensed that he had changed over the past months; his earlier hostility towards her seemed to have evaporated and she had the feeling that he would have liked to – what? She didn't quite know. She only knew that she felt so safe and protected in his presence, with her hand still held captive in his that she was sorry when the supper interval ended and the orchestra struck up again.

'I can see old Pinkerton weaving his way over to claim you, Jo, so unfortunately our little tête-à-tête will have to come to a close,' he said ruefully, giving her hand a squeeze before reluctantly letting it go. He stood up and helped her to her feet as her next partner came to claim his dance. 'But don't forget the last waltz is mine,' he bent and whispered in her ear.

'My turn, Silkin,' the man said, swaying a little on his feet. 'You mustn't monopolise the little lady. Old Abe might have been happy enough for you to take his name when he adopted you but I doubt he'd be so happy if he realised you'd also set your sights on his wife!' He gave a wheezing chuckle and offered his arm to Joanna. 'Come along, my pretty, you'll be safe enough with me.'

101

Joanna shot a quick glance in Lynwood's direction, but he was glowering at the other man with an expression of pure venom on his face. 'If I were you I should watch your tongue, Pinkerton,' he said through gritted teeth, then turned and shouldered his way through the crowd.

Joanna never knew how she got through the rest of the evening even though Gertrude was often at her side to make sure she said and did the right thing. She didn't know which she hated most, having her toes trodden on and her breasts covertly squeezed by sweating dancing partners or being watched with open disapproval by their jealous wives. At the end of the evening she was relieved to relax into the safety of Lynwood's arms for the last waltz.

'It's been quite an ordeal for you, hasn't it, Jo?' he whispered down at her.

She gave him a tremulous little smile. 'Yes. I don't know how I'd have got through it if you hadn't been here. And Gertrude, of course. I've hardly seen Abraham. I thought he would ... I don't think he realised—'

'Uncle Abe's not much of a one for dancing, he's more at home playing host at the card tables. Not that he's a gambling man,' he added hastily, uncharacteristically defending his godfather. 'Any road, he knew you'd be all right with Aunt Gertie and me keeping an eye on you.' He bent his head and kissed her swiftly on the cheek. 'In truth, I have great difficulty in keeping my eyes off you,' he said softly in her ear and gathered her even closer, making her excitingly aware of every contour of his body. She closed her eyes and gave herself up to the dreamy rhythm of the waltz, the feel of his arm holding her, his hand warm in hers.

All too soon the dance ended and he spun her round and round until she fell against him, dizzy and breathless. Then, with a quick but unmistakable squeeze he set her back on her feet, keeping her within the circle of his arm just a moment longer than was strictly necessary.

'Uncle Abe's waiting for you, Jo,' he whispered, nodding towards the door. 'Unfortunately, he has first claim on you. Come, I'll take you to him.'

They crossed to where Abraham was waiting for her to join him in bidding their guests goodnight. As the two men stood together it struck her how old and heavy-jowled her husband was in contrast to his young and handsome godson, and not for the first time she had to fight the comparison.

Abraham smiled at her as he took her arm and guided her to stand with him by the front door. She felt so tired and emotionally drained that she could hardly stand, but she managed to smile back at him and brace herself to shake endless hands and murmur endless goodnights. After the last guest had gone she remembered, even without being prompted by Gertrude, to thank the staff for all their hard work. Then she felt her duty was done.

'Is that all, Abraham?' she asked, looking round. 'Is there anything else I should do, or ought to have done?'

He frowned. 'Was the evening so onerous, my love?' he asked a shade tartly. 'I thought you were enjoying yourself.'

'Oh, yes, I did, dearest. It was an unforgettable evening,' she said truthfully. 'But I'm very tired now.'

'Then run along to bed, my love,' he said, placing his hand over hers as it lay on the newel post. 'I shall remain below for a night-cap.' He nodded complacently. 'Yes, it was a most successful evening, wasn't it? And everyone came who was invited.' He nodded, obviously gratified, and repeated, 'Yes, a most successful evening.' He patted her hand and watched affectionately as she mounted the stairs. Then as he turned to go into his study he noticed that Lynwood was standing in the shadows, watching.

'Come and have a night-cap, my boy,' he said.

'Thanks all the same, Godfather, I think I've had enough for one night,' Lynwood answered uncharacteristically, moving towards the stairs.

'I said, come and have a night-cap. I wish to speak to you.' Abraham didn't raise his voice but his tone brooked no argument.

Half an hour later Lynwood flung himself out of the study and up to bed, his face like thunder, whilst Abraham remained sitting in his armchair twisting his whisky glass in his hand, deep in thought.

He'd been a fool. When he married Joanna he hadn't foreseen a problem with Lynwood. In truth he had fondly imagined that by this time she would be looking forward to the birth of a son, *his* son, so she would be totally preoccupied. Instead of which, to his eternal humiliation, he had failed to even consummate the marriage, with the result that now he was consumed with jealous envy, which he tried very hard to keep under control, every time Lynwood so much as looked at Joanna. The lustful look he was increasingly detecting in the boy's eyes was not entirely due to his own jealous imagination, of that he was quite certain. And in all truth, who could blame him, young and hot-blooded as he undoubtedly was?

He drained his glass and stared into it thoughtfully. Perhaps he should try to exercise his conjugal rights again. A child to look forward to would ... He shuddered. No, not even for peace of mind could he risk repeating that humiliating charade. He must trust that his warning to Lynwood, that if he so much as laid a finger on Joanna he would be sent to live and work with the manager at the Button Factory, would be sufficient. Seth Mortimer was a surly man with a slovenly wife and six children who lived in the dark manager's house in the yard of the Button Factory overlooking the stinking River Don. He was reasonably confident. Living in the over-crowded, squalid, industrial area of the town was not a prospect the boy would relish after the luxury of Cliffe House, leaving aside the fact that he would be forced to take more interest in buttonmaking, which he openly despised.

Abraham closed his eyes. Suddenly, he felt very old and tired. Levering himself up from his chair he left his study and made his way upstairs to his lonely bed, where he lay staring up into the darkness until dawn began to break.

As for Joanna, she fell asleep the moment her head touched the pillow and dreamed erotic dreams of Lynwood that left her consumed with guilt and made her extra attentive and loving towards her elderly husband in the days that followed.

Reassured, Abraham responded in the only way he knew. He showered her with gifts, he gave her a clothing allowance that would have bought a new outfit every week had she taken advantage of it, he took her to the theatre and the music hall, which she loved. In short, he pampered and petted her and gave her everything she could possibly want – except for one thing, and for that he felt a permanent sense of shame and failure.

In one sense, Joanna was totally happy. Her life was a round of extravagance and pleasure. She had only to breathe a desire for something and Abraham bought it for her. She loved clothes and pored over fashion magazines so that she soon became the best-dressed woman in the whole of Sheffield. Wives who had previously been 'not at home' when she left her card were now only too happy to receive her and learn from her which were the newest materials and styles.

To her credit, in her new, opulent life she didn't forget her old friend Martha. Although she never again dared to venture back to the farm she made sure that regular hampers were delivered with whatever delicacies she thought might make Martha's life more bearable: thick stockings, warm slippers, woollen shawls and petticoats, as well as parcels of food small enough to hide from Saul's suspicious eyes, but large enough to share with Tom if she felt so inclined. If indeed Tom was still at Bradshaw's Wheel. That was something Joanna had no way of knowing. Sometimes, standing at the window and looking down at the Porter Brook, with Bradshaw's Farm on one side and the Bradshaw Wheel on the other it seemed that her life there had been nothing more than a bad dream and her friendship with Tom a distant memory.

Tom had been a good friend, she thought, turning away from the window, but he had never filled her mind the way Lynwood now did.

Lynwood. He was the only cloud on her otherwise bright horizon. She couldn't understand him at all. At the party he had been so attentive she had almost had the impression that he was in love with her; even now the memory of the way he had looked at her, the way he had held her, the way he had whispered in her ear brought a warm glow to her cheeks and a stab of what she could only call excitement in her body. Yet since that night he had completely ignored her. In fact for months now he had hardly spoken to her at all. Indeed, she hardly saw him except at dinner, when he would eat his meal in virtual silence and then excuse himself. He was always out with his cronies or, when he couldn't avoid it, at the Button Factory with Abraham. She always knew when he had been there because he could be heard banging about and shouting at the servants to bring him water for his bath so that he could wash the stink of the place off and swearing at them if they took a moment longer than he expected.

Sometimes, after a day at the factory, Abraham would try to talk to him about the business over dinner, but he refused to answer other than in monosyllables, and kept his eyes on his plate.

'Are you not interested in what Abraham is saying to you, Lynwood?' Joanna asked one evening. She was tired of being ignored and desperate for a kind word or look from this young man who had previously been so charming and attentive to her and who still roused feelings in her that were all the more pleasurable because she knew they were forbidden.

He looked up at her and then away quickly to Abraham. 'I'm sorry, Uncle Abe, what were you saying?' he mumbled.

'I was saying that Mortimer is a good fellow. Keeps the workforce under control.'

'Mortimer?' Lynwood looked blank.

'The manager!' Abraham's patience was wearing thin. 'He has a firm hand. He needs it too. He's a good man, is Mortimer. Knows the trade from start to finish. He started as a lad and worked his way up so there's nowt he can't set his hand to.'

'Good for Mortimer.' Lynwood helped himself to more cheese.

'There's no need for you to behave like that, my lad. It 'ud be more to your credit if you took a bit more interest in what goes on down there.' Abraham's accent broadened with his irritation.

Lynwood shuddered. 'I'm sorry, Uncle Abe, but it's not what I'm used to. The place is dirty and smelly. And the noise! Oh, it's all right for the people that work there, I don't suppose they even notice it. But the stink when they're boiling up the bones!'

'You'll not mek bone buttons without boiling t'bones, lad. And remember, where there's muck there's brass! And those workers you're turning your nose up at are them as mek t'brass for you to spend on fine clothes and cock-fighting. And don't think for a minute I don't know about that!' Abraham drained his glass and thumped it down on the table. 'But this is not fit talk for a lady's ears.' He turned to Joanna and said more gently, 'Let me refill your glass, my love. I've heard that red wine is good for the voice, and I want you to sing for me after dinner. Your music teacher tells me he's very pleased with your progress.' He smiled at her lovingly then turned back to Lynwood. 'I shan't expect you to stay, Lynwood. I've no doubt you've got what you consider to be more important things to do.'

Lynwood leaned back in his chair, picking his teeth. 'That's where you're wrong, Uncle. I should very much like to hear the nightingale sing.' He bowed his head in Joanna's direction. 'That is, if neither you nor she has any objection.'

Joanna flushed with pleasure. 'I have no objection,' she replied.

Later, when she sat down at the piano with her music she was disconcerted to see that Lynwood had positioned himself in line with the piano so that his head was always visible over the music desk and it was impossible not to be aware that he was watching her all the time. This made her so flustered that she kept playing wrong notes and when she went to turn the page of her music she knocked it on to the floor in the middle of a song.

'Allow me.' Lynwood jumped to his feet and helped her to pick up the sheets of music.

'Thank you,' she murmured, her eyes briefly meeting his.

'I see you have the music to "Drink to me Only",' he remarked softly as he handed the music back to her. 'It is one of my favourites. Perhaps you would sing it—' he glanced over to where Abraham was gently dozing, '— especially for me.' He resumed his seat and said more loudly, 'Joanna has a very sweet voice, Uncle Abe.'

Abraham came to with a start and cleared his throat loudly. 'Indeed yes, she has. What are you going to sing for us now, my love?'

She began to sing, 'Drink to me only with thine eyes and I will pledge with mine,' carefully not taking her eyes from the music in front of her. When she had finished Lynwood clapped his hands. 'Such beautiful words and beautifully sung,' he said, smiling at her in an embarrassingly intimate manner.

Flushing to the roots of her hair and with her heart thumping painfully, she went over and sat down by her husband's side.

'I sang it specially for you, Abraham,' she lied, taking his hand in hers.

'Thank you, my love,' Abraham said, patting the hand he held with his free one. 'You have a sweet voice.'

'Indeed, yes. A sweet voice. But how could it be anything else, coming from such a sweet lady?' Lynwood agreed, still smiling at her, but now his smile was bland and courteous, with nothing in it that even Abraham could object to. He got to his feet. 'And now, if you will both excuse me I have just remembered an appointment ...' He left the room, but not without a sly wink in Joanna's direction behind Abraham's back.

And so it went on. It was disconcerting. She didn't know what to make of the man. And what made matters worse was the fact that as time went on she found herself watching for him to return home each day because he looked so handsome and dashing on a horse. And although it made her feel guilty and embarrassed and disloyal to Abraham she seized grate-fully on every tiny, seemingly innocent remark that he occasionally threw out at the dinner table, that she knew had a meaning for her alone.

She was falling in love with him. She knew it and she suspected that he did, too. But she realised that he was too much of a gentleman to take advantage of his elderly godfather so he never tried to arrange secret meetings, never again kissed her or tried to hold her hand.

Sometimes, in fact more and more often as time went on, she found herself wishing that he would.

Chapter Twelve

In spite of her secret and seemingly unrequited love for Lynwood Joanna was happy. She had a lifestyle beyond anything she could ever have dreamed and a husband who doted on her. In turn, she adored him as she might have adored an elderly, beneficent uncle, and would have died rather than cause him anger or sorrow. And when, as often happened, she was overcome with guilt over her secret thoughts and dreams of Lynwood she made up for it by being extra affectionate towards Abraham, thus salving her conscience and delighting him at the same time.

Life was both harmonious and sweet.

Lynwood was less contented. His godfather's ultimatum after the New Year party had both shocked and frightened him. The last thing he wanted was to be incarcerated in that hell-hole of a button factory and the thought of it was quite enough to cool his ardour for Joanna. Or so he believed. But he couldn't resist the odd innuendo, the sly wink that he knew would bring that attractive blush to her cheek. Neither could he stop dreaming about ways of getting her into his bed even though his sexual appetites were well taken care of at the highly select – and expensive – house of Madame Dupont, situated discreetly on the outskirts of Chesterfield. The situation was both infuriating and frustrating and at times he contemplated going right away – joining the army, even. But he enjoyed his present lifestyle too much to give that thought more than passing consideration. He knew when he was well off. He had plenty of money, congenial drinking and gambling cronies and a comfortable home, so he obeyed his godfather's commands and endured his frustrations with as good a grace as he could muster.

In the summer of her nineteenth birthday, when they had been married for three years, Abraham took Joanna to the south coast for a holiday, intending to stay three weeks but staying six because Joanna was so delighted with life in Brighton. He even allowed her to go bathing, hiring the bathing machine with the most buxom woman attendant he could find so that there was no possible risk of harm coming to his precious wife. Joanna so enjoyed the experience that she wanted to go every day and tried to persuade Abraham to do the same.

'Bathing in the sea is very good for your health, Abie,' she pleaded, using her pet name for him. 'Even the dear Queen does it.'

'I'm glad you enjoy it, my little love,' he said with a smile, but refused to dip even a toe into the waves.

In the afternoons they visited the Pavilion and explored the tiny alleys where he bought her necklaces and brooches; they walked on the seashore and in the evenings they attended plays and concerts.

'You spoil me, Abie,' she laughed, draping the pretty scarf he had just purchased for her round her shoulders.

'Nonsense. You have brought great happiness into my life, my little love,' he answered truthfully. But he seemed preoccupied and when she questioned him he admitted that he felt unwell. 'I'm concerned at leaving the business for so long, too. I left Lynwood in charge, but—' he sighed, 'I fear Lynwood and Mortimer don't see eye to eye in a great number of things ...' He shook his head sadly.

'If you are making yourself ill by worrying about the Button Factory we must go home immediately,' Joanna said at once. 'I shall arrange for our bags to be packed and we'll leave in the morning.' She put her head on one side and studied him. 'No, you don't look at all well, Abie. Perhaps the bracing sea air doesn't agree with you.'

He sighed. 'No, I don't think it's that. I rather think it's all the rich food we've been having. It's given me a touch of indigestion, although I hate to admit it.' He rubbed his chest.

110

'I shall call Dr Marfleet the minute we get back,' she said decisively.

Dr Marfleet prescribed complete rest for a month, confining Abraham to his room. Joanna sat with him endlessly, reading to him or sitting by the window where he could see her, quietly sewing, always ready to jump up and attend to his needs.

Lynwood paid his godfather fleeting visits, ostensibly to report on progress at the Button Factory, but in reality to feast his eyes, however briefly, on the lovely Joanna. He said he couldn't bear the atmosphere of the sick-room, but actually he was afraid that if he stayed long Abraham would ask him questions about the business he couldn't answer.

One afternoon Gertrude arrived to visit her sick brother. She came to Cliffe House less often now that Joanna was used to running the household, even to the extent of becoming proficient in keeping the household accounts, something Gertrude herself had never wholly mastered.

'Oh, you're not looking too bad, Abe,' she said, giving him a perfunctory peck on the cheek. 'You've been indulging in too much of a good thing, I'll wager, that's what's wrong with you.' She winked at Joanna over her shoulder.

'Yes, you're quite right. Too much rich food when we were in Brighton,' Abraham answered seriously. '"Dyspepsia", the doctor called it.'

Gertrude snorted. 'Ha! Well, if that's what he says—' she looked over at Joanna, sitting by the window. 'You're looking a bit peaky too, love. Are you under the weather, as well?'

'Me? Oh, no. I'm perfectly all right, thank you, Gertrude.' Joanna said in surprise.

'I daresay you could do with a bit of fresh air, any road. Cooped up here in the sick-room all day.'

'Aye, that's what I keep telling her, Gertie, but she'll never leave me on my own,' Abraham said, gazing fondly at his wife.

'Well, you're not on your own now. I'm here.' She turned to Joanna. 'So why don't you go and tek a turn round the garden, love? It'll do you good. I'll keep an eye on his nibs, here.'

'Yes, you do that, my love,' Abraham said, smiling at his

wife. 'You spend far too long sitting here with me.'

'But I never mind sitting with you, Abraham,' she said, not quite truthfully, because it had to be admitted that at times she felt trapped and stifled by the sick-room atmosphere and longed to be out in the fresh air.

'And I'm always glad of your company, my love. But do as Gertie says and go for a walk in the garden. It's a lovely day and I want to know if the Michaelmas daisies are out.'

'Very well, Abraham. I'll pick a bunch for you if they are. If Bragg doesn't mind, that is,' she added laughingly.

'I must say this marriage of yours has worked far better than I ever imagined it would, Abe,' Gertrude said after she had gone.

'Yes, Joanna's a delightful lass,' Abraham said, his eyes half closed. 'She's brought me great happiness.'

Joanna fetched a shawl and went out into the garden. It was one of those beautiful days in mid October, often known as St Luke's little summer, when the weather was as sunny and warm as a summer's day. She strolled along the terrace where the geraniums cascaded in their urns and across the lawns where the Michaelmas daisies were indeed flowering amongst the dahlias in the herbaceous border. As she walked she held her face up to the sun and took deep breaths of the clear fresh air. Oh, it was good to be free.

She lifted her skirts and ran through the gap in the hedge to the little arbour in the far corner of the garden, almost hidden in the last of the rambler roses. This was one of her favourite places, it was here she used to come to practise her arithmetic when Abraham was teaching her to manage the household accounts and here she would come with a book, ever grateful at the horizons he had opened up for her in teaching her to read. She felt a sudden stab of guilt. It was wrong of her to resent being trapped in the sick-room with Abraham. She had so much to be grateful to him for that it was a small price to pay. The drudgery from which he had rescued her now seemed like a distant life. Indeed, in her contentment she had almost forgotten the quest for her mother, the poor drowned girl in the Porter Brook that had once been her desperate and only hope of salvation. Now it no longer seemed important.

She sat down on the stone seat in the arbour and closed her eyes, the perfume of the roses all around her.

'Oh, what a charming picture.'

She started and opened her eyes to find Lynwood smiling down at her. She hadn't heard him approach across the springy turf. Immediately, she began to get to her feet.

'No, don't get up,' he said, sitting himself down beside her. 'You're enjoying the sunshine. I'm sure you won't mind if I enjoy it with you for a few moments.'

'No. No, of course not.' For some reason she felt a little flustered, as if she had been caught out in some misdemeanour, and her heart seemed to be fluttering in a most disconcerting manner.

Fortunately, he didn't appear to notice. 'Uncle Abe seems to be improving,' he said heartily.

'Yes. He seems much better,' she answered, looking down at her hands.

'Soon be up and about again.'

'I hope so.'

'Do you? Do you really?'

She looked up at him, surprised at his question. 'Of course. I don't like to see my husband indisposed.'

He held her gaze. 'At least when he's in bed he can't watch your every move, can he?'

'Don't be silly, Lynwood. Of course, he doesn't watch my every move.' Her hand moved nervously to her throat.

'Yes, he does. He watches you like a hawk. I never get the chance to speak to you.'

'Don't be silly. You speak to me most nights at dinner,' she said with a little laugh that sounded silly even to her own ears.

He ignored her words. 'You have the most beautiful blue eyes, Jo,' he said softly.

She looked away quickly. 'You mustn't say things like that, Lynwood.'

'Why not? It's true.'

'All the same—' her voice trailed off. She gathered her shawl round her. 'I must go back to Abraham. I've been away quite long enough.'

He put his hand on her arm. 'My God, Jo, don't you get tired of being stuck in that sick-room with that old man day after day?' he said violently.

'Of course not. He's my husband. Any road, it's my duty to be there if he needs me.' She tried to get up but he held her arm.

'Duty. Is that all it is, Jo?'

She tried to shake herself free. 'I don't know what you mean. Please let me go, Lynwood.'

'What about love? Do you love him, Jo?' he persisted.

'Of course I do. He's a wonderful man. He's so good to me that I'll never be able to repay him.' Once again she tried to get up but now he put his arm round her, preventing her.

'That's gratitude, Jo. And it does you credit. But it's not love,' he said softly. He put up his free hand and plucked a rosebud and tucked it in her hair. Then he began playing with a tendril of hair at her neck. 'I don't think you really know what love is,' he said thoughtfully. Then he smiled. 'But I'd be happy to teach you.'

His face was near and he was looking at her in a way that made her insides do funny things. 'I ... you mustn't say things like that,' her words came breathlessly.

'Why not?' He bent his head to kiss the curve of her neck and went on, his voice muffled, 'God, you're such a desirable woman, Jo.' He was kissing her throat, her ear, her chin. 'And totally wasted on an old man like Uncle Abe. You need a young—' There was no further need for words as his mouth reached hers, gently teasing at first then more demanding as her lips opened willingly under his.

'You see, you want me just as much as I want you,' he whispered, his mouth against hers.

'No, it's not true,' she moaned, knowing she should push him away, yet unable to resist him as his mouth found hers again.

After a long time he lifted his head. 'I've wanted to do that for so long, Jo. And so have you,' he put his finger on her lips, then took it away and brushed them with his own. 'No, don't bother to deny it, because I know it's true. I know everything about you, Jo. I know you want me just as I want you. I've only managed to keep my hands off you because of Uncle Abe's beady eye. You see, he blackmailed me. He said if I laid a finger on you he would send me to live at the Button Factory. I couldn't bear that. I couldn't bear the thought of not seeing you, Jo. But he's safely out of the way now. He's confined to his room so he can't see us. Come to me tonight, Jo. Come to my room. Let me love you as you should be loved.' His voice was urgent as he began to kiss her again. 'Let me show you what love really is.'

'No. No, Lynwood. I can't. What if—?'

'What if you should have a child?' He was covering her face and throat with kisses as he spoke. 'What matter? It would only mean that I had succeeded where he has failed and he would never know the child wasn't his. Just think how pleased he would be. And after all this time, too!' As he spoke his hands were busy at her breasts.

Suddenly, she froze. She had been going to say what if the servants found out and told Abraham. The thought of a child being conceived hadn't entered her head. Of course, Lynwood had no idea that there had never been any possibility of this happening with Abraham and it was something she could never, ever tell him.

He lifted his head. 'What is it? What's wrong, Jo?' he asked, frowning.

She pushed his hands away. 'I must go back,' she said stiffly. 'This is all wrong, Lynwood. I should never have allowed it to happen.'

He tried to take her in his arms again. 'You couldn't have stopped it. You want me just as much as I want you. Why deny it? Come to me tonight, Jo.'

She struggled free. 'No. I can't do this to Abraham.'

He took her face in both his hands, forcing her to look at him. 'Just tell me one thing, Jo. Am I wrong? Do you feel nothing for me?'

She closed her eyes. 'No,' she whispered unwillingly. 'You're not wrong, Lynwood.'

He released her and helped her to her feet, smiling down into her eyes. 'Then sooner or later I shall find a way, Jo. Make no mistake about that.'

She went back to the house with her emotions in a turmoil. Lynwood loved and wanted her, the words sang in her ears, words she had longed to hear. Then the picture of Abraham, old and sick, rose to her mind. How could she do anything that might hurt him? She recalled the visit to Brighton, the delight he had taken in her pleasure with everything she saw. She realised that in spite of everything she really did love him dearly.

But she loved Lynwood, too. And deep inside she knew that her love for Abraham was not the real reason she had refused him. It was because she was terrified of the possible consequences. If she were to become pregnant Abraham would know it was not his child and heaven knew what he might do. That he would send Lynwood away was a foregone conclusion, but what if he threw her out, too? She could end up in the Porter Brook like her own poor mother. No, she could never allow that to happen.

All these thoughts were whirling through her mind as she crossed the lawn and hurried into the house. As she passed the long mirror in the hall she caught sight of herself: she looked flushed and dishevelled and the tell-tale rosebud was still in her hair. She snatched it out and stood looking at it for a minute, then tucked it in her bodice because she couldn't bear to throw it away. Then she took several deep breaths to compose herself, patted her hair into place and carried on up the stairs.

Abraham was asleep when she went into the sick-room and Gertrude was nodding in the chair beside him. She lifted her head as Joanna entered.

'You look as if you've been out in the sun too long, my lass,' she said, pursing her lips. 'Your face is quite pink.'

Joanna flushed even more red. 'I've been sitting in the arbour,' she said. 'Look, there are still a few roses out. I picked this bud for Abie.' She took the rosebud out of her bodice and laid it on the counterpane by Abraham's hand. It was a symbol of sacrifice, although he would never know it.

Gertrude watched but said nothing.

'Dr Marfleet came while you were outside,' she said after a bit. 'He's pleased with Abe's progress. Says he can go downstairs tomorrow for an hour.' She glanced at the sleeping man and dropped her voice. 'You know it's not dyspepsia he's suffering from, don't you? It's his heart.'

'His heart?' Joanna clapped her hands over her mouth, afraid she had spoken too loudly. 'No, I didn't know that.'

Gertrude nodded. 'I went outside and had a word with old Marfleet. He says it's just a warning. As long as he takes life gently there's no reason why he shouldn't live for years.'

'Oh, thank God for that,' Joanna breathed and was surprised to realise that she meant it. She couldn't imagine life without him.

116

Chapter Thirteen

Abraham made a good recovery, but Dr Marfleet insisted that he shouldn't resume work until after Christmas, saying that he was sure Lynwood was quite capable of keeping an eye on the Button Factory in his absence. Joanna agreed with this but Abraham was a bad patient, fretting and fuming and declaring that he was perfectly fit and what a fuss to make over a bout of indigestion.

On Dr Marfleet's advice Joanna said nothing about the real cause of his illness. The doctor had told her that knowing he had a heart condition would only worry Abraham and could delay his recovery. Indeed, this proved to be true because at the beginning of December, Abraham seemed so much better that Joanna didn't disagree when he declared that he had had enough of being treated like an invalid and was going back to his office. In truth, he had become so restless and argumentative that she thought work might be the best thing for him – and her, too. So although it was a bitterly cold morning, with frost riming the trees and making patterns on the windows, she made no objection when he called the carriage and took himself off to the Button Factory.

She watched him go with a sigh and a shake of her head. He was a headstrong man. But she had to admit that after his enforced rest he looked younger and fitter than he had done for a long time and privately she wondered if Dr Marfleet had been over-cautious in his diagnosis and the trouble was only indigestion after all. Abraham had certainly found such a long convalescence irksome. He had always been an active, energetic man and she knew how much he had hated being

117

restricted to the house. It would probably do him good to get back to work.

She watched until the carriage had disappeared round the bend of the drive and then rang the bell for Mrs Osborne, the cook, and settled down to work out with her the menus for the week. This was something she enjoyed doing. And to use her new mathematical skills she had also begun to keep a tight rein on the household accounts. This was something Abraham had never worried himself over, he had simply paid the bills Mrs Osborne presented without question. But Mrs Osborne's arithmetic was admittedly sketchy and although she could not be faulted on choosing the best cuts of meat and the freshest vegetables, she had no idea that some of the tradesmen were overcharging her shamelessly. Careful checking of the order books had soon shown this up, although it had taken quite a lot of tact and diplomacy on Joanna's part to put the matter right without upsetting Mrs Osborne or antagonising the tradesmen. But she had managed this and it pleased her that she was now able to save Abraham several pounds each month on the housekeeping bill.

It was nearly six o'clock before Abraham returned from his office.

Joanna hurried to greet him, admonishing him for being away so long, but without even his usual kiss he shrugged her off and went straight to his study, his face like thunder.

This was so unusual that Joanna was at a loss to know what to do. After several minutes of indecision, pacing up and down the hall she plucked up the courage to knock at the door. 'What's wrong, Abie?' she called. There was no reply.

She knocked again. Still no reply. By this time really worried she opened the door and went in.

He was sitting and staring into the fire, a whisky glass, already empty, in his hand. She took it from him. 'Oh, Abie, you know what Dr Marfleet says—' she began.

'Yes, I do know what old Marfleet says, but if he'd been where I've been today he'd need a glass or two of whisky to calm his nerves,' he said testily. He waved his hand towards the tantalus. 'Be a good lass and pour me another.' He looked up and gave her a ghost of a smile.

She knew better than to disobey him so she poured him

another whisky and then sat down opposite to him. 'Are you going to tell me about it, Abie?' she asked gently.

He shook his head. 'I don't know where to start.' He sighed and passed his hand across his eyes. 'Oh, Joanna, lass, I've had a dreadful day.' He took a gulp of whisky. Then another. 'I don't know why I'd convinced myself I could trust that lad. God knows he'd never given me any reason to, when I come to think of it.'

'Lynwood?'

'Aye. Lynwood. Young bugger's hardly been near the factory while I've been laid up.' He twisted the whisky glass in his hand, staring at it without seeing it. 'There's bills not paid, stuff that was ordered not delivered because of money owing, rents from Bradshaw's Wheel, the flour mill and the other one further up the Porter – not collected. If I'd been away another week I'd likely have had the bank manager up here to see me, wondering what the hell's going on.' He suddenly remembered her presence. 'Oh, I'm sorry my love. My language—'

She waved her hand. 'Don't be silly, Abie. I've heard a good deal worse than that in my time.'

'God knows how I'm going to sort out the mess he's let things get into.' He stared into the fire, shaking his head.

She went and sat at his feet, her head on his knee. 'Why don't you let me help, Abie,' she said. 'I'm sure it'd not take long for you to teach me,' she smiled up at him. 'You've often said what an apt pupil I am and how quickly I learn.'

He looked down at her affectionately. 'The Button Factory is not the place for you, my love. It's dirty and smelly and the language—'

'Oh, Abie, have you forgotten the life I was born into? It'd take more than a few curses to shock me.' She was silent for a minute, then she added, 'I should like to help you, Abie, really I would.'

It was his turn to be silent. At last he gave a sigh. 'Very well, my love, I'll take you with me tomorrow. God knows I shall be glad of a bit of help.' He got to his feet and helped her to hers, planting a kiss on her forehead as he did so. 'Have I ever told you what a great comfort you are to me, Joanna?' he said.

119

She hugged him. 'Yes, you have, dear Abie,' she replied with a little laugh. 'Many times. Now, go and get yourself ready for dinner. You know how cross Mrs Osborne gets if it's left to spoil.'

Lynwood didn't put in an appearance at dinner. This was nothing unusual but for once Abraham was annoyed.

'I wish to speak to Master Lynwood,' he said to Parker as he left the table at the end of the meal. 'No matter what time he comes in send him to my study.'

'But Abie,' Joanna protested, hurrying after him, 'surely it can wait till the morning. You've already had a long day. Shouldn't you go straight to bed?'

Abraham's mouth was a thin, hard line. 'No. I must have this out with Lynwood tonight. I've turned a blind eye to his short-comings for too long. Oh, I knew when he came here that he didn't really care about my business interests, but I persevered and tried to teach him, for his dead father's sake as much as anything. But this is the last straw, finding out that he didn't even bother to keep an eye on things when I was ill.' He reached his study door and turned to look at her. 'I'm going to tell Lynwood he must mend his ways or leave my house, Joanna. I've made up my mind and I shan't sleep until I've told him. I've had more than enough of his self-indulgence, his gambling and his—' He was going to say 'womanising' but stopped himself just in time. He patted her hand. 'You run along, dearest. Believe me, I know what I'm doing.'

Joanna was shocked. She had never heard Abraham so vindictive. And towards Lynwood, too. She could only think his day at the office had been too much for him and he was overwrought.

'Well, at least come into the drawing room for half an hour,' she pleaded. 'Knowing Lynwood he'll not be home yet.' She caught his hand. 'Come along, dear, I'll play the piano and sing to you. You like that, don't you. You always say it relaxes you.'

He snatched his hand away. 'Don't fuss, woman!' Immediately the words were out he regretted them and he kissed her. 'Oh, don't mind me. I'm a grouchy old stick tonight. Go and play the piano and sing, my love. I shall be able to hear you from my study.'

'Very well, Abie.' Knowing there was no point in arguing further, she went into the drawing room and for an hour she played and sang all his favourite pieces. Then, at eleven o'clock, she went to bed.

Lynwood still hadn't returned home.

He still hadn't returned at midnight. Joanna hadn't closed her eyes, her thoughts were in too much of a turmoil. She was certain there must be some mistake. Lynwood couldn't be as irresponsible as Abraham was making him out to be. He was not properly recovered from his illness so it was more than likely he had overlooked something. Or miscalculated. Given the chance she was in no doubt she would be able to help him smooth things over and put everything right. Unless – suddenly another thought struck her. Had Abraham somehow heard of what happened between her and Lynwood in the arbour that day? Did he think it had gone further? Was this a trumped-up excuse to rid himself of Lynwood because of it? She tossed and turned on her pillow. She couldn't believe that Abraham would be capable of such a devious scheme. He must know he could trust her.

She must have drifted off into an uneasy sleep because it was after one o'clock when she heard the sound of voices and a door slammed. She waited a few moments, then put on her robe and opened her bedroom door and peered out. Lights were blazing everywhere and the study door was wide open. On a chair in the hall Lynwood was slumped, grey-faced, a glass of whisky in his hand.

So Abraham had issued his ultimatum. Poor Lynwood. She felt a rush of annoyance. If only Abraham had waited a few days until he was quite certain ...

She went slowly down the stairs. As she reached the bottom Lynwood looked up, his faced ravaged.

'He's dead,' he announced flatly.

She stared at him in disbelief, then her legs gave way and she sank down on the bottom step, clutching the newel post, her mind racing. It was not a door slamming she had heard, it was a shot.

'Oh, God,' she moaned. 'You've shot him.'

Lynwood stared at her uncomprehendingly. 'What do you mean?'

At that moment Norbert came out of the study. He was in his dressing gown and his face was ashen but impassive. He glanced at Lynwood, then saw Joanna, still crouched at the foot of the stairs.

'Oh, Madam,' he said and for once in his life he was flustered. 'You shouldn't be here. I sent for Lily to look after you.' He looked round anxiously. 'Where is she?'

'It doesn't matter,' Joanna said dully. She looked up, her face screwed in perplexity. 'It is true? Abraham's dead?'

Norbert bowed his head respectfully and spoke in a hushed voice. 'I fear so, Madam. Osborne's gone for Dr Marfleet.'

'And the police?'

'Oh, that won't be necessary, Madam.'

She couldn't take it in. 'But he was shot—' She looked up, frowning. 'Wasn't he?'

It was Norbert's turn to look perplexed. 'Indeed, no, Madam. Whatever gave you that idea? We think his heart gave out. That's what we think. We shan't know for certain until Dr Marfleet arrives, of course.'

She leaned her head against the newel post to cool it, to make her brain work, to understand. Tears seeped out of her eyes but she wasn't crying. She was too confused to weep. She hardly noticed that Lily had come down the stairs and was sitting beside her, her arm round her, supporting her. 'Where is he?' she asked Norbert.

'In the study, Madam.'

She struggled to her feet. 'I must—'

Anticipating her action Norbert stood in her path. 'Do you think it's wise, Madam?'

'Wise? Of course it's wise. He's my husband. I need to see him.' Pushing him aside she walked across the hall like a sleepwalker and into the study, with Lily and Norbert following anxiously behind her.

She stopped when she reached the door. Just as she had left him, Abraham was sitting in his armchair by the fire. His glasses were perched on the end of his nose where they always slid down to when he was reading and his book was still on his lap. A tumbler lay on its side on the carpet in a pool of whisky where it had fallen out of his hand.

'Don't be ridiculous. He's not dead. He's fallen asleep,'

she snapped, her voice rising hysterically.

'No, Madam, I'm afraid not.' Norbert's voice was firm but gentle. 'I believe he's been dead an hour or more. You see, he left orders with Parker to ask Mr Lynwood to go to his study when he arrived home. I looked in on him before I went to bed about half an hour ago to see if he wanted anything and I thought – as you did, Madam – that he was asleep. Parker waited up for Mr Lynwood and gave him the message when he came in and Mr Lynwood went straight to the study. When he got no reply from his greeting he looked closer and realised the Master was not asleep at all, but—' he bowed his head, 'no longer in this world. Naturally, Parker immediately called me. It's been a terrible shock to us all.' He looked up. 'I'm sorry, Madam, I should have prepared you ... But it's all been so sudden.'

Joanna stood for several minutes, looking at Abraham, then leaned over and kissed his cheek. It felt cold and papery. She slid down until she was sitting at his feet, her head resting on his knee, just as she had sat only a few hours ago. 'Oh, Abie, what am I going to do without you?' she whispered. Then she began to cry.

Dr Marfleet arrived. He was not pleased at being hauled out of bed in the middle of the night, especially to a man who had disobeyed his orders, and he'd seen death too many times to be overly affected by it.

He took one look at Joanna, still sobbing at her dead husband's knee, and at Lynwood, shocked and ravaged, and sent them to their respective beds with a stiff dose of laudanum. Then he turned his attention to Abraham, pronouncing that death was due to heart failure and adding quietly to Norbert that if the stubborn old fool had done as he'd been told he would have been good for another ten years. Then he signed the death certificate and left.

Joanna slept the clock round. When she woke she felt completely drained and was glad that Gertrude had arrived and was quietly taking charge.

The next days passed in a daze for Joanna. There were black-edged letters and flowers tied with black ribbon arriving daily. Estelle came and fitted her for the black dress Gertrude had thoughtfully ordered and all the time Abraham lay in his coffin in the morning room waiting for his last journey in the purple-draped hearse pulled by plumed jet-black horses.

After the funeral there was the further ordeal of the will. Mr Garthwaite, Abraham's solicitor, came to the house and was shown into the study as the most appropriate room for such a solemn occasion. He sat behind Abraham's desk and after much throat clearing began the reading with bequests to the servants, the amount carefully commensurate with their length of service. Norbert was to receive two hundred pounds.

Mr Garthwaite waited a few moments for this to sink in, then continued, 'And to my sister, Mrs Gertrude Theakston, I leave my gold hunter watch. It will have a sentimental attachment for her as it belonged to our father.' Mr Garthwaite cleared his throat again and took off his spectacles to look across at Gertrude.

She nodded in approval. 'Thank God he didn't leave me money. I've more than I know what to do with already,' she murmured.

Relieved, he replaced his spectacles and went on, 'To Lynwood Silkin, my godson, I leave an annuity of five hundred pounds plus five per cent of my business profits from the Button Factory and rents from my properties—' He looked up as Lynwood drew in a swift breath, then went on '—provided he takes over the running of said business and maintenance of said properties in a responsible manner.' He was again silent for several minutes, then began again, 'To my dear wife, Joanna, who has brought me so much joy and happiness, I leave the remaining ninety-five per cent of my business profits and rents, together with all the property I own, including Cliffe House and its entire contents, provided she remains a widow and does not remarry. In the event of her remarriage my entire estate shall revert to my godson, Lynwood Silkin.'

Nobody spoke. Then Lynwood got up and took himself off to lick his wounds. He had hoped for better than that from the old man. When he had gone and only Joanna and Gertrude were left Mr Garthwaite cleared his throat again and said, 'I'm not sure whether I should tell you this, but Mr Silkin had recently decided to change his will. In fact it was in the after-

124

noon of the day that he died that he made the appointment to see me. His unfortunate demise precluded this, so of course the will stands as it is.' His mouth twisted 'Ironically, the appointment was for today.'

'What changes did he want to make?' Gertrude asked bluntly.

'That, Madam, I can't say.' Mr Garthwaite's tone indicated that he wouldn't tell her if he could. 'As I said, Mr Silkin wished to discuss some matter with me concerning his will. I believe it may have had something to do with Mr Lynwood Silkin, but what it was I have no idea.' He tapped the document in his hand. 'In the event, whatever his subsequent wishes might have been this is Mr Abraham Silkin's last will and testament, the terms of which I am legally bound to carry out.'

Mr Garthwaite left.

Gertrude turned to Joanna. She was sitting by the fire in Abraham's chair, pale and dignified in her widow's weeds, all her tears spent. 'Well, lass, you're a rich woman now,' she said.

Joanna nodded. 'Yes, I suppose I am.'

She had come a long way since her days of slavery on Bradshaw's Farm.

Chapter Fourteen

For nearly three months Joanna didn't leave the house. At first Gertrude, who had remained with her 'to help you over the first shock, lass,' was sympathetic and patient, but eventually her patience wore thin and one morning near the end of February she swept into the morning room, where Joanna was gazing listlessly out of the window, and announced that she was going home.

Joanna stared at her in alarm. 'Going home! But you can't, Gertrude! What shall I do without you?'

'You'll get up off your backside and get on with life, my lass, that's what you'll do,' Gertrude said bluntly.

'But I'm in mourning,' Joanna protested wildly, shaking her head. 'Abie's dead and I don't know what to do.'

Gertrude sat down on the window seat beside her and took her hand. 'I know how you feel, love,' she said more gently. 'I felt much the same when my Sam died. But you're a young woman, much younger than I was when I was left. It's not right that you should mope your life away just because Abe's gone. He'd not want that, now, would he?'

Joanna's eyes filled with tears. 'He was so good to me, Gertrude. I keep thinking I should have tried harder ... I could have made him happier if I'd tried. I know I could.' She laid her head on Gertrude's shoulder.

'Now, that's quite enough of that,' Gertrude said firmly, patting her arm. 'I know it's only natural to feel like that when someone we love dies, we all feel we could have done more for them, that we should have said this, or shouldn't have said that. I know I did when Sam died. Remorse is a natural part of grieving. But just remember, none of us is perfect, we all have our faults. You have to allow for yourself to be human, love. And if you think you fell short of what Abe expected of you – not that I ever heard him complain, mind – well, just remember he wasn't perfect, either.' She pushed Joanna away gently and took her hand in both of her own. 'Now, come on, love, shape yourself, you're a woman of property now. Don't you think it's time you took an interest in your inheritance?'

Joanna gave her a watery smile. 'You're good for me, Gertrude. And you're right, I suppose I really should go and see what's going on at the Button Factory. Abie wasn't very happy at what he found when he went there—' she swallowed '—the day he died. Lynwood was supposed to have—'

'Don't talk to me about Lynwood,' Gertrude waved her hand impatiently. 'He takes himself off in the morning before I'm up and heaven knows what time he gets back at night. I'd just like to know what he gets up to with those cronies of his.' She gave a chuckle. 'I guess he's still furious that Abe didn't leave him a bigger share in his fortune. But he never did anything to earn it so it serves him right, the lazy young tyke.'

Joanna shook her head and sighed. 'I don't know what Lynwood thinks, Gertie. I've hardly seen him since the funeral.'

The next morning, a tearful Joanna waved Gertrude off in her carriage, begging her to come and stay whenever she felt like it.

'I don't know how I'm going to manage without you, so please come back soon,' she pleaded. 'You know your room will always be waiting for you, Gertie dear.'

'We'll see, lass, we'll see.' Gertrude leaned back in her carriage with a sigh of relief. Much though she loved Joanna she was glad to be going back to her own home, where she could leave her stays off if she felt like it and belch to her heart's content.

After Gertrude had gone the house seemed empty. Joanna wandered from room to room, picking things up and putting them down again, unable to settle to anything. Finally, she did what she knew she must, she called for the carriage and instructed Osborne to drive her to the Button Factory.

Osborne helped the black-clad, heavily veiled figure into the carriage, unable to conceal his disapproval. 'Do you really

127

think you should, Ma'am? T'Button Factory's hardly the place—' He coughed. 'Surely Mr Lynwood—'

She cut him short. 'Thank you, Osborne. I know what I'm doing and it's no concern of Mr Lynwood's.'

'Very well, Ma'am. Just as you say.' He said no more.

Joanna stared out of the window of the carriage as it wound its way down into Sheffield. She had to admit that it was good to be outside the confines of Cliffe House again and as they passed the track into Whitely Woods she recalled the happy hours she had spent there with Tom, filling their always hungry stomachs with berries. She couldn't even remember what it was like to be hungry now. What had become of Tom, she wondered? Was he still tied to his miserly master, Zack Wenlock, or had he escaped down into the town to make his own way? There was no way of knowing.

The woods ended, to be replaced by hedgerows interspersed with houses that gradually became more and more densely packed as they spilled down into the town. It was almost as if the houses were sliding down the hillside to huddle together in the valley, where they were enveloped in an eiderdown of smoky fog from the factories and steel works.

Joanna almost forgot that she was in mourning and peered eagerly out of the carriage window, looking for familiar land-marks that she could remember from her market days. She could see herself now, a skinny little figure in clogs two sizes too big, hurrying along the streets, trying to protect the basket of eggs she was taking to market from the jostling, bustling crowds, and she smiled. Never in her wildest dreams had she ever imagined that she would one day ride along those same streets dressed as a lady and in her own carriage. Oh, she had so much to thank Abraham for. She lifted her head proudly. She mustn't let him down now.

The carriage wound its way through streets she had never seen before, then turned into a narrow sunless road flanked on one side by a blank brick wall and on the other by a square, blackened building with rows of identical windows on three floors.

Here Osborne stopped the carriage and got down and opened the door for her.

'This is the factory, Ma'am.'

'Oh!' She looked up at the unprepossessing building with its peeling paint and barred windows with a hint of alarm.

'Would you like me to come in with you, Ma'am?'

Hurriedly, she pulled herself together. 'No, thank you, Osborne. That will not be necessary.

'Then shall I wait here, Ma'am?'

'No. Come back for me at one o'clock.'

'But that's three hours away, Ma'am.' He was horrified.

'Well, I expect you can find something to occupy your time till then,' she said absently, her eyes still on the building in front of her.

She pushed open the door to Silkin's Button Factory, her heart thumping with a mixture of excitement and apprehension. So this was where Abraham spent his working life. Stepping inside she found herself in a stone corridor with doors on either side and a flight of stone steps at the end. An appalling smell hung everywhere and from the floor above she could hear the clatter of some kind of machinery. She waited a moment, undecided what to do, then pushed open the first door she came to. The stench was stronger here and seemed to come from two great vats that were bubbling on the stove that ran along one wall.

A man's figure emerged from the steam, snatching off a battered stove-pipe hat as he came.

'Oh, my word! Mrs Silkin, Ma'am. Us weren't expecting– Mr Silkin never said—' He ushered her out quickly and closed the door behind him. 'It's t'bones. We're boiling up t'bones for t'buttons,' he said, jerking his head back. 'Smells a bit.' He stood, embarrassed, not quite knowing what to do next.

'It's all right, Mortimer. It is Mortimer? My late husband's manager?' She had to look up at the man, he was big and burly, with hands like great hams, yet he was twisting his hat round and round in them for all the world like a schoolboy caught misbehaving.

'Ay, that's reet, Ma'am. I'm afraid us didn't know tha was intending to pay us a visit or us needn't have boiled today. Mr Silkin never said– '

'Mr Silkin?' For a moment she felt quite faint. Had the last months been nothing more than a horrible dream? Was Abraham even now sitting in his office? She put her hand to her throat. 'He's in his office?' she asked uncertainly.

'Aye, Ma'am. Hardly leaves it, he does. Please to come this way, Ma'am, I'll tek tha to him.' Flustered, the man led her further along the passage to a door near the stairs.

'Mr Silkin, Sir. Mrs Silkin is here. You'd not said she'd be coming, Sir. We've nowt ready for—' he scratched his head, totally at a loss. 'We've nowt ready, Sir,' he repeated.

'It's all right, Mortimer, you can go. I'll look after Mrs Silkin.' As he spoke Lynwood got up from Abraham's desk and began to put on his jacket which was hanging over the back of his chair.

'Lynwood! It's you!' Joanna stared at him, open-mouthed. Suddenly, she felt weak at the knees and she clutched at the door jamb for support. 'I thought, when he said Mr Silkin ... What are you doing here?'

'I might say the same thing to you, Joanna, dear,' he answered with a smile 'And with slightly more justification. Hey, what's wrong? You look as if you've seen a ghost.' Hurriedly he swept a heap of papers from a chair and pulled it forward for her. 'Sit down here.' He helped her to the chair. 'That's better. Now, tell me, what brings you here?

'I – Abraham was worried about things. He told me he was worried the night he died. I thought it was time I came to see if I could—' She licked her lips. How in the world could she sort out the mess Lynwood had made while he sat in Abraham's chair for all the world as if he owned it? Worse, how could she tell him that was what she had come for?

'Sort out the mess?' Lynwood read her thoughts. 'What mess?' He grinned at her, clearly enjoying himself.

She pulled herself together with some difficulty. 'Yes, I did come to look at the books, if you must know,' she said, sitting up straight in her chair. 'Since Abraham is no longer here somebody needs to keep an eye on things. He had already agreed that I should help him,' she added, unable to keep a note of pride out of her voice.

He sat down at the desk and leaned towards her on his elbows. 'You're very welcome to look at the books, Jo, dear,' he said. 'I think you'll find them in apple-pie order.' He tipped his chair back and ran his fingers through his hair. 'My God, they jolly well ought to be! I've worked day and night since the funeral to get everything straight.'

Her jaw dropped. 'But Abie said—'

'Oh, Jo, don't call the old man Abie.' He got up and began to prowl round the room. 'But yes, I can imagine exactly what he said. He said the business was in a mess, bills not paid, goods not ordered, etc., etc.' He swung round. 'And he was right. To my eternal shame I admit I didn't lift a finger and hardly came near the place while he was ill. I've always hated the whole business of button manufacture although God knows he tried hard enough over the years to get me interested. But it's different now, isn't it?'

She frowned. 'What do you mean?'

His mouth stretched into a wide grin. 'Well, it's ours now, Jo, isn't it? Yours and mine?'

'I don't know about *ours*, Lynwood. Not much of it belongs to you, as I recall,' she said in a small voice. 'Five per cent?'

He came over and drew her to her feet. Then he carefully lifted back the black veil that still covered her face and kissed her full on the lips.

'Then let's say I'm doing it for you, my love,' he whispered, his face only inches from hers. 'And when we're married—'

She tried to push him away, confused by his nearness. 'But I can never marry, Lynwood, you know that,' she murmured. 'The terms of Abie – Abraham's will – don't you remember?'

'Ah, yes. The terms of the will.' He surveyed her thoughtfully, his head on one side. 'Are you feeling better now?' he asked, changing the subject. 'You looked as if you'd seen a ghost when you came in.'

'Yes, thank you. It was the shock. Mortimer saying that Mr Silkin was in his office. I thought—'

'You thought it was Abraham? Oh, dear.' He made a face. 'I didn't realise I was such a poor substitute.'

'You're not a poor substitute, Lynwood. You know I didn't mean that,' she said, shaking her head.

'Good.' He rubbed his hands together. 'Well, now you're here I expect you'd like to see your inheritance. Or do you simply want to examine the books?' He lifted one eyebrow quizzically.

'Now I'm here I think I should take a look, don't you?' she said uncertainly. She let her eyes travel round the office. It was not very big and its single window looked out on to a grimy brick wall that kept most of the light out. The furniture consisted of Abraham's desk with a swivel chair behind it in which Lynwood had been sitting, a table under the window piled with papers and boxes of buttons, a chest of drawers with a cupboard on top, open to reveal papers crammed in, and the chair on which she was sitting. Stained brown linoleum covered the floor. It was quite obvious that Abraham had kept all evidence of his wealth away from the place in which it was made. The only concession to comfort was the fire burning in the grate.

'I do, indeed.' He opened the door for her and again the dreadful smell assailed their nostrils. 'You've come on a bad day,' he said cheerfully, 'it doesn't always stink quite as much as this.'

'Mortimer told me they were boiling up bones to make the buttons. It is that all they use, Lynwood? Bones?'

'Heavens, no. They make them from all sorts of other things as well: horn, pearl, stuff called false ivory – it looks like ivory but it's easier to work. Comes from the nut of the Corozo palm.'

'You seem to know an awful lot about it all.' Holding her handkerchief to her nose she followed him up the stone stairs to the floor above.

'Of course I do. I've made it my business to find out.' He smiled at her over his shoulder. 'Ah, here we are.'

He pushed open double doors and she could see men working all sorts of different machinery. There were lathes and punches, circular saws; Joanna could see a number of odd-looking hand tools and wondered what they were used for. There were buttons everywhere. Half-made buttons, buttons without shanks, buttons waiting to be drilled, buttons of all shapes, sizes and colours. But there was no time to ask any questions before Lynwood closed the door on the noise and led her on up more stone stairs. As they went they could her the sounds of raucous music hall songs and laughter but as soon as Lynwood pushed open the door at the top of the stairs there was immediate silence from the women and girls who worked there.

As soon as they saw Joanna in her black widow's weeds they all scrambled quickly to their feet and curtsyed and then stood quietly waiting.

Lynwood waved his hand. 'It's all right. Get on with your work.'

Immediately, the women, there were six of them, sat down at the table in the middle of the room and resumed their task

132

of stitching buttons on to card. Several girls, little more than children and not very warmly dressed, were busily sorting and sizing the buttons for them from the bins at the end of a long table. The room was cold, even though a small inadequate fire burned, yet the atmosphere was stuffy and there was a rank smell of unwashed bodies. Even here there were echoes of the bones being boiled two floors below.

'Seen enough?' Lynwood asked, standing in the doorway so that she wasn't able to go further into the room. 'The packing department is through that door at the end. Brown paper and string, mostly.' Obviously tired of showing her round such a cheerless place he grinned at her. 'Come on, we'll go back to the office. It's warmer there. It's no place for a lady up here, some of the songs they sing.'

Back in the office, the fire had been stoked up and burned brightly, warming the room in stark contrast to the rest of the building. Before he would let her go, Lynwood insisted on showing her the account books, the order books, the rent books from the various properties belonging to Abraham, in fact everything concerning the old man's business interests.

'There you are, you see? Everything's in apple-pie order,' he said smugly. 'I told you, I've been working like a Trojan for these past three months. Uncle Abe would be pleased with me.'

'It's a pity you didn't work like this when he was alive,' Joanna said sharply, unaccountably peeved.

'Oh, Jo. Don't be like that.' After being so pleased with himself he put on a hang-dog air. 'I'm really trying, you know.'

She burst out laughing. It was the first time she had laughed since Abraham died. 'You are indeed, Lynwood. Really trying,' she said.

He didn't like being laughed at. 'Well, at least you know your inheritance is in safe hands,' he said huffily.

She put out her hand to him, serious again. 'Yes, Lynwood, and I'm very grateful to you. I really am,' she said.

He took the hand she offered in both of his. 'I want more than gratitude, Jo,' he said and the way he looked at her sent a delightful shivery tingle through her body.

'I must go,' she said faintly. 'Osborne will be waiting.'

He didn't try to detain her.

That night he was at home to dinner.

'I thought you might be lonely now the Old Girl's gone,' he said disrespectfully as they sat together over saddle of lamb.

'That was kind of you,' Joanna said, her eyes on her plate.

'Not really. I've been waiting for her to go home so that I could have you to myself. God, I was beginning to think she'd never go!' He helped himself to more potatoes. 'We've got a lot to talk about, you and me, Jo. But it'll keep until we've finished this excellent meal. Parker, convey our compliments to Mrs Osborne in the kitchen,' he said over his shoulder.

Joanna frowned. Surely *she* should have been the one to compliment the cook?

After dinner, instead of going out with his friends, Lynwood came to sit with her in the drawing room so that he could tell her of his plans for the factory, plans which, if she was honest, she had difficulty in understanding. But her ears pricked up when she heard the words,

'And when we're married—'

'But we can never be married, Lynwood,' she said. 'I've already told you that. The terms of Abraham's will are very plain. If I remarry I lose everything.'

He leapt up and came and sat beside her. 'But don't you see? You'll lose it, yes, but only to me, my darling, so what difference could it possibly make? You know I shall always care for you so what does it matter whether the inheritance is in my name or yours?' He took her in his arms. 'You know my feelings for you, Jo. I managed to keep them under control while Uncle Abe was alive, but he's gone now so we've nothing to feel guilty about. We can be married. We can be together. All the time.' He began to fiddle with her buttons, sliding his hand inside her bodice.

'No, Lynwood,' she protested weakly, knowing she should stop him yet wanting him to continue.

'Let me come to your room tonight,' he whispered, his mouth against hers. 'Then I can show you what it's like to be loved by a real man.'

She twisted her head away. 'No, Lynwood. I could never do that. It wouldn't be right. Abie's hardly cold in his grave. It's too soon,' she cried, hardly knowing what she was saying because her body disagreed with her words.

'Very well, my love.' He began carefully and deliberately

to refasten her buttons, then his lips brushed her cheek. 'I can wait.' He put his finger under her chin, forcing her to look up at him. 'But not for too long. I want you for my own, Jo.'

'I want you, too, Lynwood,' she admitted, 'but Abraham said I was to remain a widow. The will said—'

'Listen, my darling. I believe that clause was put in the will because Uncle Abe didn't want you to marry anybody outside the family. He wanted you to marry *me*. That's why he left things the way he did.'

'Do you really think so, Lynwood?' she said uncertainly.

He bent and kissed her. 'I'm sure so, sweetheart. You don't think Uncle Abe could be such a miserable old curmudgeon as to condemn a beautiful woman like you to a life of lonely widowhood, do you? I think it was very clever of him, myself. Don't you agree?'

She nodded, still not convinced. 'Yes, I suppose you're right.'

'I know I'm right. I'll prove it to you.' He took her in his arms and kissed her until she was weak. 'You see? You're not meant to spend the rest of your life without love, my darling,' he whispered breathlessly in her ear. 'We were made for each other. We must be wed.'

'Not until my year of mourning is up, Lynwood,' she said, trying to force her mind to work rationally. 'We must wait until then.'

He released her slightly so that he could gaze down at her. 'And how do you think I'm going to wait that long, my darling. Seeing you every day.'

She smiled tremulously and put her finger to his lips. 'I know it will be difficult, my love. It will be hard for me, too. But out of respect for Abraham's memory that is how it must be.'

He kissed the tips of her fingers. 'Very well, my love. So be it. But I can't wait a full year. You'll be mine before next Christmas. That I promise you.'

Chapter Fifteen

Soon, life seemed brighter. Instead of moping about the house Joanna went about singing as she began to look forward to a life with Lynwood instead of backwards to the life she had shared with Abraham.

But in spite of his ardent wooing, which she found it very hard to resist, she was adamant that they should not be married until her year of mourning was up. And worse, in his eyes, she would not allow him into her bed until the ring was safely on her finger. He found this irritating and frustrating in the extreme and although he continued to work hard at the Button Factory – his godfather would have been proud of him, had he lived to see it – occasionally things grew too much for him and to relieve his frustrations he visited his old haunts to drink and gamble the night away.

Joanna, of course, was unaware of these 'flings'. She basked in his attentions, the flowers he bought her almost daily – despite the fact that better ones grew in her own green-houses – the gifts he lavished on her. She enjoyed their drives to the Botanical Gardens and visits to concerts, although she refused to accompany him to the music hall whilst still in mourning. Lynwood grew to hate her widow's weeds and longed to see her dressed in bright colours again. In fact, at times his patience was tried almost to breaking point by her insistence that she must observe the proprieties of mourning for her late husband. As far as Lynwood was concerned, his godfather was now out of the way so the coast was clear for him to step into Abraham's shoes, or rather his bed. And he couldn't wait to do so.

It was during one of his 'flings' that he overheard a snippet of gossip that made him prick up his ears with interest. Much later, when he had sobered up and recovered his equilibrium sufficiently to face both his future bride and Mrs Osborne's excellent dinner, he made a deceptively casual remark over the pudding.

'Are you still anxious to discover the identity of your mother, my darling?' he asked. 'Or have you given up all thought of it?'

She regarded him thoughtfully. 'No, Lynwood, I haven't exactly given up all thought of it,' she said, playing with her spoon and fork. 'But for some reason it hasn't seemed quite so important, lately. You see, Abraham gave me all I could ever want, so I didn't have to dream of being rescued by my rich relatives.' She frowned a little. 'Does that sound terribly disloyal? Of course, I would still dearly love to know who my mother was and where she came from.' She looked up at him with a smile. 'And thanks to Abraham I know my family wouldn't be ashamed to own me now.'

'I'm sure any family would be proud to claim you, my love, have no fear of that.' He smiled back at her. 'But I'm glad to hear you're still interested because I believe I may have discovered something that might help.'

Her face lit up and she leaned forward eagerly. 'Oh, Lynwood, have you really? What have you found out? Do you know who my mother is – was? Where does – did she live? Who are my relatives?'

'Hold on, Jo!' He held up his hand. 'It's only a clue and it may not lead anywhere. But I was with—' he hesitated, not anxious to reveal the kind of company he sometimes kept, 'some friends the night before last and a yarn came up about a young girl who drowned in the Porter Brook.'

'That's where my mother was found,' Joanna interrupted.

'Something like twenty years ago?'

'About that. Yes.' Joanna nodded eagerly.

He shrugged. 'Well, it may not be the same person, of course, but apparently a young girl from Chatsworth went missing about that time. She was the niece of some relative of the Duke of Devonshire, so the story goes.'

'Was she—?' Joanna hesitated, not wanting to be indelicate, 'Was there a child?'

137

'Oh, there was most likely one in the offing, as you might say,' he replied, grinning at her. 'That's the reason most young girls run away from home, or are turned out, isn't it?'

'Then you think perhaps—?' She was hardly daring to breathe.

He nodded. 'Seems quite likely, don't you think?'

She was almost beside herself with excitement and she clasped her hands together, her eyes sparkling. 'How can we find out more, Lynwood? Oh, wouldn't it be wonderful if—'

'Leave it to me, darling. I'll see what else I can discover.' He leaned down and pressed her knee under the table. 'But it'll come at a price,' he added wickedly.

That evening, in the privacy of her little sitting room, she allowed him privileges that sent his senses reeling, but to his fury she still denied him the ultimate prize. When he could stand it no more he flung himself away from her and went over to the mirror to rebutton his shirt and adjust his cravat.

'There are names for women like you, Jo,' he said savagely. 'Leading a fellow on like you do and then—' He couldn't think of a way to finish the sentence that wouldn't offend her so he left it hanging in the air.

'I do love you, Lynwood,' she said, watching him and adjusting her own bodice, her face and neck rosy from his kisses. 'You know that. I love you with all my heart.'

He turned and faced her. 'Then why in hell—?' He checked himself. In spite of being married for over four years she really did seem a little innocent. It was odd.

She went to him and laid her head on his chest. She knew she had displeased him. 'You will see what you can discover about my mother, dearest, won't you?' she pleaded.

'I told you I would,' he replied, trying to conceal his irritable frustration. He had tried every ploy until he was certain he had broken through all her defences, but at the last minute she had pushed him away and turned from him. What in hell was the woman made of? How could she expect him to wait another four months?

An idea came to him and he turned from the mirror and smiled at her. 'Once we are wed, my darling, I shall leave no stone unturned.'

Joanna capitulated. She agreed to marry as soon as it could

be arranged and the date was set for October the eighth.

She rode over to break the news to Gertrude, full of apprehension. Gertrude was a stickler for convention and she made no secret of the fact that she didn't care for Lynwood. It was not going to be easy.

There were muffins for tea. That was a good sign. Gertrude loved muffins.

'We had muffins the first day I came to Cliffe House,' Joanna said, licking her fingers. 'Do you remember, Gertie?'

'Aye, that I do. You were a scrawny little wraith, but you put down muffins faster than I could hand 'em to you.'

'I was hungry.'

Gertrude eyed her up and down, taking in the beautifully cut black bombazine dress and the jet necklace and matching earrings, the diamond rings on her fingers. 'You've come a long way since then, lass. I wasn't very happy about it at first, I'll be the first to admit, but Abe did all right by you and you made him a happy man. As his sister I couldn't ask more.' She nodded contentedly and took a noisy sip of tea.

'I'm to be wed again, Gertrude,' Joanna said after a bit. She couldn't face the delicious cream cakes until she had told Gertrude her news.

Gertrude stopped with an éclair half-way to her open mouth. 'Wed again? But my brother's hardly cold in his grave. You've surely not let any man start courting you so soon! Good gracious me, you're still in full mourning. I'm surprised at you, Joanna. Where have you been gadding off to meet this man, whoever he is?'

'I've not been anywhere, Gertie. I've—'

'Who is he, then? I hope he'll observe the proprieties and not expect you to wed for another eighteen months, at least.' Gertrude attacked the éclair viciously.

'It's Lynwood, Gertie, and we're to be wed at the beginning of October.' Joanna spoke in a rush and then waited for the explosion.

She didn't wait in vain. Gertrude turned a dull red. 'Lynwood!' She nearly choked on the éclair. 'That good-for-nothing layabout! How could you, Joanna? After all my brother did for you, picking you out of the gutter and making a lady of you. Oh, my Lord, he'd turn in his grave if he

139

knew.' She pulled her shoulders back and pursed her lips disapprovingly although the effect was somewhat lost by the blob of cream on her chin. 'And as for marrying before Abe has been dead a full year ... well, words fail me!' She peered at Joanna and finished scathingly, 'You'll be telling me next you're with child by him.' She dabbed the cream off with her napkin.

'I am not with child,' Joanna said with dignity. 'But I love Lynwood and he loves me. We see no reason to wait any longer to begin our life together.'

'Pah! You love Lynwood so you're too blind to see that what he's after is getting his hands on your fortune. Or had you forgotten you'll lose it if you remarry?' She gave a mirthless laugh. 'And once *he* gets his hands on it it'll disappear like snow in summer. Good-for-nothing layabout that he is.'

'No, I haven't forgotten,' Joanna said quietly. 'And as for being a good-for-nothing layabout, Lynwood has worked very hard at the Button Factory since Abraham died. All the books are in perfect order, I've seen them, he showed them to me.' She lifted her chin. 'And of course we've discussed the terms of the will, but as Lynwood says, what does it matter whether things are in my name or his? It makes no difference because he handles things and he'll look after me.'

Gertrude shook her head irritably. 'Oh, lass, how can you be so gullible? Can't you see—?'

Joanna stood up. 'I can see that you don't like Lynwood and never have,' she said hotly. 'You can see no good in him at all. Well, maybe he was a bit wild, maybe he didn't take any interest in Abraham's business, but I'm telling you, he's changed. He's a good, kind, caring and hardworking man and I love him. I know he would never do anything to harm me. We are to be married on October the eighth. You will be more than welcome to come to our wedding, Gertrude, provided you accept Lynwood as the decent, kind man that he is.'

'I have more respect for my brother than to attend his widow's wedding less than a year after he was laid to rest,' Gertrude said, her voice heavy. 'And I tell you this, lass, though it pains me to say it, if you wed that man you'll no longer be welcome here at my house.'

Joanna lifted her chin. 'Then I had better leave at once.

Perhaps you will be good enough to have my carriage called.'
She got up and went to the door. When she reached it she
turned. 'And you may be interested to know that Lynwood
thinks he may have discovered a clue to my family – my *real*
family. A niece of a relative of the Duke of Devonshire went
missing somewhere round the time my mother was found
drowned. He's going to investigate and see if it might be one
and the same person.' With that she swept from the room.

Gertrude stared at the closed door for a long time, her head
shaking from side to side sadly. She didn't trust the young
popinjay. Never had. She suspected he'd probably made up
the story about Joanna's mother in order to get her into his
bed sooner. She closed her eyes, hoping and praying that she
was wrong and that Joanna would be happy with him, because
in spite of everything she was very fond of the lass. But she
very much doubted that any good would come of the match.

Joanna was happier than she had ever been in her life
before. Lynwood insisted on accompanying her to choose the
material for her wedding dress; he absolutely refused to allow
her to be married in her widow's weeds. They settled on pearl
grey silk, but Joanna insisted that it should be trimmed with
black, or at least a very dark blue.

'And I shall wear my mother's cloak,' she said on a burst of
inspiration. 'It's midnight blue so it will be eminently suitable.'

Lynwood looked doubtful but when she showed it to him he
agreed that it would be ideal. It was, he considered privately,
exactly the kind of thing that a relative of the Duke of
Devonshire might have worn – contrary to Gertrude's suspicion he had not fabricated the story – and it occurred to him
that he could be marrying even more of an heiress than he
realised. The thought gave him enormous pleasure and he
went out of his way to please his charming bride-to-be.

October the eighth dawned a bright, cold day with enough
wind to blow the last of the leaves from the trees. It was as if
even the hedgerows had been decorated for the day with bright
red berries and old man's beard, and a carpet of red, orange
and brown leaves covered the ground as the carriage carrying
Joanna to the church passed Whiteley Wood.

She gathered the blue cloak round her. It was the first time

141

she had worn it since the day Martha found her and she loved the feel of the soft, thick velvet that enveloped her. Lily had hung it over a steam bath to make sure there were no creases in it and she had wanted to stitch a new clasp on to replace the broken one but Joanna wouldn't let her. She wanted to wear it exactly the way it had been when her mother wrapped her in it. It made her feel somehow closer to her mother, who she was quite convinced was the young girl who had once lived at Chatsworth, the great house some ten miles away to the south-west.

The carriage drew up at the church. There was nobody to give her away so, carrying a sheaf of lilies, a coronet of red roses securing the short white veil that covered her face, Joanna walked proudly alone through the throng of people lining the churchyard and up the aisle to meet her bridegroom, waiting eagerly at the chancel steps. She made her promises in a clear voice and looked adoringly into his eyes as he slipped the heavy gold band on to her finger, then bent and folded back her veil and kissed her lips.

'You're all mine now, Jo,' he whispered ardently and the vicar had to clear his throat loudly to remind them that the service was not quite finished.

The ceremony over and the register signed, the happy couple emerged from the church into bright sunshine, to be showered in rice as they hurried through the crowds to the open carriage that was to take them back to Cliffe House and the wedding breakfast and then for a honeymoon in Venice.

But as they reached the lich-gate there was a commotion among the waiting crowd and a voice yelled, 'Leave me alone! Let me through! I've every right to be here. I've every right to wish my daughter well!'

Joanna and Lynwood halted and Joanna scanned the crowd puzzled. Who could have called her 'daughter'? Her mother was dead, drowned. She couldn't have come to see her married. Then she saw a tall figure, dressed all in black, with a wide black hat obscuring her features, trying to elbow her way to the front whilst the churchwardens struggled to hold her back. The woman managed to shake them off and stepped in front of Joanna.

142

'You've done well for yourself, my child. I'm proud of you,' she said softly.

Joanna reeled back with a cry of horror, for the figure standing there in her stinking rags was Liddy Ingram, Liddy the witch.

'No!' she moaned, her voice little above a whisper. 'Not you! You can't be my mother. My mother is dead.'

Liddy lifted her head proudly. 'You want proof?' She rummaged among her rags then held out her hand. There in her cracked and smoke-blackened palm lay the other half of the broken clasp belonging to the midnight-blue cloak.

Joanna stared at the clasp in horrified disbelief, her hand automatically going to its other half, still attached to the blue cloak, as if to shield it. 'No! No! It's not the same!' she cried.

'Oh, yes, it's the same,' Liddy said, nodding. 'Look at it.' She held it close to Joanna's face.

'No! No! This can't be happening.' Joanna tried to clutch Lynwood's arm for support but he wasn't there. He had moved away from her side and was staring at Liddy with absolute abhorrence. Desperately, she turned back to Liddy. 'You lie. You're a witch. You must have stolen it from my mother.' She was sobbing now, the tears running unchecked down her cheeks.

'I never lie and I never steal.' Liddy spoke with dignity. She stroked the cloak Joanna was wearing. 'That cloak was mine. I knew when I gave you away that it was only right that you should one day know your true parentage. I promised myself I would wait until you were twenty-one, but this seemed as good a time as any to tell you.' Liddy smiled at Joanna through broken and blackened teeth. 'One day you may be glad I did,' she added softly.

'You can't be my mother. My mother would never have come and spoiled the happiest day of my life,' Joanna sobbed.

'I am your mother,' Liddy insisted.

The crowd had fallen silent, drinking in the scene, but now a jeering voice called, 'Who's the wench's father, then, witch? The devil himself?'

This was greeted by a roar of laughter from the crowd, which was quickly silenced when Liddy turned to the direction of the voice. It didn't do to mock witches, they remembered.

'Chickens come home to roost,' she said quietly. 'I gave my child back where she belonged.' With that she turned and strode away, the crowd parting this time to let her through.

'Oh, Lynwood.' Half-fainting, her face ravaged by disgust and horror, Joanna turned to her new husband, desperate for his support and the comfort of his arms. But to her astonishment his face was drained of colour and he pushed her away, staring at her with absolute repugnance.

'Oh, my God! To think I've just wed the spawn of a witch,' he muttered, backing away from her, his face ugly with disgust.

She sank at his feet in the mud and clutched his knees, the sheaf of lilies discarded on the ground beside her. 'No, Lynwood, it's not true. It can't be true. She's lying. I'm the same Joanna that I was yesterday, I promise you. My real mother belonged at Chatsworth, just like you said.'

He prodded her with the toe of his boot, at the same time tearing off his cravat.

'Get up,' he sneered, 'stop soiling my boots with your grovelling.'

She struggled to her feet, the tears still streaming down her cheeks, and held out her arms to him. He brushed them aside impatiently and wound the cravat round her neck, yanking it so tight that she could hardly breathe. Then he climbed up on to the wall of the churchyard and dragged her up beside him, holding her there by the ends of the cravat.

She could hardly stand. The coronet of red roses Lily had so lovingly placed on her head such a short time ago had slipped drunkenly sideways and the veil it held in place was lopsided and torn. Her face was tear-stained and dirty and the beautiful grey dress was spattered with mud and filth where she had grovelled at Lynwood's feet. She looked a pathetic sight.

'Who will buy this daughter of Satan?' he shouted. 'Who will give me tuppence for this witch's spawn?'

'I'll give tha a ha'penny,' a voice came from the crowd amid a roar of laughter.

'Mek it a penny. She looks good for a roll in t'hedge,' another called.

'She's worth a tanner,' came from a third voice. 'She'll be cheaper than t'whores at Ma Driffield's.'

144

Joanna only half-heard all this going on. She had covered her face with her hands in shame and was more than half-fainting with misery. It was only Lynwood's hand on the halter round her neck that kept her upright.

'I'll give you five shillings,' a strong voice rang out. 'You'll not get a better offer than that.'

'Aye, that you'll not,' came a rumble from the crowd. 'Let t'poor lass go. Witch's spawn she may be but she's suffered enough.'

Lynwood jerked her off the wall and undid the cravat. 'She's yours for five shillings, then, whoever you are,' he said. He took the money and stuffed it with his cravat into his pocket. Then he gave her a push towards the man who had paid him and strode off to his carriage, the same carriage, still decorated with flowers and ribbons, that was to have carried him and his new wife to begin their life together.

Still weeping, Joanna watched it disappear along the road and then, without even a glance towards the man who had put up the money, turned and ran through the churchyard to crouch sobbing by the grave she had tended all these years. The grave that for all these years she had so fondly believed held her mother.

Chapter Sixteen

A pasty-faced woman in the crowd, her figure slack from too much child-bearing, had been watching the proceedings with great interest. It was Jacob Bradshaw's wife, Bella. Bella liked watching posh weddings, she liked to see the pretty clothes and imagine herself dressed in them. More practically, sometimes you could even collect up enough of the rice that had been thrown afterwards to make a pudding. Today, of course, there had been the added attraction of the bride being Joanna Bradshaw, that was. Bella hadn't forgotten Joanna's days as a scrawny little unpaid skivvy to Saul Bradshaw, Bella's father-in-law, and she had stood outside the church, her eyes popping with amazement at the transformation, when Joanna and Abraham Silkin were wed. She hadn't really envied her then – no, that wasn't true. If she spoke the truth she'd have given her eye-teeth – if they hadn't already fallen out – to be rich and live in a big house and wear beautiful clothes like Joanna. But marrying an old man was not to Bella's taste; she had an insatiable sexual appetite and she needed a man with a bit of spark and a bit of energy left in him.

It was different this time. Because now not only was Joanna rich and beautiful, she was marrying this young, virile and handsome man, and Bella was there to watch, filled with lust and envy in equal quantities. Wild horses wouldn't have kept her away from this wedding, never mind the strict instructions from Martha to notice every detail so that she could relay the scene home, because her rheumatism was too bad for the walk to the church.

146

Well, Bella had watched the wedding and had witnessed the scenes that followed, scenes that would be talked about in Sheffield for years to come, scenes that in some ways she viewed with smug satisfaction. Pride cometh before a fall was a phrase that sprang to mind.

But her satisfaction was short-lived, to be replaced by cold fury. Because although Bella was slow-witted she was no fool and after going over the scene several times in her mind she began to realise exactly what Liddy Ingram had been saying when she spoke about 'chickens coming home to roost'.

She dredged her memory to make sure she had her facts in order. Joanna had been left in the cowshed at Bradshaw's Farm. Bella remembered it all only too well because it had happened not many weeks after she and Jacob were wed and only four months before their Albert was born. In fact Martha sometimes used to look after Albert when he was little, saying it was company for Joanna, since they were much of an age. She hitched her youngest child up further on her hip and, dragging his sister by the hand, made her way purposefully back to Bradshaw's Farm, where Jacob was supposed to be helping his father dig the last of the potatoes. As she walked she did what were for her complicated sums, working things out in her mind several times and in several ways. But the conclusion she came to every time was inescapable: her husband had fathered Liddy Ingram's child.

When she reached the farm Martha was hobbling about the kitchen making tea for Saul and Jacob, who were sitting there in their muddy boots waiting for it.

'Good! I'm glad you're all here.' Tight-lipped, Bella didn't wait to sit down but immediately launched into her story. Martha listened, her mouth dropping open as the identity of Joanna's mother was revealed.

'Liddy Ingram! Well, I never would have thought it,' she breathed. 'Not in a million years. Oh, my poor little lass. What a shock for her.'

'Never mind t'poor little lass. Never mind who her mother is,' Bella snapped. 'It's her father I'm interested in.' She turned to Jacob. 'It's you, in't it, you dirty, sneaking little rat!' She held up her hand. 'Oh, you don't need to bother denying it, I've been working it out all t'way home. Our

Albert is four months younger than Joanna so you must have been tailing that dirty old bitch at t'same time as you were having me. And to think I were daft enough to imagine I were t'only one!'

'I never did!' Jacob shouted, red in the face. 'Tha *was* t'only one!'

'Don't lie to me, Jacob Bradshaw. I know your appetite. Any road, who else could it have been? After all, your brother Caleb was too young.'

'And tha allus was a randy young pup,' Saul said, chuckling. He slapped his knee, enjoying the scene. 'Be sure tha sins'll find tha out, lad.'

'Shut up, Da.' Jacob got to his feet and wagged his finger at Bella. 'I'm tellin' tha, woman ...'

'You're telling me nowt, Jacob Bradshaw, not ever again,' Bella shouted. 'I'm off and I'm tekin' t'children with me. I'm fed up with your boozing, t'way you tip all your wages down your throat so there's nowt left for us. God knows, I'll not be any worse off wi'out you. I've only stayed with you because I thought you were faithful to me. But now I find ... and wi' that old witch ... Ugh.' She shuddered then gathered the children to her and made for the door. 'Albert and Freddie are both in work and Harry and Jim soon will be so they'll look after their old Mam and the little ones. And Jinny and Sally are out at service so I don't have to worry about them.'

'Why can't tha listen to me, woman!' Jacob shouted back at her. 'I never—'

'I've had enough of your lies, Jacob Bradshaw, and I'll hear no more. I'm going to my sister now. She'll put us up till us can find somewhere to live.' She left, slamming the door behind her.

Jacob leaned forward and put his head in his hands. 'As God's my witness—' he began.

'Never mind it, lad,' his father said, laying an arm round his shoulders. 'Your Bella's allus been hot-tempered. She'll be back. Have a cup o' tea an' leave her to cool off.'

'Tha can allus move back wi' us, lad,' Martha said, her mind ever on practicalities. 'Tha can have Caleb's room. Tha dad can do wi' an extra hand.' She poured them both more tea. Then her thoughts turned back to Joanna and the tale Bella

148

had told. 'Oh, my poor little lass,' she said, staring into space. 'My poor little lass. Whatever's to become of thee?'

Joanna had no idea how long she lay sobbing on the grave of the unknown woman, the grave she had tended so lovingly all these years, but suddenly she felt a hand on her shoulder.

'Aye, I thought I'd find you here, Jo,' a voice said gently.

She looked up and saw a young, pleasant-looking man with a shock of black hair and a well-trimmed beard. 'Tom?' she said tentatively. Then, 'It is Tom, isn't it?' She scrambled to her feet and looked at him, still not quite sure.

'Aye, Jo, it's me.' He nodded, smiling at her.

'You look ... different.' She wiped her cheeks with the heels of her hands and tried to smile back at him. 'You're a man now.'

'Aye. I'm out of my time. I've left Zack Wenlock. I'm living in the town now, making my own way, like I always said I would.' He nodded towards the expensive pearl grey dress and the blue cloak, both now crushed and liberally streaked with mud. 'You're different, too, Jo.' He put out his hand and gently removed the bedraggled coronet and veil. It had tipped rakishly over one eye. 'Except you're even more beautiful.'

'I don't feel very beautiful.' She hung her head and turned away from him. 'Did you see what happened just now, Tom? Did you see what my ... what he did to me?' she said, her voice muffled.

'Aye, Jo, I saw it,' he said grimly.

'I – can I come home with you, Tom?' she asked uncertainly. 'Just for a few days. I'd feel safe with you. He sold me.' Her voice broke on a bitter sob. 'Oh, God! Lynwood auctioned me to the highest bidder.'

'I know that.'

'How could he do such a thing to me?' Her voice rose. 'How could he humiliate me like that? Did you see who b—' she couldn't bring herself to say the word, 'who he sold me to?' Joanna glanced anxiously over her shoulder to see if Tom had been followed.

He put an arm round her. 'It's all right. You've nowt to fear, Jo. I'll look after you,' he said.

'I know you will, Tom.' She clutched his arm desperately. 'Lynwood can't do this to me, can he? It's not allowed. If we find the man, whoever he is, and pay him back I can go home.'

'Home? Home to that bastard? Who strung you up and sold you to the highest bidder?' His voice was scathing. 'My God, do you know what you're saying, Jo?'

'Oh, I'm sure he didn't mean it. He did it in the heat of the moment. It was the shock ...' her voice trailed off.

'You might think that, but you obviously didn't see his face!' His jaw tightened. 'Any road, I'd not let you go back to the bastard. I'd kill him with my bare hands first.'

Joanna wasn't listening. 'Somebody paid five shillings for me. Who was it, Tom? I didn't see.' She put her hand up to her mouth. 'What shall I do if he finds me? Shall I have to go with him?' She looked round wildly. 'Oh, God! What shall I do? I don't know where I belong any more.' She turned away from him and covered her face with her hands and began to weep again, rocking back and forth in her misery.

'You belong to me, Jo. *I* bought you,' he said quietly.

She remained absolutely still for several moments, then looked at him from between her fingers. '*You* bought me? For five shillings?'

He spread his hands. 'It was all I had in the world. If I'd had more I would have paid more.'

She dropped her hands and stared at him. He was very clean, but his coat and trousers were threadbare, the cap perched rakishly on his dark hair had seen better days and his boots were worn out and tied up with string. The hands he held out to her were calloused. Once he had been her friend, they had been all but inseparable. Now he was a stranger.

'What are you going to do with me?' she whispered.

'What do you think? I'm going to take you home with me.' He looked her up and down. 'But not dressed like that.'

'Why not?' She was affronted and tried to brush some of the mud off.

'Oh, Jo. Have some sense. That dress you're wearing must have cost more than folks where I live earn in ten years.' He pinched his lip, deep in thought. 'Now,' he said when he had made up his mind, 'go behind that big tombstone over there and take it off. You can put the cloak on afterwards.'

She frowned. 'No, I don't need to do that. I can pull the cloak round so nobody can see it.'

'It's not a case of hiding it, Jo. I've got to take it to the pawnshop.' His voice was sharp. 'I've got no money, Jo. I told you, that five shillings was all I had in the world.'

'Oh, yes. I'm sorry, Tom. All right, I'll go and take it off.'

'What I get for the dress will buy something for you to wear that's more in keeping with where we're going plus a pair of clogs instead of those silly satin slippers and with any luck a pie each for our supper.'

'But that dress cost pounds. Lynwood—' The tears began to flow again.

'What he paid for it has nowt to do with what I'll be able to get for it from the pawnshop. You ought to know that, Jo.'

She began to tug at the wide wedding ring that had only been on her finger a matter of hours. 'You might as well take this, too,' she muttered.

He laid his hand over hers. 'No, Jo. You're going to need that. Mrs Goffin, where I live, won't let you stay in my room with me if she thinks we're not married.'

'But we're not!'

'She's not to know that, as long as you're wearing a wedding ring.'

'Well, you might as well take these.' She wrenched off the triple string of pearls Lynwood had given her as a wedding present. One rope had already broken, the pearls gone.

He took them and smiled at her. 'Trust me, Jo. I'll do the best I can.' He bundled the pearls up in the beautiful grey dress and, tucking it under his arm, hurried out of the church-yard.

When he had gone Joanna wrapped herself in the blue cloak and crouched behind a tombstone. She hated wearing it because it had belonged to Liddy the witch. Her mother. *Her mother*. She had come from the body of that filthy old woman who lived in the woods. She retched at the thought. And the old charcoal burner, that grotesque figure with only half a face. Her grandfather. The words banged on her brain and she began to retch again.

But who was her father? She leaned her head against the

tombstone and tried to think what Liddy had said. Something about chickens coming home to roost. So it must have been one of the Bradshaw boys. Caleb? She shuddered with disgust but tried to make her brain work, to calculate. Caleb would only have been fourteen or fifteen at the time she was conceived so it was hardly likely. But Jacob. Yes, it could have been Jacob. The thought still disgusted her, but not as much as if it had been Caleb. Caleb who had tried to rape her. Caleb whom she had wished dead. Whom Liddy knew she had wished dead. Liddy the witch. Her mother. She began to retch again.

When she had finished, exhausted, she pulled the cloak closer round her, hating it for what it was, yet glad of its warmth and its cover. Tom could sell it later.

She closed her eyes wearily. Oh, God, what was happening to her that her wedding day had turned into such a nightmare that the clothes off her back must be sold in order to buy food? How could she bear it? She wished she were dead. She wished Lynwood had pulled the noose a bit tighter round her neck so that it had strangled her. Once again, tears began to trickle down her cheeks from under her eyelids.

Sunk in misery she waited for Tom to return. When at last he arrived he was carrying a dress of coarse greenish material, none too clean, with large sweat marks under the armpits and a torn hem.

She looked at it in disgust. 'I'm not wearing that!' she said flatly.

'Wear it or walk through the streets in your shift. Please yourself.' Tom's patience was wearing thin. He'd had to haggle to get what he wanted for the grey dress and in consequence had had to pay more for the green one. And although the old pawnbroker's eye had lit up at the sight of the pearls he had only paid a pittance for them because Tom hadn't been able to convince him that they weren't stolen. 'I don't know if the clogs'll fit but they were the best I could get. I got us a pie each, too, and I've still got a bit of money left. Here you are.' He held out a hot pie.

She shook her head; the smell of it threatened to make her retch again.

'All right, I'll save it for you for later.' He ate his own

while she changed into the green dress then bundled up the cloak to make it as inconspicuous as he could.

'Come on, now.' He took her hand and led her back through the churchyard. It was empty and very quiet now that the crowd had dispersed. The only movement came from the sparrows, busy with what was left of the rice that had been so enthusiastically thrown such a short time ago.

Numb with shame and shock Joanna allowed Tom to take her through unfamiliar streets down into the heart of Sheffield. It was a long walk and the stiff, unyielding clogs she was wearing soon covered her feet in blisters.

Neither of them spoke as she hobbled along beside him, the streets becoming ever narrower and darker and more squalid. 'Are we nearly there?' she ventured at last, glancing apprehensively over her shoulder.

'Yes. We're here now.' He turned into a passageway between two tall buildings which opened out into a cobbled yard round which three cottages huddled. There was a single drain in the middle of the cobbles, into which a gully ran from each cottage. Many years ago the cottages had been white-washed, or bug-blinded, as it was called locally, but now they were grey and peeling like the paint on the doors and windows. One cottage had a brave little geranium blooming in a pot outside the door and it was to this cottage that Tom took her.

'Try not to say owt,' he whispered as they reached the door. 'And whatever I say, don't argue.'

He led her into a dim, immaculately tidy though over-crowded room where a small, neat-looking woman was sitting by the fire in a rocking chair, knitting. She looked up as Tom walked in. 'Ee, lad, I was wondering where tha'd got to.' She gave him a toothless smile which faded as she noticed Joanna. 'But who's this tha's brought home? Tha knows my rule.'

Tom smiled back at her. 'Yes, Mrs Goffin, I know your rules and I'd not break them for all the world. But you'll not object to me bringing my wife home, now, will you?' He held up Joanna's hand, with a warning squeeze to remind her not to contradict him, to show off her brand new wedding ring.

'Ee, lad, tha's a dark horse and no mistake.' A cavernous grin nearly split the old woman's face in two. 'Tha never even

153

said tha was courtin'!' She put down her knitting and got stiffly out of her chair to squeeze herself between the table, standing in the middle of the room and the bed, covered with a patchwork quilt and pushed against the wall, to come and shake Joanna by the hand. 'I'm pleased to mek tha's acquaintance, lass,' she said formally. Then she turned to Tom. 'Tha should have let me know what tha was plannin', lad,' she said thoughtfully. 'Tha'll be needin' an extra room, I'm thinkin'.'

'It's all right, we'll manage, Mrs Goffin. I'm afraid we can't afford two rooms just now,' Tom said quickly. 'We're a bit strapped for cash at the moment, you understand.'

Mrs Goffin waved her hand. 'Tha's been with me long enough to know I'll not quibble over a bit o' rent, Tom, lad. Tha was good to me when my Harry died and I've never forgot it. Tha can have t'attic and welcome, as well as t'room tha's got. It'll need a bit o'clearin', mind, but there'll be plenty o' room for a double bed up there. And a crib, too, when t'time comes.' She smiled at them happily.

'Thank you, Mrs Goffin.' Tom squeezed Joanna's hand and nodded towards the old woman.

'Yes, thank you, Mrs Goffin,' Joanna managed to whisper.

She followed Tom up the narrow staircase in the corner of the room up to the floor above. There was a single bed under the window that looked out on to the yard, a small table and a chair. A wooden armchair stood by the empty grate and a rag rug covered the bare boards in front of the hearth. Another table, with an enamel bowl standing on it and with a bucket of water under it, stood in the recess on one side of the fireplace; a cupboard was built into the other.

Tom beamed at her proudly. 'I was lucky to get this room. It's a far cry from living up under the rafters and sleeping on straw at old Zack Wenlock's. I've a good flock mattress here and blankets, too. I've done well for myself, Jo, don't you agree?'

She looked round at the tiny room, the dark, peeling paint, the sparse, cheap furniture and the bare boards. She swallowed hard and managed to give him a ghost of a smile. 'Yes, you've done very well for yourself, Tom,' she said bleakly.

It was true. He had. But Joanna's heart cried out for the luxury of Cliffe House.

Chapter Seventeen

Tom busied himself lighting a fire while Joanna sat huddled in the chair watching him, the picture of misery.

'You could lay the table, Jo,' he said over his shoulder. 'I've a bit of cold pork and some pickle, and a loaf Mrs Goffin made.'

'I'm not hungry.'

'Are you not?' He looked at her in surprise. 'Well, I am, I can tell you. Even though I ate both those pies I bought earlier. My stomach's fair cleaving to my backbone.'

Still she sat without moving. Only her eyes moved, taking in the greyish ceiling, the chipped dark brown wainscoting and the yellowing walls above it, the crude furniture and the bare floorboards. Such a far cry from the opulence she had become used to. She felt trapped. Beaten.

Tom got the fire going then sat back on his heels and looked at her. 'Aw, come on, Jo. I know you've had a terrible time today but you're with me now. I'll look after you.'

She didn't answer but sat staring into the flames as they curled round the sticks. 'I hate it here. I want to go home,' she muttered at last.

He threw down the poker and it landed with a clatter on the hearth. 'You want to go home? Home to that bastard who strung you up and sold you like some animal at market? Who shamed and humiliated you in front of all those people?' His voice began to rise, but he checked it and said quietly. 'Have you no pride, Joanna? Have you no self-respect that you would go crawling back to that man after the dreadful thing he did to you?' He waited for her answer. When it didn't come he added, 'Any road, what sort of reception do you think you'd get if you turned up on his doorstep?'

She hunched her shoulders but still said nothing.

'Then let me tell you.' He got to his feet and stood over her. 'You'd get the door slammed in your face, that's what you'd get. For heaven's sake pull yourself together, Jo, and face the fact that Lynwood Silkin couldn't face being married to the daughter of Liddy Ingram. When he found that Liddy the witch was your mother, instead of some wayward high-born daughter from a big house, which was what he'd thought, all he wanted was to be rid of you as fast as he could.'

She shook her head. 'That's not true. He didn't mean to sell me, I'm sure he didn't,' she said, desperate for him to agree with her. 'Lynwood loves me. You don't understand. It was only the heat of the moment that made him ... He would have come back—'

'He had plenty of time to come back for you. You were in that churchyard a good long time, so he could have fetched you if he'd wanted to. But he didn't want. I saw him.' Tom shook his head. 'I'm sorry, Jo. The truth is, once he knew who you really were he couldn't get away from you fast enough.'

Suddenly, she banged her fists on the arm of the chair. 'You're horrible, Tom Cartwright. You don't know what you're talking about. You're only saying these things to make me feel grateful to you for bringing me to this hovel. Well, I don't feel grateful at all. I didn't want to come here in the first place and I hate it. Don't you realise I'm used to a big house with servants to look after me?'

'Oh, yes. I realise that. I realise that for the past four years or so you've been spoiled and petted and pampered,' he said, his voice bitter. 'Waited on hand, foot and finger. But I also remember the days when you hadn't a rag to your back and we used to scavenge the woods for berries to fill our empty bellies. I daresay you've forgotten that.'

'No, I haven't,' she said sullenly. 'But my life's changed. It's not like that now.'

'And it wouldn't be like this, in a comfortable room with someone to care for you if I hadn't come to your rescue.' His voice began to rise again. 'You'd have ended up in a brothel, that's where you'd have ended up, my lass.'

She stared at him. 'No, that's not true,' she whispered.

'I'd stake my life on it. Any of those men who were bidding for you would have sold you on to a brothel-keeper in the town and laughed all the way to the ale house with the profit they'd made on the deal.' His mouth twisted. 'Just imagine if your precious husband were to pay a visit there, only to find himself paying for the services of his wife.'

'Stop it!' She put her hands over her ears. 'You're cruel and I hate you.'

He sighed. 'Yes, Jo, I daresay you do. You hate me because you know what I'm saying is true and you don't want to face the fact.' He knelt down beside her and took her hand in his. 'I know it's hard for you, love. You've had more to bear today than most people suffer in a lifetime, but things'll look better in a day or two. And whatever happens I'll look after you. I promise you that.'

She snatched her hand away. 'I don't want you to look after me,' she said through gritted teeth.

He got to his feet again, his mouth a thin, hard line. 'Well, you've no choice. You're mine. I paid good money for you. More than I could afford,' he said bluntly. 'So you'd better get used to the idea.' He reached into the cupboard behind her and took out bread and pickle and put them on the table. Then he came back and took out a piece of fat and lean pork and two plates. A drawer in the table yielded cheap, bone-handled knives and forks.

She watched him, shocked to the core at the words he had just spoken. His face was like granite.

'I'm sorry, Tom. I—' she began, but he cut her off.

'All I will say is that the door is never locked. If you want to leave that badly I'll not stop you. But if you go I'll not have you back so think before you walk out. It's a cruel world out there.' He jabbed the bread knife towards the window and then began to cut slices of bread.

'I could go to Martha,' she ventured. 'She'd have me back.'

'Aye. You could. Back to slaving for Saul Bradshaw, up to your knees in mud every day. And to risk being raped by him. You're a comely wench now. You needn't think he'd be able to keep his hands off you if you were under his roof.'

Her face crumpled. 'Why are you so unkind to me, Tom?'

'I'm not being unkind, I'm simply trying to make you face things as they are and not the way you'd like them to be,' he said, trying to keep the exasperation out of his voice. 'I know you, Jo, I've known you ever since either of us can remember. And I know how you always dreamed of finding your mother's family. They were rich in your dream and they were going to rescue you from your life of drudgery with Saul Bradshaw. But that dream didn't come true. The truth is, your mother is still alive. She's Liddy Ingram, a charcoal burner's daughter, living in squalor in Whitley Woods.'

'Liddy the witch,' Joanna shuddered.

He shook his head impatiently. 'I don't believe she's anything of the kind. Just because she gathers herbs and makes potions doesn't make her a witch. She's helped a lot of people, Jo.'

'She knew I wanted Caleb Bradshaw dead and he died.'

'How did she know?'

'She saw me and knew what I was thinking.'

'That's rubbish. I told you so at the time. Caleb Bradshaw was killed because he was a Rattener. Folk don't like Ratteners who take their grinding bands because they can't pay their union dues, you know that as well as I do. Caleb was set upon and thrown in Porter Brook where he drowned. It had nowt to do with Liddy Ingram.'

She shrugged. 'Perhaps you're right.'

'Of course I'm right. Just because Liddy looks a bit odd and lives in the woods with her poor father folk call her names. She was kind enough to us when your foot was poisoned, wasn't she?'

Joanna nodded. Then her eyes filled with tears again and she plucked at the hated green dress. 'I don't know what my Abie would say if he could see me now,' she whispered.

He turned from putting pork on to the plates and regarded her thoughtfully. It had always been his opinion that Abraham Silkin had married Jo for purely selfish reasons. Tom had no doubt the old man had been fond of her, but she had been almost a toy as far as he was concerned, and that was how he had treated her, as a pretty little thing to dress up and show off, proof that there was still 'life in the old dog'. But he didn't voice his opinion. He contented himself with saying, 'He's not here any more.' He sat down at the table. 'Draw your chair up and have summat to eat. You'll feel better for it.'

She did as he suggested and found to her surprise that she was hungry. She was even more surprised to find that Mrs Goffin's bread was very good and the pork was tasty. 'I suppose I should be grateful to you,' she said grudgingly when she had finished.

'I don't want your gratitude, Jo. I just want you to accept things as they are and help me to make the best of them. It isn't going to be easy. Not for either of us,' he added almost under his breath.

When the meal was finished and cleared away he lit the lamp and then took out an exercise book and a stub of pencil and a ruler and sat down at the table again.

'What are you doing?' she asked when her curiosity overcame her.

'Geometry,' he answered without looking up.

'What's that?'

'Lines and angles, degrees and suchlike.'

She frowned. 'Why?'

'To better myself, of course.' He put down his pencil and gave her his full attention. 'I go to the Mechanics' Institute on the corner of Surrey Street every Tuesday evening. I've learned to read and write and my teacher says I've a good head for figures.' He couldn't keep a justifiable note of pride from his voice.

'Oh.' She stared into the fire for some time, the only sound in the room the scratch of Tom's pencil and the ticking of the cheap clock on the mantelpiece. 'Where do you work? In the daytime, I mean?'

He put down his pencil again, irritation at being interrupted tempered by relief that at least she was taking an interest in something. 'I rent a hull in Arundel Street. I make pocket knives, like I've always done.'

'I see.' She said no more, but he could feel her eyes on him, watching him as he worked.

At nine o'clock he put his book carefully away. 'I don't keep late hours,' he said. 'Because I start early of a morning.'

She eyed the bed under the window, trying to pluck up the courage to voice the thoughts that had been going through her mind all evening.

He forestalled her. 'I'll turn my back while you take your things off,' he said 'I daresay you'll not find the bed as soft as you're used to but I can't help that.'

'It's narrow,' she said as she got into it. There were no sheets and the blankets were rough on her skin.

'It's wide enough,' he said, pulling his braces down over his shoulders.

'Not for two.' She turned her eyes to the wall as she spoke.

'I shall sleep in the chair.' He nodded towards the uncomfortable wooden armchair by the fire.

She swallowed and said nervously, 'There's no need, Tom. Like you said earlier, you've paid good money for me so you've every right to—'

He strode across the room and stood over her, his face a mask of fury. 'Don't ever say that to me again, Jo,' he said, and his voice was shaking with rage. 'I'll not use my home as a brothel. I'll not come to your bed because I've "bought" you. That's not what I gave my money for so don't insult me by imagining it might be.' He turned away from her and said in more even tones, 'When I come to your bed it will be because you want me there and not for any other reason. Not now. Not ever.'

With that he threw himself in the chair and settled himself as best he could and covered himself with his coat.

'You could cover yourself with that, if you like,' she ventured, pointing towards the velvet cloak, still lying bundled up on the floor.

'No thanks. It's too fine for the likes of me. Shall I cover you with it?'

'No!' She hesitated. 'Yes. Then you can have the blanket.' It was the first time she had thought of Tom above herself.

He unrolled it and laid it over her. 'It's a beautiful cloak, all lined with silk. I wonder how Liddy came by it,' he mused.

'Stole it, I expect.' She shuddered as the cool silk touched her.

'Liddy said she never stole and she never lied. I heard her say those very words.'

'And you believed her?'

'Yes, I did.'

'Then you're a bigger fool than I took you for, Tom Cartwright.'

'A lot of things I may be, but I'm nobody's fool, Joanna,' he said quietly. He picked up the discarded blanket and settled himself back in the chair. He blew out the candle and was soon asleep.

Not so Joanna.

She lay staring up into the darkness. Tonight she should have been lying between silken sheets with Lynwood, completing the act of love they had both so long desired, but which she had denied him until the ring was on her finger. She thought of his smiling face, his teasing lip, his experienced hands. Had she been wrong to make him wait? Would it have made any difference?

Remembering the hatred and disgust in his eyes she realised that it would not.

As it was, he had rejected her in the most humiliating and degrading way imaginable and that was why she was now in this squalid room, lying in a hard and lumpy bed, covered with this hated velvet cloak that had belonged not to some fine but wayward lady but to Liddy the witch. She ought to hate him. Perhaps she did. In truth she felt too numb to know what her feelings were.

She stared up at the grey square that was the window. What was to become of her? How could she bear to stay in this dreadful room? Yet how could she escape? Where could she go? The questions circled round and round in her head as the tears dripped on to her pillow. And the answer, when it came, was no comfort. There was no escape. She had nowhere else to go. Grudgingly she forced herself to admit that she was lucky Tom had rescued her. At least he had once been her friend. And would be again if only she would let him.

At last, as a grey dawn crept into the little room, she closed her eyes and slept.

When she woke Tom had gone, but the fire was lit and the kettle was singing. A bucket of clean water stood beneath the bowl in the corner

She got up and struggled into the horrible green dress,

161

fumbling with the hooks and shedding tears of self-pity because Lily was not there to help her. Then she washed her face and stared into the little mirror over the wash-bowl. A pale face with purple shadows under the eyes looked back at her, a woebegone face, petulant and pouting with misery. Well, that was exactly how she felt. She looked round for a comb but there wasn't one so she dragged her fingers through her hair to try and give it some semblance of neatness, then sat down in the armchair and stared into the fire.

Suddenly, she was jerked out of her self-pity by a banging on the ceiling below.

She went to the door and called, 'Were you banging for me?'

'Aye, lass. I've just mashed. Thought tha might like a cuppa tea.' Mrs Goffin stood at the foot of the stairs with the teapot in her hand.

'Oh, thank you. Yes. I'll come down.' Again, Joanna raked her fingers through her hair and went down to the room below.

It was even more cramped than Joanna had realised. There was hardly room to walk round the table because of the furniture crammed in. The bed was against one wall, with a horsehair couch under the window opposite, a marble-topped chiffonier just inside the door. The fourth wall was taken up by the kitchen range with the rocking chair beside it. Everywhere was as neat as a pin and Joanna couldn't help thinking it was a good thing Mrs Goffin was so small or she would never have fitted in.

The old lady was standing at the table, which was covered by a white cloth, pouring tea. A plate of oatcakes was on the hearth, keeping warm. Mrs Goffin picked them up and offered one to Joanna. 'I can't get out much these days, my legs are bad,' she explained. 'But I like to do a bit o' baking. That's how I spend my days, baking and knitting.'

'These are very good,' Joanna said, finishing the first one and taking a second.

Mrs Goffin nodded with satisfaction. She sat in her rocking chair and began to rock back and forth. 'I'm glad young Tom's wed,' she said, munching and nodding her head in a little bird-like gesture. 'He's a good lad and deserves a good wife.' She put her head on one side. 'I'm surprised he's never mentioned he was courtin'.'

'We've known each other since we were little.' Joanna quickly changed the subject. 'May I have another of your lovely oatcakes?'

'Aye, lass. As many as you like.' Mrs Goffin was silent for a few minutes. Then she said, 'Has tha been up and given t'attic t'once-over?'

Joanna shook her head. 'Not yet.'

'Nay, I guess there's not been time.' Mrs Goffin gave her a conspiratorial smile. 'Perhaps tha can tek a look while Tom's at work. See what you think. Tha can do it up and furnish it as tha like. I'll not charge any extra for it. Tom was good to me when my Harry died and I'll be glad to pay him back.'

'That's very kind of you, Mrs Goffin.'

Mrs Goffin shrugged. 'Well, I've nobody else, have I? My Gertie died when she were but a lass and she were t'only child we were blessed with. Another cuppa tea, lass?'

'No, thank you, Mrs Goffin.' Joanna put her cup back on its saucer with a clatter and got to her feet. 'I have to go. I've just thought of something I must do. Somewhere I must go.' She hurried out of the door, leaving Mrs Goffin gasping after her in astonishment.

Of course there was somewhere she could go for help after all, she realised as she hurried along the street as fast as the ill-fitting clogs would allow. It was Mrs Goffin talking about her little daughter, Gertie, that had reminded her. Gertrude. When she knew what Lynwood had done Abraham's sister would surely take her in and care for her.

Why hadn't she thought of it before?

Chapter Eighteen

It was a long walk and Joanna had no money to take the horse bus even for a short distance to help the journey along. But her spirits were high. Gertrude would take her in, she was sure of it, when she knew the terrible thing Lynwood had done to her. She hurried as best she could along the cobbled streets in the clogs Tom had bought for her, struggled up sharp steep hills and dragged her way up less steep but longer, even more tedious, inclines. As she walked she kept her mind off her aching limbs and blistered feet by thoughts of the warm bath Gertrude would insist on giving her, the scented water, the soft towels, Gertrude's maid fussing round her – oh, the luxury of it!

It was two hours before she finally reached Blatchford House on the Glossop Road, where Gertrude lived. It was even bigger than Cliffe House and had an imposing driveway up to the porticoed front door.

Joanna went confidently up the steps and rang the bell.

After several moments a manservant opened the door. Joanna recognised him from her stay with Gertrude before her marriage to Abraham.

'Ah, good morning, Jameson,' she said briskly, but with a smile. 'Is Mrs Theakston at home?'

Jameson stared at her, outraged by her impertinence in using his name, 'T'tradesmen's entrance is round at t'back. And for your information Mrs Theakston will never be at home to t'likes of you.' With that he slammed the door in her face.

Shocked and furious, she took a step back and stared up at the house. Then she went forward again and rang the bell again and again, making sure that it jangled and pealed through the house.

It was opened again almost immediately.

'I wish to see Mrs Theakston,' she said with a lift of her head. 'I am Mrs Abraham Silkin, her sister-in-law.'

Jameson looked her up and down, a sneer on his face. 'And I'm t'Duke of Devonshire,' he said and once more closed the door in her face.

She stared at the closed door for several minutes. The great temptation was to kick it but her feet were too sore after walking for hours in the hated clogs. She looked down at herself. In the horrible shabby green dress and with not even a comb to put through her hair it was not really surprising that Jameson hadn't recognised her.

If she was to see Gertrude there was nothing for it but to swallow her pride and go round to the kitchen door. Somebody there would surely recognise her.

Fortunately, Agnes, Gertrude's maid, was there, making her mistress a cup of chocolate. She took a bit of convincing that the grubby, ill-clad creature standing before her really was Madam's sister-in-law although she had already heard the story of the bride sale – such news travelled on wings – but in the end Joanna managed to win her over and persuade her to take her to her mistress.

Gertrude was propped up in bed in a pink satin bed jacket trimmed with swansdown. She had had a bad night and had consequently woken with a sore head and a temper to match.

'Get out! Who do you think you are, marching into my bedroom like this?' she demanded as Joanna walked into the room ahead of Agnes. Without waiting for an answer she turned to Agnes. 'How dare you let this creature into my house, Agnes, let alone allow her up into my private bedroom!'

Agnes bobbed a nervous curtsy. 'Oh, Ma'am, I'm sorry. I thought it'd be all right. It's Mrs Abraham, y'see, Ma'am. Your sister-in-law,' she whispered

Gertrude peered at Joanna distrustfully.

'It's true, Gertrude. It's me. Joanna.' Joanna stepped forward, her hands outstretched. 'I know I don't look very smart, but there's a reason for it. I need your help, Gertrude. I'm desperate. Can't you see?'

Gertrude put both hands up to fend her off, her face a mask of disgust. 'Don't come near me. I want nowt to do with you. I told you the last time you were in this house you wouldn't be welcome again. Take her away, Agnes.'

Joanna couldn't believe what Gertrude was saying. The number of times she had been in this very same room, trying on dresses, drinking chocolate in cosy intimacy; the lingering smell of Gertrude's Cologne brought happy memories crowding back in stark contrast to the reception she was receiving now.

'But Gertrude ... I need help,' she pleaded, tears beginning to flow.

'Well, you'll not get it from me. And it's no good you starting to grizzle, neither. I told you that if you were bent on wedding that shiftless layabout, Lynwood, before a decent time of mourning for my dear departed brother had elapsed I would have nowt more to do with you.' She folded her be-ringed hands across the rolls of fat over her stomach.

'But Gertrude, you can't have heard what happened. Lynwood used me very badly. We were hardly wed when he—'

Gertrude nodded. 'Oh, aye. I heard all about it. I heard he couldn't wait to be shot of you once he knew who your mother was. The tale was all over Sheffield by nightfall.'

'But, Gertrude, he *sold me!*' Joanna cried desperately.

'Aye. I know that, an' all. Serves you right. I only hope the feller that bought you thinks he's got his money's worth.'

Joanna spread her hands. 'Why won't you take pity on me, Gertrude? Why won't you take me in?'

Gertrude took a long draught of chocolate, then with great deliberation put the cup back on the tray, the stern look on her face somewhat marred by the moustache of chocolate on her upper lip.

'I'll not take pity on you and I'll not take you in because you were disrespectful to my dear departed brother,' she said heavily. 'You wed Lynwood Silkin – a ne'er-do-well if ever there was one – in what I said at the time was unseemly haste. Well, you can repent at your leisure. Not mine. I wish to have nowt more to do with you. Ever. And if you dare to come to this house again I shall have you thrown out.'

'But Gertrude. For Abraham's sake—'

'For Abraham's sake!' Gertrude struggled up straight on

166

her pillows. 'You would have done well to think of Abraham, my lass, before you put another in his place and him hardly cold in his grave.' She plucked at the sheet. 'I shall never forgive you for that. Never, as long as I live.' She lay back and closed her eyes. 'You can rot in the gutter and I'll not lift a finger to help you, so never think I might. Now get out of my sight and don't ever come back.' She paused. 'Send her out through the scullery door, Agnes. We don't want the likes of her being seen in our nice, clean kitchen.'

Totally humiliated, Joanna had no choice but to allow herself to be pushed ignominiously out into the basement area. As she went up the slippery stone steps one of her clogs fell off and she had to go back and retrieve it, knowing that even the scullery maid was watching and grinning with contempt.

She began the long walk back to the town, back to the squalid little room where Tom lived, because there was nowhere else she could go. Her only consolation was that it was downhill most of the way now. Downhill in every sense, she realised with unconscious irony. As she walked she went over and over in her mind the scene in Gertrude's bedroom. She still couldn't believe that Gertrude, who had always been so kind and generous towards her, had turned into such a hard, vindictive woman and refused to help her. Indeed, thinking about it, Gertrude had almost seemed to gloat at her misfortune.

She trudged on, footsore and dispirited. She was getting hungry too, and to add to her troubles it was beginning to rain. By the time she reached the town it was raining quite hard. She remembered that Tom had turned into a little road somewhere near St Peter's Church when he had taken her to his lodging the day before, but then she had been too shocked to take much notice of where they were going and now all the little crofts and alleys looked alike. Before long she was completely lost in a maze of streets that she didn't recognise at all. The spire of the church sometimes appeared near by, sometimes further away so that she seemed to be going round in circles and there were not even landmarks that she could recognise from her days walking to the market with eggs because this was never the way she had come.

She remembered that Tom had told her last night that if she walked out he wouldn't have her back, so if she wasn't there

when he arrived home he wouldn't come to look for her. He
would think she had run away, he wouldn't know she was lost
and desperately trying to find her way back. But how could
she find her way back when she didn't even know the name of
the yard where he lived? All she knew was that he worked in
Arundel Street, but she didn't know how to get there, either.
She began to panic and tried to run but she didn't know which
direction to run in and anyway her feet were too sore. She
hurried on, peering this way and that, fear rising like bile in
her throat. All the streets seemed to look much the same, rows
of back-to-backs, interspersed with alleys that led to more
back-to-backs or the odd shop.

She went into a shop that looked slightly less dingy than the
rest.

'Can you tell me where Mrs Goffin lives, please?' she
asked the fat woman she could only just see behind stacks of
tins and packets.

'No, love. Don't know nobody by that name,' was the
answer.

She walked on through street after dingy street, often
covering the same ground again before she realised it, trying
first one shop and then another, always with the same result.

She was beginning to despair when she tried a tiny little
shop on a corner of Campo Lane.

'Oh, aye,' a customer who was standing and gossiping said,
'I know Sary Goffin. She helped all my bairns into t'world.
She lives in Sackitt's Yard.'

'Oh, thank you. Can you tell me where it is?' Joanna asked
eagerly.

'What d'you want to know for?' The woman looked her up
and down, her glance lingering on her stomach.

'I – we have a room at Mrs Goffin's house, my – er – my
husband and I.' She blushed. 'I – we've not been wed long and I
don't know my way round these parts very well yet.' She smiled
tremulously. Although it was true it didn't sound very convincing.

The women in the shop, there were four of them by now,
laughed and one of them said, 'He'll have to tie tha to
t'bedpost wi' a bit o' string. Stop tha strayin'.'

'Aw, give over, Hatty. Coom on, love, foller me,' the one
who had spoke first said. 'I'll show tha t'road. Sackitt's

168

Yard's off Hawley Croft. It's nobbut a step from here.'

Gratefully, Joanna went with the woman and found she had been only a stone's throw from Sackitt's Yard all the time. She thanked her and went into the cottage with the geranium at the door. Mrs Goffin was dozing by the fire, her knitting on her lap.

Joanna squeezed between the chiffonier and the table to the stairs and crept up to Tom's room, careful not to wake the old woman. Suddenly, the room no longer looked so bare and uninviting; it was a refuge and she was glad to be there. She sat down on the bed and kicked off her clogs, exhausted and hungry after her long, fruitless expedition. She still couldn't believe that Gertrude could have been so heartless and cruel to her, and tears of self-pity began to well up inside her once again.

She lay down on the bed and, curling herself into a ball, she sobbed out her misery at the nightmare into which her life had been so unexpectedly and cruelly plunged. And all because of Liddy the witch. She shuddered. How she hated that woman. It was bad enough, God knew, that Liddy was her mother, but why in heaven's name had she chosen to reveal herself after all this time? And on that day of all days? Why couldn't she have kept her dreadful secret to herself? The questions went on and on, round and round in her mind until she was exhausted.

She didn't realise she had fallen asleep until she woke and found the light was growing dim. She peered at the tin clock on the mantelpiece and found it was four o'clock. She rubbed her eyes. She must have been asleep for hours. She sat up and took a deep breath. The sleep had done her good, she felt stronger now and a little less inclined to burst into tears whenever she thought of the plight she was in. Crying wasn't going to help the situation, she told herself firmly. Tom had been kind enough to take pity on her and rescue her from what could only have been a worse fate and it was up to her to make the best of it.

Full of her new resolve she lit the fire with the sticks and coal from the bucket already waiting on the hearth. Then she filled the kettle from the bucket of water in the corner and put it on the trivet. The flames gave the room a soft light and once the kettle was singing it was really quite homely, she told herself. She hobbled about, making her rumpled bed and

169

looking for other things to do. But there was nothing. The room was Spartan in its furnishings but everywhere was clean and tidy, with not a thing out of place and not even a cobweb to be seen.

She sat down again and waited for the kettle. When it began to sing she poured a little water into the bowl that stood on the table in the corner so that she could wash her poor blistered and bleeding feet. Then she sat by the fire, savouring the luxury of soaking them in the warm water.

Suddenly, she heard his voice greeting Mrs Goffin and his step on the stair. Guiltily, she tried to pull the skirt of her dress over the bowl and her soaking feet so that he shouldn't see them.

'Ah, you've got the fire going, that's good,' he said as soon as he came into the room. 'I stopped off at the pie-seller's. Nice hot pies ...' He frowned and stared at her skirt, awkwardly spread to hide the bowl. 'What's the matter, Jo? Is something wrong with your feet?'

'No. Well, they were a bit dirty. I was just washing them. If you'll turn your head I'll dry them.' He did as she asked and she took them out of the water and began to dry them on her petticoat.

When she had finished he picked up the bowl to empty it out of the window.

'This water's all bloody, Jo,' he said. 'Let me see those feet.'

She tucked them up in her skirt. 'No. It wouldn't be right,' she protested.

'Oh, don't be daft, Jo. I've walked barefoot with you enough times in the past to know what your feet are like.' He came over and knelt down and took both her feet in his hands. By the light of the fire she could see that his face was grey with fatigue. 'They're in a terrible state, Jo. They're all blistered and raw. It's those clogs I got for you, isn't it?'

She shrugged. 'Well, I've not been used—' She bit her lip and started again. 'They're a bit uncomfortable, that's all.'

He stood up. He towered over her and for the first time she realised how tall he had grown since last she saw him. 'I'll go and get some salve from Mrs Goffin. She's got cures for everything, has Ma Goffin.'

170

He went downstairs and came back a little later with the salve. 'Give me your feet, Jo.'

She tucked them under her petticoat and held out her hand. 'It's all right. I can do it for myself, Tom. You don't have to—'

'Don't be daft,' he said again. Deftly, he smeared on the soothing balm. When he'd finished he looked up at her and grinned. 'This reminds me of the day I took you to Liddy—' his voice trailed off. 'I'm sorry. That wasn't very tactful.'

'It's all right, Tom. Yes, I remember it, too. She was very good to us that day, wasn't she?' Joanna stared into the fire. 'She must have known all the time that I was her daughter. Yet she never said anything.'

He nodded. 'I seem to remember her looking at you with a strange expression on her face while you were unconscious. Almost as if she was trying to burn your image on to her memory now I come to think of it, although that didn't occur to me at the time. But yes, as you say, it was odd.' He sat back on his heels. 'These feet need binding. They look painful. We need some rag.'

'It's all right. I've got some rag. Turn your back.' She pulled up her skirt and began to tear up the expensive embroidered petticoat she was still wearing from her wedding day. As she ripped apart the delicate fabric it was as if she was tearing up the last remnants of her life at Cliffe House.

When she had finished Tom took the strips and bound up her feet. 'There, now,' he said, getting to his feet. 'Does that feel better?'

She stretched them out and nodded blissfully.

'Come and eat your pie then, before it gets cold. Are you hungry?'

Joanna looked up at him and smiled. 'Starving.'

'Good.' He put his head on one side. 'That's the first time you've smiled since I brought you here, Jo,' he said thoughtfully.

'Is it?' She hobbled to the table, embarrassed.

They ate their meal, which consisted of the pies and some more of Mrs Goffin's oatcakes. Then Tom made some tea.

'I'll take a look at those clogs,' he said as they sat drinking their tea, Joanna in the wooden armchair, Tom on the bed. 'I'm sorry they made your feet so sore. I guessed when I bought them that they wouldn't fit too well, but they were all I

171

could get. I didn't realise they'd be so bad. After all, you only walked from the churchyard at Ranmoor in them. That's less than two miles.' He picked one up. 'Perhaps I can file a bit off the inside. That might make them a bit better.' He looked up and said proudly, 'You'll be able to have some proper shoes as soon as I get paid for the batch of pocket knives I'm finishing. They'll be softer for you. With any luck I should have some money by the end of the week.'

Joanna bit her lip. Tom was being so kind to her and showing so much concern for her welfare that she knew she had to tell him the truth, regardless of the consequences.

'It's not just the walk from the churchyard that crippled me, Tom. It was my own fault I got sore feet. I walked quite a long way today,' she admitted.

'Oh, where did you go?'

She closed her eyes, unable to face him. 'I went to see Gertrude, my late husband's sister. I hoped she would take me in. But she refused to have anything to do with me. And then I got lost on my way back.' She paused, fighting the desire to cry again. 'I knew you had said if I left you'd not have me back and I thought if I couldn't find my way you'd think that was what I'd done and I'd have nowhere to go at all. And then I found somebody who knew Mrs Goffin and she showed me the way home.' She opened her eyes and looked at him. 'Now you know the truth. I would have stayed with Gertrude if she'd taken me in. But she wouldn't have me.' She squeezed her eyes shut. 'She said some dreadful things to me. Things I would never have believed of her.' She opened her eyes again and looked straight at him. 'So I came back. Can I stay, Tom? Can I stay with you?'

He smiled at her. 'Do you realise what you've just said, Jo?'

'What do you mean?'

'You just said that somebody who knew Mrs Goffin showed you the way home. *Home*, Jo. Yes, lass, as long as you regard my humble room as home you're more than welcome to stay.'

Chapter Nineteen

Joanna didn't find it easy. Life was cramped in Tom's room and she longed for the high, spacious rooms, the huge staircase and the extensive gardens of Cliffe House. She missed being fussed over and pampered by Lily, her little maid, and she wondered what had become of the girl now that she, Lily's reason for being at Cliffe House, was no longer there. She hated the fact that the sun never seemed to shine through the haze of smoke and fog that permanently blanketed the town and as winter drew on and the roads and alleyways became thick with mud and slime she noticed, although this didn't seem to trouble other people, the all-pervading stench of rotting vegetation and worse. That she seemed to be the only person to notice this she put down to the fact that it was a stench very like the stink of the yard at Bradshaw's Farm, a stink she was never likely to forget.

Some days she was sunk in despair and misery and she would sit, staring at the wall, tears of self-pity coursing down her cheeks, wondering how she was going to escape this life into which Tom had 'rescued' her. She would dream of Lynwood finding her and going down on his knees to beg her forgiveness for the terrible mistake he had made in wanting to get rid of her. And when, after a suitable time, she had forgiven him he would take her back to Cliffe House where she belonged and they would live happily ever after.

At other times she became almost frantic with hatred and fury. She hated Liddy Ingram, the mother whose ill-timed revelation of their relationship had ruined her life. She hated the life she was being forced to lead. But most of all she hated

Lynwood, the man she had idolised and who had professed to love her so much, yet had cast her off her like an old shoe. No, worse than that, had discarded her in the most humiliating way possible, degrading her with never a thought for her feelings. She vowed that she would never forgive him. Never.

As her spirits seesawed Joanna tried very hard not to let it show that so many things in Tom's life irked her. The cramped room, the fact that every drop of water had to be fetched from the tap in the yard, the midden, not cleaned nor emptied often enough and shared with three other families. She realised he was doing his best for her and tried to make allowances for the fact that he had no idea of how far his 'best' fell short of what she had become used to in these past years. But since she had nowhere else to go she gritted her teeth and tried not to complain.

But they argued continually.

First it was over the bed. Tom insisted that she should have it because he was quite comfortable sleeping in the wooden armchair night after night.

'That's not fair,' she reasoned. 'You are at work all day. I've seen how you come home every night nearly dropping with tiredness. You need a good night's sleep. You should have the bed.'

'I'm all right, I tell you,' he growled, yawning widely.

'No, you're not. Just think about this, Tom. Where would we be if your hand slipped and you cut it badly because you were overtired? Those knives you work on are razor-sharp.'

'I'll not cut myself. I'm used to working with them.'

'Oh, for God's sake don't be so pig-headed and arrogant, man! You're only human. Any road, it's all right for me. I can sleep during the day. I can lie on the bed all day if I want to so it'll be no hardship to me to sleep in the chair at night. I've got my—' the word stuck in her throat but she carried on, 'mother's cloak. I can wrap that round me. You must have the bed, Tom.'

'How can I sleep in a comfortable bed knowing you're sitting up on a hard chair all night?'

'Then I'll lie on the floor.' She gave an exasperated sigh. 'Oh, for goodness sake, Tom. Be reasonable.'

He was silent for several minutes. Then he said, 'We'll take it in turns.'

'Good. It's your turn tonight.' It never even occurred to her that part of the reason Tom couldn't sleep was the fact that she was lying so tantalisingly near to him just a step across the room.

That night Joanna curled up on the floor in front of the dying embers of the fire wrapped in the blue velvet cloak, and quickly feigned sleep. Tom hesitated for some time, then realised he was beaten and got into the bed. That night he slept so solidly that he was late for work the next day. Joanna didn't wake him although she was up early, stiff and sore from her hard bed. But Tom was not happy with the situation and at the end of the week, as soon as he had been paid for the batch of penknives he had finished and received advance payment for the next lot, he bought a double bed.

'Don't worry, Jo,' he said, with only the merest trace of bitterness in his voice as she helped him to carry it up to the attic and put it together. 'I'm not expecting to share it with you. I've got my own bed.'

'I didn't say a word,' she protested.

'You didn't have to. I saw your face. But you must agree it would have looked odd to Ma Goffin if I'd bought a single bed.' He bounced up and down on the sagging springs and lumpy mattress. 'Lord, she'd have a fit if she knew we were living here together unwed! She have us out of here so fast our feet wouldn't touch the ground.'

Joanna giggled and twisted her wedding ring round on the finger. 'I've already noticed her looking to see if my waistline is beginning to bulge.' She avoided looking at Tom as she spoke.

He got to his feet. 'Well, she'll wait a long time for that, won't she,' he said, his voice expressionless.

They went downstairs to what was now their living room to eat the stew that Joanna had prepared and Mrs Goffin had cooked on top of her kitchen range. Neither of them knew that Mrs Goffin had added herbs and flavouring to the rather insipid mess of vegetables Joanna had taken down to her.

'This is good, Jo,' Tom said, helping himself to more. 'When did you learn to cook like this? Surely, not at Cliffe House?'

A shadow crossed her face. 'No, I didn't have to do

175

anything there.' She closed her eyes, remembering. Then with an obvious effort she put those thoughts behind her and said, 'I tried to remember what Martha used to do. But this tastes different, somehow. It's much nicer than what she used to make.' She poked about on her plate. 'I didn't put these little green bits in.' She looked up and they said together, 'Mrs Goffin!' and laughed.

Then Tom because serious. 'Do you mind, Jo?'

'Mind what?'

'That Mrs Goffin interfered with what you made?'

'No. I shall ask her what she put in so I can do it myself. It's delicious.' She gave herself a second helping and Tom a third.

'Careful, Jo. There won't be enough for tomorrow,' Tom warned. 'And I've not a lot of money left now I've bought the bed.'

'I've still got some potatoes and an onion and I can go to the market and get some carrots. I know my way there now and I've still got tuppence left from what you gave me today.' She leaned her elbows on the table. 'I wish there was something I could do to earn some money, Tom,' she said. 'I feel so useless.'

'You scrubbed out the attic and you keep this room clean.'

She shrugged and looked at her hands, no longer soft and white. 'That doesn't take long.' She didn't tell him she had found that immersing herself in scrubbing and cleaning was the best way to work off her hatred and frustration.

Tom regarded her thoughtfully. She seemed to have settled down to life with him remarkably well, considering what she had become used to in the last five years. Nevertheless, he had been very careful not to speak of that life and she never spoke of it, either. They lived for the present, he simply because he was happy to have her near and to care for her, she, he suspected, because she was waiting. For what, he had no idea. Neither, he rather thought, had she.

'I've been thinking, Jo,' he said, when the meal was cleared away and the plates washed. 'It's time you paid your mother a visit.'

'*What?*' Joanna had been sitting and gazing into the fire. Now her head shot up and she looked at him in amazement.

'Go and see Liddy the witch? After what she's done to me? You can't be serious, Tom.'

'Yes, I am. I've thought about it a lot. And I think you should go. After all, she is your mother.'

'I don't need reminding of *that*. It's something I'd prefer to forget, if you don't mind.' She hunched her shoulders and set her mouth in a straight line. 'I'm not going to see that woman so you needn't try to make me. I shall never forgive her for what she did to me. I want nothing to do with her. Nothing. Ever.' Each word was punctuated with a thump of her fist on her lap.

Tom sighed. He had known mention of Liddy would provoke yet another argument, but it was something that he felt needed to be said. He picked up his pipe from the hearth. It was his one luxury, a pipe of tobacco after his evening meal, and he savoured it. He rammed a few shreds of tobacco into the bowl and lit it with a spill from the fire. It was not until he had got it going to his satisfaction that he began again.

'She must have had a reason for doing what she did,' he said carefully.

'Yes. She wanted to humiliate me. Well, she managed that, all right, didn't she! Showing all the world that I was the daughter of a witch. *And* she turned the man I loved away from me.' She blinked away the tears that threatened, furious with Tom. 'Why did you have to remind me about that terrible day?' she cried.

'Because I think you ought to go and see Liddy,' he persisted quietly.

'Well, I'm not going, so you can save your breath,' she said. 'Any road, I couldn't walk there in these clogs.'

'Then go and buy yourself a pair of shoes.' He reached in his pocket and handed her a shilling.

She looked at it but didn't reach out for it. 'I thought you said you'd no money left,' she said.

'I said I'd not a lot left. Not that I had none at all. There's enough for you to buy shoes. I'd have bought them for you but—' he made a face. 'Well, I didn't do very well with the clogs, did I?'

She looked down at her feet. 'They're not so bad now my

177

feet are used to them,' she said. 'As long as I don't walk far,' she added quickly.

'That's what I thought.' He threw the shilling and it landed in her lap. 'So get yourself some shoes and go and see your mother.'

'I'll not visit that old witch.' Her mouth was still set in the stubborn line he was beginning to recognise.

'Ma Perkins, the pawnbroker, has some shoes in her window. I'm sure you'll find a pair to fit.' He took the last draw of the evening on his pipe and laid it very deliberately on the hearth. 'I'm doing my best for you, Jo,' he said, his voice quiet. 'I've thought about this a lot and I'd not say you should go and see Liddy if I didn't think it was the right thing to do. She must have had a reason for doing what she did. I think you should go and find out what it was. That's my last word on the subject. Now, will you go to your bed and leave me to go to mine? I've to be up early in the morning.'

'Yes. I'll be glad to get away from you telling me what I should and shouldn't do.' She got to her feet and flounced over to the stairs in the corner. 'Just remember I'm not your wife, Tom Cartwright,' she shouted. 'I'll not be ordered about by you.'

'If you don't keep your voice down Mrs Goffin will hear and you'll be ordered out into the street,' he shouted back at her.

'Oh, you always think you know best, don't you!' She took off her clog and threw it at him. It was only meant as a gesture but she had flung it harder and more accurately than she intended and it hit him on the head.

For a second she froze, watching as he put his hand up to where the clog had hit him. His expression was one of disbelief.

'Oh, Tom, I'm sorry. I shouldn't have done that.' She rushed across to him. 'I didn't mean to hit you, honestly I didn't. I don't know what made me throw it. Oh, you've gone dreadfully pale. Let me see. Is there a bump?'

He pushed her away and got to his feet. Now she realised that his face was drained of colour because he was white with fury. 'Don't you ever do that to me again, Joanna,' he said, towering over her, his eyes narrowed. His voice was ominously quiet, which was far worse than if he had shouted at her. He went on, 'I've given you lodging in my room, I've gladly looked after you and cared for you these past weeks because I—' he hesitated, 'Well, I've been happy to help you. I've even put up with the way you argue and disagree with everything I say because I know you've had a rough time and you're finding things difficult. But if you're going to start throwing things at me I don't want you here. I'm not a violent man, I've seen too much violence in my time, and I'll not have it in my house.' He turned away from her, his expression one of disdain. 'Now, either go to bed or get out. You can please yourself which it is.'

She knew she had gone too far and she put her arms round him and laid her head on his chest. 'Oh, Tom, I'm so sorry. Please forgive me. I'll never do anything like it again. I promise. I don't know what came over me.' She looked up at him, totally contrite, her face streaked with tears.

He stared down at her. God, didn't she know what she was doing to him? Had she no idea how much he loved her? How much he wanted her? How he longed for her in his bed? Surely she must hear his heart hammering against her ear. He closed his eyes. It would be so easy now. All he had to do was to put his arms round her and bend his head— But he wasn't sure that he could stop at a kiss and he had promised himself – and her – that he would not take her to his bed until she was willing.

With iron self-control he took her arms and placed them at her sides. Then he took a step back. 'You'd better go to bed,' he said, his voice not quite steady.

Chastened and for some reason oddly disappointed, she went up to her attic, where she lay for a long time staring up into the blackness. She had never seen Tom so angry, and all because she refused to visit Liddy the witch, the woman who had ruined her life. For once she allowed her thoughts to roam to the realms of how things would have been if Liddy hadn't appeared. Married to Lynwood, cherished and loved by him, and living at Cliffe House. She thought of days spent calling on ladies who didn't really want to see her and entertaining them in return when they called on her. No, that was unkind and only part of the story. She thought of nights with

Lynwood, spent between scented silken sheets . . .

She thumped her pillow; it was harsh and filled with prickly straw, a far cry from soft down and silk. Oh, Liddy Ingram had a lot to answer for. But she would go and visit her since Tom had been so determined that she should. And when she got there she would tell her just how much she hated her and how she had ruined her life.

With that she turned over and fell asleep. She dreamed she was lying in a huge soft bed between silk sheets and Lynwood was beside her, whispering to her, stroking her, kissing her. She said his name, over and over again, but then, as a shaft of moonlight caught his face she could see that it was not Lynwood at all. It was Tom.

She woke with Tom's name on her lips and it was a long time before she slept again.

The next day Joanna set off to see Liddy Ingram. It was a frosty morning and as she walked along the streets her breath was cloudy on the morning air. She carried the blue cloak over her arm, determined to return it to its rightful owner, but eventually she was glad to put it round her shoulders against the cold wind that whipped through the alleyways and round corners. Stubbornly independent, she hadn't stopped to buy shoes as Tom had ordered, but wore the uncomfortable clogs for the journey. At the back of her mind was the hope that when he saw her raw and bloodied feet he would feel guilty and be sorry he had made her go; nevertheless she had prudently wrapped her feet in the last of her fancy petticoats before putting on the clogs so that they shouldn't be too painful.

Her step slowed as she walked up Hangingwater Lane. She was nearing the end of her journey and she was a bit nervous. She had come determined to tell Liddy Ingram what she thought of her, but what if she really was a witch? What if she were to cast some kind of evil spell on her?

She stood on the bridge over the River Porter, undecided what to do. The sluice that directed the water to the dam that fed Bradshaw's Wheel had been closed and the dam drained so that it could be repaired. It was lined or 'puddled' with clay and the retaining wall at the end was built of huge dressed stones. All the men who worked in the grinding hulls were in the dam now, re-puddling the base and sides and making sure all the leaks were plugged. It was work that had to be done from time to time because if the dam were to burst tons of water would flood the valley, but while the work was being carried out no money was being earned so every man had to do his share. Joanna could see both Saul and Jacob Bradshaw working there with the others now, up to their ears in clay. Nobody would stop until the work was done and the sluice gates opened again to fill the dam.

On the other side of the river smoke curled up from the chimney at Bradshaw's Farm. Martha would be there. She hadn't seen Martha for such a long time and Saul was safely occupied. She turned down on to the well-trodden path to the farm.

Chapter Twenty

Martha was in the kitchen making bread. She looked older, thinner and more wizened than ever. But her face lit up when Joanna walked in at the door and they hugged and kissed each other, getting covered in flour and laughing and crying all at the same time.

When they had got their first greetings over Martha made a pot of her thick black tea and they sat at the table together talking about everything and anything except what was important to them both.

'I saw Saul at the dam. He's covered in mud so I reckoned it was safe to come and see you,' Joanna said.

'Aye, there was a bit of a leak. They'll none of them be finished for hours yet. Ee, it's good to see you, lass.' Martha got to her feet and fetched a tin of cakes.

Joanna watched her, frowning. 'Your rheumatism is bad, Martha. You can hardly walk.'

'Some days it's worse than others. I manage. Look at you. You're thinner than ever, lass. Have one of my special cakes. You allus liked them.'

'Yes. I've missed them.' Joanna took a cake and bit into it. 'How do you manage? The dairy and everything? Who takes the eggs to market? You can't walk that far now, I'm sure.'

'No, I can't. I get a lift on the carrier's cart. And he brings me back afterwards.' Martha smiled. 'I've seen you at the market. Twice. But you didn't notice me.'

'But I looked for you! I'd have bought your eggs. I thought you'd stopped coming. You must be in a different place. Why didn't you call out to me?'

Martha picked up her cup and examined the contents. 'I wasn't sure you'd want to see me.'

'I'll always want to see you, Martha.' She gazed out of the window at the yard. It was well swept and scrubbed. 'I thought of coming back to you after . . .' she paused, 'but Tom said I shouldn't. He said Saul would—'

'Aye. He's right. Saul would give you no peace. You'd be nowt but a slave here and he'd not keep his hands off you. Not now you've grown into such a lovely lass. Not even knowing— He's nowt but an animal, that man.' Martha spoke in a low voice but her tone was vicious. She was silent for several minutes, then her face broke into a smile. 'So you're with Tom now, love?'

Joanna nodded. 'He bought me. For five shillings. Like a prize heifer,' she said bitterly. She looked out of the window. 'Of course you'll have heard all about that.'

'Aye, lass, I heard. It were a bad business. But I was glad to hear Tom rescued you. He'll look after you. He's a good lad, is Tom.'

'I'll not be staying with him for long. Only until I can—' her voice trailed off. 'The yard looks better than I've ever seen it,' she said briskly, changing the subject. 'All scrubbed and clean.'

'Jacob sees to it. He lives here now. He's a good help.'

Joanna raised her eyebrows. 'But what about Bella? And the children?'

'She left him and took them with her.'

'Because of what happened that day?' There was no getting away from the subject. 'Because of what Liddy the witch said?'

'Aye.'

Joanna leaned her head on her hands. 'Oh, God. What a mess! And to think I'd always imagined I was high-born and belonged in a big house with servants and a carriage. I thought that was why I felt so at home at Cliffe House. Oh, how are the mighty fallen!'

'No call to be ashamed of your roots, love. My Jacob's a good lad,' Martha said primly. 'He allus did right by his children.'

Joanna looked up, her face wet with tears. 'He didn't do right by me, did he?'

'How could he? He'd no way of knowing you were his.' Martha leaned over and laid her gnarled hand on Joanna's, smiling. 'But it pleases me more than I can say to think you're my flesh and blood, lass.' Then she became serious and shook her head. 'I can tell you Jacob was reet cut up when Bella left and took the children. He denied everything, of course, insisted she'd got the wrong end of the stick and it were nowt to do with him, said he'd never been near Liddy. But he would say that, wouldn't he? Wouldn't want to admit he'd been with her at the same time as he were going with Bella.' She shrugged. 'Any road, it's over now. Bella's gone and Jacob's back here, helping his dad. Mind, he's a changed man. Never goes out and doesn't have to lot to say for himself.'

'But it's not over, Martha,' Joanna said vehemently. 'I'm here. And I have to live with the fact that Jacob is my father and even worse, that my mother is that filthy old witch who lives in the woods.' She shuddered with disgust.

'We don't know the whole story, lass,' Martha said. 'And to her credit Liddy didn't try to keep you with her. Just imagine what your life would have been like if she had.'

'Oh, Martha, don't. I can't bear even to think about that,' Joanna groaned.

'But she didn't. She gave you to me. She knew I'd care for you and love you.'

Joanna gave her a watery smile. 'And I'll always be grateful to you for that, Martha dear.' She looked away, her eyes bleak again. 'But I shall never forgive that woman for what she did to me. She'd kept quiet about it for all those years, why couldn't she carry her secret to the grave? And if she needed to tell me why couldn't she have done it quietly, so nobody else needed to know? Why did she have to appear on my wedding day, of all days? Oh, Martha, I was so shamed.' She covered her face with her hands and began to sob.

'Aye, but your new husband shamed you even more, didn't he? Auctioning you off to the highest bidder, indeed! And him not married to you for more than five minutes. What he did was the real shame.' Martha shook her head sadly. 'Oh, aye, Bella was there. She told me all about it.'

'I didn't blame him, Martha. It was the shock of finding

out— I don't think he realised what he was doing,' Joanna protested defensively.

'That's as may be.' Martha was clearly not convinced. 'Have you seen him since? Has he come looking for you?'

'No. At least, not as far as I know. But how can he? He's no way of knowing where I am, has he? Sheffield's a big place.'

Martha sniffed. 'There's ways and means of finding out if he'd been of a mind to.'

Joanna nodded. 'Maybe.' She drank the rest of her tea in silence, then got up to go.

Martha put out her hand. She couldn't let Joanna go on a note of animosity. 'Thank you for coming to see me, love,' she said. 'It's been a treat to talk to you.'

Joanna went to her and put her arms round her. 'I'd come more often if I could, you know that, don't you, Martha?'

'Aye, I know that, love. I understand. If it weren't for Saul—'

Joanna turned away and picked up the cloak that had fallen to the ground when she first came in. 'I was really on my way to see Liddy, but when I saw Saul was up to his eyes in mud working on the dam I knew he'd be there for several hours so I thought I'd be safe to risk coming here.'

'Aye. I'd never have let you stay, else.' Martha raised her eyebrows. 'You say you're on your way to see your mother?'

'Don't call her that!' Joanna snapped.

Martha put out a hand and fingered the rich velvet of the cloak. 'Ah, that brings back memories. You were such a little scrap, wrapped up all warm and cosy in that cloak when I found you. I wonder where Liddy came up such a beautiful thing. It must have cost a pretty penny.'

'Stole it, I shouldn't wonder.' Joanna bundled it up so that the red silk lining was uppermost.

'Liddy's never been known as a thief and it's wrong of you to suggest she might be,' Martha said sternly. 'And she did the best she could by you, whatever you might think of her. It must have been a terrible hard thing to do, to give up the baby she'd carried under her heart for all those months. I don't think I could have done it.' She shook her head. 'You mustn't think too hardly of her, love.'

185

'If you say she did the best she could for me then – although I think she just wanted to be rid of me – why did she do what she did to me twenty years later?' Her shoulders sagged. 'Not that I care any more. I'm only going to see her because Tom said I should, not because I want to.' She gritted her teeth. 'But while I'm there I'm going to make her tell me why she chose to ruin my life.' She closed her eyes. 'God, to have done a thing like that she must hate me almost as much as I hate her,' she said from between her teeth.

'That's no way to talk, love,' Martha said, her voice soft. 'Don't go to her with hate in your heart.'

'Then I'll not go at all,' Joanna said.

'Now you've come this far to see her you must finish the journey,' Martha said with a sigh. She got to her feet and kissed her. 'God bless you, child.'

Although she couldn't see them from the path along by the river Joanna could hear the sounds of the men still working in the dam as she walked back to the road. Her father would be working there, she realised with a shock. Her father, Jacob Bradshaw. Over the years she had had little to do with him but she had always liked him better than his boorish brother, Caleb. Or his disgusting father, Saul. But to learn that Jacob was her natural father turned her stomach and she didn't look back when she reached the road but plunged into the track through Whitely Woods towards the clearing where the charcoal burner and his daughter lived. Her mother. She shuddered with revulsion.

The wood had hardly changed in the five years since she had last been there with Tom to gather berries and sometimes to walk by the river, little more than a deep, fast-running stream here. Some places were a little more overgrown perhaps, and here and there a tree had blown over in the wind and lay gathering moss, and there were several clearings where the charcoal burner had coppiced the woods for his charcoal. She walked through the dead and rustling leaves, reviving memories of the dreams that had centred round the poor drowned girl in the river, whose grave she had tended so lovingly for all those years and around whom she had woven all her hopes for the future. The girl's identity would now

186

never be known, yet the dreams Joanna had cherished had sustained her through the harsh years at Bradshaw's Farm. In a way those dreams of living in a large house with servants and beautiful clothes had come true, thanks to Abraham Silkin. Her eyes filled with tears. 'Oh, Abie,' she whispered, 'if you could see me now!'

She knew she was nearing the place where the charcoal burner lived because of the pungent smell of smoke, stinging her nose and making her eyes water. As she reached the clearing she could see the old man, his stove-pipe hat balanced on the top of his head, grey hair wisping from under it, sawing wood on the far side of the smouldering stack, near the hut where he lived with his daughter. There was no sign of Liddy.

Her whole body seemed to sag with relief, making her realise just how tense and nervous she had been at the thought of confronting Liddy. Now, at least she could tell Tom she had paid the old witch a visit. It wasn't her fault if she wasn't at home. She dumped the cloak unceremoniously in the fork of a tree, then sick with relief she turned to go back the way she had come. But her path was barred by the filthy, black-clad figure of her mother standing and watching her, a basket of herbs in her hand. The sight made her start so much that she nearly fell over.

'You crept up behind me!' she said furiously, clutching at a branch to keep her balance. 'You made me jump!'

'I was interested to see where you were going,' Liddy answered, staring at her coolly.

'I came to see you.'

'Yes, I thought as much. Well, here I am. What do you want with me?'

Joanna felt uncomfortable. Even in her tattered black cloak and hat, with her greasy hair falling in rat's tails over her face, Liddy was in imposing figure. Drawn up to her full height she was nearly half a head taller than Joanna and as she looked down her nose her expression held no hint of recognition, but bordered on hostility.

'You know who I am?' Joanna asked uncertainly.

'Of course.' There was the merest inclination of Liddy's head. She waited. 'Well?' she said at last.

187

'I've brought your cloak back. I stitched the other half of the clasp back.'

'It's yours. You should keep it.'

'I don't want it.' Suddenly, a blast of cold wind rustled through the trees and Joanna gave an involuntary shiver.

'It would warm you. It would keep out the wind.'

'I don't *want it*, I tell you!' Joanna licked her lips, plucking up the courage to say what she had come to say. 'You ruined my life,' she blurted out. The words hadn't come out right. They sounded petulant instead of accusing.

'Did I?' Liddy raised one eyebrow.

'You know perfectly well you did. On my wedding day. Didn't you see what happened after you ... after you *appeared?*'

Liddy gave a sigh but said nothing.

'Didn't you see how I was strung up and sold like a pig at a market? And all because *you* chose that moment to reveal yourself as my mother!'

'I'm sorry—'

'Sorry! It's a bit late for saying that! Why did you do it? Why did you choose that day, of all days? It was a cruel, evil thing to do.'

Liddy was silent for several seconds, staring at Joanna and with a shock the girl realised that she was looking not into black eyes, as she had always thought, but blue ones, the mirror of her own. 'You could say it was a test,' Liddy said at last. 'I needed to be sure you were doing the right thing.'

'I don't understand what you're talking about,' Joanna snapped. 'Any road, why should you care what happened to me? You'd never bothered before. You didn't come near when I married Abraham.'

'That shows how little you know.' Something, a softening of expression, it could hardly be called a smile, crossed Liddy's face.

'Well, your test as you call it failed.' Joanna's eyes filled with angry tears. 'Because of what you did to me I've lost everything, my beautiful house, all my money, my new husband, and I'm reduced to living in poverty and misery. Why, in God's name, did you choose my wedding day of all days to tell me I was the spawn of a witch?'

Liddy gave an almost imperceptible wince. Then she shrugged. 'That's only what people choose to call me. They're glad enough of my help when they need a cure for their ailments.'

'You cast spells. God knows, you cast an evil spell on me, that day,' Joanna said savagely.

'I cast no spell on you, my child,' Liddy said, her voice low.

'Don't call me that!'

'But you are my child. And I am your mother. One day you will be glad of what I did that day.'

'*Never!* You've ruined my life. Don't you realise that?' Joanna didn't wait for any more but pushed past Liddy and rushed back the way she had come, her eyes full of angry tears.

Liddy watched her go. Then she said quietly. 'You'll be back, my child. You'll be back.'

Chapter Twenty-One

Joanna began the long walk back to the town in a seething fury, almost blinded by tears of frustrated rage. That dreadful, horrible, hateful old witch! How could she have done such a wicked thing to her own daughter? Worse, she didn't care about the life she'd wrecked. She had shown not the slightest hint of remorse at what she had done. What price motherly love, Joanna thought bitterly. She wished she had never gone to Whitely Woods to see her. It was all Tom's fault for insisting that she should go.

To add to her rage, the hated clogs had begun to chafe her heels as she walked and although she refused to admit it, even to herself, she was missing the thick, comforting warmth of the velvet cloak. The green dress that Tom had bought for her was no protection against the keen north wind that had sprung up, chilling her bones and whistling round her ears till it made her head ache. She tried to hurry, both to generate a little warmth and to escape the snow clouds that were gathering ominously, but before long the first flakes of snow began to fall and before she could reach Sackitt's Yard it was snowing heavily.

She lifted the latch with fingers that were stiff with cold and almost fell into Mrs Goffin's room. After the bitter cold outside it was warm to the point of stuffiness. Surprised as much by the blast of cold air as Joanna's sudden entry the old lady looked up from her knitting and beckoned her over to the fire.

'Ee, lass, look at tha. Tha's nowt better than a snowman, and starved to death wi' it. Come over here and sit by the fire and get thyself warm, do.'

Joanna sidled past the furniture to the stairs. She didn't want to stay and talk to Mrs Goffin, her head was throbbing too painfully from coming into the warm room after the cold air outside.

'No, it's all right, thanks, Mrs Goffin. I'd best go on up and get some dry clothes on and the fire going. Tom will be frozen when he gets in. It's snowing really hard now.' She could hardly speak, her teeth were chattering so much.

'Aye. Tha'd best get them damp things off.' Mrs Goffin nodded sagely. 'Tha don't want to catch tha death.'

Joanna dragged herself up the stairs. The room was nearly as cold as the air outside but Tom always left sticks and coal ready for her to light the fire so it shouldn't take long to warm up. She took off her dress and because she had nothing else to put on sat huddled in the blanket from Tom's bed. It was not a very thick blanket and she still shivered as she sat impatiently watching the flames lick round the sticks and coal. It seemed to be taking an age for the fire to warm the place and her headache was getting worse. She filled the kettle from the bucket in the corner and put it on the hob. Perhaps a cup of tea would warm her.

'Joanna, love,' Suddenly, Mrs Goffin's voice called from the bottom of the stairs. 'I've a bowl of my nice soup to warm tha. Will tha fetch it? My legs are too crammocky to climb t'stairs to bring it up.'

'Oh, that's very kind of you, Mrs Goffin.' She got to her feet and went down the stairs, still wrapped in the blanket. The soup smelt delicious.

'I'll send some more up when Tom gets back,' Mrs Goffin smiled her toothless smile, 'but I reckon tha can do wi' a drop now.' Her smile faded. 'Tha looks a bit peaky, lass.'

'I've got a bit of a headache and I can't seem to get warm,' Joanna admitted, warming her hands round the soup bowl.

'Well, away wi' tha, then, back upstairs and sup t'soup. It'll warm tha cockles.' The old woman watched as Joanna remounted the stairs, then went back to her knitting.

Joanna drank the soup gratefully. It was very good, but she still felt cold and shivery and the fire didn't seem to be throwing out much heat. She piled on most of the coal from the coal bucket, enough usually to last all evening, but even so the

191

room seemed to get no warmer. She pulled the blanket more closely round her and sat on the floor, resting her throbbing head on the seat of the armchair. Even as she sat there icy fingers seemed to be playing up and down her spine, chilling her even further.

Of course, it was all Liddy's fault. And Tom's, because he had persuaded her to go to see her. She was a witch, everyone knew that, so it was hardly surprising that she'd cast a spell on her. Very likely she would die. It didn't matter. Dying would be preferable to living in this hovel with a man who used to be her friend but now she didn't even like very much. She didn't like him very much because he made her do things she didn't want to do. Like going to see Liddy the witch. Her mother. Who'd put a spell on her that made her feel cold. And ill. It was all Liddy's fault. All Liddy's fault she felt so ill. And Tom's. It was his fault, too.

She was still sitting there, muttering the same things over and over again when Tom arrived home from work. He had brought more of Mrs Goffin's soup up with him and he placed it on the hearth so that he could look at Joanna.

'Jo! Whatever's wrong? This place is like an oven yet you're sitting there wrapped in a blanket.'

'I can't get warm,' she muttered through chattering teeth. 'It's all your fault. And hers. You made me go there and now she's cast a spell on me. It's made me ill. I should never have gone. She doesn't care about me. She hated me. That's why she spoiled everything for me.' Tears of weakness coursed down her cheeks.

'You're ill, Jo.' Tom helped her to her feet. 'Come on, get into my bed. That's right. Wait a minute and I'll fetch your cloak. That'll keep you warm.'

She tried to shake her head, but it had something like a lead weight rolling around inside it. 'You can't. I gave it back to her,' she whispered.

'You did *what?* You mean to tell me you walked all the way home from Whitely Woods in that thin dress and no shawl? In this weather?' He stared down at her. 'Whatever possessed you to do such a stupid thing, Jo?'

'It was hers. I don't want anything of hers.'

'My God, sometimes you do some stupid things, Jo.'

She closed her eyes and muttered, 'She's wicked. She cast a spell on me. It's your fault. You made me go. I expect I'll die.'

He sat down on his heels beside her and put his hand on her forehead. It was burning even though she was still shivering with cold. 'Don't be daft. Of course Liddy didn't cast a spell on you. You've caught a chill, Jo. I expect you caught it by walking through the streets with no coat. And all because you were too pig-headed to keep that cloak.'

'I didn't want it. It was hers, so I gave it back to her,' Joanna explained feebly. 'I don't want anything that reminds me of her.'

'I don't care who it belonged to, nor what it reminded you of. It was a good, warm cloak and you were a fool not to keep it. I'll never be able to afford to buy you another one as good. Oh, sometimes you make me despair, Joanna.' He got to his feet with a degree of impatience. 'I'd better go and see if Mrs Goffin's got a potion I can give you. She's got cures for most things. With a bit of luck she'll soon have you well again.'

She didn't open her eyes. 'I don't want to be well. I want to die.'

'Don't talk rubbish. I'll not let you die.' His voice softened and he laid his hand on her burning forehead. 'I love you far too much to let you die, Jo,' he said softly.

He went downstairs and after a few minutes came back with something in a mug which he forced between her lips. It tasted foul and in her fuddled state she was certain it was poison that Liddy had made up for her. She didn't care, in fact she was happy to drink it. When she was dead Tom would understand. With that she fell asleep.

She had no idea how long she slept for. All she knew was that every time she opened her eyes Tom was there, wiping her face with a cool cloth, moistening her lips with water, or forcing her to drink more of the foul-tasting medicine. He changed the sweat-soaked bed for lavender-smelling sheets borrowed from Mrs Goffin and he washed her and put her into a clean shift that he bought from the pawnshop because she had neither the strength or the will to do it for herself.

All Joanna's efforts were being channelled into keeping Liddy the witch away from her bedside. Whether her eyes were open or closed she could see the black-clad figure in her battered straw hat. She was always somewhere in the room, standing by the fire, sitting at the table or squatting in the corner. The worst time was when she came and bent over the bed, a leering smile on her face that revealed her broken and blackened teeth, her blue eyes mocking through her curtain of rat-tailed hair.

'Don't let her touch me,' she would scream, panic-stricken. 'Don't let her take me away.' Then she would feel strong arms round her, holding her, keeping her safe, and the vision of Liddy would recede, only to return again and again.

Then one morning she woke just as grey fingers of dawn were creeping into the room and discovered that Liddy had gone. Carefully, she turned her head to look round the room, but there was no sign of her. She struggled up on to one elbow, anxious to make quite sure she wasn't crouched in a far corner, waiting to come out at her, but there was nothing there. Only Tom, dozing in the chair by the remains of the fire.

She fell back on her pillow. 'She's gone,' she whispered weakly. 'Oh, thank God, she's gone.'

Tom was by her side in a flash. 'It's all right, Jo, I'm here,' he said, taking her hand and watching her anxiously.

She smiled at him. 'Yes, it's all right. She's gone. At last she's gone.' She licked her lips. 'I'm very thirsty, Tom.'

Tom brought her a cup of water and held her up so that she could drink it. Then he lowered her gently back on to the pillow.

She put her hand up and touched his face. 'Your beard needs trimming,' she murmured, then she fell into a gentle, healing sleep.

Tom stood looking down at her, his eyes moist. After days and nights watching over her he was exhausted, but she was going to live and he was thankful. He dragged himself up to the attic and flung himself down on Joanna's bed and slept his first proper sleep for over a week.

With Tom's care and the help of Mrs Goffin's nourishing broth Joanna's recovery was speedy. Before long she was able to tell him of her terrible nightmares, of Liddy the witch's constant and terrifying presence during her illness.

But what neither she nor Tom ever spoke of were the things he had done for her at that time, intimate things of which she was only dimly aware. She had vague memories of her fevered body being sponged with warm water, of her linen being changed, and she realised that only Tom could have done these things. The knowledge hung between them, an unspoken barrier of embarrassment.

As soon as he was able Tom went back to work in his hull in Arundel Street.

'I'll be home late,' he told Joanna,' because I've got behind with my work. I've an order for a dozen lobster knives that should have been finished days ago. They'll pay well but I'll not get the money till I deliver them.'

'I'm sorry, Tom. It was my fault you couldn't go to work,' she said, feeling guilty.

'I'm not blaming you. You couldn't help being ill, Jo,' he said. He picked up his bag and slung it over his shoulder. 'I've been thinking,' he said, not looking at her. 'It's not right the way you were treated by that man.' He always called Lynwood 'that man' as if he couldn't bear to speak his name. 'He's no right to your fortune. From what you've told me you're a rich woman. You shouldn't be living from hand to mouth in two rooms like this.'

'Abraham's will said that if I remarried everything would go to Lynwood,' she said flatly. 'Well, I did remarry. We both knew what would happen but Lynwood said it wouldn't matter because he would always look after me. He said Abraham had put that clause in his will to prevent me from marrying anybody else. Lynwood said Abie wanted me to marry him.' She made a wry face. 'And I was fool enough to believe him.'

Tom frowned. 'You could always go to the lawyer who drew up the will, Jo. Tell him what happened. I'm sure it's not legal, what that man did to you.'

'Yes, I suppose I ought to do something,' she said with a sigh. 'I realise I'm being a drain on you, Tom. I'm sorry.'

He flushed angrily. 'I didn't say it for that. I don't want your money, Jo. All I want is justice for you. I want you to be able to buy a decent dress and a pair of shoes instead of having to pick over second-hand goods at the pawnbroker's.'

His voice dropped. 'You deserve better than that, Jo.'

'Maybe I do.' She shrugged. Then she pulled her shoulders back. 'But I'll not go begging to Mr Garthwaite and have him say "I told you so" in that horrible way of his. He warned me against marrying Lynwood in the first place but I wouldn't listen.'

'But if it's your due—'

'I'll not go, Tom.' Her voice rose and she banged her hand down on the table. 'I'll go begging in the street before I ask him for a penny. Even if I am entitled to it. And that's my last word.'

He sighed and hitched his bag further on to his shoulder. 'As you will, Jo. I can't stand here arguing with you, I've my living to make. I don't know what time I'll be back.'

He left then and she began to tidy up the room and make his bed. Then she went up the narrow stairs to tidy her own room. She smiled wryly to herself. After all the intimate things Tom had done for her during her illness there had been no question of him wanting to share her bed once she had recovered. She was puzzled over this, and even a little disappointed if she was honest. After all, she told herself, no woman likes to think she is totally unattractive to a man and it would have been good for her self-esteem to have been able to refuse him.

When she had finished the tasks she had set herself, taking the slops down to the stinking midden, and fetching clean water from the tap in the yard for herself and for Mrs Goffin and staying for a brief chat with the old woman, she sat down at the table and reviewed her situation.

Clearly Tom found her a burden. But at the moment she had nowhere else to go. Lynwood didn't want her and her pride would not let her go to Mr Garthwaite for help. There was only one thing for it, she must find work for herself and in due course perhaps a room of her own. For some strange reason this last thought gave her no pleasure.

She brushed her hair carefully and put on the shawl that Tom had borrowed for her from Mrs Goffin. It was faded and shabby but neatly darned. She didn't know where she might find work although she was sure it wouldn't be difficult because she could read and she could write a fair hand, thanks to Abraham. He had also taught her simple arithmetic. She made a face. That she could also sing and play the piano a little was likely to be of limited value in finding work in this area of Sheffield.

She left the house and walked through narrow ginnels to streets that were almost as narrow. She walked along Campo Lane, past St Peter's Church, and eventually found herself in Fargate, busy and noisy with traffic. On the corner was Coles' Department Store and she remembered very well shopping here with Gertrude, buying dresses, gloves, shoes, parasols on the merest whim. In another life. She walked up and down for some time, then plucked up her courage and went inside. Nobody would recognise her from the old days she was sure and her skills would be appreciated.

The scene inside the store immediately took her back to the days when she had money to spend and a carriage waiting at the door. The distinctive smell, a mixture of wax polish, gas mantles, which kept the shop brightly lit and sparkling all day, leather and what she could only describe as 'newness'; the tall chairs by the counters so that ladies could sit and choose at their ease and leisure. Suddenly, a flood of nostalgia swept over her for the days when her elderly, doting husband was still alive.

A floor walker in a black swallow-tail coat approached her before she had taken more than three steps inside the store.

'What do you want?' he asked rudely, looking down his nose at her.

'I'm looking for work. I can read and write a fair hand and my arithmetic is good. Could you take me to your employer, please?' She spoke quietly but with authority.

For a moment he was taken aback. Then he looked her up and down. 'You've got a nerve,' he said, his lip curling as his eyes rested on the darns in her shawl, the frayed and mud-spattered hem to her faded green dress. And the clogs. 'Coming in here dressed like that and expecting work. This is a high-class establishment, I'll have you know.' He raised his eyebrows. 'But of course, Madam, if you have suitable refer-ences—?' His voice was heavy with sarcasm and he gave a supercilious smirk as he saw her face fall. 'No, I thought not. Then, this way, if you please.'

Joanna tried to draw herself up to her full diminutive height

197

as he almost frog-marched her to the door. 'Do you realise who I am?' she asked, trying to sound imperious and at the same time to twist round and look up at him.

'Who you are is of no concern to me. My concern is for the good name of the store.' She found herself bundled unceremoniously out into the street.

She was so humiliated she hadn't the courage to try another shop and she walked up and down for a long time wondering what to do. A group of buffer girls passed her, laughing and joking together. Clad in their filthy buff brats and red head rags, their faces and hands black from the work they did, they stood out from the rest of the passers by and Joanna was tempted to ask if there might be work with them. But they had gone before she could pluck up the courage to speak to them.

She made her way down Surrey Street and found herself in Arundel Street, where Tom worked. Perhaps she should go and ask his advice. He might know where she could find some kind of work. At least it would let him see that she was making some effort to become independent and less of a burden to him.

There were several tall tenements set round cobbled yards in Arundel Street. Once they had housed families but now they were given over to industry. Each group of tenements was called a 'wheel' from the water power which in the past had driven the machinery there and they were named after whoever had either owned or previously lived there. The rooms in the tenements were all made into small workshops or 'hulls' which were rented out to the 'Little Mesters', all self-employed craftsmen in aspects of the silver industry. She walked along the street, passing Black's Wheel, Collis Wheel, Shenstone Wheel and several others where the name boards had faded so much they were indecipherable. Joanna recalled that Tom had spoken of working at Fenwick's Wheel and she walked up and down until at last she found the fading board with that name on it above the main door.

She was directed to Tom's hull on the third floor and she went up the three flights of narrow, grimy stairs to reach it, rehearsing what she would say to him over and over in her mind as she went.

To her surprise, as she got near she could hear voices raised.

'I don't want your bloody money!' That was Tom's voice; he was obviously in a temper.

'Be reasonable, man. I was shocked at the time. Didn't know what I was doing. Well, now I've had time to cool off and think about it. I was wrong and I want to put things right. She's my wife and I want her back.'

Joanna froze. It was Lynwood's voice.

He went on, 'I'm offering you your five shillings back. That's what you paid for her, isn't it? Well, I wouldn't want you to be out of pocket.'

She heard the chink of money.

'I've told you, I don't want your bloody money.' The coins were swept on to the floor. 'I bought her and she's mine. You're not having her back.'

'I'll give you double what you paid for her,' Lynwood pleaded.

'You'll give me nowt. She's mine.' She could hear the rage in Tom's voice. 'You were eager enough to sell her to me, as I recall.'

'Oh, come on, man. It all happened in the heat of the moment, you must realise I didn't mean—'

Joanna gritted her teeth. How dare they! She was not a commodity to be bought and sold like a pound of lard, she was a *person* with a right to a say in her own life. She didn't wait to hear any more. Almost blind with rage at the way the two men were haggling over her she rushed down the stairs, nearly tripping and falling on the way, and out of the yard. She remembered seeing a notice chalked up on the wall of one of the tenements while she was looking for Fenwick's Wheel saying LASS WANTED and she ran up and down the street until she found it. Then, fuelled by her temper and regardless of the consequences, she went in. Whatever the job was, she would take it.

Chapter Twenty-Two

Blagg's Wheel, where Joanna had seen the advertisement, was at the opposite end of Arundel Street to where Tom worked. The yard looked bleak and shabby and not much sunlight reached it. It was deserted except for a blacksmith working at his forge.

She went over to him and pointed to the message scrawled on the door. He pointed to some stairs in the corner.

'Harry Smithers, that's who's asking. Tha'll find him up there.' He continued his work.

Joanna thanked him and mounted the stairs. She was still too furious at what she had heard outside Tom's hull to stop and think twice about what she was doing. How dare they treat her as nothing more than a chattel to be passed from hand to hand on a whim. She would show them . . .

As she reached the top of the stairs a girl came out of a room on her right, tears streaming down her face and her mouth set in a tight line.

'I've come to see Harry Smithers,' Joanna said.

'Tha's bloody welcome to him, miserable old bugger. He's in there,' the girl jerked her thumb over her shoulder, indicating the room she had just left. 'In a right old mood he is, too, so I should watch out, if I was you.'

Joanna knocked at the door and a gravelly voice told her to enter.

Harry Smithers was a coarse-looking man of around forty, with a belly that put a great strain on his waistcoat buttons. Before he went to seed he had been a handsome man and he cherished the fond remnants of his looks by making sure that a lock of hair – one of the few he had left – fell forward over his forehead. He was sitting at a table strewn with papers.

'Well?' he said rudely, then peered at her. 'Who are you?'

'You're advertising for a lass to work here,' Joanna said, holding her head high and staring him out. 'I've come for the job.'

He looked her up and down and then shook his head. 'You're too old. I'm looking for a young errand lass to train.'

'Too old for what?' Joanna said, infuriated by his manner. 'I'm not daft. I've got skills. But if all you want is an errand lass then that's what I'll do. I'll run errands.'

'Skills? What skills have you got? Look at your hands, soft as a baby's bum. If you'd ever done a day's proper work you'd not have nails like that. Oh, I can tell as soon as look at you that you'd never last five minutes in this job.'

Joanna looked at her hands. Ever since Gertrude had shown her how to care for them she had been proud of her hands and nails. Now they were putting her at a disadvantage. 'Just because my hands are clean it doesn't mean I can't do a day's work,' she said indignantly. 'You might at least gave me a try.'

He sucked his teeth thoughtfully. 'All right. Try this, then. Where have you come from? What can you do? Have you learned a trade? Are you a glazer? Polisher? Transfer sticker? Mirror polisher?' He shot the words at her like bullets.

Joanna was bewildered. She had never heard any of these terms. She lifted her chin. 'I've none of those trades but I'm willing to learn,' she said.

He shook his head. 'Nay, I can't afford to pay you while you're spoiling good work. And you'd not want to work here for errand lass's money so don't waste any more of my time arguing.' He pulled forward a well-thumbed account book and began to frown over it.

Joanna stared at the book for several moments.

He looked up. 'I said you could go. I've nowt more to say to you.'

'Very well.' She went to the door. 'But you'll never get that book to balance till you add it up right. There's a mistake in the left-hand column. It's five pounds out.' She went out, closing the door behind her. That would show Harry Smithers she wasn't quite such a fool as he took her for, she thought savagely, clattering her way down the stairs. Trying to make out she wasn't capable of learning a trade, nor of doing a day's work ...

He was at the top of the stairs calling her back before she reached the yard.

This time his manner was quite different, almost apologetic. 'To tell you the truth, I could do with a bit of help with all this paperwork,' he said, waving his hand across the cluttered table. 'My brother always looked after this side of things but, well, we had a bit of a dust-up last week and he walked out on me. Started up on his own over on t'other side of t'town, he has, rotten bugger. And left me with all this to sort out.' He spread his hands. 'I've got eight women working for me and everything they do is what I've taught 'em. I know every aspect of my trade. People trust me, they know I'll turn out first-class work.' He scratched his head. 'But I can't make moss nor sand of these bloody figures.' He ran his fingers through his sparse hair, then remembered his kiss curl and automatically pulled it forward. He looked up at her 'I'll be glad to give you a job. When can you start?'

'What will you pay me?' It was the first word she had spoken since she got back into the room.

His expression because cagey. 'Well, till I see how things are going ... Shall we say five shillin' a week?'

'That's not a lot. I'll bet your brother didn't work for that.' She knew she had the upper hand.

'He was bleeding the business dry, was Sid. And all to get enough money to set up on his own. You've no idea—'

'Seven and six. For a start.'

'Oh, I don't know—' He turned his mouth down at the corners.

'Suit yourself.' She turned to leave.

'No. Wait a bit. Yes, all right. Seven shillin'. But for Gawd's sake don't tell them out there what I'm paying you.' He jerked his thumb towards the door.

She sighed. 'I said seven and six. But all right. Seven shillings.' She was tired of haggling.

'When can you start work?'

She took off her shawl. 'Right now.'

With a huge sigh of relief he got up from behind the desk. 'I'll leave you to it, then,' he said and escaped to his workshop.

Joanna sat down, her heart in her mouth. She had no idea what she was supposed to do. She had got the job because she had happened to spot an error in addition in one of the columns, reading it upside down. She could have been wrong. Quickly she added the column up again, the right way up. No, she hadn't made a mistake, there was a five-pound error. But what it all meant she had no idea.

Slowly and laboriously she began to sort out the mess of papers on the desk, matching figures to invoices and bills and putting them in their respective columns. By the end of the day she was just beginning to understand the rudimentary book-keeping system that 'Sid', Harry Smithers' brother, had been using.

Harry was so pleased with what she had achieved that she had no difficulty in persuading him to pay her a shilling in advance out of her wages. On her way home she bought two lamb chops and a spray of winter jasmine from the flower-seller on the corner of Surrey Street and Fargate. She hadn't before realised just how much she missed the masses of flowers that were brought into Cliffe House each day from the gardens there.

Thinking of Cliffe House reminded her yet again of the scene she had heard earlier in the day outside Tom's hull. The thought of being haggled over like a pig at market still made her blood boil, but she decided that the best thing was to bide her time and say nothing until Tom spoke of it, as he surely would.

She reached the lodgings and after a brief word with Mrs Goffin went upstairs. She lit the fire and found a jam jar for the jasmine. The bright yellow of the flowers and the flames shooting up the chimney made the room look quite cosy and welcoming and she hummed to herself as she went about preparing the meal for herself and Tom.

It was quite late when he arrived back and he was grey with fatigue. With only a brief greeting he threw his bag down in the corner and went over and washed at the bowl in the corner. Then he combed his hair and his beard and sat down at the table, his neat appearance only seeming to emphasise his exhaustion.

'Chops?' he looked up inquiringly as she put his plate in front of him. 'And flowers? How did you manage that, Jo?' He frowned and said sharply, 'You didn't borrow money from Mrs Goffin, I hope.'

'No, I didn't borrow money from anybody. I've found myself work.' She was so pleased with herself she couldn't help smiling.

He didn't smile back. Thoughts tumbled through his tired brain at such a rate that he needed time to sort them out. If Jo had found work did that mean she would want to leave? She couldn't leave, she belonged to him. The bargain he had made with Silkin was as binding as marriage vows. But did he want to keep her against her will? Silkin wanted her back. Should he tell her? Would she go back to him if she knew? He closed his eyes. Oh, God. Now he had got her back after all these years he couldn't bear the thought of losing her again.

Joanna touched his arm. 'Are you all right, Tom? You're not cross because I've found work, are you? I thought it was time I did something to earn my keep, I've been a drain on you for quite long enough.'

He passed his hand across his face. 'No, I'm not cross Jo. Just bone weary. It's been a long day.' He gave her a ghost of a smile. 'Where is this work you've found?'

'At Harry Smithers, in Arundel Street.'

He frowned. 'How did you manage that? You don't know anything about what they do there, Jo. They work with acids, etching the marks on knives, things like that. It's highly specialised work.'

'What makes you think I couldn't learn?' Her voice was sharp. Then, seeing how tired he was her voice softened. 'He advertised for an errand girl but when I answered the advertisement he said I was too old. Then I discovered he needed someone to sort out his accounts.' She made a face. 'You could say I don't know anything about that, either, but Abraham taught me a bit and it's surprising what I'm finding out for myself. At least I know more about it than he does. He can't even add up.' She lifted her chin. 'He's paying me seven shillings a week, Tom, so I shall be able to pay my way.'

He flushed. 'I don't need you to pay your way, Jo. The lobster knives I'm working on should be ready tomorrow. And I've got plenty of other work.' He leaned forward. 'I'm building up my business, Jo. I'm getting myself known as a good craftsman. If I work hard I shall prosper. We won't live in these rooms for ever. I'll find us a nice house—'

She closed her eyes. He simply didn't understand, but there was no point in arguing with him when he was so tired. So she merely said quietly, 'I want to pay my way, Tom,' and left it at that.

After they had eaten she washed up and tidied the room, by which time Tom had fallen asleep in the chair by the fire. She touched his shoulder.

'I'm going up to my room now, so you can go to bed.'

He laid his hand over hers. 'Thanks, Jo. I'll be glad to. I need to make an early start in the morning.'

She took a candle and went up the narrow stairs to her room under the eaves. As she lay in the wide bed she recalled the warm strength of Tom's hand as it had covered hers, his rough, calloused palm; craftsman's hands. She supposed she had noticed it because he so rarely touched her except by accident. Theirs was a strange relationship, she mused, almost like brother and sister. Yet not quite. Brothers weren't afraid to hug sisters and sisters weren't too shy to kiss brothers. She sighed up into the darkness. It seemed a very long time since she had been hugged by anybody. Or kissed. Not since Lynwood ...

Dreamily, she began to re-live Lynwood's ardent love-making, the feel of his arms round her and the touch of his lips on hers. But as she drifted off into sleep it was not Lynwood who held her in strong arms but Tom. Tom who she belonged to, not because he wanted her but because he had bought her for five shillings.

Five shillings she would repay and then be free. Free to leave Tom and return to Lynwood, who regretted the way he had treated her and wanted her back.

It took longer to save the money than she expected. Each week, when she received her wages from Harry Smithers she put aside five shillings to give Tom, but as the week went on it somehow always disappeared. First she bought a shawl so that she could give back the one Mrs Goffin had lent her. It was a warm paisley shawl that she had seen in the window of a small shop in Fargate. Then there were shoes to buy so that she could discard the hated clogs. And a new dress. And underclothes.

She dressed herself in her new clothes one Saturday afternoon and with her week's pay in her pocket set off for Cole's Department Store. Let that snooty floor walker try to turn me out now, she thought, her lip tightening.

She walked in, her head held high. Oh, it was good to smell again those once familiar smells, and to walk down the polished aisle with its strip of thick Turkey carpet down the middle. She smiled triumphantly to herself as the same floor walker who had turned her out so unceremoniously such a short time ago now came up to her and bowed obsequiously as he pulled forward one of the tall chairs by the glove counter for her to sit on. She spent a happy half hour trying on gloves and hats and when she had made her purchases waited for the floor walker to open the door and bow her out of the store.

After that, she visited the store every Saturday afternoon. There was always something she could buy, stockings and handkerchiefs, small items of jewellery, all manner of things that she had bought without thinking twice when Abraham was paying the bills. As well as buying these things for herself she bought a patchwork blanket for Tom's bed. It brightened up the room as well as giving him extra warmth at night. Then there was a plush tablecloth for the table, and a rug for the hearth. The chest of drawers for her attic bedroom came from the second-hand shop on the corner of Campo Lane; the ones in Cole's were too expensive.

She was careful that she never, ever got into debt, she never bought anything until she could pay for it in full. But she had no experience in handling money; living on Bradshaw's Farm she had never had any to handle and married to Abraham there had been no need because everything had gone on his account. The result was that money burned a hole in her pocket and although she always intended to save five shillings to give to Tom, somehow by Saturday night there was never much of it left.

Tom watched with interest, saying little. He was glad she was taking an interest in her appearance, although privately he was of the opinion that she was dressing herself a little too smartly for the area in which they lived. Yet she was too open and friendly with the neighbours for them ever to accuse her of 'getting above herself'. Then he began to torture himself with fears that she might be buying herself all these new clothes because she had somehow learned that Silkin wanted her back and she wanted to do him credit, but he couldn't think how she could have heard of his visit to the hull that day.

When she began to buy items to brighten up their lodgings his fears abated a little and he even began to cherish the fond hope that she might not be looking to leave him after all, but was becoming contented with their life together, such as it was, a life that was so much more than he had ever dared to hope, yet so much less than he could have wished.

But when the armchair appeared he decided she had gone too far.

'It's for you to sit in when you come home tired,' she explained when he protested.

'I have my bed. I can lie on that. And the wooden armchair is very comfortable.'

'Not as comfortable at this.' She stroked the back and arms. 'Sit in it, Tom. Try it.'

He sat in it. It was indeed very comfortable. The most comfortable chair he had ever sat in, upholstered in red plush, with a buttoned back and padded seat and arms. 'Where did you get it? How much did it cost? Do you owe money on it?' He shot the questions at her like bullets out of a gun.

'It's not new,' she countered.

'It's almost new. Where did you get it?'

'I bought it from the second-hand shop on the corner of Campo Lane. The same place as I bought my chest of drawers. They have some nice things there.' She lifted her head. 'I paid for it. In full.' She turned away. 'You don't need to know what it cost. It's a present. Your birthday present.' She grinned at him, pleased with her sudden burst of inspiration.

'It's not my birthday,' he said with a sigh.

'How do you know that? It could be. You don't know when your birthday is, so today is as good a day as any to celebrate it.' Impetuously, she flung her arms round his neck and kissed him on the lips. 'Happy birthday, Tom.'

He got hold of her arms and pushed her away. 'Don't ever do that,' he said, roughly, his jaw tightening as he turned away from her.

'Oh! I'm sorry, Tom.' She slumped down at the table. 'I didn't mean to offend you.'

He took a deep breath. 'You didn't offend me, Jo. It's just—' he looked at her, sitting there, a picture of dejection, and he was sorely tempted to open his heart, to tell her how hard it was to live so closely with her, yet never holding her the way he longed to, loving her, giving her his children. But he was so afraid that if he spoke of these things it would ruin the fragile relationship they shared now and she would go, leaving him bereft. So he shrugged. 'It's nothing,' he said.

'And will you keep the chair?' she asked anxiously. She smiled at him. 'I had the most awful trouble getting it up the stairs.'

He smiled back at her. She was looking at him with the eagerness of a puppy who had stolen a chop and desperately wanted to be forgiven. God, if she only knew how much he loved her. 'Yes, I'll keep it. Thank you, Jo.'

Chapter Twenty-Three

Tom never, ever mentioned the fact that Lynwood had visited him that day when he was working in his hull. He couldn't bring himself to speak of it because he knew Joanna too well to be deceived by her expression, in spite of what she might say. She had said several times that she hated Lynwood for what he had done to her, but he was not convinced that deep down she might not still love him and hope one day to return to him. So he kept his own counsel and prayed that he had seen the last of the man, secure in the knowledge that Joanna knew nothing of his visit.

And Joanna never, by a word or gesture, let Tom suspect that she did know. But the knowledge of what she had heard that day hung over her and she couldn't help thinking about it. Often. The trouble was, the more she thought about it the more it clouded her vision and made her less certain of her feelings towards Lynwood. Of course, she hadn't forgotten the terrible, cruel thing he had done to her on their wedding day. And in her more rational moments she could hardly believe that she had loved him so much that she had agreed to flout convention and marry him before the statutory year of mourning for her first husband was up, allowing him – she could now see – to diminish the value of her life with her beloved Abie. It was also a source of great regret to her that she had alienated herself from Abraham's sister. She had always been very fond of Gertrude, who had treated her almost like a daughter and been a good friend to her when she needed it most. A friendship that was lost for ever, and all because Lynwood had been too impatient to wait those few extra months.

Looking back at the way he had humiliated her on their wedding day, the day that should have been one of the happiest in her life, she knew she should hate him. She *did* hate him. It was a vile, unforgivable thing he had done to her and even now if she closed her eyes she could see the look of loathing on his face when he realised that she was the daughter of Liddy the witch, and could feel the cruel yank of his cravat round her neck as he hauled her up on the wall for all to witness her degradation. She still remembered the despair that had filled her until her old friend Tom came to her rescue.

But Lynwood wanted her back. She had heard him tell Tom as much. He had admitted his mistake. He regretted his impetuous action. He still loved her. Sometimes, picturing his laughing face, remembering the feelings he could arouse in her with no more than a look, his persuasive tongue, she wondered if she would be able to resist him if he said these things to her face. Could she forgive him for what he had done to her and go back to him? Back to the warmth and excitement of his arms, back to her old life of ease and luxury at Cliffe House where servants were there to attend to her every need? It was a tempting thought.

She consoled herself with the thought that if Lynwood loved her as much as he had professed to he wouldn't take Tom's refusal to hand her over for an answer. He would be back. He would find her. And by that time she would be free and she would have her answer ready.

While she waited for him to come she continued her life with Tom and her work at Blagg's Wheel, working for Harry Smithers. She tried not to spend the money she earned, anxious to pay Tom back his five shillings, but a coat in Cole's caught her eye one week, which took most of her wages, and there was usually a trinket, or a pretty scarf to tempt her. She even bought Tom a cambric shirt, one week.

He shook his head when he saw it.

'Now when do you think I'd ever have cause to wear such a fine thing, Jo?' he asked ruefully.

She shrugged. 'I don't know. But I've bought myself some nice things so I thought I'd buy something for you. I thought you might like it, that's all.'

'I do like it. It's the finest shirt I've ever seen.' He touched it gently with his calloused hand. Then he smiled at her. 'It's kind of you to think of me, but I think you should take it back to the shop you bought it from. Shirts like this are not for the likes of me, Jo. Shirts like this are for gentlemen.'

She smiled back at him. He called himself a journeyman, but he was far more of a gentleman than a good many men she had met who laid claim to the title.

He gave it to her and she took it upstairs and laid it in the drawer with the things she had bought for herself, the clothes she called her 'Saturday clothes', clothes that she was careful not to wear for work because she didn't want to appear different to the other girls.

So she continued to wear the same old green dress that Tom had bought for her on her wedding day because then she looked like everybody else at Harry Smithers' acid etching works. She didn't have to worry if it got spattered with acid or lime when she took a few minutes from her office to watch the team of girls at work etching the marks on to the knives and razors. She was fascinated to watch them; each girl had her own task, her fingers flying with long practice. Maggie printed the transfers, six at a time, on to tissue with ink made from a brew of beeswax, Swedish pitch, soot and turpentine. Then they were cut up and whetted off on to the knife, careful to make sure that the imprints were straight. Florrie did the varnishing, which had to be just the right strength or the acid would go through it and ruin the knife, then dried so that the next girl could do her part, using paraffin to release the ink without affecting the varnish. Other girls worked with lime, to clean the knife blades and kill any grease, and nitric acid, which ate into the mark without harming the rest of the knife, then finally it was cleaned with spirits. It was all highly skilled yet because they were on piece work they had to work quickly to make any money. The fact that they were working with dangerous acids on blades where one slip could have the top of a thumb or finger off made no difference to the speed at which they worked. Maggie could stick on nearly a gross of transfers in fifteen minutes and often her fingers bled from the pressure. And if there was an accident and a girl lost a finger or got badly burned with acid, the rest would have a whip round of a few coppers to 'tide her over' till she could get back to work.

Joanna appreciated the fact that although she didn't actually work with the etching team but in a separate office, doing what they called 'book work' and working out their wages, the girls accepted her as one of themselves. They taught her about knives, how every part has its own name: the handle was called the bolster, and there were many different designs of bolster, all with their own name, and the blade which had a mark side and a pile side, and some had to be marked on the mark side and some on the pile side. Then there were all the different kinds of knives ... Sometimes Joanna's head reeled with their explanations, which made the girls laugh.

'Aw, come on,' they said. 'It's as clear as mud when you get used to it.'

Every day, during their dinner break, they all sat together round the fire in their filthy hull, surrounded by their work, lethal-looking knives in various stages of completion. But when the weather began to get warmer, they went out into the yard and sat on the wall. This was their opportunity to catch up on the gossip while drinking the thick soup that Molly the errand girl fetched from Mrs Blatch's pie shop round the corner. Rumour had it that Mrs Blatch made the soup in the copper she used for boiling the clothes on Mondays, but nobody was ever allowed in the dark, cavernous back regions of her shop to find out whether or not this was true. Not that they really wanted to know. Mrs Blatch's soup was very good and quite thick enough to make a meal from, whatever utensil it was made in.

They were sitting on the wall one day enjoying the first warm rays of spring sunshine shafting bravely through the layer of smoke and fog that permanently blanketed the town.

'How's your sister now, Florrie?' Maggie asked. Maggie was the girl who had rushed out of Harry Smithers' office in tears the day Joanna had arrived. Whatever the problem had been it must have been solved satisfactorily because Maggie was always cheerful and happy in her work.

Florrie dipped a crust of bread in her soup and sucked it. 'She's better. T'rash is all gone. Liddy said it were shingles.'

Joanna's eyes widened at her mother's name but nobody else seemed in the least surprised. In fact, several of the other girls nodded sagely.

'Did she gi' her owt for it?' one asked.

'Oh, aye. She made her up some stuff to rub on t'blebs and gie her summat for t'pain an' all.'

'Aye, she's good, is Liddy.' They all nodded in agreement.

'Folk say she's a witch!' Molly, the new errand girl said in a hushed whisper.

'That's only because she looks a bit odd and lives wi' that poor owd dad of hers in t'woods,' Maggie said. 'But she's all right.' She gave a laugh. 'She's helped me out a time or two, I can tell you.' She winked and made an oval over her stomach.

'Me, too,' Florrie said with a nod. 'She's all right, is Liddy. I'd trust her where I wouldn't trust t'quack, I can tell you. She cured my mum when her legs all swelled up.'

Joanna said nothing. She had never considered Liddy as anything but a figure to be feared; a strange-looking oddity who lived in a hut in the woods and dabbled in herbs and possibly witchcraft. To think she was so highly thought of in the town as a healer was something quite new to her and put a totally different perspective on this creature who was her mother.

'Ee, do you remember the time Liddy turned up at that big wedding?' One of the girls said with a laugh.

'Oh, aye. It were the talk o' t'town for weeks. It were t'boss o' Silkin's Button Factory getting wed, weren't it? Put his bride up for auction straight away when he found out she were Liddy's daughter, rotten bugger.'

'Fancy Liddy having a daughter. What man 'ud want to risk having a go at her,' Florrie said with a shudder.

'Some men'll have a go at anything, randy sods.' Maggie drained the last of her soup. 'I wonder what happened to her?'

'Who?' The others were still laughing at her joke.

'T'lass. Her daughter.'

'Lord knows. Probably on t'streets by now.'

'Well, it didn't do him much good, neither, by all accounts. T'Button Factory's not doing too well, from what I hear,' a girl called Kath said. 'My aunt was laid off only last week.'

'Serve him right if it goes bust.' Maggie got to her feet. 'Come on, time to get back to work. Old Skinflint's looking out of his window wi' his watch in his hand, mean old bugger. He gets his pound o' flesh wi'out watching to see we don't

213

take an extra two minutes over our dinner break.'

They all went back to their respective jobs. Joanna sat at her desk, her pencil twirling in her hand, mulling over in her mind the things she had heard. It was surprising what you could hear if you kept quiet, she thought to herself with an inward smile and she wondered what they would have said if she had revealed the fact that she, whom they knew as Mrs Joanna Cartwright, was the bride who had been so cruelly sold that day.

Neither would they have recognised as Mrs Joanna Cartwright the smart young woman who walked along Fargate, gazing into the shop windows as she went, the following Saturday afternoon. It was Joanna's little charade, her pretence at stepping back into the life of luxury she had once known, that she indulged in each week. This was when she frittered away her week's earnings. Tom knew nothing of this, he worked all day on Saturday and by the time he returned home she had put all her finery away, annoyed with herself that yet again she had spent the money she was so desperately anxious to save to buy back her freedom and independence.

Today she was carrying the pretty little parasol she had bought the previous week. It matched the pale blue dress with the ruched front and the little blue hat that tipped forward over one eye. She felt very pleased with herself and quite confident as she walked into Cole's Department Store and wandered around looking at everything from feather beds to feather boas. Gradually, over several weeks, she had bought some pretty matching china, garlanded with tiny pink and yellow roses. She had bought plates, cups and saucers, a milk jug and sugar basin, and today she completed the set with a teapot. The floor walker nodded deferentially to her as she walked proudly out of the store and came face to face with Gertrude.

Her first instinct was one of joy and her face lit up with pleasure as she stepped forward to greet her.

'Oh, Gert—' her voice trailed off as Gertrude stopped, lifted her chin and looked right through her, then turned away and walked into the store, cutting her dead.

Joanna made her way back along Fargate, the teapot clutched under her arm, her parasol in the other hand, utterly shamed and mortified. Suddenly, she could see her behaviour for what it was. Play-acting. She was no longer a lady and it was no use trying to pretend that she was. She could no longer expect to move in the circles she had previously enjoyed. It was a salutary lesson.

When she got home she carefully laid her smart clothes away in the drawer and put on the striped dress she had bought from the pawnshop to replace the old green one and began to prepare Tom's meal.

She never went back to Cole's Department Store again. Indeed, she never again dressed up and went on her Saturday afternoon excursions. She was too fearful that she might meet someone else she had once known and receive the same treatment Gertrude had given her.

Joanna deluded herself when she thought Tom knew nothing of her Saturday adventures. It was not difficult for him to guess something of what she was doing, from the drift of perfume that greeted him when he arrived home, the new purchase – there was nearly always something to brighten up the room, even if it was only a bunch of flowers. Lately she had been buying delicate china which he was half afraid to handle. He understood her motive for buying these things. When she had begun working he had refused to take any of the money she earned towards her board and lodging despite her arguments, saying it was his pleasure to provide for her. So she was asserting her independence in the only way she could. He didn't mind. At least it meant she was making no effort to leave. She had been with him nearly six months now and although he had rashly promised himself – and her – that he would never take her for himself until she was willing, it was an increasingly difficult promise to keep. At night he would lie in his narrow bed thinking of her, wanting her, with only the steep wooden stairs between them. The temptation to take those stairs three at a time and gather her into his arms was at times almost too much to resist. In fact, the only thing that held him back was the knowledge that such an action would drive her away, out of his life for ever. That was more than he could even bear to think about.

When she got home from work at one o'clock the following

Saturday, instead of passing through Mrs Goffin's over-furnished room with no more than a brief word, Joanna sat down on the sofa to talk to her.

'Not rushing off to get yourself all dressed up today, lass?' Mrs Goffin asked, obviously pleased. 'You look a reet treat in them smart things.' She sighed. 'I used to be smart, once-over, when Goffin was here. He used to get me nice things to wear.' She got to her feet with difficulty. 'If you're not in a hurry will you stop and have a drop of soup wi' me? I'd be glad o' t'company.'

Joanna took off her hat. 'Yes, Mrs Goffin. I'll be pleased to.' In fact, the thought of the empty Saturday afternoon stretching ahead had filled her with dread, mostly because she had been wondering if she would be able to resist the temptation to dress up and go shopping as usual.

The soup was good. 'You'll have to tell me how you make it,' Joanna said, holding out her mug for more.

'Aye. They all like my soup. Goffin used to say I made t'best soup in all Sheffield, although I don't know how he'd know that, I'm sure, since he never tasted anybody else's.'

'How long has he been dead, Mrs Goffin?' Joanna asked, cradling her mug in her two hands.

'Oh, Goffin's not dead, love. He's in Australia. He promised he'd send for me when he could, but of course I'd not go now even if he did, my legs are too crammocky.' She gave a sigh and looked down at her hugely swollen ankles.

'How long has he been gone?'

'Ee, must be near on twelve year.'

'That was brave of him, to go off to a strange country like that. What was his trade?'

Mrs Goffin threw back her head and laughed. 'Ee, he didn't go from choice, love,' she said. 'He were transported. On a convict ship. He were a pickpocket by trade. Well, he'd thieve anything, but pickpocketing was his main thing. Made a good living, too, he did. While it lasted. But he were caught in t'end and sent off to Botany Bay.' She lumbered to her feet again and fished in the cupboard by the side of the fireplace. 'I had a letter, once-over. He must have got someone else to write it, Goffin didn't know how.' She peered at it and then smiled up at Joanna. 'He said he'd let me know when he got there safe,' she said with a satisfied nod. 'I don't read, myself, but you can read it if you like.'

Joanna took the letter. It had been written on a scrappy, yellowed piece of paper in large, badly formed letters. It was clear from the state of it that it had been lovingly handled over and over again. 'Would you like me to read it to you, then?' she asked.

'Aye, that'd be nice. I'd like to know what he said.' Mrs Goffin folded her arms over her stomach, prepared to listen.

Joanna scanned the letter in horror. It said baldly that Samuel Goffin had died of a fever eight days into the voyage and had been buried at sea. She licked her lips, trying to think what to say.

'I can't read it very well,' she said, playing for time as she held it towards the light from the window. 'Ah, yes. It says that the voyage was good, the sea was calm all the way.' She paused. 'They landed in Australia safely.' She couldn't invent anything else because she had no idea where Australia was, nor what it was like. 'He sends his love and hopes to see you before too long,' she added hurriedly.

Mrs Goffin nodded happily. 'That's what I thought it said,' she said, taking the letter back and folding it lovingly. 'I know I shall never see him again, but it's nice to know he's safe, even if it is on t'other side of t'world.'

'And you've not even got children to be a comfort to you, Mrs Goffin,' Joanna said sadly.

'Nay, lass, after our Gertie died me and Goffin weren't never blessed wi' any more.' She gave a shrug. 'Maybe it's as well. He used to knock me about a bit when he was in t'drink, I'd not have wanted to see him tek it out on bairns.' She glanced at Joanna's waistline. 'I see no sign of you podding up, love,' she said and from the tone of her voice it was impossible to take offence. It was quite plain that she regarded Tom and Joanna as her family now.

'No, not yet.' Joanna got to her feet, escaping before there were any more questions. Nor likely to, the way we live, she thought as she went up the narrow stairs to her room. For some reason she couldn't fathom this last thought gave her no pleasure.

217

Chapter Twenty-Four

Now that she no longer went on her Saturday afternoon shopping expeditions Joanna found that the little carved box she had bought to save money in, which had so far remained for the most part empty, was beginning to fill. She still couldn't resist buying something on her way home with her week's wages – having money in her pocket had never lost its novelty. Usually it was a bunch of flowers from the flower-seller on the corner or a pair of kippers as a treat for Tom's tea. Once she even bought a new tin kettle for Mrs Goffin. But she no longer felt the urge to spend every penny as soon as she earned it. The result of this was that before long she had more than enough money in the box to give Tom the five shillings he had paid for her and buy her freedom.

Every week she would count the money carefully and then sit and look at the growing heap of coins. All she had to do was give Tom what he was owed and then she would feel free to walk out and never come back. The knowledge was comforting and she always thought, next week I shall do it. Yet for some reason she never did, but instead replaced the money carefully in the box and put the box in the drawer with the neatly folded clothes she now never wore.

She spent most of her Saturday afternoons with Mrs Goffin, who taught her to cook tasty meals from practically nothing as well as giving her a knowledge of herbs and their use as remedies. As she learned the benefit of lemon balm or lavender for headaches, borage to reduce fever and the many uses of thyme, from cleaning wounds to curing coughs and colds, Joanna thought of Liddy, branded as a witch for using these

218

very remedies, and again she saw her mother in a new light.

Joanna helped Mrs Goffin, too. It was some time since the old lady had been able to give her room what she called 'a reet good turn out' so one afternoon Joanna piled all the furniture on the bed and scrubbed the floor while Mrs Goffin sat in the corner sorting out the boxes that had been stacked under the sofa and sideboard and hadn't seen the light of day for years. Then everything had to be moved to the other side of the room, including Mrs Goffin and her boxes, so that Joanna could move the bed and scrub that part of the floor. By the time she had finished the whole room sparkled, there was a sackful of rubbish to be thrown away and Mrs Goffin's face was a picture of delight. After that, Joanna made a point of keeping the room neat and clean and in return Mrs Goffin baked her a cake each week.

'You and Mrs Goffin get on well together, don't you, Jo,' Tom said as he helped himself to another slice of her seed cake. It was a Saturday evening in late July, his week's work was finished and he had been well paid for it. Joanna was sitting opposite to him across the table and the room was homely and comfortable as only a woman could make it, brightened by the bunch of daisies she had bought on her way home from work. No man could ask for more, he thought contentedly, smiling across at her, except ... Resolutely he turned his thoughts away; taking Joanna to his bed, holding her, loving her, occupied his thoughts far too often for his peace of mind.

'Yes. She's a dear old soul.' Unaware of his thoughts, Joanna poured more tea from the teapot, bought the fateful day she had met Gertrude, into the pretty matching cups. 'She reminds me a bit of Martha,' she said, her head on one side, the teapot still in mid-air. She stayed like that for a few seconds, then put the teapot down. 'Only Mrs Goffin's a better cook. Did I tell you I saw Martha at the market the other day, Tom?'

'No. I thought you said she'd stopped coming.'

'I thought she had, because I hadn't seen her for several weeks. But she'd been ill. She says she's better now but she looked very frail.'

'What about Saul?'

'Oh, he's still the same as ever, never satisfied with what

he's got, always wanting more, she said. But Jacob looks after her and does most of the heavy work.' She leaned her elbows on the table. 'Apparently Saul's drinking a lot these days. He never used to get drunk when I lived there, at least, not often.' She grinned. 'Martha always used to say he was too mean to spend the money.'

'Maybe he's got more to spend now.' Tom moved over to his comfortable chair by the hearth, which Joanna had decorated with a fan of green and red paper for the summer months. He bent and picked up his pipe and lit it.

Joanna shrugged. 'If he has, I don't know where he gets it from. Martha says the farm doesn't pay.'

'He still works over at Bradshaw's Wheel though, doesn't he?'

'Yes. But that never paid much, as I remember.'

Joanna collected up the dirty platters and washed them up, then threw the water out of the window, wide open because of the oppressive heat. Then, after swatting a fly that was buzzing lazily round the room she sat down in the wooden armchair opposite to him and picked up her knitting. This was yet another skill Mrs Goffin had insisted on teaching her, saying 'It'll come in handy when you've bairns. You'll be able to knit nice warm things for 'em. There's nowt like wool for keeping bairns nice and warm.'

Joanna had protested. 'But I'm not —'

'I know, love,' Mrs Goffin had cut her off with a wink and a knowing smile. 'But you will be. In time.'

One thing Joanna had learned was that it was pointless to argue with Mrs Goffin, so now, to please her, she was knitting patchwork squares for a blanket that she knew would very likely be big enough to cover Paradise Square, never mind a cradle, before it was needed.

Suddenly, there was a step on the stair and a knock at the door.

They exchanged puzzled glances. It couldn't be Mrs Goffin, she couldn't climb the stairs and nobody else ever visited them; people who needed to see Tom saw him at work and Joanna had no friends except those at Blagg's Wheel.

Slowly, she put down her knitting and went over to open the door.

220

Tom was watching and saw her flush and put her hand to her throat.

'You!' she whispered. 'What are you doing here? What do you want?'

Frowning, Tom got up from his chair and strode over to the door to see who it was she was talking to. His face darkened when he saw who it was.

'Silkin! I thought I'd told you—' He glanced at Joanna, who looked as if she was about to faint. 'Oh, I suppose you'd better come in. We can't stand talking at the door.' He put his arm round Joanna and led her to sit on the bed. 'You sit there, love. I'll fetch you a drink of water.'

Lynwood came in and shut the door and then stood leaning against it, his arms folded. 'Quite a touching little domestic scene,' he said sarcastically.

Tom waited until he was sure Joanna was all right, then he turned to him. 'I'd be glad if you'd state your business and then go, Silkin. I may as well tell you from the beginning that you're not welcome in my house.'

'Hardly a *house*, Cartwright,' Lynwood said with a sneer. 'You don't even have a front door. I had to squeeze my way between that old woman's furniture down below to reach the stairs to this poky little room.' He looked round. 'God! Is this the level you've brought Joanna down to!' He turned his gaze back to Tom. 'And it's *Mr* Silkin to you, if you don't mind.'

Tom kept his temper with difficulty, telling himself no good would be served by knocking the man down. 'Very well, *Mr* Silkin. You're not welcome in my *home*. It amounts to the same thing.'

'I take it you've never told Joanna I came to see you in the hovel you work in?' Lynwood asked.

'No, I did not,' Tom answered.

'I thought as much. That's why I've come here tonight. In my opinion she should be allowed to make up her own mind.' He strode across the room and stood looking down at her. 'I've come to tell you I'm sorry I did what I did on our wedding day, Jo. I acted in the heat of the moment and I've regretted it ever since.' He spoke in short, barking tones as if it went against the grain even to speak the words. He held out

221

his hand. 'I'm willing to let bygones be bygones and take you back,' he added magnanimously.

She looked up at him, a puzzled frown on her face. He looked much the same as ever; his suit was immaculately pressed and his linen snowy white. His hair was a little longer than she remembered, but it was carefully styled in what she supposed was the latest fashion, oiled so that it lay close to his head and fell curling under at his neck. It didn't suit him.

'You're willing to let bygones be bygones? What do you mean by that, Lynwood?' she asked.

'I mean I'm willing to forget the past eight months, the fact that you've been living in this hole with him,' he jerked his head in Tom's direction.

'But where else would I be living? You sold me to him, don't you remember? You sold me to the highest bidder. With a halter round my neck, like a prize pig at an auction. Surely, you can't have forgotten that, Lynwood.' Her voice was quiet, she spoke in an almost bemused tone.

'No, of course I haven't forgotten,' he said impatiently. 'It was a stupid thing to have done, I realise that now, but I acted in the heat of the moment. But it's all in the past now. I'll make it right with him.' Another jerk of his head in Tom's direction.

'And how do you intend to do that?' She was still speaking in the same bemused tone.

He tossed his head. 'Oh, we'll come to some arrangement.' He smiled down at her and held out his hand. 'Come along, now, darling, get your things. I haven't got all night to waste. No, on second thoughts there can't be anything here you'd want to take back to Cliffe House.' When she didn't make any attempt to move he bent down towards her and said encouragingly, 'I love you, Jo. I want you back.'

She put her head on one side and looked up at him. 'Do you, Lynwood?'

His smile froze and he frowned impatiently. 'Do I what?'

'Do you love me?'

'Of course I do, you silly little goose. Why else do you think I've traced you to these squalid back streets? It's taken me all this time to find you. But now I've come to rescue you and take you back where you belong.'

Slowly, she got to her feet and went over to the door. He followed her eagerly. 'That's my girl. I knew you'd see sense.'

She paused with her hand on the door knob. 'Would you like me to wait outside while you and Tom haggle over me?' she asked, gazing up at him.

He gave a slightly uncomfortable laugh. 'Oh, I shouldn't think that would be necessary. I'm sure we—' he hesitated, noticing for the first time the cold gleam in her eye. He put his hand on her arm. 'Look, I've said I'm sorry, Jo. What more do you want?'

'I want you to get out of this room and never come back, Lynwood, that's what I want,' she said quietly.

'But I'm willing to take you back. For God sake, I *want* you back, Jo. I've come to fetch you,' his voice had lost its arrogant edge and was pleading.

'But I don't want to come with you. Can't you understand, Lynwood?' Her lip curled. 'Any road, what's made you change your mind? Don't you realise I'm still the same person I was when you sold me? I'm still the daughter of Liddy the witch. And that's what you couldn't stomach, as I remember. Being married to the daughter of a witch.'

'Oh, Jo.' He ran his fingers through his hair. 'I told you. I did it in the heat of the moment. I was a fool. I realise now that it doesn't matter who your mother is. It's you I love and I want you back.'

'It matters to me,' she said bitterly.

Tom had watched the two of them, saying nothing. Without realising it he had been holding his breath throughout the entire exchange, but now he let it out in a great sigh and came over and laid his arm across Joanna's shoulders. 'I think Jo's given you her answer, Silkin – sorry, *Mr* Silkin,' he said.

Lynwood rounded on him. 'You keep out of this, Cartwright,' he said venomously. 'It's got nothing to do with you.'

'You're wrong. It's got everything to do with me,' Tom answered. 'Jo belongs to me now and I'm not letting you take her away from me.' His hand tightened on her shoulder.

'But she's my *wife*, damn you!'

'You should have thought of that before you sold her to

me,' Tom replied. 'She's *my* wife now.' He felt a thrill of pride as he said the words, even though he knew they were not strictly true.

Lynwood turned and his gaze swept Joanna from head to toe, resting insolently on her waistline. 'Are you with child?' he barked. 'Are you having this man's bastard?'

Joanna opened her mouth but before she could speak Tom said, 'If you take her back that's a risk you'll have to take, isn't it?'

Lynwood glanced at Tom. 'It wasn't you I asked.' He turned back to Joanna. 'Well, are you with child?'

Joanna licked her lips. 'No. That is, I don't think so.'

'But you're not sure?' Lynwood looked at her closely and when she didn't answer he turned away. 'Perhaps I'm not so keen to have you back after all,' he said scathingly. 'For if I did, how could I ever be sure I wasn't bringing up his bastard!' He jerked his head in Tom's direction.

'In that case perhaps you'll be good enough to leave before I throw you out,' Tom said through gritted teeth.

He turned to go. 'You'll not get another chance,' he called to Joanna over his shoulder as he went down the stairs. 'So it's no use you coming crawling back to me when you change your mind.'

Tom closed the door quietly and went back to his armchair. Joanna sat down on the bed, her hands between her knees, trembling slightly. Neither of them spoke for a long time.

Then Tom said, 'If he'd known how we live he wouldn't have needed to ask if you were with child.' There was bitterness in his voice.

'It would have made no difference. I still couldn't have gone with him,' she said.

He looked up. 'Couldn't? Why not?'

'Because I wasn't free to go. You'd paid him for me. Five shillings.' The bitterness was in her voice now.

He waved his hand. 'You know that wasn't important, Jo.'

'Oh, but it was, Tom. It was very important to me. Something I could never forget.' She got up from where she was sitting on his bed and went up to her room. When she came back she was carrying the little carved wooden box that held her money. She knelt down beside him and held it out to him. 'You'll find five shillings in there,' she said quietly.

He stared in astonishment, first at her and then at the box. He waved it away. 'Don't be daft. I don't want that, Jo.'

She put it in his lap. 'But I want you to have it, Tom.'

'Why, in God's name?'

'Take it. Then I'll tell you.'

'Oh, very well.' With a resigned sigh he took the money out of the box and put it in his pocket. 'There. Does that satisfy you?'

'Yes. It does.'

'I can't see why it should,' he said, shaking his head in bewilderment. 'What difference does it make?'

She lifted her head and smiled at him. 'Because now I'm free, Tom. I don't belong to you. I don't belong to anybody except myself. I'm free to choose what I do and where I go.'

Tom didn't return her smile. He realised he had fallen into her trap and was about to lose her. He cleared his throat. 'I see. Well, you know where to find me if you ever need me, Jo,' he said gruffly. 'I didn't realise how you felt. I thought you knew you were always free to go, if that's what you wanted. I would never try to keep you here against your will.'

'Thank you, Tom. I appreciate that.' She took the empty box from him and got to her feet. She looked at it for several minutes then took it back upstairs. When she came down again Tom was still sitting where she had left him. He was holding his pipe clenched between his teeth but making no attempt to light it.

He took it out when he saw her and said, 'Have you decided where you'll go? What you'll do, Jo?' He tried to make his voice matter-of-fact although he was dying inside.

She nodded. 'Yes, Tom, I've decided.'

He took a deep breath. 'So? Are you going to tell me, or are you just going to—' he hesitated, 'disappear from my life?'

She went over and knelt at his feet again. 'It rather depends on you, Tom. But if you'll have me I shall stay here with you. I shall stay with you and care for you and if you're willing I shall bear your children.' She looked up at him. 'Will you have me, Tom?'

He didn't answer for several minutes. His heart was too full. But he had to be sure.

'I can never give you the life you've been used to these past years, Jo. You understand that? If you stay with me you'll never live in a big house, with servants to wait on you hand, foot and finger. There'll be no money to spare for the frills and furbelows you've become used to. I'm an honest working man, good at my trade and I can never pretend to be other than that.'

She got to her feet and turned away from him. 'You're saying you don't want me. I understand, Tom. And I don't blame you, really I don't.'

He got up and stood behind her. 'I'm saying nothing of the kind, Jo. You must know I want you more than anything else on earth. But I love you far too much to let you blind yourself to the reality of what life with me would be.'

'I've lived with you for the past eight months, Tom,' she said quietly. 'And I've been happy. Happy in a way I never imagined. I've come to realise what a fine man you are, and I've grown to love you.' She blushed. 'I want to be your wife.'

He put his hands on her shoulders and gently turned her round to face him. Her cheek was wet with tears and gently he wiped them away with his thumb. 'Oh, Jo, I've waited so long to hear you say that,' he whispered as he bent and very slowly, as if he couldn't really believe it was happening at last, put his lips to hers.

Chapter Twenty-Five

That night, when Joanna went up the stairs to her attic bedroom Tom was right behind her.

As they reached the top of the stairs she hesitated, then turned to face him.

'Tom, you will be . . . gentle with me, won't you? You see, I've never—' she paused, staring at the candle flame that was making their shadows dance on the bare walls, too shy to meet his eyes. She spoke with some reluctance. She hated the thought of being disloyal to Abraham's memory, to reveal her elderly husband's inadequacy, but she realised that even if she said nothing Tom would know. 'When he . . .' She paused anxiously.

Tom was watching her, his eyes full of longing for this girl – this woman now – whom he had loved ever since he could remember. He put out his hand and gently tucked a tendril of her hair behind her ear. 'You've no need to worry, I'd never willingly do anything to harm you, Jo, my love, surely you must know that,' he said softly, bending to kiss her.

She put her finger on his lips. 'No. Wait. I must tell you, Tom. I want you to know. Abraham never . . . he couldn't, you see . . .oh, he tried two or three times . . . but it was no use. I think after that he was too embarrassed to try again. He never said anything, never made excuses, but afterwards he always slept in his dressing room.' She had spoken rapidly, jerkily, anxious to say what must be said. Now she turned her head away. 'We never, ever talked about it. It's just the way things were and I . . . we accepted it. Nobody knew – well, perhaps Norbert did but he was too discreet to say anything.

And of course I never told Lynwood. He wouldn't have understood.'

Tom pulled her head down on to his shoulder and stroked her hair, staring at the blank wall behind her. Although she didn't realise it, she had answered the question that had tortured him most about her relationship with Lynwood. He had been quite prepared to believe that the blackguard had seduced her, in fact at first he had been afraid that Joanna might already be carrying Lynwood's child; this was the only reason he could think of for such a hasty marriage. He still remembered the blessed relief he had felt when he finally knew that his fears were groundless.

He felt suddenly guilty that he should have doubted her and humble in the face of her innocence. He buried his face in her hair and held her close. 'Thank you for telling me, Jo. But it will be all right. I promise it will be all right. Just trust me.' He leaned over and blew out the candle, then gently, with trembling hands, began to undress her.

The next morning he was late for work.

Soon after he had gone, when Joanna tripped down the stairs at her accustomed time, she was humming happily to herself. As always, when she went through Mrs Goffin's room on her way to work Mrs Goffin was sitting up in bed wrapped in a shawl and drinking a cup of tea.

'You sound cheerful this morning, lass,' she said as Joanna greeted her.

'Well, it's a lovely morning, Mrs Goffin. Listen, can't you hear the birds singing?' Joanna beamed at the old lady.

'Aye, I can, that.' Mrs Goffin nodded and took another slurp of her tea. She watched thoughtfully as Joanna went out of the door. She looked different today, somehow, she had a bloom on her that was almost radiant. And Tom had been late for work. Never in all the years he had lived there had he been late for work before. He was a stickler for good time-keeping, was Tom.

Mrs Goffin slurped thoughtfully at her tea. Something had happened between the two of them, that was sure. Something that had put a smile on Joanna's face and made Tom late for work. In Mrs Goffin's mind there was only one explanation for that. But it was getting on for a year since Tom had first brought her here as his bride so that couldn't be the explanation.

She leaned across the table and poured herself more tea. It must have something to do with that posh fellow who had come to see them last night. Mrs Goffin hadn't liked him, nor the way he had looked down his nose at everything when she'd directed him up to their room. He'd taken himself off in a high old paddy, whoever he was. She hoped he wouldn't come back, even though it must have been something to do with his visit that had brought that sparkle to Joanna's eye.

She finished her tea and folded her hands across her chest. Joanna would tell her about it. When she was ready.

But Joanna said nothing. Her new happiness with Tom was too precious to be shared. And if his lovemaking was less expert than Lynwood's teasing advances had been the consummation of their love was everything she could possibly have desired.

Sometimes, as she busied herself about the two rooms they shared, sweeping floors, pulling down cobwebs, emptying slops and carrying up clean water, she was amazed at her own contentment. It seemed like another life – in truth, it had been another life – when she had lived at Cliffe House, waited on by servants, her every whim anticipated by Abraham, never having to lift a finger for herself. It had been pleasant while it lasted, although if she was painfully honest sometimes she had been just a tiny bit bored with so little to do except spend Abraham's money, Oh, how she had enjoyed that! That was why curbing the urge to spend all the money she earned at Blagg's Wheel had been so dreadfully difficult. Thinking back, it was quite frightening how it had slipped through her fingers each week. But now she hardly ever bothered to look in shop windows and was learning to manage very carefully the money Tom trusted her with every week to buy their food and provisions. Her biggest thrill came when she had a few coppers left over at the end of the week.

She still worked at Blagg's Wheel for Harry Smithers, keeping his accounts straight. At Tom's insistence she kept aside the money she earned, putting it into the little carved wooden box as security against a rainy day. Sometimes she had the beginnings of an urge to take it and go on a spending spree, but then she would think about it and realise there was nothing she really needed; the trinkets and folderols she had felt so compelled to buy in the past no longer held the same fascination for her and there was nothing more that she could buy for their little home without making it as overcrowded as Mrs Goffin's room.

The only thing that began to worry her was the stink of the hull at Blagg's Wheel. The mixture of acids, varnish, beeswax, turpentine and smoke from the fire, blended with unwashed bodies and other human smells suddenly began to nauseate her. She took bunches of herbs to work with her and hung them near her desk and made sure that her own clothing had been laid in lavender when it was washed to try and make the place smell a little fresher, but it made little difference.

Of course the girls at work noticed, especially as the weather became hotter. They teased her as they sat on the wall eating their dinner, because Joanna was fanning herself with a sprig of rosemary as she nibbled at a lump of bread and cheese. It was a particularly hot day, the air was thick and stifling as the hazy midsummer sun tried to burn a hole in the blanket of smog that perpetually covered the town. It was on days like these that Joanna felt a pang of nostalgia for the fresh, clean air at Cliffe House, or the cold sparkling water of the Porter Brook, where as children she and Tom sometimes used to dangle their feet.

'You're getting mighty fussy, Josie.' This was the name the girls had chosen to call her by. 'Look at you! Your office upstairs stinks of thyme and lemon balm. And now you're fanning yourself with rosemary. What's up wi' you? Have you been getting charms from Liddy the witch or summat?'

She tried to smile, but Maggie was sitting next to her and the smell of her breath was making her stomach turn. She couldn't understand why she had never noticed it before. Maggie always ate a lot of garlic. 'I just like to make the place smell better,' she said weakly. 'You must admit it doesn't smell very sweet up there. Mind you, it doesn't smell all that good down here with the stink of the blacksmith's forge.'

'I can't smell owt,' one girl lifted her head and sniffed loudly.

'Well nowt different to the usual,' another said with a laugh. 'We can allus smell Maggie's garlic.'

'It's good for the rheumatics,' Maggie said, totally unrepentant. 'Want some?' She fished in her pocket.

'No thanks.' They all waved her away, wrinkling their noses. Joanna nibbled on the crust of her bread.

'Don't you want that, Josie?' Polly nodded longingly towards the bread and cheese in her hand.

'No. I'm not very hungry. You can have it if you like.' Joanna handed it to her, glad to be rid of it. Even the smell of the cheese seemed to turn her stomach today, probably because it was so blisteringly hot.

'I think I'll get a bit of tripe on my way home tonight,' Maggie said thoughtfully. 'My man's partial to a bit of tripe cooked with onions and garlic.'

Suddenly, at the thought of tripe, Joanna's stomach finally rebelled and she leaned over the wall and began to retch. Maggie supported her until she had finished, then sat her down on the backless chair someone had produced and gave her a few sips of the water someone else had run for. Then she dipped her sleeve in the cup and wiped Joanna's face.

'There, that's better. You're getting a bit o'colour back into your face now,' Maggie said, standing back and regarding her. 'Have you felt like this for long?'

Joanna nodded weakly. 'Yes, for nearly a week now. It must be something I've eaten. I can't think what else it could be.'

'Can't you?' Maggie said dryly. She raised her eyebrows at the other girls then leaned forward and whispered in Joanna's ear. 'How long since you last saw your monthlies, lass?'

Joanna frowned. 'I can't remember. It must be—' She flushed. In truth she had seen nothing since Tom had come to her bed. She had given this no thought at all, except to be glad, anxious as she was that nothing should hinder their loving.

'You're in pod, lass, that's what's wrong wi' you,' Maggie said with a laugh. 'I'm surprised you've not been caught before. How long have you been wed?'

Joanna tried to marshal her thoughts. A baby. Tom's baby. She felt a rush of love for him and instinctively her hand went to her stomach to protect the precious thing it held. Then she frowned and rubbed her forehead with her fingers. What was Maggie talking about, lucky she hadn't been caught before? She must have fallen right away. Then her mind cleared and she pulled herself together. Of course, to the outside world she and Tom had been married for nearly nine months.

She smiled wanly. 'Getting on for a year. Well, it'll be a year come the beginning of October.'

'You've been lucky, then. Me, I fell the night I was wed,' Maggie said. She burst out laughing. 'And if it weren't for dear old Liddy and her "mixture", I'd have been falling ever since. And that doesn't always work!'

There was a ripple of laughter and agreement as they all slid off the wall and began to straggle back up the stairs to resume work.

Maggie lagged behind. 'Are you all right now, lass?' she asked Joanna. 'Or do you want to go home?'

'Oh, I couldn't go home. Not just because I feel sick. What would the others think?' Joanna said with a laugh. 'They never stop work until they're in labour and they're standing all day, not sitting down, like me.'

'Well, you're not used to it, are you?' Maggie said and Joanna realised that in spite of their friendship the girls still thought of her as being 'different', 'a cut above'.

By way of celebrating her precious news Joanna bought two of the special meat pies Tom liked best on her way home from work. She also bought a geranium in a pot and stood it on the window sill. Then she prowled about the room, smoothing the patchwork quilt spread over the couch that had replaced Tom's single bed under the window, plumping up the cushion at its head, straightening the rag rug at the hearth, and all the while listening for his tread on the stair and rehearsing in her mind the calm and matter-of-fact way she would tell him she was pregnant.

But when she heard his step everything went out of her mind and she flung her arms round his neck the minute he was inside the door.

'Oh, Tom, what do you think?' She kissed him, her face radiant. 'I'm to have a child! Our child! Oh, Tom, I'm so happy I could die.'

He held her close, trying to feign as much excitement and joy as she was showing, hiding the thoughts that immediately began to tumble through his head . . . so happy she could die. Women did die in childbirth. But not Jo. Please God, not Jo. Not now they had found such happiness together. He went cold at the thought. His mind ran on. He would have to be careful in future. Up to now they had simply enjoyed their lovemaking with no thought of the days to come. But once this child was born . . . visions of a hoard of bare-foot, hungry children and Joanna bowed down with constant child-bearing because of his selfish lust made him screw up his eyes in pain.

'What is it, Tom?' She reached up and touched his face. 'Aren't you pleased at the idea of being a father?'

He bent his head and kissed her tenderly. 'Of course I'm pleased, Jo.' He laid his hand gently on her stomach. 'Every man wants a son to carry on his name.' His faced relaxed and broadened into a smile. 'Even if it's only the name that was given to him in the workhouse.'

She smiled back at him. 'What's in a name? Whoever he was, your father must have been a fine man to have fathered a son like you, Tom.' She drew away from him. 'But you must be hungry. And I've bought some of your favourite pies for supper. To celebrate. They're in Mrs Goffin's oven. I'll go and fetch them while you get yourself cleaned up.'

'Have you told her?'

'Not yet.' She gave him another hug. 'It's our secret for the moment. She'll find out soon enough.'

It wasn't until they sat down at the table a little later that Joanna noticed the rag round Tom's thumb and the awkward way he was holding his knife.

'What's the matter with your thumb?' she asked, frowning towards it.

He glanced down at it. 'Oh, nowt much. I caught it with a blade I was working on and nicked it a bit. It was a daft thing to do. I should have known better after all this time. It'll mend.'

'Let me look at it.'

'After supper.'

But after supper he had other things to do and by the time they went to bed Joanna still hadn't managed to examine it.

233

'It's all right. I can look after it,' he said, putting it behind his back when she protested the next day. 'I'll get some stuff from Mrs Goffin, she's got a cure for most things. Don't fuss, woman.'

But the thumb didn't mend and a few days later it had swelled up like a balloon.

'Mrs Goffin says it'll be all right as long as I keep it bound up,' Tom said impatiently when Joanna again tried to look at it. 'It's only a canker. Grinders get them all the time from the swarf. It's just a nuisance because it slows me up, that's all.' But he was very pale and Joanna noticed how he winced if anything touched it.

She spoke to the girls at work about it. They seemed to have a fund of cures, some of them quite horrific, often handed down from their mothers.

They all shook their heads. 'Sounds nasty,' one said. 'Sometimes they do go bad, then it's the very devil to get them right.'

'He needs to see Liddy,' Maggie said sagely. 'Like Biddy says, it sounds like a nasty one. Get your man to go and see her. She might look a bit odd but that's because she lives in the woods with her poor old dad, but she's all right.' And she proceeded to give Joanna careful directions to Whitely Woods.

'I didn't tell her I knew those woods like the back of my hand,' Joanna laughed as she told Tom what Maggie had said. 'And she'd have been even more surprised if she'd known Liddy was my mother. When will you go and see her, Tom? Tomorrow?'

'No. I'm not going at all.' He was showing a surprising streak of obstinacy. 'And I don't like you discussing our affairs with those people.'

'Oh, Tom, don't be silly. They're the lasses I work with. They're a good bunch. Any road, you'll have to do something. Look at the state of your hand.'

'It's better than it was.'

'Don't talk such rot, Tom. Even I can see that it's worse.' Joanna tried to get hold of it but he winced and drew it away. 'The stuff Mrs Goffin gave you isn't doing any good at all.'

'I can't afford to take the time off. I've got a lot of work on at the moment. Now leave me alone.' It was the first time he had raised his voice to her. He turned his head away. 'I think I'll go to bed.' He mumbled and went heavily up the stairs.

That night, for the first time he made no attempt to make love to her, but lay tossing and turning, in obvious pain from his hand. The next day he had gone to work before she woke.

She got up and dressed, turning over in her mind what she should do, how she could overcome this stubborn streak in Tom, a streak that seemed to get worse with the state of his hand. She talked it over with Mrs Goffin.

'I think you're right, lass, it is getting worse,' Mrs Goffin said. 'The stuff I gave him doesn't seem to be doing any good at all.'

'The lasses at work say he should see Liddy the witch,' Joanna said tentatively, watching for Mrs Goffin's reaction.

Surprisingly Mrs Goffin agreed with her.

'But the trouble is he refuses to go,' Joanna said, her face creased with worry.

'Then you must go for him,' Mrs Goffin told her. 'If you can tell her what the trouble is she'll likely be able to tell you what to do for him.' She shook her head. 'It's beyond me, I'm afraid.'

Joanne sent a message to Blagg's Wheel, saying she wouldn't be in that day and set off for Whitely Woods. She was not looking forward to confronting Liddy, remembering the last time they had talked, but she reasoned that there could be no harm in asking her advice. And it was not as if she was asking favours because she had brought money in her pocket to pay Liddy for her help.

She stepped confidently into the wood, but by the time she reached the clearing where Liddy lived with her father she found herself trembling and her mouth was dry.

She came upon Liddy sooner than she had expected, sitting in a clearing on a fallen log with her father. They were eating bread and cheese. As Joanna approached Jack got up and walked away, reluctant to let anyone see the difficulty he had in chewing his food with his disfigured jaw.

Liddy remained where she was sitting, watching Joanna approach. She waited until Joanna was standing in front of her before getting to her feet.

'So,' she said with a nod. 'Things haven't worked out so

badly for you, after all, have they? Tom is a good man and you'll have a child next year. It's as I expected.'

Joanna wasn't listening. 'Tom is ill,' she said in a rush. 'His hand is badly poisoned. I wanted him to come to you about it but he wouldn't.'

'He brought you to me once, when your foot was poisoned, as I recall. He had faith in my cures then,' Liddy said dryly.

'It's not that he has no faith in your cures. He's stubborn. He insists it will heal with Mrs Goffin's salve. But it won't. I can see that it's getting worse and even Mrs Goffin admits that her salve isn't helping.' Joanna's eyes filled with tears. 'I know your cures work. And the lasses I work with swear by you.' She stared at the ground. 'The good things they say about you make me realise how mistaken I've been over the years.'

A sudden shaft of genuine pleasure crossed Liddy's dirty face, but Joanna was still staring at the ground and didn't see it.

Suddenly she looked up. 'Will you help Tom, Liddy?' Her eyes filled with tears. 'I don't know what I would do if I lost him.'

Liddy closed her eyes. 'It needs cutting,' she said, her voice almost a chant. Her eyes snapped open. 'Will you cut it?'

Joanna swallowed, then nodded. 'If I have to. If he'll let me.'

Liddy stared at her. Then shook her head. 'He'll not let you. Wait here.' She strode off into her hut. After several minutes she came out again with a small carpet bag.

'What do you want me to do?' Joanna asked, praying that whatever it was, her courage wouldn't fail her.

Liddy rammed her battered old straw hat further on to her head. 'Nothing. I'll do it. I'm coming with you.'

Chapter Twenty-Six

Liddy hardly spoke as she accompanied Joanna back to the town. She strode along, her old black cloak streaming out behind her, the carpet bag clutched in her hand, looking neither to right nor left as she went and taking no notice of the stares and gibes that her odd appearance inevitably provoked. Her only defence seemed to be that she took such long strides that Joanna had to take little running steps every now and then in order to keep up with her. It was not until some time afterwards that it occurred to Joanna that Liddy had never once asked the way but had gone unerringly through the narrow streets and ginnels until she reached Sackitt's Yard. Only then did she turn.

'Which one?'

Joanna nodded towards the step where the geranium still bravely bloomed.

Liddy stood aside. 'You'd better go first.'

Completely ignoring Mrs Goffin, whose face was a picture of amazement, Liddy followed Joanna through her room and up the stairs to wait for Tom to return home from work.

But he was already there, lying on the sofa, his eyes closed and his face flushed with fever. 'I couldn't work. I had to come home,' he said, his voice thick. 'You were right, Jo. It's bad.'

Joanna knelt down beside him and took his good hand in hers. 'It's all right, Tom, I've fetched Liddy. She'll make you better.'

Liddy looked down at him, then laid her hand on his forehead. 'It's poisoned his blood. He may have left it too late,' she said and began to rummage in the carpet bag.

The next half-hour was a nightmare. Whilst Liddy lanced Tom's hand and forced out the stinking pus that was poisoning his system he held on to Joanna's hand, squeezing it tightly when the pain got unbearable so that even though her delicate stomach rebelled at the stench she couldn't move and had to swallow the bile that continuously rose in her throat.

When Liddy had finished she placed leaves carefully on the wound and called for clean rag to bind it. Then she sat back on her heels and stared at Tom. His face was ashen except for a trickle of blood on his chin where he had bitten his lip through.

'I'll make up an infusion for him to take to clear the poison out of his system,' she said, rummaging in her bag again. 'I'll need hot water.'

'I'll fetch some from Mrs Goffin. Her stove is always alight, even in the hottest weather.' Joanna took her kettle and hurried downstairs.

The old lady was full of questions which Joanna answered as briefly as she could before hurrying back upstairs. Liddy went to the table and stood there for several minutes, pounding and mixing, adding water and stirring. Then she asked for a bottle and poured the decoction into it and shook it violently. Then she handed it to Joanna. 'Shake the bottle well, then give him a tablespoonful. Every hour, on the hour for the next twenty-four. Don't miss. Then every three hours, day and night.' She studied the bottle. 'There'll not be enough there. He'll not be out of the woods for several days yet. I'll make some more up and you can fetch it tomorrow or the day after.' She picked up her carpet bag.

'You're not going?' Joanna said anxiously. 'I – we haven't paid you.'

Liddy looked at her and her eyes seemed to bore right through her. Then she looked away. 'I'll take no money from kin,' she said and before Joanna could recover from her surprise she was gone.

For the rest of the day Tom lay like someone dead, his eyes closed and his face as white as the pillow Joanna placed under his head.

Every hour she held up his head and trickled Liddy's

238

medicine between his lips, making sure he swallowed every drop. All night and throughout the next morning she sat in his armchair, watching him, afraid to close her eyes in case she missed the time for his next dose. Twenty-four hours, almost to the minute, after Liddy had left he opened his eyes for the first time.

'I'm very thirsty, Jo,' he croaked.

She was at his side in a second, holding a drink to his lips. 'It's time for your next dose,' she said when he had taken a few sips.

'Dose? What dose?'

'The dose Liddy left for you.'

'Liddy? Has she been here?'

'Yes. Don't you remember?'

'No.' He frowned. 'The last thing I remember is looking at my hand and realising it was too painful and swollen to hold my tools with. Then I noticed I'd got two left hands and there were two grinding wheels. I knew then that something was badly wrong and I ought to do as you said and see Liddy. I came home to tell you but you were at work so I thought I'd lie down till you got back. I don't remember anything else.' He closed his eyes, exhausted and licked his dry lips.

Joanna moistened them again. 'I wasn't at work. I was fetching Liddy.' Only just in time, too, she realised. 'Here's the medicine she left for you.' She held the spoon to his lips.

'Ugh!' He made a face. 'It's vile!'

'Is it? Well, you've already had a dose every hour and haven't complained. I've been giving it to you since twelve o'clock yesterday.' She smiled down at him and smoothed his damp hair back from his forehead. 'You should sleep now, love. You haven't got to have any more of this till three o'clock.' She held up the bottle; it was more than three parts empty and it was doubtful where there would be enough to last through until the next day.

'Thank God for that. Oh, Jo, I feel awful.' He frowned. 'I can still see two of you.'

'You'll be better soon, love. Get some sleep.' She sat down in the chair with the bottle in her hand, undecided what to do. It would take her more than three hours to fetch more medicine from Liddy, it was a long walk to Whitely Woods, and

239

Tom was not yet recovered enough to take the medicine for himself. She held up the bottle. There were at least three more doses in it; perhaps by the time he had taken them she would feel safe to leave him. She got to her feet and put the bottle on the table and stood looking down at him. He was sleeping fitfully, turning his head from side to side restlessly and his face was hollow-cheeked and gaunt. She rubbed her own aching head. She was tired, so tired, both from lack of sleep and anxiety. If Tom should die . . . A tear slid down her cheek and she squeezed her eyes tightly shut against the thought. It was more than she could bear and she knew that she mustn't leave him yet, but must stay with him, to hold on to him, to make sure he didn't slip away while she wasn't there.

She sat down in the chair again, watching him, never taking her eyes from his face.

An hour later she woke and shook her head to clear it. She hadn't meant to go to sleep, she had meant to keep watch over Tom. She went and knelt by his couch, to make sure . . . but he was all right, still asleep, still tossing his head. She got up to go to the bowl in the corner to get some water to bathe his brow when out of the corner of her eye she saw a figure in the corner.

It was Liddy, standing there just as she had seen her when she was ill. She passed her hand over her eyes, this was no time for hallucinations. She had to be strong for Tom's sake. She blinked and looked into the corner again. Liddy was still there, standing just inside the door with her carpet bag in her hand and her old black straw hat rammed firmly on her head. She could even smell her, a mixture of smoke, herbs and dirty clothes.

Distressed, she passed her hand over her eyes. 'Oh, God, Liddy's here. Now I'm seeing things again,' she murmured.

'Don't be ridiculous, of course you're not seeing things. I've just got here.' Liddy's voice was sharp. She put her bag down on the table. 'Father and I were coming to deliver a load of charcoal for the steel works so it wasn't much out of my way to bring Tom some more physic.' She fished in her bag and brought out another bottle. 'Anyway, I wanted to see him.' She went across and looked down at Tom. Then she put her hand on his forehead. 'Fever's lessening. He'll do.' She

240

turned to Joanna. 'What did you mean, saying you were "seeing things again" when I got here?' she asked curiously.

'Nothing. Nothing at all.' Joanna was suddenly embarrassed.

'Tell me.'

'It was while I was ill. Not long after Tom brought me here.' She shrugged, fiddling with the blanket covering Tom so that she didn't have to look at Liddy.

'Go on.' Liddy was watching her keenly.

She shrugged again. 'I was delirious. I kept seeing—' she paused uncomfortably, then straightened up and looked directly at Liddy. 'Well, if you must know, I kept seeing you. Wherever I looked you were there, in the room, watching me.' She covered her face with her hands. 'It was awful. It frightened me.'

Liddy nodded. 'That's interesting.' She was quiet for a minute, then she gave an apology for a smile. 'I'm sorry if it upset you. It shouldn't have done. I was only watching over you.'

'You were *here*?' Joanna said, her eyes wide. 'Tom never said—'

'Of course not. He didn't see me.'

'I don't understand.'

'You will, when your child is born.' Liddy nodded to where the child lay under Joanna's heart. 'But I hadn't thought the bond would be strong enough for you to actually see me,' she said thoughtfully.

'You mean you weren't actually here?'

'Only in spirit. You were never out of my thoughts.'

'I didn't realise you even knew I was ill,' Joanna whispered.

'I know everything about you. I always have.' Suddenly, Liddy's mood changed. She picked up her carpet bag and said briskly. 'I shan't come again. He'll mend now. Goodbye.'

She was gone before Joanna could speak.

Tom mended slowly. His legs were weak, he had no strength in his arms and he tired quickly. He fretted and chafed at his inability to get back to work and he took it out on Joanna. She tried to be patient and to see his bad temper as a sign that he was getting better, but sometimes she found herself shouting back at him.

'If you hadn't been so stubborn and pig-headed in the first place you wouldn't have been so ill!' she yelled one day when he was fuming at his enforced inactivity. 'And if I hadn't fetched Liddy you'd have been dead by now!'

'Perhaps it would have been a good thing. What good am I doing, sitting in this chair like an old man,' he shouted back at her.

She gritted her teeth. 'Don't you ever say that to me again, Tom Cartwright,' she said, her voice shaking with fury. 'What about me? What about our child? Instead of sitting there and feeling sorry for yourself because you can't work why don't you use your energy to get your strength back. For *our* sake, if not your own!'

He held out his arms and she went and sat on his lap. 'Oh, Jo. I'm sorry. I'm a selfish clod. And you're quite right, I should be thinking of you.' He buried his head in her breast. 'I've never even asked you how you're managing since I've not worked. Forgive me, Jo. I'm not myself.'

'I know that, love.' She looked down at his hand, fumbling with the buttons on her bodice and smiled, 'but you're beginning to act more like the old Tom.'

'I'm beginning to feel more like him, too,' he said with a grin, sliding his hand inside and beginning to kiss her white throat. 'I'm sure this'll do me more good than all Liddy's physic.'

'You mustn't tire yourself.' But it was only a half-hearted protest as he tumbled her on to the couch and began to make love to her.

Joanna had returned to work as soon as Tom was fit to be left alone and she became used to finding him there when she returned at night, sitting in his chair smoking his pipe or at the table, poring over the books he had borrowed from the Mechanics' Institute. It was with something of a sense of loss that she came home the day he began work again, knowing that she would find the room empty.

'That man came,' Mrs Goffin said, bursting with the news, as soon as she got inside the door. 'Brought a parcel. I told him you weren't home but he went up to your room just the same.'

'Man? What man? I don't know any man,' Joanna said, frowning.

'That posh man – you know, that man who came to see you once before.' Mrs Goffin was nodding at her, willing her to remember.

'I don't even remember any man coming.' Then her face cleared. 'Ah, yes, now I do. What did he want?'

'He wouldn't say. Went up to your room, he did. I couldn't stop him, lass.'

'It's all right, Mrs Goffin. I understand. Well, I wonder what he came for?'

'Doubtless you'll find out when you get up there. Then you can come and tell me.' Mrs Goffin happily resumed her knitting.

Joanna went up the stairs and opened the door. There, on the table was a large box. Puzzled, she opened it and found that it was full of fruit: apples, pears, dates, hot-house peaches, even a pineapple. She was still unpacking it when Tom came in.

She turned to him, her face lighting up. 'Oh, you left work early. That's good.' She leaned over to kiss him.

'What's this?' he asked.

'Lynwood brought it. Look, hot-house peaches. I haven't had a peach since—' she quickly bit into one to cover her thoughtlessness. She knew Tom didn't like to be reminded of her life at Cliffe House.

'How often does he come here?' Tom's face was dark with suspicion.

Joanna didn't notice. She was still busy with her peach. 'He hasn't been before.' She wiped the juice from her chin with the palm of her hand and began to rummage in the box again.

'Then why did he come today? Did you tell him I'd be back at work?'

She stopped rummaging and stared at him, puzzled. 'What do you mean, Tom? I haven't seen Lynwood at all. I didn't see him today. I don't know when he came. Mrs Goffin told me he'd been and left a parcel, that's all. Oh, look, here's a note.' She pulled out a scrap of paper. 'It says, "We've got a glut of fruit so I thought you might like some. I know you always liked peaches. L."' She looked up. 'There, that's all there is to it. Wasn't that nice?'

Tom flung himself down in his chair. 'Oh, yes. Nice that he can rub it in that I can't afford to buy you hot-house fruit. Nice that he can remind you of the life you used to lead. Nice that he can—'

'Stop it, Tom!' Her face was pale with rage. 'Stop being so childish and jealous. I can't help it if Lynwood brings us a box of fruit they've no use for, can I?'

'He could have sent someone with it. He didn't need to come himself,' Tom muttered.

'Oh, don't be so stupid. What difference does it make? I've told you enough times that Lynwood means nothing to me now. If he did I'd have gone back to him months ago as he wanted me to.'

'Why don't you, then? He can give you a better life than I can. Living in two rooms in this squalid little cottage, when you could be living in a mansion with servants to wait on you hand and foot.'

'Have I ever complained?'

He had the grace to look sheepish. 'No.'

'Then perhaps you're saying these things because you want to be rid of me.' She folded her arms and looked straight at him. 'You've only got to tell me, Tom. I wouldn't want to outstay my welcome.'

Immediately, he got to his feet and came over to her. 'I'm sorry, Jo. I'm a miserable sod,' he said as he tried to take her in his arms. 'You know I can't bear the thought of losing you.'

She stood rigidly in the circle of his arms. 'Then why can't you trust me, Tom?'

'I do, Jo. I do.' He dropped his hands. 'It's just that all this has come after a hell of a day at work. I can't get my hand to hold things properly yet. I'm so slow—' He stared out of the window. 'To tell you the truth, Jo, I'm frightened, because I don't think I'll ever work properly again.'

Now she put her arms round him and laid her head on his chest. 'It's your first day back, love. Have a little patience. Don't forget you've been very ill.'

'Yes, I know. But it's hard,' he said with a sigh.

She reached up and kissed him, then stroked his beard. 'Whatever happens I shall always be here, by your side, Tom. You need have no fears over that.'

Chapter Twenty-Seven

January was cold and snowy. Each night Joanna battled her way home from work through the icy streets, glad to reach the warm fug of Mrs Goffin's room for a cup of tea before going upstairs to light her own fire. Mrs Goffin hated the cold; she seemed to shrink into herself when the north wind blew outside. She complained that this winter was affecting her more than any previous one that she could remember.

Joanna and Tom both worried about her. Tom made sure she always had plenty of fuel handy and Joanna shopped for her, fetched clean water and emptied slops so that she had no need to venture outside her door. But although she was physically frail there was nothing wrong with Mrs Goffin's mental abilities and she somehow seemed to gather all the gossip of the neighbourhood without ever leaving her chair. She regaled Joanna with her day's gleanings over a cup of tea every evening before she would allow her to carry on up to her room and in this way Joanna always knew who had given birth, who had died, who was '"up for one" an' her not wed, the shameless hussy', whose husband had beaten the living daylights out of her, and where to go to get the best price for a blanket whether buying or selling.

But one evening when Joanna arrived home there was no tea tray on the table and she received no answer to her greeting although Mrs Goffin was sitting in her armchair by the fire as she always was, her knitting in her hands.

Joanna put her bag down on the table with a thump. 'Good evening, Mrs Goffin,' she said, more loudly this time, watching for the old lady to give a start and say, 'Mercy me, I must have dropped off for a second,' as she often did.

But she didn't move. Frowning and with a cold feeling at the pit of her stomach Joanna edged her way round between the table and the bed and laid her hand over Mrs Goffin's. It was quite cold.

All at once, her legs wouldn't hold her up and Joanna sat down on the bed, staring at her old friend. It wasn't possible. Mrs Goffin couldn't be dead. People didn't die sitting in an armchair, they had to be ill. She got to her feet and looked into the old lady's face. She looked different, somehow so peaceful, and the years seemed to have dropped away because many of the lines on her face seemed to have smoothed out. She must have been very pretty when she was young.

Still refusing to believe that she was dead Joanna picked up the piece of mirror that Mrs Goffin kept on the table beside her and held it in front of the old lady's mouth, hoping desperately that her breathing, however shallow, would cloud it. But there was nothing. When there could be no shadow of doubt she put down the mirror and leaned forward and kissed the pale face.

'Dear Mrs Goffin. We shall miss you so much,' she whispered, tears beginning to trickle down her cheeks.

She was still sitting on Mrs Goffin's bed weeping when Tom arrived home an hour later. He came and sat beside her and his tears mingled with hers when she told him the news, but at last he pulled himself together and said, 'Come on, Jo. Dry your tears. There are things to be done and there's nobody but us to do them. First we must find someone to lay her out.'

Joanna sniffed and gave him a watery smile. 'Mrs Wagstaff. Campo Lane. Mrs Goffin was talking to me about her only the other day. She said, "Aye, Mrs Wagstaff helps folks into the world and out of it."'

Tom smiled at Joanna's mimicry. 'I'd better go and fetch her while you look for the laying out clothes, I'm sure Mrs Goffin has them all ready somewhere.'

'Yes, she's told me where they are. They're in a box under her bed. She showed them to me once. All snowy white, they are.'

'Well, you find them while I fetch Mrs Wagstaff. Did Mrs Goffin say what number?'

Joanna shook her head.

'It doesn't matter. Someone's sure to know.'

It was left to Tom to arrange and pay for her funeral, because Mrs Goffin had no family. But she had many friends and they all came to see her buried in St Paul's churchyard, which was sufficiently close for Tom and three other strong neighbours to carry the coffin without the added expense of a hearse.

As soon as the funeral was over Tom went to see the landlord and asked to take over the tenancy of the cottage.

'Ee, lad, as long as t'rent's paid I'm not bothered who lives there,' the landlord said, surprised Tom had even asked.

'So it's ours now?' Joanna asked, her eyes shining, when he came back with the news.

'Yes, Jo. It's ours.' The smile on his face nearly reached his ears.

'Dear Mrs Goffin. She was a terrible old busy-body. I shall miss her being here to keep us up-to-date with all the gossip,' Joanna said, as she and Tom began to sort through Mrs Goffin's possessions.

'We'll miss her for a good deal more than that, Jo,' Tom said as he began to dismantle the old lady's bed. 'She was a kindly soul and she looked upon us as her family.'

Joanna straightened up and laid her hand on her swelling belly. 'She was so looking forward to our baby. It's a shame she didn't live to see it born.'

Tom got to his feet and gave Joanna a hug. 'Yes, but isn't it wonderful to think we've got the whole house all to ourselves, Jo,' he said excitedly. 'Look how much more space there is in this room already now that Mrs Goffin's bed's out of the way.'

'Yes, but we've still got those boxes to go through. Goodness knows what she kept in them.' Joanna lifted one on to the table and peered inside. 'This one seems to be full of silk handkerchiefs. That's odd.'

'This one's got a lot of oddments, purses, wallets . . .'

'Money in them?' Joanna looked up expectantly.

He shook his head. 'No. Ah, wait a minute, look, here's half a guinea hidden in a corner!'

Joanna helped him to rummage in the box. 'I've found a

silver watch and chain.' She held it up.

Tom frowned. 'Where on earth do you think all this stuff came from?'

Joanna frowned with him. Then her face cleared. 'Of course, Tom! Mrs Goffin's husband was a pickpocket!' Her voice dropped. 'These must have been some of the things he stole over the years.'

'Ah, yes.' He nodded. 'You know, I often wondered what she lived on. She never seemed to be short of money, yet I knew she couldn't live on the rent I paid her.'

'Well, here's the answer. Over the years since her husband was transported she must have been selling off the things he stole in order to live. Is there anything else, Tom?'

'No, I don't think so. This was the last box.'

'Well, considering he's been gone over twelve years she must have had quite a store of things for there to be anything left at all!'

Tom spread his hands. 'What shall we do with it all, Jo?'

'I think Mrs Goffin would like you to have the watch, Tom. And the half guinea will pay for the funeral. As for the rest—' she shrugged. 'I don't think a few silk handkerchiefs would fetch a lot and apart from that there are only two wallets and a purse. They're all empty and the purse has got a hole in it.'

Tom grinned. 'Poor Mrs Goffin. She was fast coming to the end of her wealth, wasn't she?'

'Yes, but she'd done very well to make it last this long. Twelve years is a long time.' As she spoke Joanna was folding the handkerchiefs into a pile.

'Either that or her husband was a very good pickpocket.'

'Oh, yes. Mrs Goffin said he was. She was very proud of him. One of the best she said he was.'

'Only till he got caught!' Tom said with a laugh. 'Oh, come on, Jo, we've still got work to do.'

That evening, tired after their day spent making the cottage into their own, Joanna sat on one side of the range in Mrs Goffin's armchair, stitching for the coming baby, and Tom sat opposite to her in his own armchair, which he had carried down from their old living room upstairs, smoking his pipe, a book in his hand, the kettle singing on the range.

Joanna put her work down in her lap and gazed round the

room. The curtains were drawn against the dark winter night, the lamp cast a pool of gentle light over the room, glinting on Mrs Goffin's chiffonier, which Joanna had polished until she could see her face in it. 'We've really made this house our own now, Tom,' she said, nodding towards their own pretty china, sparkling behind the glass doors of the chiffonier and thinking of their old living room upstairs, already transformed into the bedroom.

His gaze followed her and he nodded happily. Then he raised his eyes to heaven. 'Oh, thank you, Mrs Goffin,' he said fervently. 'Thank you for your kindness towards us and thank you for leaving us a comfortable home for our children to be born into.'

'Amen to that,' Joanna said quietly and picked up her sewing again.

Every Friday morning on her way to work Joanna called in at the market to buy vegetables. She also bought meat when she could afford it, otherwise bones to stew. And eggs. She always went to Martha's stall and bought eggs whether she could afford them or not. Apart from the fact that she knew the eggs from Bradshaw's Farm were good, it was a way of making sure that she never lost touch with her old friend.

Martha had recently taken to bringing a stool to sit on at the market when she came in on the carrier's cart and she was sitting muffled in several layers of shawl when Joanna visited her stall on a frosty morning in early March.

'I can't stand for too long now, my legs are too bad,' Martha told her by way of explanation. 'But never mind me, lass. How are things with you? The bairn must be due shortly, by the look of you.'

'Yes, only another three or four weeks, I think,' Joanna said happily. 'Tom's made a cradle ready for it. And we've got so much more room now we've got a whole house to ourselves.' She became serious. 'Of course we miss Mrs Goffin, but—'

'Aye. I understand, lass,' Martha said, patting her hand. She nodded contentedly. 'I'm glad you and Tom are settled so well. I allus thought you two were right for each other although at one time as you know I had hopes of seeing you

250

and Caleb wed, and that I'll not deny. But it's as well, the way things turned out, wi' Jacob being—' she left the sentence hanging. Even now she couldn't bring herself to speak of Jacob as Joanna's father.

'Jacob is still with you? He helps you on the farm?' Joanna said quickly. She didn't want to be reminded of being fathered by Jacob Bradshaw.

'Aye. He's a good lad, is Jacob. One o' the best,' Martha said, anxious to show her son in a good light. 'He works all the time. But quiet. Very quiet. He misses Bella and the bairns still.' She shook her head, her mouth turning down at the corners. 'Ah, it were a bad day for him as well as you, love, Liddy the witch turning up on your wedding day like she did.'

'But in the end it turned out to have been a good day for me, Martha. I can see that now, although I didn't think so at the time,' Joanna said gently. 'But Liddy knew. That's why she did what she did. She knew Tom would come and rescue me.'

'Aye. That's as maybe.' Martha's tone was bitter. 'All I can say is it was a pity Bella was there to hear what Liddy said. After all, young men allus sow their wild oats. There's no harm—' she shrugged. Suddenly she shot a glance at Joanna. 'Any road, how would you know what Liddy had in mind that day?'

'Because she told me so herself.'

'Oh, she did, did she?' Martha looked at her sharply. 'Well, you seem to have changed your tune some bit about her,' she said almost accusingly. 'I mind the time you'd not got a good word to say for her and you were afeared to go anywhere near her if you could help it.'

'It's different now. She saved Tom's life.' Again Joanna changed the subject. 'Jacob may not be very happy but things are better for you now he's come home, Martha, aren't they? With your bad legs you'd never manage these days without his help. Does he still work over at Bradshaw's Wheel, too?'

'Aye. They both do, Saul as well. But it's in a sorry state now old Silkin's gone.' Martha shot her a guilty glance. 'Sorry, love, I mean Mr Silkin, your late husband. He allus used to make sure everything was in good order, but the young one never pays any mind to it. He doesn't seem to care that the roof needs seeing to and the wheel's all silted up and broken. Oh, the men who work there do what they can to keep it running, well they will, won't they, it's their living, but it all needs money spent on it and from what I hear Young Silkin is more fond of spending his money on horses and drink than on the places that make his money for him. Even the Button Factory's not what it was, from what I hear.'

'Oh, dear,' Joanna said carefully. Martha wasn't usually as forthcoming as this. But today she seemed anxious to talk, to unburden herself, and she looked pinched up and even more wizened than usual. 'Are you ill, Martha?' she asked anxiously.

Martha's face broke into a smile. 'No, love, I'm not ill, I'm just having a bit of a moan, that's all. Don't mind me. The cold gets to my bones in this weather. And Saul—' she broke off.

'What about Saul?'

Martha sighed. 'I don't know. Sometimes he's like a bear with a sore head, nobody can do anything right for him.'

'But he was always like that when I was there,' Joanna said, raising her eyebrows. 'What's different?'

Martha leaned forward. 'It's not just that, lass. He goes about muttering to himself and looking over his shoulder, as if he thinks somebody's following him.' She shook her head. 'I sometimes wonder if he might be going out of his mind.' She leaned back and her shoulders sagged, as if a weight had been lifted off them.

Joanna didn't know what to say. 'Does he still hit you?' she said at last.

'No. Not these days. He doesn't bother.' Martha shrugged it off, the least of her worries.

'Well, that's something, I suppose.' Joanna stared at her, undecided. 'Is there anything I can do for you, Martha?' she said at last.

Martha pulled herself together with an effort and smiled at Joanna. 'No, there's nowt, love. It's just the cold weather getting to me.' She peered in her baskets. 'There, I've sold all t'eggs, so I'll be glad when t'carrier comes to tek me back. But that won't be till he's finished in t'Drover's Arms.' She waved Joanna away. 'But you'd best be on your way to work, lass. You'll be late and then you'll get the sack and you don't want that.'

'I'll be leaving work soon, any road. Tom says I've not to work once the baby's here. He says it's my place to stay at home and look after it.'

'Aye. Sensible lad. As long as you can afford it, that is.'

'He's doing really well now,' Joanna said proudly. 'He does a lot of work for Wolstenholmes. They send a lot of stuff to America so they're happy to take nearly everything he makes.'

'I'm glad to hear it, lass. But you'll still come and fetch your eggs from me, even after you've left work, won't you? That's what makes my day, seeing you looking so blooming.'

Joanna leaned over and kissed her. 'Of course I will, Martha. I shall bring the baby so you can watch it grow.'

'Ee, lass I'll look forward to that,' Martha said.

Joanna's baby was born on a warm, sunny day at the beginning of April. She had no inkling the birth was imminent when she kissed Tom goodbye on the doorstep on his way to work, but as she turned to go back into the house to get ready for her own day's work at Blagg's Wheel something in the corner, something lodged between the step and the yard, caught her eye. It was a small bottle and it was as she bent to pick it up that the first pain struck.

She carried the bottle indoors and sat down at the table, rubbing her side where the pain had been, wondering if she had imagined it. There was a note tied to the stopper. It said, 'A teaspoonful every hour will ease your labour. L.'

Joanna stared alternately at the note and the bottle. It was from Liddy, there was no doubt about that and it hadn't been there last night, of that she was sure. She unscrewed the stopper and sniffed. It wasn't unpleasant, it had an aromatic, earthy kind of smell. She got up and put the bottle in the cupboard by the fire, ready for when it should be needed, and carried on getting ready for work. She was just pinning on her hat when another, sharper pain struck. There was no doubt this time, the pains had begun. She fetched a teaspoon and poured herself a dose of Liddy's mixture. If it did no good she was sure it would do her no harm. And one thing was certain,

253

she realised, as yet another pain struck, whether by design or accident Liddy had certainly timed it well.

Between the pains she called her neighbour to summon Mrs Wagstaff and while she waited she busied herself preparing for the birth, keeping Liddy's bottle and a teaspoon handy in her pocket. By the time Mrs Wagstaff arrived there was a pan of water bubbling on the stove and everything was ready.

'What's tha tekin', there?' Mrs Wagstaff, a sinewy woman with darting black eyes asked as Joanna measured herself another dose.

'It's supposed to help ease my labour.'

'Pah! T'Bible says thou shalt bring forth t'fruit o' thy womb in travail. Where did tha get that jalop from?'

Joanna hesitated. 'Liddy gave it to me,' she said, her tone defensive.

'Oh, aye, let's have a look.' Immediately Mrs Wagstaff's tone changed and she unstoppered the bottle and sniffed. 'Aye, a drop o'good, that. Mind and keep tekin' it.' She handed it back almost reverently. 'Coom on, now, up them stairs. I can tell the pains is gettin' stronger already.'

Joanna's son was born late in the afternoon.

'Ee, that jalop Liddy gie' ye was a drop o' good stuff. I dunno what was in it but I've never birthed a first one so easy before.' Mrs Wagstaff said admiringly. 'Your man'll be fair knocked out when he gets home tonight and find's he's got a son.'

Sleepily Joanna gazed at the tiny child cradled in the crook of her arm. Her baby. Hers and Tom's. With a contented sigh she fell asleep.

And this was how Tom found her when he arrived home from work. As soon as he had set foot in the yard he had been greeted by everyone clamouring to tell him the good news and patting him on the back as if he had managed the whole process alone, but as soon as he could get away he bounded up the stairs to see his child and even more important, to make sure that Joanna was safe and well.

He kissed her tenderly and smoothed her sweat-soaked hair away from her brow. 'Thank God you're safe,' he breathed, 'and the lad, too.' He closed his eyes briefly. 'I have so much to be thankful for.'

Joanna stretched out her hand and took his. 'We both have, love.' She shifted a little so that he could see the baby better. 'I think I should like to call him Jack, if you don't mind, Tom,' she said thoughtfully.

'Whatever you will, my love,' he said. 'Jack's a good name. But is there any particular reason?'

'Yes. I should like to call him Jack, after his great-grandfather.'

Tom frowned. 'But he hasn't got . . .'

'Jack Ingram, Liddy's father. He's our baby's great-grandfather.' She looked down at the baby. 'I think it might please Liddy,' she said softly.

The next morning when Tom opened the door there was a bunch of wild violets on the step. He took them up to Joanna.

'I don't know where these came from,' he said, 'but they smell of springtime.'

'Oh, I do.' Eagerly, Joanna held out her hand for them. 'Liddy will have brought them for the baby.'

Tom laughed. 'Don't be silly, Jo. How would she know he's born? He's not twenty-four hours old yet. Who can have told her?'

Joanna smiled and shook her head. 'I don't understand it, either, Tom, but it seems there are some things Liddy doesn't need telling,' she said.

Chapter Twenty-Eight

For Tom the best part of each day was when his work was done and the evening meal cleared away. Then he would sit in his armchair, smoking his pipe and watching Joanna feeding their son, a contented man. He appreciated that he had much to be grateful for; he had a roof over his head, a loving little family, as much work as he could handle, and could rightly and without arrogance boast that he was one of the best makers of penknives in the whole of Sheffield.

Although little Jack was not yet three months old, so not of an age to appreciate it, he was already the possessor of a tiny, ten-bladed penknife, the handle of which was inlaid with pearl; a work of art that had been proudly and lovingly crafted by his father.

Tom was quietly musing on these things as he puffed his pipe one evening in July. It had been a hot sticky day and he had been glad to come home to the relative coolness of the house. Even so, Joanna had propped the door to the yard wide to catch what little air there was.

She had just finished feeding Jack and laid him in his cradle when there was a knock at the open door.

She peered out. 'Lynwood!' Her hand flew to her bodice to make sure it was properly buttoned after Jack's feed. 'How nice to see you,' she added lamely.

'May I come in?' Hesitantly, Lynwood stepped over the threshold.

Seeing who it was Tom got to his feet, annoyed that his precious evening's peace was spoiled.

'Is there something you're wanting, Silkin?' he asked, immediately on the defensive.

Lynwood gave a slow, ironic smile. 'Now that's hardly a question you'd be wanting me to answer, Cartwright, is it?' he said, his gaze resting on Joanna, making her blush. His tone changed. 'Would you object to my sitting down for a few minutes?'

'If you must.' Tom indicated the couch under the window, then resumed his own seat, still prickly and suspicious.

'God, the town stinks even worse than usual in this heat,' Lynwood said, fanning himself with his hat. 'But I suppose you don't notice it when you live in it all the time.' He turned to Joanna, his tone changing. 'I heard you'd had a son, Jo. I've brought him a small gift.'

Tom's fist crashed down on the table. 'My son needs nothing from you, Silkin,' he said, not quite shouting the words. 'And if you don't like the smell of the place you're not forced to visit.'

Joanna laid her hand on Tom's arm and said quietly, 'Don't be like that, Tom. If Lynwood has been kind enough to bring Jack a present it would be churlish of us to refuse it.' She smiled at Lynwood. 'It's kind of you to think of him, Lynwood,' she said eagerly. 'What have you brought him?'

Lynwood reached into the bag at his feet. 'It's nothing much. Just a silver tankard. I had it made for him. Look, it's got his name, Jack Cartwright, on it.' He beamed, clearly delighted to have brought the gift.

'Oh, Lynwood, it's beautiful,' Joanna said. 'Look, Tom, isn't it beautiful?'

Tom glanced at it. 'Very nice,' he growled, Lynwood's words 'nothing much' and 'just a silver tankard' sticking in his craw.

'I've brought a few of the new season's vegetables from the kitchen garden, as well. And the first strawberries. I know how you love strawberries, Jo.'

'Oo, lovely. Thank you, Lynwood.' Joanna felt as if she was being tugged in two. Lynwood was almost pathetically pleased to have brought the gifts and she was genuinely grateful to him. Quite obviously it had never entered his mind that Tom would feel patronised by his actions. But at the same

257

time, she hated to see Tom offended, which clearly he was, and she could quite understand his animosity. No man likes to have his inadequacies pointed out to him.

She studied Lynwood. He was as well turned out as ever, but from the way his clothes hung on him he had lost quite a bit of weight and his face had become quite lantern-jawed. He seemed more subdued, less full of himself than Joanna remembered. Suddenly, in spite of the way he had treated her in the past, she felt sorry for him.

'Would you like a cup of tea, Lynwood? I'm afraid that's all we have. We can't afford wine.' As soon as she had said the words she could have bitten her tongue out. 'But Tom makes very good beer.' Belatedly, she tried to make amends and smiled at Tom.

His face was like granite.

But Lynwood didn't appear to notice. 'I'd very much like some of Tom's beer,' he said, almost over-eager.

Joanna reached down mugs from the shelf and poured two mugs of beer and gave one to Lynwood and the other to Tom.

'This is uncommonly good beer, Cartwright,' Lynwood said, draining his mug at a draught and pushing it over for more.

Tom didn't reply, still not convinced he wasn't being patronised, and the two men drank in silence for several minutes, with Joanna watching them both like a cat watching a mouse, almost holding her breath as she waited to see what would happen next.

Suddenly, Lynwood stared into his beer, then put down his mug carefully, saying in a thoughtful tone, 'You may be surprised at this, but I'll not pretend I don't envy you, Cartwright.'

'You don't need to tell me that, Silkin. But you had your chance and threw it away, so I'd be obliged if you'd drink your beer and leave us in peace,' Tom said shortly.

Lynwood held up his hand. 'No. Hear me out. You're a lucky man. You've a snug little house here, a woman who dotes on you, a trade at your fingertips and a son to carry on your name.' He shook his head. 'No man could ask for more than that.'

Tom's hackles rose. 'Are you making fun of me, Silkin,

258

because I'm only a humble maker of penknives?'

Lynwood looked quite shocked, yet at the same time puzzled. 'Indeed, I'm not, Cartwright. The skill you bring to your craft is well known. What I'm saying is, you're making something of your life, which is more than I can claim to be doing.'

Tom was not to be mollified. 'Then you're hard to please. You've got a large house to live in, a button factory to keep you in luxury, not to mention the various other businesses that your godfather left you – most of it stolen from Jo, if I may say so. What in tarnation's name more can you want?'

Lynwood drained his mug and put it down on the table. 'You don't understand, do you? What's the point of all that when I've no aim or direction in my life?' he said bitterly. 'Oh, I've got money, more than I know what to do with, but what's the good of that when I've nobody to spend it on, nobody to care whether I live or die, nobody to please but myself, when all I do is rattle around in a house full of servants with nobody to call my own.'

'It was you that made that choice. Nobody else,' Joanna said softly.

He looked at her and his eyes were full of pain. 'Yes. And it's a choice I've regretted every day of my life since.'

Joanna took Tom's hand. 'Well, there's no going back on it, Lynwood. I belong to Tom now and I shall never leave him.'

Lynwood nodded, defeated. 'I know. I can see it would be useless to try and persuade you to come back to me. As for the money your husband—' he shrugged, 'I might as well call him your husband, because although you've never been churched that's what he is – the inheritance your husband says I cheated you out of, I'd be more than happy to—'

'We want nothing from you, Silkin,' Tom said quietly. His temper had cooled and he was beginning to see this wealthy young man for what he was, lonely and rudderless. 'We don't need your money. We've everything we need, thank God.'

'But you'll not refuse the present for Jack?' Lynwood asked anxiously.

Joanna picked it up. 'Of course not. Thank you, Lynwood. And thank you for the produce from your garden. It was kind of you to think of us.'

'I think of you all the time, Jo.' Lynwood turned his head and studied Tom. 'And you, too, Tom. You're a lucky swine.'

Tom nodded. 'I know it.'

Lynwood got to his feet. 'Thank you both for your hospitality. It's been a privilege to be here and talk to you.' He gave a crooked smile. 'But I must be careful not to outstay my welcome.'

Tom drained his own beer, then took out his handkerchief and mopped his beard with unnecessary thoroughness.

'There's no need to go yet,' he said at last and with obvious reluctance. 'If you've nowt better to do you could stay and help me finish the keg of beer. It's time it were emptied.' In his embarrassment his speech had coarsened.

Lynwood's face lit up like a small boy presented with a bag of sweets. 'Thank you, I'd be more than pleased to.' He held out his mug. 'It's very good beer. And you make it yourself?'

'Oh, aye. I've always got some brewing in the cellar. It's better'n what you can get in t'beer shop.'

'How do you make it so good? Is it the hops?'

Tom hesitated fractionally, then said, 'Come and have a look. I'll show you.' The two men went off down to the cellar. After some long time Joanna heard a burst of laughter and by the time they stumbled back up the cellar steps they had their arms round each other's shoulders and were none too steady on their feet.

'I shall keep you to that. Next time you come, then, Lynwood,' Tom said owlishly, wagging his finger at Lynwood as he staggered off to try and remember just where it was he'd left a small lad holding his horse some two hours before.

Lynwood raised his hand. 'Aye. I'll remember to bring a pack with me. Goo'night, Thomas.'

'Goo'night, Lynwood.'

Tom came back into the room and slumped down in his armchair. 'Poor devil,' he said, shaking his head. He wagged his finger at Joanna. 'He's got no proper friends, that's his trouble.'

'Did I hear you say he'll be coming again, Tom?' she asked carefully.

'Aye. He's going to teach me to play cribbage. I've allus

wanted to learn but never seemed to find the time.' He picked up his pipe from the hearth and began to ram home the tobacco. 'Poor devil,' he said again. 'Got no proper friends. That's his trouble. Got no proper friends.'

Joanna said nothing but she sent up a silent prayer of gratitude as she reached over and took a large ripe strawberry and bit into it. Then she picked up her mending.

She never discovered what had gone on between Tom and Lynwood that night, but from then on whenever Lynwood called Tom made him welcome and showed no sign of resentment when baskets of fruit and vegetables from Cliffe House made their appearance.

For his part, Lynwood was careful not to visit too often and never to offend Tom by allowing his generosity to overstep the mark.

Joanna was glad there was no longer rivalry and suspicion between the two men. She was aware that Lynwood loved her; how much he had loved her had only dawned on him after he had lost her, but he never by word or gesture gave Tom cause for jealousy. Whatever had been said that night in the cellar over Tom's beer must have cleared the air and left Tom secure in the knowledge that Lynwood was no threat to his happiness with Joanna.

As for Joanna's own feelings towards Lynwood, in private moments she sometimes wondered what life with him at Cliffe House would have been like. She was realistic enough to suspect that he would probably not have been entirely faithful to her, had they stayed together. It had always been Lynwood's nature to hanker for what he couldn't have so once she was his he could easily have lost interest in her, leaving her to end up with a life as empty and lonely as his patently was now. She gave a contented sigh, watching the two men drinking beer and laughing together over their card game, and a rush of love for Tom filled her. Liddy had been right, she was much happier with things as they were.

Each Friday she took little Jack to the market with her, mainly to buy eggs from Martha. But on two Fridays at the end of the summer Martha wasn't there. Enquiries to the carrier elicited the information that she wasn't at the end of the road where she always stood when he passed so he took it she'd no eggs to sell and didn't wait.

But Joanna wasn't happy at this explanation, so she made a little nest for Jack in the corner of her shawl and, travelling part of the way on the horse bus – a real treat – and the rest of the way on foot, she made her way to Bradshaw's Farm.

As she went she managed to convince herself that she was no longer afraid of Saul Bradshaw. Why should she be? If he put a foot wrong he would have Tom to deal with, Tom had already convinced her of that in no uncertain terms. So she held her head high, Jack cradled comfortably on her hip, and walked across the bridge that spanned the Porter Brook. She paused here for a moment and watched the water being diverted from the little, fast-flowing river through a simple goit to keep the dam that fed Bradshaw's Wheel filled. Although in her childhood she had taken the working of the wheel for granted as she stood watching now she was fascinated by the fact that the water was taken from the little river and stored in the dam and, when it had been used to turn the wheel, diverted back into the river to flow on its way, its work done.

'It's clever, Jack, isn't it?' she said, hitching the baby further on to her hip. 'I'd never really thought about it before.'

She carried on over the bridge and down the little lane on the other side of the Brook to Bradshaw's Farm.

Martha was sitting in her rocking chair by the fire, rubbing her hands to try and get some warmth into them although the weather was still warm outside. Her fact lit up when she saw Joanna.

'Ee, love, fancy you coming all this way to see me.'

'Well, you haven't been to the market. I thought you might be ill.' Joanna went over and kissed her.

'No, not really. The old rheumatics make my knees crammocky, that's all. I thought I'd give it a miss for a week or two.' She struggled to get to her feet. 'Hold on a minute, I'll set t'kettle on th'hob. You'll stay and have a cup o'tea, won't you, love?'

'Yes, I'll be glad of one, carrying this lad. But I'll mash, Martha. You hold Jack.' Joanna put the baby on Martha's lap.

'You've no need to bother. Call Edie in from t'dairy. She'll do it.'

'Edie?'

'Aye. Sin' I've not been able to work in t'dairy I managed to persuade Saul to get a young lass from the work'us to give a hand. She's a likely lass, half-starved when we got her o'course but she's fillin' out.'

As if in answer to her name a girl who looked to Joanna no bigger than the milk churns she had to handle came into the kitchen.

'I've done that, Missus. Oh, I beg pardon.' She sketched a curtsy in Joanna's direction.

'It's all right, Edie. This is Mrs Cartwright, come to see me. Just mash t'tea then you can go and peel tatties ready for supper in back scullery.'

'Very well, M'm.'

Martha sat cuddling Jack and watching her little maid scuttle about taking down cups and pouring tea. When she had gone, taking a mug of tea with her at Joanna's suggestion, Martha smiled down at Jack. 'Ee, he's a bonny lad and no mistake.' She looked up at Joanna. 'My great-grandson. Ee, I never thought to see t'day I'd have a great-grandson.' She saw with dismay the expression of distaste that crossed Joanna's face at being reminded who her own father was and said hurriedly, 'He's t'image of Tom, too. Although he looks better fed. Young Tom spent most of his time half-starved.'

Joanna sipped her tea, smiling to herself. Martha had taught Edie to make tea every bit as thick and black as she made it herself. She nodded. 'Yes, do you remember how I used to take him baked potatoes and we used to eat the berries in Whitely Woods?' She paused and gazed out of the window, the teacup still in her hand. 'He always said he'd wed me. I used to laugh at him.'

'Maybe one day you will, love,' Martha said thoughtfully.

Joanna looked at her in surprise. 'What do you mean? Oh, I see. Yes, I suppose we might get wed one day. To tell you the truth I'd forgotten we weren't.'

It was true.

She poured more tea and they sat drinking it and reminiscing while Jack fell asleep on Martha's lap.

263

They had been talking for some time when a heavy step in the yard made them both turn to the door apprehensively.

'Aye, it's about time for Saul to come back,' Martha whispered. 'Pour him a mug o'tea, love, that'll sweeten him a bit.'

Even as she finished speaking the door opened and Saul came in.

He glared at Joanna, then frowned and said to Martha. 'Who's this?' Then, as his mind cleared, 'What's she doing here?'

'I came to see Martha,' Joanna replied without raising her voice. 'And I can speak for myself, thank you.'

His lip curled. 'Ha, pride comes before a fall. Took a tumble in t'world, didn't tha, wi' tha high and mighty ways. Got left at t'church door. Oh, aye. I heard. It were all over t'town. Serve tha right, stuck up bitch.' He stared at her plain blue gingham dress and cotton shawl. 'None o' tha fancy trappings now, I see. Not on what Tom Cartwright can provide.' He went on mumbling, repeating himself over and over. 'Stuck up bitch. Serve tha right. Stuck up bitch. Come down in t'world.'

'Tom and I do very well. We have all we need.' Her voice shook with fury that he should speak so disparagingly of Tom. She went on, 'I may say he provides for me better than you've ever provided for Martha. And he doesn't treat me as a slave the way you always did, you great bully.' She got up from her chair, her chin held high. 'I only hope you treat young Edie better than you ever treated me.'

'Why you little—' he lunged at her but she side-stepped him.

'Don't you dare touch me! Tom said I was to tell him if you tried to as much as lay a finger on me. He's a fine man,' she looked Saul up and down, he was showing signs both of age and debauchery and his movements were slow and sluggish, 'he'll have no trouble dealing with you.' She turned to Martha. 'We must go. I'll come and see you again, Martha, dear.'

'Oh, I shall be at t'market next week, lass,' Martha said, returning her kiss and giving one to Jack before relinquishing him.

Proudly, Joanna wrapped the baby in her shawl and walked

264

past Saul, her head high. He stared at her, then at the baby, screwing up his eyes and even stepping forward to get a closer look.

'Aye, tek a look at your great-grandson,' Martha said proudly, 'he's a bonny lad and no mistake. A real chip off t'old block.'

Joanna was watching Saul. His face was flushed a dull red as he looked from her to the baby and back as if he wasn't quite sure what he was seeing. 'Did you not know I was a mother now?' she said, shielding the baby from his gaze.

He shook his head, all the bluster gone out of him. 'No. No, I never knew.'

'Oh, that piece of news wasn't all over t'town then,' she said, imitating his voice.

He slumped down on his chair. 'Where's my tea?'

'Here. Right in front of you.' Joanna leaned forward and pushed the mug over to him, misjudging the distance so that the whole lot tipped into his lap.

With a roar of rage he got to his feet. 'You bitch—!'

But she had gone, slipping out of the door with a triumphant smile on her face.

Chapter Twenty-Nine

Joanna left the farm and went back up the lane. When she reached the bridge she hesitated. Liddy had never seen Jack. Maybe she wouldn't be interested, but after all, he was her grandson so she had a right to see him. And Jack Ingram might be pleased to know that his great-grandson was named after him.

Slowly, she turned and made her way into the wood by the track the charcoal burner used with his horse and cart. She was hardly a hundred yards into the wood when she saw the scarecrow-like figure of Liddy striding towards her.

'I knew you'd come today. I've been looking out for you,' Liddy said by way of greeting.

Joanna frowned. 'How could you have known? I've only just made up my mind to come.'

Liddy shrugged. 'Maybe I made it up for you.' She spoke in a matter-of-fact way but the words still sent a chill down Joanna's spine.

'I've brought my baby to see you. I thought it time you saw your grandson.'

A smile of genuine pleasure lit up Liddy's grimy face. 'Thank you, my girl.' She craned her head to look at little Jack. Then she made an impatient gesture. 'Oh, come and sit on that log over there so I can take a proper look at him,' she said.

They sat down and with a great effort Joanna steeled herself to say, 'Would you like to hold him?'

Liddy looked down at her filthy skirt, then at her grimy hands. 'Better not,' she said sadly, scratching herself. 'I wouldn't want to dirty the boy.'

Impulsively, Joanna put him on Liddy's lap. 'He'll wash,' she said with smile.

Liddy watched the baby in her arms for several minutes, and when she handed him back Joanna was surprised to see tears making a river down her cheeks. 'What do you call him?' she asked.

Joanna laughed. 'Don't you know? You seem to know everything else about me.'

Liddy shook her head, smiling through her tears. 'No, I don't know that.'

'We've called him Jack, after your father.'

'Oh!' Liddy's hand flew to her mouth. 'Oh, I don't know what to say.' She shook her head, her face crumpled as she tried not to burst into tears. 'Oh, thank you, my girl. Thank you.'

'I thought your father might like to see his great-grandson,' Joanna said softly.

Immediately, Liddy shook her head. 'No. No. That would never do.'

'But why not? Are you afraid his appearance might frighten the child?'

'Yes!' It was almost as if she latched on to this as an excuse, but then she looked away. 'No. It's not that,' she said, honesty getting the better of her.

'What is it, then?'

'He doesn't know.' The words were wrung out of her.

'Doesn't know what?' Joanna frowned, puzzled.

'Doesn't know about you.'

'I don't understand. How could he not know? Weren't you living here in the wood with him when I was born?'

'Oh, yes. We were living here, the two of us. In the hut, where we'd lived ever since we came here. But it wasn't difficult to hide. I'd always worn clothes that didn't fit properly, loose, baggy things.' She shrugged. 'I've never cared much what I looked like. But they came in useful then. They hid the fact that I was pregnant so he never noticed and I never told him.'

'But when I was born? Surely, he must have found out then?' Joanna could hardly believe what she was hearing.

Liddy shrugged again. 'It was the middle of the night. I

267

went outside. You were born under a bush. I wrapped you in my mother's cloak and . . . well, you know the rest.'

Joanna was silent for a long time, digesting Liddy's story. She had never felt so close to her mother before and now, at last, she felt able to ask the question that had always puzzled her.

'Liddy, the women in the town have great regard for you and your cures. They swear by your "women's physic" to save them from unwanted pregnancies. Why—?'

'Why didn't I use it on myself?' Liddy interrupted. She gave a wry smile. 'When I found I was pregnant I thought long and hard about it. A baby was the last thing I wanted, living in this place. But then I thought to myself, I can't do it. I can't destroy this life inside me. I've never before had anything of my own to love and care for. Never. This baby will be mine and nobody else's. I shall love it and look after it. Oh, I made such plans,' she said, her voice dreamy. 'I was going to leave this place and make a proper home for us, somewhere in the country—' Her voice changed. 'Then you were born. It was a freezing cold March night and you were such a tiny little scrap. I realised that the hut where we lived was no place to take a baby. God, what sort of life would you have had, living like we do? Of course I'd realised by that time that I couldn't leave the old man, he could never have managed without me. So I wrapped you up and gave you back where you belonged. I knew Martha would love you. She'd always wanted a daughter.' She turned and looked at Joanna for the first time. 'Your life with the Bradshaws may not have been easy, Joanna, but it was a damn sight better than it would have been here with me. And him.' She jerked her head in the direction of the charcoal burner's hut. Suddenly, she got to her feet and said briskly, 'Thank you for bringing the lad to show me, but it's better you don't bring him again. I wouldn't want him to know about me and be ashamed.'

'I'm not ashamed, Liddy,' Joanna said quietly.

Liddy flushed with pleasure, then her mouth twisted. 'You were once, as I recall.'

'Ah, but I know you better now.' Joanna stood up and made a nest for Jack in her shawl. 'Have you always lived like this, Liddy?' she asked, carefully not looking at her.

'No, of course not.' Liddy gathered her tatty old cloak round her and strode off into the wood. 'My mother was a lady,' she called over her shoulder.

Thoughtfully, Joanna made her way out of the wood. There were so many things she would have liked to ask Liddy, so much she had left unsaid. She wondered if she would ever know her mother's whole story.

Joanna's daughter was born when Jack was not quite two years old.

'It would be nice if the new baby came on Jack's birthday, wouldn't it, Tom?' Joanna said as she kissed him goodbye one morning in late March. 'I think it's due in about a month and that would make it round about that time.'

'I don't mind when it comes as long as it arrives safely,' Tom said, laying his hand on her swollen belly. 'Oh, what's this on the step?' He stooped and picked up a small brown bottle and handed it to her.

Joanna took the bottle and sniffed it. Then she smiled. 'Liddy's been here,' she said. 'It's more of her mixture to help with my labour.'

'But how did she know you're pregnant?' Tom said with a frown.

Joanna shrugged. 'I don't know, but apparently she does.' She smiled. 'But she hasn't timed it very well this time, has she? I've still got a month to go.' She put the bottle in the pocket of her apron and patted it. 'But it'll keep till it's needed.'

Joanna spent the day cleaning the house in a fever of activity. She washed curtains and bed covers, scrubbed floors and polished all the furniture. When Tom arrived home she was beaming with satisfaction at what she had achieved.

He wasn't so enthusiastic. 'You'll be making yourself ill, Jo. You should be getting more rest.'

'Rubbish. If I worked down a coal mine—'

'But you don't work down a coal mine and I think you should get more rest.' He kissed the tip of her nose.

'I will,' she promised. 'Tomorrow.'

But during the night, after only three doses of Liddy's mixture, Sarah Jane was born.

'I thought you said you weren't due for another month,' Mrs Wagstaff said, as she cleaned the baby up and laid her in her mother's arms. 'There's nowt early about this one,' she said, raising her voice above the baby's yells, 'she's a bonny full-term if ever I saw one.'

'It seemed you knew better than I did when she was due, Liddy,' Joanna whispered, gazing down at the tiny puckered face.

'Eh? What's that you say?' Mrs Wagstaff put her hand to her ear.

Joanna raised her voice. 'I said she's beautiful. Call to Tom to come and see her, will you? But tell him to look on the doorstep before he comes up.'

It was no surprise when he walked in with a tiny bunch of violets in his hand.

Joanna took them from him, her eyes shining. 'Liddy must have searched very hard to find these so early in the year,' she said, as he bent to kiss her.

'What's wrong with kissing me properly?' she asked indignantly as he gave her a chaste kiss on the cheek. 'Don't I deserve a proper kiss after giving you this beautiful daughter?'

'Aye, you do, my love. But I've got a bit of a cough, must have caught a chill or summat and I wouldn't want you to catch it.'

She pulled him down to her. 'It's a bit late to worry about that, Tom Cartwright. If I'm to catch anything from you I'll have caught it by now.' And she kissed him soundly on the lips.

Lynwood came to see the new baby and was delighted when Tom asked him to be her godfather.

'I'll be honoured,' he said, 'if you're sure it's what you want, Thomas?' He was always very careful not to take Tom's friendship for granted.

'Oh, we're quite sure, aren't we, Jo?' Tom put his arm round Joanna.

When Joanna nodded happily, Lynwood said, 'Then I must find my little goddaughter a special present. I can't buy a lass a tankard, now, can I?'

'Nowt too expensive, mind,' Tom warned.

Lynwood smiled. 'All right, Thomas. Nowt too expensive.'

The next time he came he brought the baby a silver bracelet with her name on it. 'Is it all right?' he asked anxiously.

'What do you mean, is it all right?' Jo said with a laugh. 'Of course it's all right. It's beautiful.'

'What I meant was, will Thomas think it's too . . . well, too expensive?'

Tom came up from the cellar with two foaming mugs of beer. 'What's this about Thomas?' he asked, looking from one to the other.

'Lynwood's worried about the bracelet he's bought Sarah Jane,' Joanna said. 'He's afraid you'll think it was too expensive.'

Tom grinned. 'I've come to think that nowt but the best is good enough for my daughter,' he said happily. 'Here, lad, drink to her health. I think we should—' he never finished what he was about to say because a fit of coughing racked him. 'Tek no notice,' he panted, when the spasm was over. 'A drop of beer went down the wrong way, that's all.'

Joanna frowned. She hadn't seen him put the beer mug to his lips so how could he choke on it?

After that she watched him carefully. He had occasional bouts of coughing but always seemed to find a reason: he'd choked on a drink, a bit of smoke from his pipe went down the wrong way, most people who smoked pipes coughed in the morning, it helped to clear the tubes – there was nothing at all to worry about.

But Joanna did worry. In the back of her mind there was always the fear of the dreaded grinders' asthma, the disease that was a constant hazard for grinders, bent over their grindstones and inhaling the dust from them all day. Penknife-making didn't involve perpetual grinding although a certain amount had to be done, but surely not enough to put Tom at risk.

Her other fear was that he might have contracted consumption. There was so much of it about in the town and there seemed to be no cure except to go where the air was pure and clear. There was fat chance of pure, clear air in the middle of smog-ridden Sheffield.

When he began to lose weight Joanna said, 'You must do something, Tom. You're not well. Why don't you go and see a doctor?'

271

'We've no money for doctors, love. Doctors are for rich people.' He gave a little cough. 'We do all right on what I earn, but once the quacks get hold of you they bleed you dry. They're not getting hold of me.'

Joanna watched him, weighing her words. 'We could ask Lynwood,' she said tentatively. 'I'm sure he'd be glad to help. He might even know someone—'

Tom's face darkened and he thumped his fist down on the table. 'I've never yet asked Lynwood for owt and I'm not about to start now,' he said. 'He's a good friend to us and I don't mind when he brings a few bits from the garden at Cliffe House that he's no use for, or the odd present for the children. But I'll not ask for owt for myself and I'll not have you asking, neither. It'd spoil everything. Any road, if I went to the quack he'd likely tell me to rest up and I can't do that, I've got a big order for one of the big steamship companies to get finished.'

'So you realise you're not well, then?' Joanna said quietly.

'Aye, I'm a bit under the weather, but nowt that a bit of sunshine won't cure.'

'Why don't you go to see Liddy, if you won't see a doctor? She can cure most things.'

'Oh, stop blethering, woman, and leave me alone.'

That night Joanna lay awake staring up into the darkness and listening to Tom's laboured breathing for a long time. Of course it had been too good to last. She and Tom were so happy together, they had a comfortable little house – oh, it was not very big and not in a very nice area and it was difficult to keep the midden down the yard even half-way fresh, but it was home – two healthy children and – she put her hand on her stomach – she was almost sure there was to be a third, even though Sarah Jane was not yet six months old. She didn't mind that, she loved her children, but without Tom life didn't bear thinking about. He *was* her life. Her life and her love.

Her cheeks wet with tears, she felt for his hand.

The next day, after he had gone to work she left the children with the woman next door and went to see Liddy, confident she would have a cure for Tom. But for once it seemed Liddy had failed to know what was in her mind and wasn't there. The clearing where she and her father lived was empty, although the horse was grazing lazily among the trees and the cart, ready loaded with charcoal, was waiting near by. The door of the hut was closed. It was all very strange, and Joanna hesitated, half minded to go and knock on the door. But supposing Jack Ingram was there, on his own, what reason could she give for her intrusion on his privacy? And Liddy might be annoyed if he was upset.

Disappointed and vaguely worried, she retraced her steps out of the wood. She had just reached the edge of the wood and turned into Hangingwater Lane when she was relieved to see the familiar black-clad figure striding along the road towards her. But for once Liddy looked almost presentable, her face had been washed and her hair combed and her clothing was more or less neat. She was even wearing a new pair of boots.

'You've been to see me?' Liddy asked as soon as she was close enough.

'Yes.'

'Well, I wasn't there.'

'I found that out.' Joanna looked her up and down. 'You're looking very smart today, Liddy.'

'I've been to a funeral.'

'Oh.'

'The old man's. My father. He dropped dead last week. I buried him today.' She spoke in a matter-of-fact tone as if it was of no particular importance.

'Oh, I'm sorry, Liddy.'

'You needn't be. He was a miserable old devil.' All the same there was a glint of tears in her eyes.

'I'll walk back with you. I expect you're feeling a little lonely,' Joanna said.

'I'm used to that. But it's kind of you.'

They walked in silence into the wood and sat down on the log where they had sat before. 'He was a soldier, you know,' Liddy said after a while. 'Served with Wellington. He was a Captain in the Dragoons, a handsome man by all accounts. That was before he got shot in the face, of course.'

'Do you remember it?'

'No, I was only a baby. We lived in London. I don't remember that, either. In Grosvenor Square.' She gave a hollow laugh. 'My mother was the daughter of a diplomat, can you believe! There was plenty of money in the family, so I'm told, and of course they didn't want Sylvia to marry young Captain Ingram.' Her voice changed, became higher and extravagantly refined. 'What! Marry a common soldier? Marry a man with no connections and no prospects? My deah, that would never do!' Her voice changed back to her normal tone. 'But love conquers all, so they say, although I've never found it so. Anyway, they eloped and her loving family disinherited her. I don't think she ever saw any of them again.'

She paused for several minutes and Joanna waited, not wanting to risk interrupting Liddy's narrative. After a time she went on,

'I think they were happy enough, until he came home wounded, that is. Then he became something of a recluse. Understandable, when you think about it. He had difficulty in making himself understood, people couldn't bear to look at him – he couldn't even bear to look at himself, so he had all the mirrors taken down – he couldn't eat properly. It must have been a terrible time for my mother. Her handsome husband had come home from the war dreadfully disfigured, in mind as well as body, he couldn't get work so there was no money to pay the rent and they had a small child. She must have been at her wits' end. It was to her credit that she stayed with him.'

'She must have loved him very much,' Joanna said quietly.

Liddy nodded. 'Either that or she had nowhere else to go.'

'You don't remember any of this?' Joanna asked.

Liddy frowned. 'Not really. I do have some vague recollections of going to a big house with high rooms and long windows looking out on to lawns and gardens, I think my mother went to ask her parents for help and took me with her thinking it would soften their hearts. But it didn't. They refused to have anything to do with us.' She shrugged. 'So we moved from lodging to lodging, each one worse than the last. I don't really know how we came to end up here in Whitely Woods. To tell the truth I hardly remember living anywhere else. But it was something my father could do for a living, at the same time keeping himself relatively hidden away, so I suppose it was better than a debtors' prison. I know my mother hated it.' She spread her hands. 'Poor Mama. Just imagine. After the life she'd been used to, being forced to live in this hovel. No wonder she pined away and died.'

'How old were you when she died?'

Liddy looked blank. 'I don't know. I'm not even sure how old I am now. I suppose I must have been something like twelve? Fourteen? Something like that. Anyway, I was old enough to work with my father and look after him.' She stared into the distance. 'He was a miserable old devil but he was never unkind to me. He never, ever laid a finger on me, never beat me. I think he was fond of me, in his way. And it's funny, I never really thought of him as being ugly. I suppose you get used to these things. It used to upset me when children called him names or ran away, frightened.' Her voice died away and they both sat silent, each busy with her own thoughts.

'Thank you for telling me, Liddy,' Joanna said at last. 'I always thought it strange that you should be living like this. Your speech, the way you hold yourself, your manner . . . it didn't seem to fit, somehow. Now I know why.'

'Well, you've a right to know. I've always meant to tell you.'

Joanna smiled. 'And of course, it explains the blue velvet cloak.'

Liddy nodded. 'It was my mother's. The one thing she refused to part with. I think she always cherished the hope that one day she would wear it again. But of course she never did. I did think of having her buried in it when she died but it seemed a waste, somehow. But it seemed fitting to wrap you in it. Something of your grandmama's.'

Joanna hung her head. 'I'm sorry I threw it back at you. I wouldn't have done if I'd known.'

'I understood that. But it's yours. You must have it back. Sometime.' She gave a deep sigh. 'But not today.' She got to her feet and Joanna rose with her. 'Thank you for keeping me company. It helped. Like I said, he was a miserable old devil but I expect I shall miss him.'

'Will you stay here?'

Liddy looked at her in surprise. 'Where else would I go?'

'You could go anywhere you liked.'

She shook her head. 'No. I feel safe here in the wood with my herbs and potions. People like to come to me for their cures. They feel brave, coming to Liddy the witch with their troubles.' She shrugged. 'Anyway, it's all I've ever known.'

Joanna leaned over and kissed her cheek. 'I shall come and see you sometimes and if ever you need me you've only got to call me.'

'I guess I needed you today,' Liddy said with a smile, putting a hand to the place Joanna had kissed. 'There's no one else I could have talked to.'

'But I didn't know,' Joanna protested.

'You came. That's the important thing.'

Joanna turned to go. Somehow, in spite of her anxiety over Tom she couldn't bring herself to trouble Liddy for a cough cure. Not today.

Chapter Thirty

Joanna's second son, Paul, was born when Sarah Jane was barely eleven months old. Unlike her first two pregnancies, Joanna had been sickly and listless the whole time, hardly able to make the effort to keep the house clean and the family fed. Added to this the winter had been particularly long and harsh, with thick depressing fogs and snow that piled in filthy heaps at the side of the road and made walking treacherous and slippery.

It was an anxious time, too. Unable to face the long trip to Whitely Woods to see Liddy, Joanna worried about her mother, living alone now in her isolated cabin. She worried about Tom, too. His cough seemed to be getting worse, although he insisted it was improving.

The highlight of their week was when Lynwood came to see them. He paid them a visit most weeks, and usually brought Joanna some delicacy or other to tempt her appetite. It was a measure of Tom's concern over her that he didn't discourage this and showed nothing but relief when she took a few bites of a hot-house peach or ate a morsel of smoked salmon.

The two men always played a hand of cribbage – this was ostensibly Lynwood's reason for visiting – and at least once during the evening he would casually offer Tom a fill of tobacco from his pouch, saying with a laugh, 'Have some of mine. At least I smoke a decent brand. What's that vile muck you smoke? Horse shit and tram tickets?'

'It's good honest shag,' Tom laughed back at him, a laugh that ended in the usual fit of coughing.

'God, listen to you! That muck you smoke's rotting your

lungs,' Lynwood said. 'Take another fill for later.' He spoke teasingly as he pushed his pouch across the table, but deep down he was anxious about his friend.

'I'll be better when the summer comes,' Tom said. 'We'll *all* be better when the summer comes,' he added with a sigh, glancing at Joanna, looking tired and pale as she sat with a pile of mending untouched on her lap.

The night Paul was born was a night of thick, damp fog that enclosed the world in a shroud of silent stillness. Mrs Wagstaff, the birthing woman, demanded to be paid extra for turning out in such dreadful weather. But the next morning Tom discovered that the vile weather hadn't prevented two bottles being left on the doorstep, one to ease the birth pains and the other labelled in neat copperplate handwriting, '*To help you regain your strength*'. Nobody saw Liddy come and go but there was no doubt that it was she who had left them. Joanna heaved a sigh of relief. At least now she knew that Liddy had survived the winter.

Paul was a sickly child, unlike the other two, and despite Liddy's physic Joanna took a long time to recover from his birth. The fact that the other two children were healthy and boisterous didn't help because it meant that there was no peace to be had anywhere in the little house. Joanna became more and more depressed; she felt down-trodden and ill and perpetually worried about Tom.

'Things will get better when the summer comes, my love,' Tom said, trying desperately to cheer her up.

'Oh, yes. That's what you always say. "When the summer comes!"' Joanna mimicked sarcastically. 'Only the summer never does come here, does it? You can't ever see the sun for the smog. The only way we can tell that summer has come is that there's no air and the place is full of flies.'

Tom tried to take her in his arms. 'I'm sorry, sweetheart. It's all my fault. I should never have—' he broke off with a fit of coughing that seemed to rack his thin frame.

Joanna was immediately contrite. 'No, it's my fault. I'm bad-tempered and ungrateful. We've got three lovely children and a roof over our heads. And each other.' She held him close. 'As long as we have each other, Tom, we'll survive.'

Tom stared out of the window. The way things were going

278

he wondered just how long that would be. Of course, it was all his fault. He should never have saddled Joanna with three children in under three years. But he loved her so much and that love demanded fulfilment, a fulfilment that she craved as much as he did.

Lynwood began to visit more often, sometimes twice a week. He was desperate to help but knew he must be careful not to offend Tom's fierce independence. So he contented himself with small gifts and in the darkness of his lonely bed at night he had guilty thoughts of Joanna coming back to him, should Tom die, as he surely would if that cough didn't improve. He had treated her badly once; if he was given a second chance he would make up for that, he swore to himself. God knew, he had suffered for his sin, seeing her living in that tiny hovel with Tom, making the best of the squalor they were forced to endure, the flies, the stink. Sometimes it almost turned his stomach to walk though the yard to reach the door. No wonder the baby was sickly. And the thought of Tom sharing her bed . . . He turned over in an effort to rid himself of the picture the thought conjured up. Yet he liked Tom, loved him, even, as a man loves a brother. And he had great respect for his independent spirit. In fact, it had been Tom's example that had made him look at his own life and realise what a wastrel he had become since losing Joanna.

Now, he was a reformed character. He took an interest in the Button Factory, he knew every process in the making of buttons of every kind, and as the factory prospered again he was gradually finding the money to repair Bradshaw's Wheel and the other Wheels he owned on the Porter Brook, one which drove a flour mill and another cutlers' wheel further up river. There were also a couple of small shops that paid rent.

He had let Cliffe House run to seed at first, not caring that the servants were robbing him blind and pleasing themselves whether they worked or not. But not any more. The house shone with polish, the glass sparkled, the carpets were well brushed, the gardens were well tended, everyone was well fed; he checked the housekeeping accounts every month to make sure tradesmen were not overcharging and that everything was running smoothly and nothing was wasted. Oh, he was a model master. His only problem was that there was no mistress of the house to enjoy the fruits of his labour. She was living in squalor . . . His thoughts had turned full circle.

Deliberately, he began to think of the next day. It promised fine and spring-like. He had recently bought a new hunter, he enjoyed his horses, always had. A good gallop over the hills would blow the cobwebs away after the dreary winter. On that thought he fell asleep.

It was the last day of April. At last Joanna was beginning to feel a little more energetic. Today she had given the living room a spring clean and even found time to do a batch of baking as well.

She was serving a mutton pie she had made.

Tom held up his hand. 'Don't put too much on my plate, love. I'm not very hungry.'

She paused, a second piece of pie poised over his plate. 'What's the matter, love? Aren't you well?'

'A bit tired, that's all.'

'It's fresh pie. I made it today. To Mrs Goffin's recipe.' She smiled at him encouragingly.

'Well, just a morsel more then.' He said it more to please her than because he wanted it.

She cut another small piece and put it on his plate, then finished serving the children and sat down at her own place, unbuttoning her blouse so that Paul could suckle while she ate her own meal.

'I wonder where Lynwood's got to. We haven't seen him for nearly a month,' she remarked, leaning over to wipe a dribble of gravy from Jack's chin as she spoke. 'I wonder if he's ill.'

'There's a lot of sickness about,' Tom said. 'Perhaps he's afraid he'll pick something up if he comes here. Any road, the weather's been pretty foul up till now, perhaps that's what's kept him away.'

'That's more likely. I wouldn't have thought—' she broke off as there was a loud rap at the door. 'Perhaps that's him now.'

'No, he usually taps and walks in these days.' Tom scraped his chair back and went to the door.

He stood talking for several minutes. Joanna craned her neck to see who it was he was talking to but the lintel was in the way and she could neither see nor hear anything.

Eventually, he came back and sat down, chewing his beard thoughtfully. 'That was Lynwood's groom. What's his name? Osborne.'

'Oh, what did he want? Did he bring a message?' Even after all this time Joanna knew better than to sound too eager. Tom was a jealous man.

'Yes. Came to tell us that Lynwood's had a riding accident. That's why he hasn't been to see us lately. So he wants us to go and see him.'

'When? Did Osborne say?'

'Yes. He said he had orders to take us back with him but I told him we'd go tomorrow.'

'Oh, Tom, you shouldn't have said that,' Joanna said. 'If Lynwood wants us to go tonight, then we should go.'

He shrugged. 'Well, you know me, Jo. I don't like being ordered about.'

'This is different. Lynwood's been very good to us these past years and he's never asked anything in return. What sort of accident was it? Is he badly hurt?'

'I don't know. Osborne didn't say. Just said it was a riding accident.'

She got to her feet. 'You'd better go and see if you can catch Osborne. He'll hardly have had time to turn the carriage round. Tell him to wait. We'll be out in ten minutes.'

Still he hesitated.

'Oh, go on, Tom,' she pleaded. 'I think we owe Lynwood that much. And any road, it'll be better to ride in a carriage than take the horse bus and walk.'

'Very well.' Reluctantly, Tom went to call Osborne. While he was gone Joanna bustled around. She fetched a bowl of water and washed the children's faces and tied them into clean pinafores. Then she hitched the baby on to her hip and caught Sarah Jane round the middle so that she could carry her on her other arm.

'Hold on to Mama's skirt, Jack,' she called. 'We're going for a ride in a real carriage. What do you think of that!'

'Ride in a carriage,' he kept repeating, trotting behind her as she hurried across the yard to meet Tom, already on his way back.

'You've not given me time to change into my Sunday suit,' Tom complained as she handed Sarah Jane over to him.

'Don't be daft. Has Lynwood ever seen you in your Sunday suit when he comes to play cribbage with you?'

'No, but that was in my house. I've never been to his house before. I should have put my Sunday suit on.'

'There's no time. We mustn't keep Osborne waiting any longer.' She gave him a push towards the carriage.

It was a strange sensation, riding again in the carriage she had so often used as Abraham Silkin's wife. She touched the pale satin lining. It looked as if it had hardly been used since she last travelled in it. She studied her little family. Tom's face was set like granite, he was clearly not happy at being summoned so peremptorily and not given time to change into his Sunday suit. The two older children, in clean pinafores, their bare feet hardly reaching the edge of the seat, were sitting perfectly still, like small statues, too over-awed by the fact that they were riding in a real carriage to even turn their heads to look out of the window. Paul had fallen asleep on her lap, lulled by the motion.

They reached Cliffe House and the front door was opened before Osborne had time to let down the carriage steps. Norbert came out to greet them, his face impassive. He was far too well trained to show any glimmer of what his feelings might be at ushering in the former mistress of the house in her well-worn grey dress, with her retinue of three poorly dressed children and a man in his working clothes.

He led the way up the stairs. Jack dragged at Joanna's hand, savouring the feel of thick Turkey carpet under his bare feet and Sarah Jane, on her father's arm, gazed wide-eyed in wonder at the sparkling silver and glass. As for Joanna, it was almost as if she had never been away. Nothing seemed to have changed. She almost expected to see Abraham appear at the head of the stairs saying, 'Ah, there you are, my little love.'

She gave herself a mental shake. Things had moved on a long way since those days. She was no longer the pampered wife of an old man. That had been in another life.

Norbert knocked on Lynwood's door and announced them.

'Oh, come in, come in. Don't stand on ceremony,' Lynwood's voice sounded tetchy. But he managed something of a pleased smile when he saw them.

Joanna was shocked. He was lying propped up in bed, his face almost as white as the pillows, except for an angry-looking graze stretching from his chin to his brow.

'Take the children down to the kitchen, Norbert,' he ordered weakly. 'I've something important to discuss with my friends. Ask Mrs Osborne to feed them. That should keep them happy, children are always ready for food.'

He watched as Norbert took Paul awkwardly from Joanna.

'I'll bring the other two,' Joanna said quickly.

'No. No. Norbert can manage one on each arm,' Lynwood said impatiently. 'And Jack can follow him.'

Sarah Jane looked back uncertainly at her mother.

'It's all right, darling. Mama will come and fetch you soon,' she said, smiling at her encouragingly. Jack wasn't a bit worried, the thought of walking again on the soft Turkey carpet was keeping him happy.

'Norbert's not used to children, you can see that, can't you,' Lynwood said when they had gone. 'But he'll learn.'

'I don't see why he should,' Joanna said. 'He's a man's servant.'

'Come and sit down,' Lynwood said, ignoring her last remark. 'No, not there, over here, where I can see you.' He pointed to the brocade settee placed by the side of the bed for their benefit.

They sat down, side by side, Tom sitting bolt upright, his hands clasped between his knees, clearly uncomfortable in such opulent surroundings. Joanna was more relaxed, though slightly wary.

'No doubt Osborne has told you what happened?' Lynwood said wearily.

'He said you'd taken a tumble from your horse,' Tom answered.

Lynwood made a face. 'It was a bit more than a tumble, I fear. I was riding Jason, my new hunter. He's a fine horse but inclined to want his head. I used to take him out for a gallop every morning. We were still getting to know each other, you understand.'

They both nodded, although neither knew much about horses.

'Well, what happened was very simple, really. Jason caught his foot in a rabbit hole and went down and I went over his head.' He paused. 'Broke his leg, poor devil and had to be shot.'

'And you?' Joanna prompted.

'Me?' He paused again, his mouth working. When he had it under control he went on, 'The fall broke my back.'

Joanna's hand flew to her mouth. 'Broke your back! Oh, Lynwood! Oh, my God.'

He gave a mirthless smirk and went on as if she hadn't spoken, 'Unfortunately, there was no question of them shooting me. They don't treat humans who break bones as kindly as they treat horses.'

'That's no way to talk, man,' Tom said quietly, his face pale with shock.

'Why not? It's true. What have I got left to live for? Tell me that. Do you realise my legs are completely useless?' His voice rose on a note of near hysteria. 'I'm going to be stuck in a bath chair for the rest of my life! Do you understand? For the rest of my life!' A tear trickled down his cheek and he turned his head and brushed it away, hoping they hadn't seen it.

'There must be something—' Joanna began helplessly.

'There's nothing to be done.' Lynwood cut across her words. 'The doctors have agreed on that, and God knows, enough doctors have pushed and pummelled me about over these last weeks to make sure there's no doubt. Not that I could feel much,' he added gloomily.

'Oh, Lynwood.' Impulsively, Joanna reached over and took his hand. 'And to think we didn't know. When did all this happen?'

Lynwood frowned. 'About three weeks ago, I think. One tends to lose track of time just lying here, helpless.'

'And to think we'd no idea. We remarked on the fact that you'd not been to see us recently, but thought perhaps the weather— We would have come before if we'd known, wouldn't we, Tom,' She turned to him as she spoke.

'Aye. We would, man,' Tom nodded. The news had shocked him into forgetting his surroundings and he got up and sat on Lynwood's bed. 'If there's anything we can do, man, you've only got to say,' he said, his face creased with concern. 'Not that there's likely to be much *we* could do, I guess you've got about everything you need here to make your life as comfortable as it can be.' He gave a little smile. 'Perhaps I can come and play the odd game of cribbage with you, when you feel up to it.'

'I'm afraid I'm going to ask more of you than that, my friend,' Lynwood said carefully.

'We'll do what we can, you know that,' Tom said.

'Wait until you've heard what I'm going to say.' He looked from Tom to Joanna and back again.

'Well?' they both said.

Lynwood licked his lips. He was obviously getting tired. He closed his eyes as if to gain strength, then opened them and took a deep breath. 'I want you all to come and live here, at Cliffe House, with me,' he said.

Joanna and Tom stared at him; they were speechless. Tom regained his wits first. 'We couldn't do that, man,' he said, aghast.

'Why not?'

'Well, because ... because ... well, it wouldn't be right, would it?'

'I can't see why not.' Lynwood put his hand up to his brow. 'Look, I'm not in a fit state to argue with you at the moment. Come and see me tomorrow and we'll talk about it again.'

They both got to their feet. 'Yes, that's probably the best thing,' Joanna said.

'But don't reject the idea out of hand,' Lynwood said quickly. 'Just think what it would mean for the children to have the gardens to play in. And lovely fresh air to breathe. The fresh air would do Thomas good, too. It would help to get rid of his cough.' He closed his eyes, then opened them again. 'And I would so much like Joanna to have what's hers. She should have been mistress here, I should never have robbed her of that. It's always on my conscience.'

Joanna made a deprecating gesture. She didn't know what to say.

'You seem to have thought it all out, man,' Tom said after a bit.

'I've had plenty of time, lying here. It's the only thing that's stopped me from going out of my mind, planning and dreaming about having you here to live.' He went on, his voice dreamy. 'We'll be able to play cribbage, Thomas, and I'll teach you to play chess. And backgammon.' He saw the expression on Tom's face. 'I know you'll want more than that, Thomas. A life of indolence wouldn't suit you at all. But you could have a workshop in one of the outhouses, if that's what you'd like – maybe later on you could even tutor me in some of your skills.' He went on, warming to his subject, 'And when they're old enough the children can have a governess to teach them so that they grow up well-read and able to write and count. And Joanna,' he smiled at her, 'you managed the house once so it would be no hardship to take up the reins again.' He held out his hand and she took it. 'I should like to know you were here, Jo, and would come and sit with me sometimes.' He covered her hand with his. 'I don't need to tell you how I feel about you, I think you know. It would be such a comfort to me to know you were always here.' He turned his head to look at Tom and his mouth twisted wryly. 'Don't let that worry you, my friend. I'm content to come a bad fifth, after you and the children, in her affections.' He closed his eyes. 'I can't talk any more. Go away and think about it. Let me know tomorrow. I just hope to God you'll find it in your hearts to answer yes.'

Chapter Thirty-One

Tom and Joanna hardly exchanged words during the journey home, they were each too busy with their own thoughts. The children were less restrained. Over-excited by the good things they had been given to eat and the wonderful grassy places where they had been allowed to play they bounced up and down on the seats of the carriage, giggling and laughing, until Paul and Sarah Jane fell asleep and Jack became quiet and pale.

'I hope he's not going to be sick,' Joanna whispered absent-mindedly to Tom.

'We're nearly home now,' Tom said, keeping his eye on his elder son.

Their fears were groundless. Although Jack was a bit quiet and wobbly on his feet for a few minutes after he was lifted down from the carriage he soon regained his colour and began to chatter about what he had seen and done at Cliffe House.

'Can we go back to that big house, Mama?' he asked anxiously as later she tucked him into his little bed in the attic. 'I should like to see the puppies again. There were five of them and so new they hadn't even got their eyes open. I should like to see them with their eyes open.'

'We'll see, darling,' Joanna said, kissing him goodnight. She gazed round the room. It was as comfortable as she could make it, with two truckle beds, one for Jack and the other one where Sarah Jane was curled up like a petal, with her thumb in her mouth, fast asleep. A chest of drawers stood between the beds and there was a rag rug on the floor. There was no room for anything else and the ceiling was so low that Joanna could only stand upright in the middle of the room.

She could honestly say that this had never worried her before, but after a few hours in the lofty rooms at Cliffe House the contrast struck home. She noticed that there was a damp patch in the corner, too, where a tile on the roof had come loose. She hadn't seen that before. Thoughtfully, she went down the narrow uncarpeted stair to the floor below. Here the double bed she shared with Tom was pushed up against the wall to make room for the baby's crib and a wardrobe that Tom had bought cheaply although it was really too big for the room. It was an ugly wardrobe.

She shook herself mentally as she went down the next flight of stairs to the living room. These things had never worried her before, so why should she suddenly start noticing them now?

She spent a sleepless night listening to Tom coughing restlessly beside her. There were so many things to be considered it was difficult to see the right way forward, but as the night progressed she weighed everything in the balance and made her decision. But it was Tom who would make the ultimate choice and she wouldn't try to go against his wishes.

As soon as it was light he got up and went downstairs. She followed him.

'Well?' she said, crossing her fingers behind her back. 'What have you decided?'

He didn't answer at once but picked up his pipe from the hearth and knocked the dottle out. Then he rammed home tobacco and lit it. As usual the first draw of the day made him cough. When he had recovered his breath he said quietly. 'I've thought about it all night and my answer is yes, Jo. I think we should do as Lynwood asks and go and live at Cliffe House.'

She hadn't realised that she had been holding her breath waiting for his answer, but now she let it out in a long, relieved sigh and nodded slowly. 'I think so, too.'

'It's what Lynwood wants and if it will help him— God knows he'll need all the help and support we can give him, poor devil,' he said. In fact, he was being less than honest. His concern was more for Joanna than for Lynwood. He reasoned that if they moved to Cliffe House Lynwood would provide her with the security she would need if – when – he died. Because for some months now he had been trying to come to terms with the fact that his cough was not getting any better. He was dying. He gave himself a year at the most. It would help to ease the pain of leaving her a little if he knew she would be well cared for.

She nodded again, anxious not to appear too eager, knowing that Tom's jealousy still lurked just beneath the surface. 'Yes, I'm sure it will benefit Lynwood,' she agreed carefully. Her face brightened. 'And it will be so much better for the children.' The thought of them growing up strong and healthy through running around the grounds of Cliffe House and breathing fresh clean air made its own powerful argument. But like Tom, she was concealing her real reason. She had become increasingly worried about Tom's health and she was convinced that the only thing that would help his chest would be to get him out of the smog-filled atmosphere of the town. Sheffield was filthy. Standing in the grounds of Cliffe House, on top of the hill, she had been able to see very clearly the pall of foul air hanging like a dirty blanket over the valley in which the town stood. She had thought then that if only Tom could get away from that he might stand a chance of recovering. Now they had been offered that chance and she was desperate to take it.

'Lynwood will be relieved,' Tom said, his voice devoid of expression.

Joanna relaxed and uncrossed her fingers. 'He will, indeed.'

A month later they moved into Cliffe House.

To Joanna it was almost as if she had never been away. The house was as familiar to her as the back of her hand, she remembered the names of all the servants and they soon accepted her as surrogate mistress. What they said about her behind her back she neither knew nor cared as long as they treated her family with respect. She even found that her clothes were still in her closet where she had left them, although they hung a bit loose on her now, and Lynwood insisted on Lily being found and brought back.

'But I don't need a maid, Lynwood,' she said, appalled, worried at what Tom might think.

'Of course you do. How else will you manage all those fastenings women seem to need to fix their clothes with. And who will look after your hair?'

'I can do it myself. I always do.'

He shook his head. 'No, no, no. You must have it looked after properly.' He leaned forward and took a strand in his hand. 'You used to have such pretty hair. Now your curls have all gone and it's all lank and lifeless. You've been quite ill, haven't you, Jo?'

'Not really. Just a bit under the weather.'

'Well, we'll soon put some roses in your cheeks.' He smiled at her, then grimaced with pain. 'Can you move my pillows a bit? It's making my neck ache.'

She supported his head while she plumped his pillows.

'Ah,' he said, 'This brings back memories. Unfortunately, they are only memories. Burying my head in your bosom no longer has the effect it once did.' He closed his eyes and sighed with relief as she laid his head gently back on the pillows. 'Have Tom's suits arrived yet?' he asked without opening them.

'Yes. At least, two of them are ready.'

'Good. Tell him to put them on and come and show me. One at a time, of course.' He smiled at his own joke. Already he was beginning to get more colour in his cheeks and seemed to have regained the will to live. He opened his eyes and waved his hand to shoo her away. 'Go on, Jo. Go and tell him,' he said, with a trace of his old impatience.

'Very well.' She picked up her skirts and went to look for Tom. Today she was wearing a mulberry and pink striped redingote. It had always been one of her favourites and she savoured once again wearing skirts that swished and rustled as she walked and that billowed as she ran lightly down the wide staircase. Over the years she had schooled herself not to miss the rich opulence of Cliffe House and never to make comparisons, and she could lay her hand on her heart and say that she had been contented enough in the little house she had shared with Tom. But she couldn't deny that it was good to be back.

She found Tom in the outbuildings, looking for a suitable place for a workshop.

'Lynwood wants you to try on your suits, Tom. He's

anxious to see you in them,' she said, tugging at his arm.

'What, now?' He frowned. 'Oh, very well.'

He wiped his hands on his breeches and followed her into the house, taking off his boots as he went through the boot room and padding behind her in his stockinged feet.

In their bedroom she watched as he struggled into the unfamiliar fashions of the day, the tight purple kerseymere trousers with instep straps, the frilled cambric shirt, the striped silk waistcoat and the braid-trimmed jacket, the side-laced boots with cloth tops.

'You look very smart, love,' she said encouragingly as she helped to tie his cravat.

'I feel like a pox-doctor's clerk, if you want the truth,' he said grumpily, tugging at the waistcoat. 'This isn't me, Jo. I'm a working man, not some poncing dandy.' He turned this way and that, flexing his broad shoulders in the soft stuff of the jacket. 'When I was measured for these things the tailor took one look at my hands and you should have seen the expression on his face.' He held them up. 'Look at them, workman's hands, rough and calloused. Why should I be ashamed of them because some prick with a tape measure looked down his nose at them?'

'You've nothing to be ashamed of, love,' Joanna soothed.

'I know that. When he took out a penknife to sharpen his pencil I nearly told him it was one of mine, one that I'd fashioned from a lump of steel, from start to finish. *That's* workmanship, for you, not tiffling about with a tape measure all day, getting a cheap thrill out of taking inside leg measurements.'

Joanna burst out laughing. 'Oh, go on with you. Go and show yourself to Lynwood. I think he fancies a game of backgammon or cribbage or something.'

Tom went off, his jaw set. He wasn't happy at Cliffe House. He didn't like being dressed in clothes he wasn't comfortable in at someone else's expense. He didn't like having to be on hand whenever Lynwood called. He didn't like having nothing to do for the rest of the time. And when he offered to help the gardener he received such a shocked response that he never asked again. In short, he was like a fish out of water at Cliffe House. But he was determined to make the best of things, for Joanna's sake.

He consoled himself that it probably wouldn't be for long, although God knew he didn't want to die.

Joanna watched him go off to Lynwood's room. She knew he wasn't happy and she had the dreadful feeling that they were beginning to grow apart. And the reason wasn't simply that they had moved into grand, unfamiliar surroundings. It went deeper than that.

Since Paul's birth, four months ago, there had been no lovemaking. Joanna had always liked to sleep curled up in Tom's arms and if this led to a sleepy coupling, as it often did, it was no more than an expression of their profound love. But now Tom was afraid of making her pregnant again. He couldn't bear the thought of her being made old before her time with too frequent child-bearing so he had schooled himself not to touch her. His kisses were now hardly more than a quick peck on the cheek and he rarely even put his arm round her in case it led on to other things. He had even taken to sleeping on the far side of the bed – not difficult in the enormous feather bed they now shared. Joanna hated this and she knew that he did, too. It was putting a strain on them both at a time when they needed to be close and united.

Joanna realised that the remedy lay in her own hands so as soon as she was able she slipped away to visit Liddy. This was not too difficult because Whitely Woods was not far away from Cliffe House.

When she arrived Liddy was sitting on a bench in the sunshine outside her hut, smoking a clay pipe and whittling a piece of wood. She moved up to make room for Joanna.

'Come up in the world, haven't you?' she said, taking in Joanna's blue tarlatan dress with its ribbon trimmings. She smiled, revealing her broken, blackened teeth. 'I expect my mother used to wear dresses like that at one time.'

'I need your help, Liddy,' Joanna said.

'Of course you do. You need some of my women's physic. I don't know why you've never asked for it before.' She got to her feet, holding her side.

'Are you in pain, Liddy?' Joanna asked with a frown.

'It's nothing. I strained my side lifting the timber.' She

disappeared into the hut.

'You still make charcoal? Yes, I suppose it's your living.' Joanna gazed round the clearing, waiting until Liddy came out again. 'You don't need to do this heavy work any longer, Liddy,' she said carefully. 'I'm sure we could help you.'

Liddy drew herself up to her full height. 'I don't need help from any quarter,' she said proudly. 'I have all I need. And as for money—' She paused, clearly weighing her words, 'I suppose somebody should know and you have a better right than anyone else. When I'm gone you'll need to dig under the cabin floor. There's more money there than I'll ever need.'

Joanna gaped. 'I never meant—'

Liddy waved her silent. 'It'll be yours when I'm gone, what's left after my funeral's paid for. And I want a proper funeral, mind. Plumed horses. The lot!' She bared her black teeth again in a smile. 'But I'm not going yet, so don't get excited.' She showed Joanna two bottles. 'Get a bit of sponge and soak it in this stuff,' she shook the first bottle. 'Put it . . . well, you know where to put it, don't you?' She made a graphic and unmistakable gesture. 'If ever that one doesn't work you take a dose of this one. That should shift things.'

'Thank you, Liddy,' Joanna said taking the two bottles gratefully and putting them in her reticule.

'Tom's not happy, living at the big house, is he?' Liddy re-lit her clay pipe and puffed on it thoughtfully.

'He's not well. His cough—'

Liddy took the pipe out of her mouth and made an arc with it, dismissing Joanna's words. 'His cough will get better now he's breathing good air,' she said. 'It goes deeper than that.'

'He has no need to be jealous of Lynwood, if that's what you're thinking,' Joanna said with a frown.

'That's not what I was thinking,' Liddy said. 'Has he got a workshop yet?'

'No. There hasn't been much time, what with one thing and another. Lynwood—'

'Aye. Lynwood calls the tune, doesn't he? That's what sticks in Tom's craw. You'll need to be patient with him. He's not finding life easy.'

'I know, Liddy.' She blushed. 'That's why I came and

asked for your stuff.'

Liddy patted her shoulder. 'Sensible lass. You've got the right idea.' She looked at her closely. 'Are you happy, my girl, back living at the big house?'

Joanna thought for several minutes. 'Yes, I think I am, because I know it's so much better for Tom and the children to breathe the good, clean air.'

'That's not what I asked. Are *you* happy, my girl?'

Joanna smiled. 'Yes, I must confess I feel quite at home at Cliffe House.' She picked up a fold in her skirt. 'I love wearing these lovely clothes and bathing every day, feeling clean and sweet-smelling.'

Liddy nodded approvingly. 'That's what my mother could never get used to, not feeling clean. She used to bathe in Porter Brook every day, winter and summer. Probably that's what helped to kill her.' She shrugged. 'It's never bothered me. But I'm glad you're at home at Cliffe House. It shows you've something of your grandmother in you. I like that.' She nodded, well satisfied.

That night, as Tom donned the night-shirt he had taken to wearing in deference to his new life and got into bed, he found Joanna lying there naked.

'Oh, Jo,' he groaned, 'you're not being fair to me. God knows, it's difficult enough as it is without—'

'It's all right, Tom. I promise you it's all right. I went to see Liddy today. She gave me something to make sure there'll not be another baby.' She held out her arms. 'Come to bed, my love . . .'

Tom whistled as he went about the house the next day.

'You're mighty cheerful, my friend,' Lynwood said grumpily, as Tom helped to lift him out of bed and into his bath chair. He banged the wicker arms of the chair. 'Christ, I hate this bloody thing.'

'I know you do but without it you'll never move outside this room. I'm going to take you down to the paddock to see the horses.'

'I don't want to see the bloody horses. It was a bloody horse that broke my back.'

'Well, it's time you took a look at the accounts for the Button Factory.'

'I'm not interested.'

Tom sighed. 'I can't do everything, Lynwood. You've got to make some effort for yourself.'

'Joanna will help you. Uncle Abe taught her to figure.' He closed his eyes. 'I'm sure you and Joanna can see to things between you.'

Tom looked at him, alarmed. 'This is no way to talk, man. Come on. Whether you like it or not I'm taking you down to the stables. I've found one that'll do me nicely for a workshop and I want to show it to you.'

'That's it, then, isn't it? If you say that's what we'll do, then that's what we'll do. I don't have any say in it, do I? I can't bloody well walk away and say no thank you, I just have to make the best of it.' Lynwood set his mouth in a thin, hard line.

Tom walked round to the front of the wheelchair and looked down at him. 'Yes, that's just what you've got to do, man, make the best of it,' he said, his voice like steel. 'Like I'm having to. I'm a common working man, Lynwood. I'm not used to parading about in posh clothes and having nowt to do all day except be at your beck and call and it takes some getting used to, I can tell you. But I'm trying. God knows, I'm trying. And if you did the same we'd all be a lot happier. Jo and I came here to please you, Lynwood. Don't make our lives more difficult than they have to be.'

Lynwood stared at him in amazement. 'Don't you like it here at Cliffe House, then?'

'I didn't say that. But it isn't easy, knowing that the servants snigger behind my back because I don't use the right fork.' He saw the expression on Lynwood's face. 'Oh, don't worry, I'll stick it out and in the end I expect I'll get used to it, but just don't imagine that all the adjustment's on your side. Because it isn't.'

Lynwood was silent for several minutes. Then he said, 'Let's go down to the stables. And then perhaps we can take a turn round the garden and see how the artichokes are doing.'

Chapter Thirty-Two

Over the next six months things began to get slightly easier. Tom's outburst had given Lynwood pause for thought and he gradually became a little more resigned to his life in a wheelchair and began to take an interest in things outside his sick-room.

As for Tom, choosing an outhouse for a workshop was as far as he got; he was kept far too busy with Lynwood's affairs, because once he became resigned to his restricted life Lynwood took great pleasure in teaching him all he knew about the running of the Button Factory. Tom found this far more interesting than he had expected and spent extra time there, learning about the various processes involved in the making of buttons so that he could discuss matters with Lynwood and even suggest ways in which things could be improved. Eventually he became so knowledgeable that even the manager was not above asking his opinion on various matters.

Then there was the estate. Pushed in his wicker wheelchair by Tom, Lynwood toured the gardens most days, even in the worst of weather. He became fascinated by things that had never interested him before, indeed, things that he had never before noticed, like the colours of the changing seasons. With the warm autumn colours, as the leaves carpeted the orchard in bright red and yellow, and the hedges became bright with red and orange berries, Lynwood had an idea he might like to take up painting and capture the scenes on canvas. But snow had covered the garden before he could begin and he fumed at being stuck indoors and having to watch the children making snowmen and playing snowballs from his window instead of being out there, helping them.

He had become very fond of the children and at Joanna's suggestion he made pencil sketches of them playing in the garden. With practice these became quite good and he had them framed to hang round his room. He was inordinately proud of the six-bladed penknife that Tom gave him to sharpen his pencils with.

'You made it yourself, Thomas?' he asked when Tom first gave it to him, turning it over and over in his hands and examining the inlaid mother-of-pearl handle.

'Yes, of course I did. That's what I've done all my life, make penknives.'

'But the handle . . . all inlaid with mother-of-pearl. Did you do that, too?'

'Aye. It's done with a tool called a parsee. Quite tricky.'

Lynwood opened and closed the knife several times. 'Works like a dream.'

'It'll have your finger off like a dream, too, if you don't handle it right,' Tom warned.

'It's a beautiful piece of work. I shall treasure it.' Lynwood looked up. 'You're a clever bugger, aren't you?'

Tom shrugged. 'Zack Wenlock taught me well, even if he half-starved me in the process.'

'Well, you're not half-starved now,' Lynwood said with a laugh.

Tom didn't laugh. 'No. I'm not making penknives, either.'

Whilst Tom was out at the Button Factory, or collecting the rents from Bradshaw's Wheel and the other Wheels on the Porter Brook, Lynwood kept Joanna busy learning the money side of the various business affairs. At first she refused to take much interest, but in spite of herself she found the accounting system quite fascinating, especially as Lynwood was so keen to teach her.

'I shall soon know as much as you do, Lynwood,' she laughed one day.

'Good. Then I shall be able to devote my life to becoming a great painter,' he replied.

Sometimes the three of them would make plans for repairs and improvements to the properties. The floor around

Lynwood's wheelchair would be strewn with papers on which rough plans had been drawn, scribbled over and drawn again, or with costings and estimates and the odd pencil impression of new buildings that Lynwood had sketched. They passed many a pleasant winter evening this way.

'I don't suppose anything will come of them,' Tom said privately to Joanna, 'but it makes a change from backgammon or cribbage.'

'I thought you enjoyed a game of backgammon,' Joanna said.

He shrugged and gave a sheepish grin. 'I do. But he always wins. I owe him hundreds of pounds.'

'You don't play for money, Tom?' Joanna asked, aghast.

'Not proper money. We keep a running account.' He laughed. 'I usually win at cribbage so that makes it roughly equal.' He saw her expression. 'Don't worry, Jo. Money never changes hands.'

'Oh, that's all right, then.'

Tom shook his head. 'No, it's not really, is it, Jo? I'm not very happy at Lynwood paying us for being here and doing next to nothing. After all, we're fed and housed, we shouldn't expect to be paid as well. Paid generously, at that.'

Joanna laid her hand on his arm. 'You earn your money, Tom. You practically run things here. If anyone wants to know anything who do they come to now? You. And Lynwood is happy for it to be this way. As for your friendship, even Lynwood couldn't put a price on that.'

He nodded and looked at his hands. 'It's just that it doesn't feel like work to me.'

'Only because you don't get your hands dirty,' she laughed.

Things didn't always run smoothly, however. Joanna was furious when Lynwood insisted on engaging a nursemaid for the children.

'They're *my* children. I can look after them,' she fumed.

'Of course you can, Jo. You're a wonderful mother and they love you to distraction,' Lynwood said with a winning smile. 'It's really Mrs Osborne I'm thinking of.'

'What do you mean?'

'Well, they spend quite a lot of time with her when you're working here with me, don't they?'

She thought about it. 'Yes, I suppose they do,' she conceded grudgingly.

'There you are, then. If they had a nursemaid she would be responsible for them when you were busy instead of Mrs Osborne. That's all, Jo.' He smiled at her again.

She smiled back. It was good to see him cheerful again. 'Very well, Lynwood.'

He rubbed his hands together. 'Good. I thought perhaps Lily's young sister. She seems a likely lass. What do you think?'

She lifted her eyebrows. 'You've got it all worked out, haven't you?'

'I have plenty of time to think about these things when I can't sleep.'

'Well, if she's as good a nursemaid as Lily is as my maid I'll have no complaints.'

'Good. I'll tell Lily to fetch her over.'

So Lily's sister Primrose was engaged. The children loved her on sight and Joanna had to admit that it all worked very well. She made sure that she still had plenty of time with them, but sometimes she was kept so busy that she found herself glad that they were taken off her hands for a good part of the day.

Lynwood seemed to think of everything.

'Are you happier here at Cliffe House now, Tom?' Joanna asked one night as they lay close in the big bed, sleepy after lovemaking. 'I know you didn't like it at first. Being at Lynwood's beck and call all day and having to dress like a gentleman. But we've been here a year now and it seems to be working quite well.'

'Aye. It's not so bad,' he answered with a sigh. 'It's surprising what you can get used to when it comes to it. And Lynwood seems a bit more settled now he's faced the fact that his life is never going to be any different, poor devil. He doesn't have so many of those black moods, when he won't speak to anyone.' He sighed. 'It's funny, really. He seemed a lot better after I pointed out that things weren't all honey for us, either. I didn't like doing it, mind, but he got me on the raw, that day.'

'I know, love. But I'm sure it was better to get it out into the open.'

'Aye, it doesn't do to brood on things.' He gave a little cough.

'Your cough's much better now, Tom. It must be the fresh air. I've noticed, you don't cough much at all now.'

'Aye. I've noticed it, too. It's only when I go down into the town to the factory now. Or into the hulls on Porter Brook. It's the dust. It gets on to my chest. But a walk round the estate and a chat with the gardeners soon clears it again.'

'Perhaps it's as well you've never found time to make a hull here at Cliffe House then,' she said, snuggling closer to him.

'Oh, I'll find the time. Eventually. It's not right for a man like me to do nowt.'

'You do plenty, Tom Cartwright. You're always busy.'

'Yes, but it's not what I call real work.'

'Oh, go to sleep. I'll not argue with you any longer.' She snuggled even closer to him.

He turned and nibbled her ear. 'There'll be no sleep for me, woman, nor you neither, if you hold me like that,' he whispered, beginning to kiss her again.

They always woke early and it was Tom's habit to go along to Lynwood as soon as he was dressed. He knew that Lynwood slept badly, even with his nightly sleeping draught, so he was always glad of company as he drank his early morning tea.

This morning he met Norbert coming out of Lynwood's room.

'The master's still sleeping, Mr Tom,' Norbert said quietly. 'I thought it best not to disturb him. It's not often he gets such a good night's sleep.'

Tom frowned. 'Are you sure he's all right, Norbert? He never sleeps this late.'

Norbert began to look alarmed. 'I don't know, I didn't really look. He didn't speak like he usually does, so I thought he was still asleep. I put the tray down without drawing his curtains back because I didn't want to wake him. He was perfectly all right when I left him last night.'

'You're probably right, Norbert. He's sleeping late. But I'll just check on him, if you don't mind.' Tom went into

Lynwood's room with Norbert close on his heels.

Lynwood was lying back on his pillows, a half-smile on his face. Tom touched his face. It was quite cold.

'Pull back the curtains, Norbert,' he said urgently. 'I can't see—' As light flooded into the room they could both see that Lynwood's face was as white as the pillow on which he lay.

'Is he ill, Mr Tom?' Norbert said anxiously. 'He's very pale.'

Reluctantly, because he knew what he would find, Tom leaned over to feel the pulse in Lynwood's neck. 'It's worse than that, Norbert,' he said quietly, straightening up. 'Much worse. I'm afraid he's dead.'

'But how? Why? He was perfectly all right when I brought him his sleeping draught last night.' Norbert's face was a mask of fear and disbelief. He babbled on, almost incoherent with shock. 'And it was the same as he had every night. A single dose in a packet. I left it with his milk, all ready for him to take.'

Tom shook his head. 'No, that shouldn't have killed him,' In something of a daze he pulled the sheet up to cover Lynwood's dead face.

It was then that he saw the blood. He was amazed that he hadn't noticed it before. It had soaked through the thick towel Lynwood had wrapped round his wrists, it had covered his night-shirt and seeped down on to the bedding where he lay in a pool of his own blood. The stain had spread upwards through the blankets and was just beginning to seep through the thick quilt.

'Christ!' Tom swore. 'He's cut his wrists! God, he's cut his wrists! He's taken his own life.' He sank down on his knees beside the bed and put his head in his hands.

Norbert couldn't look. He went to the table beside Lynwood's bed and moved things around, hardly knowing what he was doing.

'The master must have been planning to do it,' he said, after a minute. 'Look, he'd saved up his sleeping draughts. There are five empty packets here. He must have kept them back so that he could take them all at once.'

'And then he cut his wrists to make sure. Oh, there's no doubt what his intention was. He'd planned it down to the last

301

detail.' Tom got slowly to his feet. 'Better not touch anything until the doctor has been. Will you send someone to fetch him, Norbert?' He passed his hand across his face, still unable to fully take in what had happened. 'Not that there's anything he can do. It's far too late for that.' Now he covered Lynwood's face with the sheet and they left the room, locking the door behind them.

The full horror of what had happened hit Tom as he tried to break the news to Joanna and he couldn't stop shaking. She held him close, trying to make sense of what he was trying to say, yet refusing to believe it when she did. 'What do you mean, dead? He can't be dead. There must be some mistake. Let me go and see him.'

'No. No. You can't go in there. It's not ... Oh, Jo. It's dreadful. Dreadful that he should have been so unhappy that he took his own life. And that he had planned it all makes it even worse.'

They held each other close. Tom was still shaking with shock and now great shuddering tears racked his body. But Joanna didn't cry. Her tears would come later. For the moment she felt numb and empty and an overwhelming sense that they had somehow failed Lynwood.

'We think we know somebody so well,' she said in a dull voice, 'yet when it comes to it we don't know them at all. We thought he had come to terms with his life, he had seemed quite happy these last months, yet he must have known what he was going to do all the time. And we had no idea. No idea at all. Oh, Tom. How could we have not known he was so miserable?' Now her tears began to flow and it was Tom's turn to comfort her.

'We didn't know because he was careful that we shouldn't,' he said, holding her close and stroking her hair.

The doctor came. When he had finished his examination he called Tom to one side.

'It was very plain that he planned his suicide down to the last detail,' he said. 'It appears he took an overdose of his sleeping draught and before it could take effect he cut both wrists. He even had the forethought to wrap his hands in a towel to minimise the ... er, what shall I say? Mess.' He cleared his throat. 'Not that anything could have done that, of course.'

Tom nodded. There was nothing he could say.

The doctor went on. 'I've left the knife for the coroner to see.'

'Knife?'

'The knife he used. A small penknife with a mother-of-pearl handle.'

Tom covered his face with his hands. 'Oh, Christ. He used the knife I gave him. It was one of mine. One I made myself.' It was the ultimate irony.

Lynwood's funeral was quiet. As a suicide he had to be buried in unconsecrated ground. If Joanna noticed that his grave was quite near to the grave of the unknown woman she had tended for years, thinking it was her mother, she never said and Tom didn't remind her.

After the funeral Mr Garthwaite, the solicitor, read Lynwood's will. In it he left everything he possessed jointly to his 'dear and trusted friends, Joanna and Tom Cartwright, as a token of my great love and esteem and in hopeful reparation for any harm I may have done to them in the past. I hope that they will enjoy being masters of Cliffe House and will be happy to continue to run the estate in the way I have schooled them over these past months whilst I was planning my demise. Let there be no remorse or regret over my death. It is as I wished. All I hope is that they and their children will have fond and happy memories of me. Lynwood Silkin.'

They received the news in stunned silence.

It was not until Mr Garthwaite had gone that Tom said, 'Lynwood must have been planning to do this right from the time he asked us to come and live here at Cliffe House, Jo.'

'If only we'd realised that we might have been able to stop him,' she said wretchedly.

'But that's not what he would have wanted.' He held her close and stared out of the window. 'Of course, with hindsight I can see it all now. He planned it all very carefully. He asked us to come and live with him for company, but really it was so that he could teach me how to run things ready for when he was gone.' He gave a wry smile. 'There's not a lot I don't know about buying raw materials for button-making now and I'm in process of getting the flour mill back into production after the fire they had there last year. Then there's Bradshaw's Wheel, although they don't like me poking my nose in there, even if I am trying to improve things.' He looked down at her. 'And he's gradually handed all the book-keeping over to you, Jo.'

She nodded. 'Yes, but I thought he was only teaching me because it gave him something else to do. I went along with him to humour him more than anything.' She turned and buried her face in Tom's chest. 'Oh, Tom. What shall we do without him?'

'We'll do what he's asked us to do. We'll run the estate for him. What else can we do, my love?'

There was a discreet cough from behind them. They both turned and found Norbert had come into the room.

Norbert cleared his throat again. 'May I just say, Sir, that with your permission I shall be only too happy to serve you as I served my two previous masters, Mr Abraham and Mr Lynwood.'

'Thank you, Norbert.' Tom said gruffly. 'I would be very grateful.' It was an unexpected compliment from the old man.

Norbert cleared his throat again. 'And the rest of the staff say they hope you will continue to avail yourselves of their services, Sir,' he turned to Joanna, 'and Madam.'

Joanna inclined her head. 'Thank you, Norbert. Will you tell the staff that we shall be more than happy for things to continue in the usual way. Please convey our thanks for their loyalty.'

Tom waited until the door closed behind Norbert, then he slumped down on a brocade settee and said, 'It's no use. I shall never get used to it.'

'Never get used to what, love?' Joanna asked with a frown.

'Never get used to having servants at my beck and call. It's not right, somehow. I'm not a gentleman, I'm a common working man.'

'Not any more, my love. Thanks to Lynwood you're a man of property.'

He shook his head. 'It's an awesome thought, Jo.'

Chapter Thirty-Three

A week later, at eight o'clock in the morning, Tom and Joanna were married. They were married in the Church of St Peter and St Paul in the middle of the town. Tom had chosen this church partly because it was not far from Sackitt's Yard where they had first set up home together, but mostly because it would have been too painful to marry in the church where so recently Lynwood's funeral service had been held, particularly as it was the same church that had seen Joanna's first travesty of a wedding.

Joanna had agonised over what she should wear. She couldn't bring herself to be married in deepest mourning, even though Lynwood had only just been laid to rest, yet a pale colour would have been disrespectful to his memory. But her marriage to Tom was too important, too special to allow etiquette or custom to mar the day, she wanted to look her best for him. In the end she settled for a dark blue silk dress with a slightly paler underskirt, caught up at intervals with tiny blue bows. With it she wore a tiny blue hat with a veil that perched jauntily over one eye. She carried a posy of white rosebuds.

They travelled to the church in their own carriage, picking up Martha, dressed in the first new clothes she had ever worn in her life, along the way. Then, witnessed only by the verger, grumpy at having to start his day's work so early in the morning, and Martha, Tom slipped the ring on to Joanna's finger. It was the same ring he had removed and put in his waistcoat pocket just before they left Cliffe House. It was the first time it had been off her finger since Lynwood had placed it there some six years before, making vows he had never

305

kept. They had agreed that it had served her well in their years together so far so what was the point of tempting fate by choosing a different one?

They left the church hand in hand and climbed back into the carriage, Tom tall and distinguished-looking in his dark, braid-trimmed frock-coat, doeskin trousers and snowy white frilled shirt, his grey-streaked beard and hair freshly trimmed, Joanna, her figure still almost girlish in her narrow-waisted crinoline in spite of having borne three children.

'Now we are really man and wife, Jo,' Tom whispered as he bent his head and kissed her.

She touched his cheek. 'It won't make any difference. I've never felt that we weren't, Tom,' she replied, softly. 'But I'm glad.'

They took Martha back to Cliffe House with them for breakfast. When they arrived nobody appeared to have thought it strange that the Master and Mistress had gone out so early, the Master looking as smart as paint and as proud as punch and the Mistress out of mourning already and looking all dewy-eyed and excited. And if Mrs Osborne had cooked the kidneys in a rather special sauce and the kedgeree had a slightly alcoholic flavour, if the boiled eggs looked unusually festive with tiny bows round their middles and the bacon was a particularly tasty gammon, nobody remarked on it and Parker served it up with his habitual deadpan expression.

It was only afterwards, when Martha declared she had never tasted such food in the whole of her life and couldn't eat another morsel, when Joanna rang the bell for Osborne to bring the carriage round to take her home, that Parker, with a discreet cough and a slight inclination of his head, said, 'May I on behalf of all the servants say how delighted we are on this happy occasion to offer you both, Sir and Madam, our very sincerest congratulations and good wishes.' He tried to maintain a dignified, impassive face as he spoke but found it impossible and beamed at them both in turn.

'Why, thank you, Parker,' Joanna said, surprised. 'We didn't realise—'

'I think a small glass of sherry for the servants before dinner tonight would be appropriate, don't you, Jo?' Tom asked, with a lift of one eyebrow. 'To drink the health of Mr and Mrs Cartwright?'

'That would be much appreciated. Thank you, Sir. And shall I put a bottle of champagne on ice for Madam and yourself, Sir?'

'What a good idea. Yes, thank you, Parker.'

Parker composed his face and silently left the room.

Tom shook his head. 'That's one thing I don't think I'll ever get used to. Servants. How did they know where we've been?'

'They'd only have to look at you,' Martha said with a laugh. 'You look like a newly-wed.'

'Servants always know everything,' Joanna said happily. 'But it doesn't matter. Just as long as they don't tell the children their mama and papa have only just got wed!'

'I think I should go and see Liddy, Tom,' Joanna said one evening over dinner, when Lynwood had been dead and they had been married for nearly three months.

'Oh yes? What makes you say that?' he asked, too preoccupied with his own thoughts to listen with more than half an ear.

She gave a small shrug. 'I just think I ought to. I haven't seen her for quite a long time. I ought to tell her about Lynwood.'

Tom looked up and smiled. 'You think she won't have heard?'

She toyed with a forkful of sponge pudding. 'Well, yes. But not from me. Any road, I've never been to tell her we're properly wed now.'

Tom threw back his head and laughed. 'I'll be surprised if she doesn't know that, too.'

'I daresay you're right.' She screwed up her face. 'I just feel I should go and see her. After all—'

'Then go, my love. There's nothing in the world to stop you.' He cut across her words, a hint of impatience in his voice.

She heard it and looked at him, frowning. 'What's wrong, Tom? Aren't you well?' she asked, immediately concerned.

He sighed. 'Oh, it's not that. I'm perfectly all right.'

'Then what is it?'

'Only that I must pay a visit to Bradshaw's Wheel tomorrow. I hate going there every month. Old Zack Wenlock touches his forelock to me now. I loathe him doing that – for God's sake, he taught me my trade!'

'It's only because—' she bit her tongue. It was no use saying it's because you dress like a gentleman, that would be like a red rag to a bull, so she contented herself with, 'It's only because you collect his rent.'

'I collect Saul Bradshaw's rent but he doesn't touch his forelock. Far from it. He shouts and swears at me like a madman, and calls me a jumped up pipsqueak as well as other things I wouldn't like to repeat at the dinner table. I could knock him down.' He clenched his fist. 'God help me, one day I shall, too.'

Joanna treated him to a wicked smile. 'That would hardly be seemly, coming from the master of Cliffe House, now, would it?'

He gave her a sheepish grin back. 'That's another thing I can never get used to.'

'That's Saul's trouble, Tom. Neither can he!'

The next day Joanna walked to Whitely Woods. The leaves were beginning to turn, orange and yellow and coppery brown as autumn approached and as she walked they rustled under her feet. She had brought a basket with her and she picked the most succulent blackberries she could find so that Mrs Osborne could turn them into bramble jelly. Now and then she popped one into her mouth, remembering how she and Tom used to collect blackberries for Martha as children, eating them as they went to fill their ever hungry bellies. In spite of the twists and turns her life had taken since then she and Tom were still together, just as he had predicted, although to her shame she had ridiculed the idea at the time. And now they were properly, legally, man and wife. She couldn't imagine life without him.

She reached the clearing where the cabin stood but there was no sign of Liddy. There was no smoke coming out of the kiln chimney, no stack of wood waiting to be burned. Everywhere was clean-swept and quiet. The cabin door was ajar.

Gingerly, Joanna went to it. She had never been inside Liddy's hut and she was reluctant to enter it without Liddy's permission.

'Liddy?' she called, pushing it open a little more and peering into the gloom. 'Are you at home?'

'Yes, child, I'm here.' Liddy's voice sounded weak as she answered.

'May I come in?'

'Of course, child.'

Joanna dipped her head to get through the low doorway and for the first time stepped inside Liddy's hut. It smelled of herbs and smoke; smoke from years of charcoal burning and smoke from Liddy's pipe. It smelled of other things, too, that Joanna tried not to identify.

As her eyes became accustomed to the gloom she could see that the hut held little more than a table and a bench, a rough hutch that was hung on the wall to keep the food away from the rats and rabbits and a bunk bed along the far wall. A shelf above the table held a few pots and pans and a candle in a candlestick. Just inside the door was an iron wood-burning stove for cooking and heating. There was an old tin kettle on the hob but the fire was out and the kettle was cold.

She peered into the gloom again and could make out a figure lying on the bunk. She went over and saw that Liddy was lying there, covered with the blue velvet cloak.

Joanna knelt beside her. 'You're ill, Liddy. Oh, why didn't you send for me?'

Liddy smiled and put out a skeletal hand. 'Why did you come today?'

'Why? To tell you that Lynwood is dead and that Tom and I—'

'But I know all that, don't I? I know Lynwood is dead. I know you and Tom were married a week later.'

'Yes. I thought you'd know. You always seem to know.'

'So why did you come?'

Joanna frowned. 'Well, I hadn't seen you for some time. I just thought I should—'

Liddy smiled again. 'You just thought you should. That's right. That's how it is with you and me, child. You came because I needed you.' She was silent for several minutes.

Then she said, 'I'm dying, child. It won't be long now. I wanted you to know.'

A finger of ice touched Joanna's heart. 'No. No, Liddy. You can't die. I don't want you to die.' The words were wrung from her, surprising even herself because they were true.

'That's the nicest thing anybody's ever said to me,' Liddy said with a satisfied smile.

Joanna turned to look round the cheerless cabin. 'You know about herbs, why can't you treat yourself?' she asked desperately. She stood up. 'I'll collect them for you if you're too weak. Just tell me which ones to get. I'll make you a potion. You've only got to tell me—'

'I'm past that, my child.' Liddy's voice was barely more than a whisper.

'Then let me take you back to Cliffe House. There's plenty of room. Warmth and comfort and good food will soon make you better.' Joanna put her hand out and stroked the grimy forehead. 'I must do something for you, Mama,' she said gently. 'I can't just leave you here.'

Liddy caught her hand. 'You've done all I could ever have wished, my child,' she said quietly. 'Hearing you call me Mama is enough.'

'What have you got to eat?' Joanna brought conversation down to earth to prevent herself from bursting into tears.

'I'm not hungry. I don't need food.'

'I shall bring you soup. Every day. You must eat,' Joanna promised.

Liddy sighed. 'If it pleases you, child.'

'And a doctor. I'll call a doctor.'

Liddy's eyes flashed with a trace of her old spirit. 'Don't you dare! I'll have no man prodding me about. Anyway, it's too late. I doctored myself until—' she closed her eyes. 'It's too late for doctoring now.'

Joanna cried when she told Tom of her visit to Liddy.

'I never thought I would mind,' she sobbed. 'I can't believe she's the same person we were so frightened of when we were children. Liddy the witch we used to call her. Just because she looked strange and gathered herbs. Oh, I was so cruel. How could I have been so heartless? Poor Liddy. She had a dreadful life.'

310

'We didn't know that at the time, did we? And you've made up for it since, love,' Tom said, smoothing her hair.

From them on Joanna took soup to Liddy every day and fed her with it. Then she cleaned up the cabin as best she could and made Liddy a more comfortable bed with the blankets and pillows she brought with her.

'There's no need,' Liddy protested as Joanna tucked her up between the blankets. 'I've lain on a bed of bracken and lady's bedstraw all these years. A few more weeks won't hurt me.'

'Then think of it as pleasing me,' Joanna said, placing a feather pillow under her head.

'Very well, child,' Liddy sank gratefully into the comfort.

One afternoon, a bright day in late October, with a chill wind blowing away the last of the leaves that still clung to the branches, Liddy didn't move when Joanna entered the cabin.

'Liddy?' Joanna called, her voice uncertain.

'I'm still here, child.'

Joanna went to her and managed to pour a dribble of soup into her mouth.

'No more,' Liddy whispered.

Joanna laid her gently back on to the pillow. 'Can you talk, Liddy?'

'Yes. A little.' She paused, gathering her strength. 'There's something you need to know.'

'Yes. It's not that I want to pry, but—'

Liddy gave a ghost of a smile. 'Ask, child. Don't beat about the bush.'

'Very well.' The words came out in a rush. 'Were you in love with my father, Liddy? With Jacob Bradshaw?' Joanna saw a frown cross Liddy's brow. 'Don't answer if it's painful,' she said quickly.

Liddy's head moved slightly in a negative gesture. 'Not Jacob Bradshaw. He isn't your father, child,' she said, her voice barely above a whisper. 'I thought you knew that.'

Joanna's eyes widened. 'But I've always thought . . . You said you returned me to where I belonged. So who else could it be? His brother Caleb was too young—'

'Saul Bradshaw. He's your father.'

A groan escaped Joanna's lips. 'Oh, my God! Saul Bradshaw!'

311

Liddy smiled. 'He was a handsome man in those days, Joanna. A handsome man.' She closed her eyes. 'He saw me bathing in Porter Brook one evening. He must have known I went there to bathe—'

'And he—?'

'Only the once. But it was enough.' Her voice had a trance-like quality. 'I wasn't unwilling. God help me. I never went there to bathe again.'

'Saul must have known who I was when Martha found me,' Joanna breathed.

'Why should he? He'd probably forgotten. I don't suppose I was the only one. Anyway, how was he to know there was a child?'

'He hated me.'

'I know. If I'd realised what you would suffer at his hands I would never have—' Liddy's breathing was becoming shallow as she struggled to talk.

'Martha loved me,' Joanna said simply. 'She tried to make my life easier.'

'Martha's a good woman.'

'Do you think she suspected?'

'No. Why should she?' She lifted her hand weakly. 'You know the truth now, Joanna, but it's all in the past. Let it lie.' Her eyelids fluttered. 'A sip of water—'

Joanna lifted her head and held the cup to her lips. Then she laid her back gently on the pillow. 'There. Now you can sleep.'

'Yes, now I shall sleep.' Liddy closed her eyes and Joanna took her hand and held it.

Liddy died so quietly that Joanna had been sitting beside her for some time before she realised what had happened. Gently, with tears running down her face, she released her hold and went to fetch water, which she heated on the fire she lit outside the hut. Then she carefully washed her mother's body and combed her hair and wrapped her in the blue velvet cloak. Afterwards, as she stood looking down at her she could see that the years had fallen away and she was looking into the face of a woman who might have been a beauty, had her circumstances been different. She bent and kissed her cheek and then left the cabin, closing the door quietly behind her.

312

Tom was in complete agreement that Liddy would be buried from Cliffe House. Accordingly, her body was brought there and her coffin was placed in the drawing room until the day of the funeral. Then, in a hearse draped with purple silk and drawn by four plumed horses whose coats had been burnished till they looked like ebony, her body was carried to the churchyard. On the coffin rested a large sheaf of lilies on which a black-edged card read 'In loving memory of my mother. Joanna.' At the head of the cortège the undertaker's mute, an underfed lad recently rescued from the workhouse, walked solemnly, his tall hat draped with black crepe and resting on his ears. He was followed by the undertaker himself, a sour-looking man carrying a black cane. Joanna and Tom followed the hearse in their own carriage, also suitably draped in black.

As the cortège travelled along Hangingwater Lane it paused for a moment, by arrangement, at the entrance to Whitely Woods. Then it continued on its way to the graveyard, where Lydia Ingram was laid to rest beside her father.

Joanna was amazed at the number of people that lined the route the cortège took. Men as well as women were there, in their Sunday best, anxious to pay their last respects to the strange, outlandish-looking woman who had lived out her life in Whitely Woods. The woman they all knew as Liddy the Witch.

Chapter Thirty-Four

When Liddy's funeral was over Tom and Joanna went back to Cliffe House. They ate a quiet luncheon, then sat together, talking over Liddy's unfortunate life.

'I'll go and see to the cabin,' Tom said at last, getting to his feet.

Joanna followed suit. 'I'll come with you, Tom.'

'There's no need, love,' he said gently. 'You'll not want to see—'

'I want to come. She was my mother.'

'Very well, lass.'

They changed into everyday clothes and Tom collected up a spade and a rake, then together they made their way to Whitely Woods, walking side by side in the late autumn sunshine, with no sound but the song of a blackbird and the whisper of their feet rustling through the dead leaves that carpeted the wood.

Liddy's cabin stood in its clearing, empty and forlorn. With her no longer there it looked what it was, a rickety old shed with a tiny chimney poking out of the top. Beside the door and leaning at a crazy angle was the bench where she used to sit and whittle pieces of wood, mix up her herbal remedies or sit quietly smoking her clay pipe. Joanna felt hot tears rise at the back of her eyes at the scene.

Tom gripped her arm, understanding. 'I'll get the stove out first. It's no good leaving it inside because it won't burn. Then we'll—'

'Yes.' She nodded quickly. 'What will you do with it?'

'I'll bury it. That's the best thing. That's why I brought the spade. You fetch plenty of bracken and pile it inside the hut while I dig a hole for it.' He looked down at her. 'Are you sure there's nothing inside you want, love?'

Joanna shook her head. 'There's nothing there for me to want, Tom. I found the money she'd buried. Like she said, there was enough for the kind of funeral she'd asked for. Well, almost. Other than that she had nothing. Nothing at all.'

'And are you quite sure you want me to—'

'Yes, Tom. I want you to get rid of all traces of her.' Her mouth hardened. 'I couldn't bear the thought of people from the town coming up here and snooping round to see how she'd lived. She was such a private person she would have hated that. And so should I.'

'Very well.' Tom found a spot where the ground was soft and began to dig the hole while Joanna fetched bracken and dried leaves and piled them inside the hut. Tom dragged the stove out and broke it up as best he could and put it in the hole and covered it up.

Then as Joanna watched he disappeared into the cabin. Smoke was already billowing out through the door when he came out again and he came and sat beside her on the trunk of a fallen tree, his arm round her as they watched the flames begin to lick round the doorway.

It took a surprising time to burn. To take Joanna's mind off what was happening Tom began to tell her of plans that were forming in his mind.

'You know I've never really felt happy since we've lived in the big house, Jo,' he began.

'Yes, love, I know.' She glanced at him. 'But you wouldn't really want to go back to Sackitt's Yard, would you? Your chest is so much better now and the children—'

'I know all that, Jo. You don't have to persuade me that Cliffe House is a better place for us all. It's just – well, I don't feel comfortable living in such luxury.'

'You'll get used to it. You *are* getting used to it. You don't have any trouble knowing which knife and fork to use now . . .'

'Oh, I don't mean things like that.' He brushed her words aside. 'It's that I feel I ought to give something back for all the good fortune we've had.'

She frowned. 'But there's nobody to give it back to. Abraham and Lynwood are both dead.'

'I don't mean that, Jo. I mean, well, I've had this idea.'

She turned her eyes away from the flames that were at that moment leaping about the thatch of the cabin roof to look at him. 'Yes?'

He took a deep breath. 'There are several good craftsmen at Bradshaw's Wheel. Zack Wenlock's not as young as he was but he's still one of the best penknife makers in Sheffield, and that chap who makes scissors – Fred Ormsby – he's another. I don't count Saul Bradshaw, I wouldn't wish my worst enemy on him as an apprentice.'

'What are you trying to say, Tom?'

'I'm trying to say that I – that is, we could take lads from the workhouse and put them as apprentices to some of the men who work in the hulls at Bradshaw's Wheel. I guess Jacob Bradshaw could take one, even if his father wouldn't.'

'They'd say they couldn't afford to,' Joanna said flatly. 'Any road, look how you were treated by Zack Wenlock when you were apprenticed to him. I'm surprised you've forgotten that.'

'I haven't forgotten, Jo,' he said quietly. 'That's what I'm coming to.' He turned to look at her. 'If *we* paid the men to take the lads and teach them a trade, paid them well so they felt it worthwhile, it would give lads from the workhouse a good start in life. Well a few of them, any road.'

'And you'd be there to keep an eye on things. To make sure they were treated well.' Joanna nodded slowly. She stared as the roof of the cabin crashed in sending a cascade of sparks into the air, illuminating the fading evening light. 'Do you really think it would work, Tom?' she said after a bit.

'I don't see why not.' He grinned at her. 'I could even take a lad on myself. If I haven't forgotten all my skills, that is.'

'I doubt you'd have time for that, love. Not with all the other things you have to look after, these days.' She patted his knee. 'How would you go about it?'

'Well, first we'd have to do a bit of work on the buildings there. And the water wheel. And I think the dam itself needs a bit of looking to. Then, if we said that any man who was willing to take on a lad could have his hull rent free *and* be paid for the lad's keep, I don't think we'd have any trouble finding takers.' He was warming to his idea. 'Of course, we'd have to make sure the lads were well treated, I'd not want to see them half-starved like I was, but I don't see why it shouldn't work, do you, Jo?'

'I think it's a wonderful idea, Tom. And just like you to think of it.' She leaned over and kissed him.

'Well, at least I'd feel a bit more comfortable with myself if I could do a bit for a few little lads,' he said gruffly. He got up and began to rake over the ashes that were all that remained of Liddy's cabin. When he had finished he went over to Joanna and held out his hand.

'Come on, love. It's getting dark. We've done all we can here,' he said quietly.

Joanna got to her feet stiffly, her face wet with tears. She knew she would never again come back to the clearing in the woods. That part of her life was over, but thanks to Tom a new chapter would soon begin, because she was already thinking of ways in which she could ensure that the lads he was speaking of had comfortable lodgings, either with the wives of their masters, or even in dormitories converted from some of the outbuildings at Cliffe House.

Each busy with their own thoughts, they didn't speak as they left the wood and it was by common, unspoken consent that they turned their steps not towards Cliffe House but to Bradshaw's Farm to see their old friend Martha.

'I promised I'd tell her about Liddy's funeral,' Joanna said as they walked along the lane beside the Porter Brook, the dam rising darkly above them on the other side of the river. 'Her rheumatism was too bad for her to come to it.'

'She might give us a cup of her thick tea,' Tom said, in an attempt to make Joanna smile. 'My throat's so dry after all that smoke that I'd be glad of even that!'

Joanna did smile. 'Oh, Tom, Martha's tea's not that bad.' She thought for a minute. 'Well, perhaps it is.'

To Joanna's consternation Martha was not alone. It was later than either she or Tom had realised and Saul and Jacob were both there, sitting at the table eating platefuls of steaming rabbit stew, whilst Martha sat opposite picking at her share while Edie, her little maid, waited on them.

They all looked up as Tom and Joanna knocked and walked in.

'Tha might wait till tha's invited in,' Saul growled when he saw them.

'Don't be like that, Saul. The lass is allus welcome here,' Martha rebuked him.

'Not while I'm here, she's not,' he muttered. 'Miss High and Mighty, come to flaunt how well off she is, livin' in that big house and wearin' fancy clothes an' riding in a carriage.' He began to gesticulate and shout. 'And all at *my* expense! If I hadn't let her go out o' the goodness o' my heart to old man Silkin where would she be now? Tell me that!' He didn't wait for an answer, but turned and jabbed his spoon in Tom's direction. 'And as for Nimrod, there ... that jumped up clever-clogs, for ever snoopin' round in his posh clobber now he's come up in t'world: "I've come for the rent, Mr Bradshaw. Two months, I believe,"' he mimicked. 'Does he think I've forgot how he used to work in Zack Wenlock's hull wi' t'arse out o' his trousers?'

'Oh, give over, Pa,' Jacob said wearily. 'You're allus on about summat or other. Give it rest, can't tha.' He turned to Joanna and Tom, who were still standing in the doorway, Joanna frozen to the spot in horrified recognition of her relationship to the man who ranted and raged before her eyes, Tom holding her firmly by the arm. 'Sit down, both of you. Ma, pour 'em a cup o'tea. They look as if they could do wi' it.'

Saul turned on his son. 'Who d'you think you are, orderin' folk about in my house!' He had a dangerous, wild glint in his eye.

'Tek no notice of him,' Jacob said, making room for Joanna beside him at the table. 'You sit by Ma, Tom. That's it.'

'Ee, it's good to see you both,' Martha said softly, one eye on her husband. 'Did the funeral go all right?'

Joanna leaned forward. 'That's what we've come to tell you about, Martha. There were hundreds of people.'

'We don't want to know nowt about it,' Saul interrupted rudely. 'That woman caused more trouble than Soft Joe in this place.'

Joanna stared at him. 'Liddy never did anybody any harm,' she said hotly.

'A big funeral, was it, love?' Martha said in an effort to defuse the situation. 'I saw the procession go over the bridge, all the horses with their plumes and the big black hearse—'

'And that's another thing!' Saul's fist crashed down on the table. 'I'm not slavin' my guts out over there in that hull and then that jumped-up pipsqueak there—' he glared in Tom's direction, '– come an' teks half of it to spend on a posh funeral for a bloody old witch.'

'Liddy was my mother,' Joanna answered with a lift of her chin. 'She paid for her own funeral. And she wasn't a witch,' she added firmly.

'A likely story. Where would the likes of her get money to pay for a funeral like that? Any road, she was a witch so she'd no right to a funeral like that. *And* paid for wi' my hard-earned brass,' he jabbed his finger at his chest. 'I work my guts out—'

'Liddy paid for her own funeral,' Tom repeated, raising his voice above Saul's. 'Joanna just told you that.'

'An' I just said I don't believe it,' Saul sneered. 'No. It was you paid for it. Wi' *my* brass! You paid for a posh funeral for that dirty old bitch . . .'

'Pa! Give over.' Jacob laid a restraining hand on his father's arm but Saul shook him off.

Joanna stood up and pushed her chair back. Her face was white but there were two red spots of colour high up on her cheeks. 'How dare you say that about my mother!' she spat. Her voice rose. 'You didn't think she was a dirty old bitch when you had your wicked way with her the summer before I was born, did you? When you spied on her bathing in Porter Brook and fancied her?' Her eyes narrowed. 'I hate to say it, it turns my stomach to even think it, but it's you who's my father, Saul Bradshaw, not your son Jacob, as you let everybody believe.'

For a long moment there was silence in the room except for the ticking of the clock on the wall as everybody stared at Joanna. Then Martha dropped her spoon on to her plate with a clatter, breaking the spell.

Saul found his voice first. 'That's a bloody lie. The boy here—' he blustered, waving his arm towards Jacob.

Jacob's chair scraped on the flags as he got to his feet. 'My

God! It was *you*, Pa! And you never said a word when they accused me! You let me tek the blame for what you'd done. You even stood by and watched my wife tek my children away and you never said a word! All these years—' His eyes narrowed as he looked at his father and for a moment Joanna thought he was going to spit at him, but he turned away. 'You're a rat, Saul Bradshaw. A bloody rat,' he said, his face a mask of disgust.

'How did you find this out, lass? Did Liddy tell you herself?' Martha asked quietly, trying to make some sense out of the shouting match going on all round her.

Joanna nodded. 'Yes. Just before she died.'

Saul heard. 'Well, she's a bloody liar. Any road you can't tek the word of a bloody old witch,' he muttered, his bulging eyes moving from side to side as if looking for a way of escape.

Joanna leaned across the table. 'Why should she lie?'

'To get back at me,' Saul shouted.

'Why should she want to do that if you'd never done her harm?' Martha asked calmly.

'Because she's a bloody witch. That's why!' Small flecks of foam were beginning to appear at the corner of his mouth. 'A lying, bloody witch!'

'People don't lie when they're about to meet their Maker,' Martha said. She got to her feet, holding on to the mantelpiece to steady herself. 'You're a wicked man, Saul Bradshaw.' Her voice was low and full of hatred. 'You must have known right from the start that the child was yours. Ever since the day she was left in the cowshed you must have known. Yet you treated her worse than you'd treat a dog. A child of your own flesh and you treated her like a slave.' She gave a mirthless laugh. 'I can see why, of course. She was a thorn in your flesh. A reminder of your guilt, of what you'd done to Liddy Ingram in your fornicating lust.' She shook her head. 'I don't know what was worse, the way you treated the child or the fact that you let your son take the blame for your fornicating sin. You let Bella believe Jacob was to blame! In fact, you encouraged her! You watched Jacob's marriage fall apart because of what *you'd* done.' Her face screwed up in disgust. 'My God, I've hated you for years, Saul Bradshaw, but never as much as at this minute!' She turned to Jacob, her voice softening. 'Go and tell Bella what's happened this day, lad. Tell her the truth.'

Jacob shook his head wearily. 'It's no use. She'll not believe me. I've tried before. God knows I've tried.'

'Then send her to me! I'll tell her! I'll tell her what a lying bastard her father-in-law is.' She waved her hand at Saul. 'Oh, get out. You make me sick to look at you.'

For the first time in his life Saul obeyed her and slammed out of the house. Jacob hesitated, looking at his mother and then at Joanna.

Tom grinned at him. 'Go on, lad, it's worth a try.'

Jacob got up, then shook his head and sat down again, his head in his hands.

Martha sank down into her chair. Joanna went over to her and put her arm round her shoulders. She had never heard Martha speak at such length in the whole of her life.

'It's all right, lass,' Martha said, patting her hand and smiling. 'I've saved that up for years. By, I feel better now! A new woman!' She stared at the door. 'He'll not show his face through that door yet awhile. And when he does—' her smile widened. 'Ah, he'll not get the better of me again!' She rubbed her hands together. 'Come on, Joanna, lass, pull t'kettle forward. That tea's stewed. We could do wi' another mashin' after all that.'

'Why don't you come and live with us at Cliffe House, Martha?' Joanna said when they were drinking more of the thick, black brew.

'Aye. You'll surely not want to stay here with Saul. Not now,' Tom agreed.

'Oh, I couldn't do that.' Martha shook her head. She was quite definite. 'I could never get used to the posh ways of the gentry.'

'We're not—' Joanna began but she couldn't go on, for in Martha's eyes that was exactly what they were now.

'Don't you worry about me. I'll be fine.' A faraway look came into Martha's eyes. 'He'll not get the better of me again and he knows it. And Jacob—'

But Jacob had gone.

Jacob left the house and hurried along the lane. Like they said, it was worth another try. And this time he'd make Bella believe him, he'd tell her she'd only to go and ask his mam. He rehearsed what he would say to her as he went. Oh, she'd believe him this time and she'd come back. And all the kids. He'd missed the kids. And all through that bloody old liar who called himself his father.

Suddenly, he realised there was a noise of what sounded like a pick-axe. He stopped and tried to peer through the darkness but couldn't see anything, so he lit his pipe and went on.

'Is it tha, lad?' he heard his father call urgently.

'Aye, it's me,' he answered. He wished he hadn't struck the match, it must have lit up his face.

'Come an' gie us a hand, lad. I'm up on t'dam. Quick now.' He muttered something else that Jacob didn't catch, but Jacob didn't wait to hear more, he was already running back and over the bridge, his one thought that the dam was breaching, which would mean disaster for Bradshaw's Wheel and the farm too, with the thousands of gallons of water that would cascade into the valley.

He felt his way along the narrow path at the edge of the dam, until he came to where his father was working.

'How bad is it?' he asked, out of breath.

'Bad? It's not bloody bad enough. I can't get this bloody rock out o' t'road.'

Jacob could hear his father grunting and straining in the darkness. 'Pa! What the hell are you tryin' to do?' He struck a match that lit up the scene just long enough for him to see that Saul was hacking away at the side of the dam. 'Christ! You can't do that! You'll kill the lot of us!'

'I'll settle for that slimy bastard.' Each word was accompanied by a swing of the pick. 'I'll mek sure he'll not tek my money for nowt and get away wi' it.'

'Pa! You're mad! If you breach the dam it's your own livin' you'll lose. And t'farm! You'll flood t'valley, you stupid bastard.' As he spoke Jacob was grappling with his father, trying to wrench the pick from his grasp.

'Mad, am I? We'll see who's bloody mad.' Muttering insanely to himself Saul hurled himself at Jacob, knocking him against the side of the dam, where water was already trickling

322

through, weakened by his efforts with the pick. A few small rocks splashed into the river just below as Jacob recovered himself and once again launched himself at his father.

It was a mistake. The impetus of Jacob's body, together with the effort Saul was making, displaced a piece of rock large enough to let the water gush out. The weight of the water in the dam behind it did the rest.

Chapter Thirty-Five

Joanna and Tom finished a third cup of black tea and got up to leave before Edie could pour yet more.

'I wish you would come home with us, Martha. I really don't like the idea of leaving you here with Saul, the black mood he's in,' Joanna said, putting her arm round the old lady.

'Neither do I,' Tom agreed. 'He's half out of his mind with rage, if you ask me, so there's no telling what he might do to you.'

'I've seen him like this before. He'll do nowt to me. You've no need to fret,' Martha said more confidently than she felt. 'Ee, it's dark out there,' she said as Tom opened the door. 'Wait. Tek the lantern. It'll see you on your way.' She laughed. 'I'd not want you fallin' in t'river. It sounds as if it's in full flood tonight. I've not heard it roar like that for a long time.' She hobbled into the cupboard under the stairs and fetched the lantern and lit it.

Tom stepped outside, cocking his ear. Suddenly, he rushed back in and snatched the lantern. 'That's not the river, it's the dam! It must have burst its banks,' he shouted. 'Quick, all of you, get out of here and up the hill as fast as you can. Come here, Martha, I'll carry you. You'll never walk fast enough. Quick, Jo, you take the lantern. Come on, Edie, we've no time to lose.' He hustled them ahead of him and with Martha in his arms began to hurry across the farmyard. The water was spreading quickly, spewing forth from the dam and swelling the river till it rose above its banks and began to flood the valley. By the time they reached the lower field it was already up to their knees and still rising. They struggled on, Edie whimpering and holding on to Joanna, who was holding the lantern in her other hand and dragged down by her long sodden skirts clinging round her legs, Tom, carrying Martha, panting behind her. They stumbled on across the lower field to where the ground began to rise and they half-ran, half-scrambled until they reached the field that Saul had once so coveted that he had sold Joanna for it, and climbed to the top of it.

'You'll be all right here,' Tom said breathlessly, setting Martha gently down. 'Now, Edie, you stay here and look after Martha.' He put his arm round the thin shoulders of the trembling little servant girl. 'It's all right, Edie, you're quite safe here. The water'll not come up this far. Not yet awhile, any road.' Edie crept into the comfort of Martha's old arms. 'We'll have to take the lantern,' he went on, 'but your eyes'll soon get used to the darkness and it won't seem so bad. Someone'll come for you before long.'

'Don't worry about us, lad,' Martha's voice was quite calm. 'If t'water comes up this far we'll just move up a bit further. We'll be all right till they come for us.'

'That's the spirit, Martha.' He turned to Joanna. 'Now, come on, Jo. We've got to get to the road, we should be able to get along the top of this field without too much trouble and it'll be easier for you to go round by the road than if you tried to climb up the cliff to get to Cliffe House.' He took her hand and began to pull her along, still talking. 'Osborne will organise help if you tell him what's happened, although at this stage I'm not sure what can be done before daybreak and we can see what the damage is.'

'Take the lantern, Tom.' Joanna thrust it into his hand. 'And be careful, love.'

He kissed her briefly. 'Don't worry, Jo.' A quick squeeze and he was gone, the light bobbing along the road in the darkness.

Joanna tried to run up the rest of the hill to Cliffe House, but the steep gradient plus her wet skirts clinging round her legs made her feel she was trying to plough through treacle and by the time she fell in the door, holding her side, she couldn't speak for several minutes but only gesticulate as to what had happened.

They quickly understood. Norbert took charge and gathered all the men together. He went with Ernie Bragg, the gardener, to help Tom, while Osborne rode down into the town for assistance. Parker was dispatched with a lantern to find Martha and Edie while Mrs Osborne prepared soup.

By the time Lily had helped Joanna into clean dry clothes the big kitchen was quiet, the only sign that anything was wrong was the row of bowls on a tray and the delicious aroma of Mrs Osborne's parsnip soup filling the air. Joanna sat down in Mrs Osborne's rocking chair, saying it was warmer in the kitchen and anyway she wanted to know at first hand what was happening.

The first people back were Martha and Edie. Parker had carried Martha on his back and he was exhausted. Even so, he put her down gently on the settle in the inglenook and after a few spoonfuls of soup went out into the night again. Edie crouched beside her, quite overawed by the enormous kitchen she found herself in.

Joanna went and sat beside Martha and fed her spoonfuls of soup because she was too cold and weak now to feed herself. Edie slurped hers eagerly. She had never tasted such delicious food and soon she began to allow her eyes to swivel, taking in the huge dresser full of matching china, the gleaming brass and copper and the huge table running the length of the room. Now she was no longer fearful for her life she was beginning to enjoy herself.

Joanna looked at the clock. The hands stood at two o'clock. She stared at the blackness beyond the window. It must be two o'clock in the morning but she had no idea how long she had been home.

'Look after Martha,' she said distractedly to Edie, getting to her feet and beginning to pace up and down.

Mrs Osborne lumbered to her feet. 'Why don't you go to bed, Madam?' she said. 'There's nothing you can do . . .'

'Don't be ridiculous, Mrs Osborne. How can I go to bed knowing my husband is—' She laid her hand on her cook's arm. 'I'm sorry, Mrs Osborne. You must be as worried as I am knowing your husband is down there, too.'

Mrs Osborne nodded; her florid face had lost its usual placid expression and was creased with worry. 'My George is not as young as he was. And he took our Alfie with him. That's both my men. And neither of 'em can swim. Never had any cause to.' She turned away and wiped her eyes with the corner of her apron.

Joanna laid her arm briefly on Mrs Osborne's shoulder; they were equals now in their anxiety for their men. 'I think we could all do with another cup of tea,' she said, knowing any action was better than just sitting doing nothing. 'And have you got any of your delicious shortbread, Mrs Osborne?'

'Aye. I allus keep some in a tin.' Gratefully, Mrs Osborne began bustling about, doing what she knew best.

It was getting light before they heard the rumble of wheels on the drive and four weary, mud-stained and soaking wet men staggered in through the door.

Joanna counted heads anxiously. Four. There should be six. 'Where's Tom? Where's my husband?' she cried, her voice almost a shriek. 'And where's Osborne?'

'The Master's at the hospital, Madam, getting Jacob Bradshaw's head stitched.'

'Is the Master all right? Not hurt?'

'No, Madam. He's been a tower of strength to us all.'

'And Osborne?'

Norbert cleared his throat. 'He's supervising . . . one of the outhouses . . . turning it into a mortuary . . . just for the time being.'

Joanna's hand flew to her throat. 'Mortuary? Why? Who's dead?'

Norbert glanced over to where Martha was now quietly dozing, lulled by the soup and the warmth of the fire.

'I'm afraid it's Mr Bradshaw, Madam. I imagine he and his son were trying to stem the flow when they got swept away.'

Joanna's shoulders relaxed and she nodded. 'Thank you, Norbert. Go and get into dry clothes, then come back for some of Mrs Osborne's soup.' She gave a ghost of a smile at the sight of Tom's normally immaculately turned-out valet looking so dirty and dishevelled. 'We can't have you catching your death of cold now, can we?'

It was daylight before Tom returned. He was grey with fatigue, his clothes were sodden and caked with mud and he'd lost his hat. Joanna went over to him and put her arms round

327

him. 'Oh, thank God you're safe, Tom,' she whispered.

An hour later, after a hot bath and two bowls of Mrs Osborne's soup inside him, Tom went along to Joanna's little sitting room where she was dozing by the fire, relaxed now she knew he was safe. He sat down opposite to her, yawning.

'Well, it's been quite a night,' he said.

She smiled at his masterpiece of understatement. 'Will Jacob be all right?' she asked.

'Oh, yes. He needed several stitches in his head but he'll be fine in a day or two.' He stared into the fire. 'They weren't going to treat him at the hospital until I told them who I was and that I would foot the bill,' he said thoughtfully.

'But they did treat him?'

He nodded. 'Oh, yes. When they knew who I was they couldn't do enough for him.' He looked up. 'Then I went to see his wife, Bella. I told her Jacob had had nothing to do with Liddy.'

'And?' Joanna prompted.

'She believed me. She hadn't believed Jacob, but she believed me.' He shook his head. 'It's quite frightening how people take notice of what I say, these days,' he said, clearly surprised.

'That's because you're Master of Cliffe House,' she said, smiling.

'It's an awesome responsibility, Jo,' he said quietly.

'So what did Bella say about Jacob?' Joanna persisted.

'Not much. But she put her coat on then and there and went to fetch him from the hospital. I'd left him there while I went to see her.'

'I suppose you could say actions speak louder than words.' She was silent for a bit. Then she said, 'Saul's dead.'

'Yes.' Tom's mouth twisted. 'He drowned like the rat he was.'

Joanna looked shocked. 'Hush. You shouldn't speak ill of the dead, love. Especially as he was trying to save the dam.'

Tom's head shot up. 'Is that what people think?' He shrugged, then his shoulders sagged. 'Well, what matter. But Jacob and I know different.'

'What do you mean?' She frowned at him.

'Jacob told me exactly what happened. He left the farm

while we were there, didn't he, to go and see Bella? Well, as he went along the lane he saw his father hacking away at the dam, muttering about getting his own back on us; well, you know how he felt about you and me, Jo. Jacob managed to get to him to try and stop him but it was too late, Saul had already made a hole in it. Jacob managed to jump aside when the whole thing went although he got hit by a rock. Any road he was able to climb up on to the bridge and cling on there. But Saul got swept away. We found him lodged in one of his own pig-sties. You could say he ended up where he belonged,' he finished grimly.

'But what about the farm? Didn't he realise what would happen to it if he breached the dam?'

'I think he was too far gone to even think about that. Not that there's much left of it, the last of the animals went some time ago. The house is still standing, although it's up to the bedroom windows in water.' He pinched his lip. 'There's a lot of work to be done on the hulls, too. When they flooded all the men's tools went, so they'll all have to be replaced.'

'And the dam?'

He passed his hand across his face. 'I'm not sure it's worth repairing.'

'Oh dear, so much for your wonderful plans for the work-house boys,' she said wryly.

He looked up. 'Oh, I shall go ahead with those. I haven't thought it all out yet, of course, but when the valley is drained and the workshops put back in order maybe we can install steam to run the stones. Apart from being safer it'll be more reliable. And perhaps we could turn the farmhouse into proper accommodation for the apprentice boys. With a matron to look after them.'

'Not Martha,' Joanna said firmly. 'She'd be too old for that.'

He grinned at her. 'I'm sure you can look after Martha, Jo. And finding a matron will be your responsibility. I'll have enough on my plate without that, don't you think?'

She smiled back at him. 'More than enough, Tom.' She raised her eyebrows. 'And has the Master of Cliffe House any other great and wonderful plans?'

'Oh, yes,' he said seriously. 'But they can wait.' He got to his feet, yawning. 'My immediate plan is to go to bed and get some sleep.'

She stood up with him, still smiling. 'Would you like me to come with you?'

He grinned and encircled her with his arm. 'I insist on it. I assure you I've no intention of sleeping for ever.'